THE CHILD WHO CAME BACK

LUCY LAWRIE

THE CHILD WHO CAME BACK

www.lucylawrie.com

Cover design by Emma Graves.

ISBN: 978-1-9989981-5-9

For Dad, with so much love.

PROLOGUE

Teresa
Eight years ago

My daughter's message, horribly wrong, had pinged onto my phone five hours ago.

I love you too

I was miles off the main road now, hurtling around bends in a wooded valley in deepest Aberdeenshire. It had been drizzling softly since Pitlochry, a fine mist that kept settling on the windscreen without triggering the wipers. Houses were few and far between, road signs non-existent. I passed a fallen tree that I could have sworn I'd noticed a few miles back, great clods of earth clinging to its upturned roots. Was I going around in circles?

Braelochie House. That was where Maisie was supposed to be – staying with a school friend and her family. Hopefully, I'd look like a total fool, turning up there wearing my pyjama leggings and an old fleece – I hadn't bothered to get dressed before running out of the house. She'd stare at me like I was nuts, her face contorted with teenage embarrassment.

Really, Mum? Really?

And I'd laugh, and make up some excuse to tell Ally's mother – a family emergency of some sort. I'd pull Maisie into a fierce, tight hug, swallowing back tears of relief. If we got back on the road quickly, we could be home by dinner time.

But I had to find the house first.

All the while, Maisie's messages played and replayed in my head – just a handful over the last four weeks.

She'd had to walk half way up a mountain to get a phone signal because the house was in a 'dead zone' and the land-line was down. But the view from up there was amazing!

She'd been trying venison and learning Scottish dancing. She'd been on nature walks and picnics and waterfall swims. They played Scrabble in the evenings as there was no television.

And then – please could she stay a teeny bit longer, since she was having so much fun?

It had all struck a slightly wrong note. As if my moody teenager had been replaced by a child from an Enid Blyton book.

And there were no waterfalls around here, no mountains. Only these winding roads that all looked the same. These dense, dark woods, going on forever. It was as if they'd sprung up to hide Maisie, like in some nightmarish fairy tale.

Why had I let her come here? Some instinct – spider-like, crawling around the pit of my stomach – told me it had been a terrible mistake.

But no. Everything would be fine. I just had to find the house.

The sat nav was telling me to do a U-turn when possible. Pulling over, I checked the address again. On the street view setting, I could see a grey turreted roof beyond a stone wall. A pale, distorted shape – a gatepost? – loomed to one side of the image.

I turned the car and drove back the way I'd come. But this time, I noticed a narrow, single-track road disappearing downhill to the right. I overshot the turn and grazed the bramble hedge that bordered the track, its thorns clawing the paintwork on the passenger side.

This morning's message should have said: 'I love you 2.'

The number, not the word.

We always said 'I love you' with numbers. It was something I'd started when Maisie was little, when she'd struggled with maths at school.

'I love you,' one of us would say.

'I love you 2,' the other would reply.

'I love you 4...'

'I love you 8...'

'I love you 16...'

And so on. She called it 'Mummy-Maisie code', and we signed off all our messages using some variation of it.

There was a metallic crunch as my left front wheel slipped into a stony rut on the track. My heart gave a sickening skip. I couldn't get stuck here, wasting yet more time, while Maisie...

But no. Maisie was fine. She'd probably just typed the word 'too' without thinking. I'd jumped to the worst possible conclusion – that the messages weren't from her at all. That she was lying in a ditch somewhere, or locked in a cellar. But I was just overreacting.

Almost certainly.

If her phone hadn't been going straight to voicemail, I could have checked with her, and no doubt saved myself a ten hour round trip.

I managed to inch the car forwards, biting down on my lip so hard that I tasted blood. After another fifty yards or so, the bramble hedge gave way to a high stone wall. And I could see gates up ahead.

Wrought iron carriage gates, padlocked and wound with a rusty chain.

A chain...?

But the name 'Braelochie House' was carved into one of the stone gateposts. So I'd found the right place.

Which meant it would be just a few minutes now – surely – until that laugh, that hug. I imagined pressing my cheek against her hair, breathing in the petal-soft scent of her. The aching pull in my chest would finally stop.

I parked up on the verge, tyres smooshing on the muddy ground. I shook the gates until splinters of paint came off on my hands, but the padlock wouldn't budge. So I climbed up the side, forcing my feet into the angles of the ironwork. I managed to haul myself sideways onto the top of the stone wall, green-brown moss smearing my leggings and the front of my fleece.

For a moment, I imagined the family spotting me, and hurrying over to help. They would explain, probably, that the main entrance was just along the road, and that people's sat navs always sent them the wrong way. They'd offer me a cup of tea and we would all have a laugh about my undignified entrance. Maisie's cheeks would burn with embarrassment, but then she'd begin to giggle, too.

I slid down the other side of the wall and hit the ground, my ankle collapsing under me with a hot, shooting sensation. Forcing myself up, I limped along the gravel driveway, which was pocked with brown puddles, bordered by straggling rhododendron bushes.

Then the house came into view. A ribcage of blackened rafters, reaching to the sky. Blind windows, covered with plywood boards. A gaping hole torn into the eastern elevation, the damaged brickwork like a mouthful of broken teeth.

Builder's railings surrounded the ruin, with signs saying 'DANGER! KEEP OUT!'. Tall spears of rose bay willow herb poked up through the gravel – nobody had been here for months.

My stomach flipped. I tried to take a deep breath, to force air into my lungs.

Perhaps the family was staying in another house within the grounds, while this building was being renovated. I followed the railings around the back of the house to make sure. Maybe another vista would open up – a sweeping driveway to the main house. Maisie had said it was a country estate, after all. But there was nothing except a small garden shed and a peeling summer house with broken windows. Within a minute, even at my limping pace, I'd circled back to where I'd started.

Why would Ally's mum have provided the wrong address? It made no sense.

The rain was falling more heavily now, dimpling the puddles on the path. I pulled my phone out and dialled Maisie's number again.

When it rang out, I called Ally's mum, using the number

she'd given me when we'd met at the school exhibition. The call went straight to a voicemail box with a generic greeting.

'It's Maisie's mum again,' I said. 'Please call me back urgently.'

If Maisie wasn't here, where was she?

Who was using her phone to send messages?

'*Maisie!*' My shout disappeared into the drumming of the rain. 'Where are you?'

My legs folded. My knees hit the wet gravel.

I was falling. Plummeting through thin air. Nothing beneath me but absence.

1

TERESA

Northumberland
Now

He arrived without warning, on a day that began like any other.

As usual, I changed bed linen and prepared welcome baskets in the morning, stopping for a late breakfast at about half past eleven. As usual, I made coffee and spread butter onto my toast, praying that my daughter hated me.

The kitchen felt warm, summer light flooding through the French windows. I tried to appreciate the fact that my coffee was hot and strong, and that my toast had popped out just the right golden colour. Mindfulness and gratitude. They were the key to *really living*, a therapist had once told me. And I did try. Because if Maisie was dead, if her life had been snatched away at seventeen, then it would be wrong for me to waste my own.

But still, I clung to the alternative explanation – that she hated me. That she had willingly put me through eight years of misery.

I carried my dishes to the sink and stood staring out of the window while I waited for the warm water to fill the basin. I could see just one dog walker out on the beach today, her labrador jumping at the white-tipped waves as they raced towards the shore.

I'd run out of tasks already. The glamping huts were spotless, and I'd confirmed the bookings for the next few days. I'd fed the chickens and watered the hanging baskets. I was grateful for these repetitive, mundane jobs. They anchored me, stopping me from being completely swallowed by the black hole of Maisie's absence.

The rest of the day loomed ahead. Perhaps I could convince myself to go out for a walk on the beach, to leave the house for half an hour. It didn't look like it was going to rain – there was enough blue in the sky to make a pair of sailor's trousers, as my grandmother used to say. Or 'silent trousers', as Maisie would have said. Once, when she was very little, she'd tried to copy Gran, and she'd got the words wrong. And the new version had stuck.

'Oh, Maisie Munchkin.' I touched my fingertips to my lips, and threw kisses towards the window, and the grey-blue sea and the endless sky beyond. Willing them somehow to reach her.

As if in response came the sharp, shrill burst of the doorbell.

'Alright, alright,' I muttered, as it sounded again, and then a third time.

'Hey there!' A blonde woman was standing on my doorstep with a little boy who was jiggling from foot to foot.

My initial thought was that she was selling meal box

subscriptions. Or maybe she was a Jehovah's Witness, here to warn me I was heading for hell.

I released a quiet sigh. 'Yes?'

'My name's Caroline.' Her voice was low and silky. 'I'm terribly sorry to turn up like this.'

She didn't look like a Jehovah's Witness. I liked her dress – a navy-blue, floral Liberty print, paired with opaque black tights and long suede boots. Her blonde mane was secured with a velvet hairband, and she had something of the air of a royal nanny about her.

'I'm afraid this is going to sound totally mad.' She squeezed her eyes shut for a moment. They were small and mole-like, set too close together in her fleshy face.

'Oh?'

'George, my little boy here, believes he used to live in this house.' She clamped a firm hand on his shoulder and he stopped jiggling.

He was only a scrap of a thing, about seven or eight, with brownish fair hair and pink, round cheeks. A perfect little groove ran from the bottom of his nose to the bow of his upper lip, making me think of an old-fashioned teddy bear with a sewn-on nose and mouth. He wore a red rucksack, its straps tightened across both shoulders.

'I see. Well, I've lived here for over fifteen years, so...' I trailed off. 'Could it be one of the houses further up the road?'

The woman shook her head. 'He means... Oh dear. He means he lived here *in another life*.'

'What?' I cleared my throat and tried again. 'Sorry. What did you say?'

'He thinks he used to live here in another life. Before he was born.'

It wasn't meal kits they were offering, then. It wasn't heaven or hell. Or at least, not in the way I'd thought. She kept her gaze on me. She'd probably trained herself not to look away. That's what scammers did, wasn't it?

'We live near Retford in Nottinghamshire – a few hours' drive away. We've never even visited Northumberland before, so it's all a bit of a mystery!'

'How strange.'

Caroline gave a baffled little shrug. 'Does the name "Maisie" mean anything to you? Or... "Munchkin"?'

My hand shot out to the doorframe.

George looked up at his mother, and then at me. His eyes were frantic, as if everything that would happen from this moment on depended on my answer.

Slowly, I shook my head. I arched my eyebrows as if I was mystified.

I'd never had to deal with this kind of thing before – with scammers or psychics or fantasists claiming to have information about Maisie. There'd been no mainstream media coverage, because the police had quickly concluded that she'd run away, had chosen to go missing.

But maybe this Caroline had seen my own appeals on Facebook, or my missing person posters. I'd fixed them to lamp posts and made smaller versions for corner shop windows and the noticeboards in leisure centres and public libraries. I still renewed them every so often, with new images. New sizes and colours and fonts. Anything to stop them from becoming invisible. My legs felt weak from the exhaustion of it all. I pressed harder on the door frame.

George was still watching me, his pupils enormous. He held his arms stiffly at his sides, but his fingers were outstretched, rigid. Almost like he was suppressing an impulse to reach out for me.

And there was something about those eyes...

I couldn't turn them away, could I? I had to know what this was all about.

'Gosh! A real mystery.' I tried to get my expression right – intrigued, a little amused. 'Well, you've come all this way. Would you like to come in for a moment?'

I stepped back and gestured into the hall. Caroline swished past me, heels clacking on the wooden floor, but George appeared rooted to the doorstep. He opened his mouth and said something, just as a delivery van accelerated away from a neighbour's driveway.

'What was that?' I asked.

He held my gaze, his eyes as round as buttons. He whispered something that sounded like 'I'm back'. And then he flew past me, running along the hall to the bottom of the stairs. He had a foot on the first step and a hand on the banister rail before Caroline caught his shoulder.

'Stay *here*,' she said lightly. Then she turned to me, her face creasing into another smile. 'Boys!'

2

TERESA

Northumberland
Now

I showed my guests into the living room – an airy space with a log-burning stove, which gave onto the open-plan kitchen at the back.

'Sit down, George.' Caroline pointed to the low wooden coffee table at the centre of the room. 'Do some drawing.'

George slid his shoes off and kicked them aside, making himself at home. He took off his rucksack and emptied the contents onto the table. I ushered Caroline towards the kitchen area and snapped on the kettle. 'Tea?'

'Lovely. Something chamomile-y if you've got it. Look, I'm so sorry about invading you like this.'

I made the tea, glancing over at George as I did so. Perhaps he was going to wait until I was distracted, and then sneak off to lift valuables from around the house. Maybe that was their plan. But he was kneeling at the coffee table, head bent low over his drawing, heels rocking from side to side.

Caroline sighed. 'It's just that Georgie has been *so* obsessed with finding this house. You really wouldn't believe it.'

No, I really didn't.

'And today I just thought... why not? I had to come up here to Northumberland anyway, to visit farm shops in the area. And George needed a break from holiday club. So we decided to make a trip of it.'

I became aware of a noise in the room. A chill crept down my arms and across my neck.

The boy was humming. Yes... George was humming the theme from *Swan Lake.*

That was... *odd.* Maisie had used a ballerina musical box to store her drawing pencils. It had been a jewellery box, really, with small compartments on the top layer, where she kept sharpeners and erasers, and two drawers below for pencils. When wound up, it had played the theme from *Swan Lake.*

Maisie had taken it with her when she'd left for her 'Scottish holiday', saying she was looking forward to sketching the scenery.

Sometimes I streamed the *Swan Lake* theme on a speaker, letting the wistful melody drift around the empty house while I was down in the kitchen or working at my desk. Just so that I could imagine she was upstairs, safe in her room, drawing.

Trying not to let my hands shake, I handed Caroline her cup of tea. 'So tell me. How did you identify *this* house as the one George has been talking about?'

'Well,' said Caroline. 'It was strange. He said the house was near "a road-that-was-only-sometimes-a-road", and you could drive out over the sea to an island.'

'Ah. So you worked out that it was on the coast. Possibly near Lindisfarne.'

'Exactly! I remembered visiting Lindisfarne on a school trip and going over the causeway. And he also remembered there was a "high, high castle" in the distance – which I guessed was Bamburgh Castle. And a "bit where cars drive over the train tracks". He didn't even know it was called a level crossing.'

'I see.'

'And he said it had "hobbity houses" in the garden.'

'Oh!' I was proud of my three glamping pods – little wooden cabins with curved roofs and round doorways, festooned with hanging baskets of petunias, verbena and trailing rosemary. And fairy lights that came on at dusk.

'Once we found the level crossing, he sat bolt upright in his seat.' Caroline's eyes widened. 'He made me drive around – here, there and everywhere. And when we drove along this road, he shouted at me to stop. "That's the exact one!" he said. So weird, isn't it?'

I opened my mouth to tell her it was no good. She wouldn't be able to scam me in this way. I didn't believe in reincarnation, or past lives, or whatever she was suggesting. I wasn't religious, or even spiritual. Not any more. Maisie had been the only thing I believed in, and she had gone.

But none of those words would come.

'Shall we sit down?' I gestured to the living room. I would play her at her own game. I would bombard her with questions until she slipped up.

'So how long has George been talking about this? About finding this house?'

'Oh, since he was three or four. At first, we put it down to his imagination. As you can see, he's a creative little chap.' She nodded towards his drawing.

My heart gave a painful thud.

He'd drawn a picture of a room. On the right was a bed, with a pink, heart-shaped cushion lying against the pillows. On the left, tucked under the window, was a desk, with a small bookcase next to it. A pink chair stood by the bed, and the wallpaper behind was patterned with pink and purple flowers, interwoven with green leaves.

He'd drawn Maisie's bedroom. The room right above us, above the smooth, white-plastered ceiling. I'd kept it the same for her. In case, by some miracle, she ever walked back in the door.

'Just look at that detail in the wallpaper,' Caroline gushed. 'And the way he's got the perspective right. He's unusually gifted for an eight-year-old, his teacher said.'

'What are you drawing, George?' I asked.

'This was the room,' he said, without looking up.

Vis was ve room. His voice sounded so young. If this was a scam, he wasn't in on it. Surely.

His pencil was flying over the paper, adding shading around the folds of the curtains. His drawing skills were extraordinary for such a young child.

'What room?' I asked.

'From before I died.'

We sat in silence for a few moments, the only sound the scratch of George's pencils and the mantelpiece clock ticking. Again, it didn't mean anything. Any of Maisie's friends would know what her bedroom looked like. They'd remember the heart-shaped velvet cushion on her bed. The wallpaper that she'd been desperate to change, because it was too 'old lady-ish'.

My eyes began to sting. How could anybody be so cruel?

'What do you mean, George? I don't understand.'

He turned and looked at me. Reproachfully, as if I was the one who was playing games.

'I *said*. The room from before I died.'

I longed to let myself believe it. To just slide into the lie, like you might slide into a warm bath.

It was impossible. Utterly impossible.

And even if, somehow, it *was* true that he used to be Maisie, then that meant only one thing. That Maisie was dead.

Too much. It was too much.

I had to get them out of the house. I stood up. 'Well, this –'

George sprang up. 'Can I go out? Out onto there?' He pointed to the decking behind the house.

I opened the patio doors, and he charged out in his socked feet. He stood on tiptoe at the back fence, gazing out to sea, the wind ruffling his hair. He held out both his hands, the fingers outstretched, like he was trying to take off and fly.

With a shrug, I turned to Caroline. 'This is all fascinating. But I don't know a Maisie.'

This would be a test. If Caroline was genuine – if she knew nothing about Maisie, and her disappearance – she'd accept that it was all a mystery, and leave.

If she was a scammer, then she wouldn't give up so easily.

Caroline closed her eyes and exhaled, her face spreading into a disappointed smile. 'I understand. We're sorry to have bothered you.' She went over to the coffee table and started sweeping George's pencils into the red rucksack, roughly folding the drawing and stuffing it in on top.

'Oh! Shall I get you a piece of card to lay that on?' I wanted to tell her not to crush his work.

'Don't worry – he never finishes them. We've got dozens of these at home.'

Dozens of pictures of *Maisie's room*?

'George!' bellowed Caroline.

He appeared through the patio doors, dancing from one foot to the other. 'What is it?'

'It's not the right house, my lovely.' She handed him the rucksack.

'But... but...'

'Why don't we visit the beach anyway, now we're here? I don't need to be at the farm shop until three. Come on now, get your shoes.'

George's teddy bear face lengthened into a frown. He picked up his shoes and made as if to follow her down the hall. But then he stopped and looked at me, his eyes pleading, his mouth turned slightly down. It made me think of a particular look Maisie used to give me when she'd been naughty, or we'd argued, and she wanted to make up. Slowly, he lifted his skinny arms and held them out towards me.

'*George*! Come on! We need to leave this lady in peace. We've taken up enough of her time.' Caroline grabbed his shoulder again.

'Oh, don't worry,' I said. 'I'm sorry it's been a wasted journey.'

George shoved on his trainers, leaving the heels squashed down.

'You might want to put your shoes on properly, so you don't get sand in them,' I said. 'The sand is quite deep when you're walking over the dunes.'

He bent over again. I had an urge to reach out my hand

and lay it on the top of his head, with its tousled hair just the same shade of fairness as Maisie's – halfway between blonde and brown. I imagined how it might feel, the silky warmth under my palm.

'Just follow the path at the end of the cul-de-sac. You'll see it – the sandy one. It'll take you to the dunes. You can't miss it.'

'Let's hope the rain holds off,' said Caroline, peering out of the door.

'Hopefully,' I agreed. 'As my gran always used to say, there's enough blue in the sky to make –'

'A pair of silent trousers,' finished George, his eyes cast down, intent on fastening his shoelaces.

3

TERESA

Northumberland
Now

I stepped back, clattering into the coat stand. The air had gone out of me, punched right out of my chest.

What on earth...?

Nobody except Maisie and I had known about the silent trousers. It had been our own little joke – a childish word mix-up that we'd repeated to each other over the years.

Of course there was no such thing as past lives. I wouldn't entertain that. But was George... sensitive? Or something like that? Had he somehow known what I was thinking, the words I'd been about to say?

I couldn't let him walk away, not when he carried this... this *echo* of Maisie inside him.

'I feel like I'm rushing you out, when you've come all this way. Would you like to see round the rest of the house, George?'

He spun around and charged towards the stairs. On the

bottom step, he turned and looked at me, and then at Caroline.

She nodded, and sat herself down on the chair next to the hall table. 'I'll wait down here. I need to phone one of my suppliers, anyway. Take your time.' She took out a phone, opened the worn leather flap of its case.

George led the way upstairs and into Maisie's room. He didn't even look surprised by it, didn't react at the sight of the wallpaper with its green leaves and intertwining pink flowers, or the heart-shaped cushion. He simply lifted her duvet and climbed into her bed. Then he closed his eyes. This boy, who'd been in constant motion since he'd charged into my house, finally lay still.

Normally, I would have flipped out if anybody had touched Maisie's stuff. But George was different, somehow. And it was more my bed than Maisie's, these days – I usually ended up climbing in there at some point during the night.

To think that I'd discouraged Maisie's nocturnal visits to my own bed, when she'd been little and unable to sleep. I'd tried to resist her wily attempts to climb in beside me, and the spurious reasons she gave – ghosts (pronounced 'goats') behind the curtains, bees in her bed. I'd carried her back to her room and disentangled her hot, clinging limbs from mine, mindful of experts' advice about good sleep practices. Now I would have given anything, anything at all.

I knelt down beside the bed and lowered my voice to a murmur. 'Munchkin?'

His eyes shot open.

Longing surged through me, uncontrolled and dangerous.

'Do you remember?' I whispered. 'Do you remember all this?'

He pulled the covers up to his chin. He had a little double chin, his jawline still indistinct with baby pudge. 'It's from the time before.'

Then, sudden as a jack-in-the box, he sprang out of the bed. He got his foot caught in the duvet and landed upside down on the carpet before scrambling up.

'Ouch! Are you okay?'

He dropped to his knees by Maisie's bookcase and looked through the books there, pulling them out onto the floor to see the covers – Agatha Christie mysteries and dog-eared copies of Enid Blyton school stories, and the Roald Dahl books.

'Where's the mouse one?' he asked.

Ve mouse one.

'Oh... I don't know.'

'Aww,' he said, rocking back onto his heels. I could see his toes wriggling in his socks.

'Do you like reading?' I began to slot the books back in their places.

'Yes. But art is my favourite subject.' He glanced up at the wall, where Maisie had blue-tacked up some of her artwork – seascapes in blues and purples and greys. The colours were fading now, bleached by the sunlight that streamed through the window in the afternoons. I had debated with myself whether to take the drawings down and store them somewhere dark.

'What about maths?' Maths had been Maisie's nemesis at school – she'd eventually been diagnosed with dyscalculia.

'Maths?' He pronounced it *maffs*. He screwed up his nose. 'No, that's my worst.'

But then again, most children would probably tell you they hated maths.

'Shall we go downstairs?'

He rose obediently and began to walk into the hall. That was when a memory surfaced – of an Agatha Christie book, one of Maisie's favourite ones. A second-hand copy of *Hickory Dickory Dock*, with a rather sinister picture of a mouse on the cover. I went back to the bookcase and tilted my head to read the spines, trying to find it. It wasn't there. Had she taken it when she'd gone away? I remembered her whizzing around the house, gathering up everything she wanted to pack, eyes wide at the prospect of her visit to the Highland castle.

'Can I see the room with the big, big wardrobe?' He was looking at my bedroom door.

I opened it, and he craned his head in, making no move to step into the room. He eyed the big mahogany armoire, which Maisie used to call 'The Narnia Wardrobe'. Then he whipped back around. 'Can I see the elephant door stop?'

The elephant door stop, a heavy, ugly, wrought iron thing, was kept in the utility room that led off the kitchen. I used it to prop the back door open when I was using the tumble drier. How had he known about that? The door to the utility room had been closed when we'd been downstairs.

I tried to think rationally. The door stop would have been visible if George or Caroline had peered in through the windows at the back of the house, if they'd had a nose around before ringing the bell.

Caroline was still settled on the chair in the hall, tapping into her phone.

'You can go and look at the elephant door stop,' I said to George. 'It's in the little room just to the right of the kitchen.'

He rocketed off. I turned to Caroline. 'It is very strange. He does seem to have a strong connection to the house. It is like... it's like he's been here before.'

I wasn't going to mention the fact that he'd drawn Maisie's room, that he'd asked for her favourite book. That he'd come out with one of her childhood sayings.

'*So* strange,' agreed Caroline, shaking her head.

I swallowed hard. 'Look... one of my glamping huts is sitting empty this weekend. Would you and George like to stay? Have a bit of an explore round the area? It's obviously a special place for him.'

Caroline's face lit up. 'Oh! How kind of you! George would *love* that.'

'And maybe I could ask around and see if anyone has heard of a Maisie who used to live here. We could try to solve the mystery.'

Or try to find out what you're up to.

I smiled brightly, and Caroline smiled back.

4

TERESA

Northumberland
Now

I took over their welcome basket at about five, ready for when they returned from their farm shop visit. Caroline's car had been gone all afternoon – I knew this because I'd been checking every five minutes, watching out of my living room window. The sky had darkened to a lead-grey now. Surely they'd be back soon.

As well as the usual contents of the basket – milk, butter, orange juice, some farmhouse cheddar, a box of cherry tomatoes and a crusty loaf – I'd added some freshly made brownies. And a box of brown speckled eggs, courtesy of Henrietta and Clarabelle, my little hens.

I turned the key to the cabin door and went in, placing the welcome basket on the small kitchen worktop.

'Hi,' said a voice.

I spun round. George was lying on his front, in the space between the bed and the wall of the cabin. His pencils and paper were spread out in front of him – he was half way through a drawing, even though the room was dim.

'Gosh!' I placed a hand on my heart, trying to catch my breath. 'You gave me a fright! Where's Caroline?'

'Still out,' he said, without looking up. 'At the farm shop.'

She'd left him here alone?

'I brought you a welcome basket. There are brownies in it, if you'd like one?'

He shook his head. 'No thank you.'

No vank you.

I went closer, perched on the end of the bed. 'What are you drawing?'

It was a picture of a pirate ship, sailing out to an island. On the stern of the ship, he'd drawn two small figures in silhouette.

'I like your picture.'

He took a pencil and added a tiny pirate hat to one of the figures.

'You've drawn the sea really well. Did you go down to the beach with Caroline before she went out?'

'We went to the sandy bit, but not the wet bit.'

'Did you not want to go with Caroline to the farm shop?'

'She said I would have to stay totally, totally still.' He held up outstretched hands, to demonstrate. 'While she was talking to them. So I stayed here.'

Something caught my eye on the small bedside shelf behind George. It was a man's watch, one of those expensive-looking Swiss ones. It had a strap of heavy platinum links, and a navy-blue face with silver hands. And were those tiny diamonds on the clock face?

I had a sudden, creeping sense that there was a man in the room, standing behind me in the shadows. A man who'd just slipped the watch off his wrist. I imagined touching it, and feeling the metal links still warm from his skin.

'What a nice watch.' I glanced behind me, just quickly.

'It's Dad's. It used to be expensive but now it's broken.' He scrambled himself around and got to his feet to show me. He lifted the watch, and the strap came away from the face. One of the links slid off and clattered onto the floor.

It seemed sad, somehow, this ruined watch. I remembered the slogan of some advert about expensive watches – something about how you never own them, but just look after them for the next generation.

Then I looked up at George's face and gasped. There was a trickle of blood running down his chin. The sleeve of his t-shirt was smeared with red where he'd tried to wipe his face.

'George! You've hurt yourself!'

'Yes.' He opened his mouth to reveal a bloody, gap-toothed grimace. 'I was jumping on the bed, and I fell off onto the floor.'

And now I looked, there was blood on the floor. I'd stood in it.

'You've split your lip! Oh, goodness. We need to sort that out. Ice and salt water. Come on, we'll go up to the house and fix you up.'

I left a quick note for Caroline.

I've taken George up to the house – he's hurt his lip. Nothing to worry about.

In the house, I grabbed a food bag from under the sink and filled it with ice from the freezer, while George spun in circles behind me, his socked feet sliding on the wooden floor. Then I wrapped the bag of ice in a clean tea towel.

'Let's go up to the bathroom. We'll bathe it and then you can hold the cold compress against it.'

He followed me upstairs, jumping from one step to the next.

'Be careful,' I fretted. 'We don't want you to have another accident.'

In the bathroom, I went straight to the mirrored medicine cabinet above the sink. 'Saline solution,' I said. 'We'll use that to clean it. And some cotton wool pads. Okay?'

I turned around. George was standing in the doorway to the bathroom, both hands on the door frame, as if the room was a whirlpool and he was trying to stop himself being sucked in.

'No!' he said. 'Don't want it cleaned.'

'Come on, now,' I said. 'Why don't you sit there, on the edge of the bath, and I'll do it for you. I'll be very gentle, I promise.'

'No!!!' It came out as a piercing shriek.

'Shouldn't we clean you up before Caroline gets back?'

But he wasn't looking at me, or listening to me at all. His eyes were fixed on the bathtub, the pupils dilated to black pools. Then he closed his eyes, as if trying to shut out what he was seeing.

'George! George, what's wrong?'

He opened his mouth as if to scream, but no sound emerged. Moments passed, and he just stood there.

Oh God, he wasn't breathing.

'George! George!' I put my hand on his shoulder and jiggled him.

Still nothing.

'Breathe!' I jiggled him again. 'You need to breathe!'

All of the pink had drained out of his cheeks. He swayed to the side. I dropped to my knees and pulled him onto my lap. Was it a seizure? Some kind of heart defect?

His body flopped back in my arms, head rolling to the side. He'd lost consciousness.

No no no no no no no.

This couldn't be happening. I couldn't lose another child.

I couldn't lose her again.

'George! Wake up!'

My phone was downstairs, I'd left it on the worktop. I needed an ambulance. I needed...

I slid his body off my knee and began to move his thin little limbs into the recovery position. His face had turned a horrible grey.

What was I going to say to Caroline? How could I tell her that her child had died in my bathroom? My heart was jumping so hard that I could barely breathe myself. Perhaps I might die, too. I might just stop. And for a moment, it seemed like a way out. I didn't really want to be here any more. Not without her.

'I'm going downstairs to grab my phone,' I managed. 'I'll be back in two seconds.'

And then he made a noise, a little moan.

'George? George?'

His chest was moving. A little bit of pink was coming back into his face.

'You're okay. You're okay.' I stroked the hair back from his forehead, tears suddenly running down my cheeks. I wiped them away with my shoulder.

'Maisie?' I whispered.

He opened his eyes and looked at me. The sadness, the weight of the whole world, seemed to hang there in those treacle-brown eyes.

I fought the urge to pull him into my arms.

'I'm here, my love,' I said. 'I'm here now.'

5

TERESA

Northumberland
Now

Instead of calling for an ambulance, which didn't seem to be needed now, I phoned my friend Sunny. He was a physiotherapist, trained in first aid. By the time he'd arrived, George was asleep on the sofa, cartoons playing quietly on the television.

'Do you think he looks okay?' I whispered. 'I've been looking it up online, and I think it sounds like breath-holding. It's quite common in young children – it's a sort of involuntary reflex when they get upset or angry. They usually grow out of it by age six, but sometimes it can go on longer.'

Sunny looked bewildered. 'Yes.' He shrugged. 'It could be that, I guess.'

'He's got a bit more colour now, but he was deathly pale. I gave him a cheese and tomato sandwich. Do you think that was okay? He says he only eats sandwiches.'

He'd picked at it suspiciously, lifting the top slice of bread and then checking under all the slices of tomato. But he'd eaten about half of it in the end, before curling up and falling asleep.

'But who *is* he, T? Why is he here in your house?'

'He's staying with his mum in one of the glamping huts.'

'And where is she? Where's the mum?'

'She's gone to a farm shop, I think. She's trying to sell them puddings.'

'Teresa.' His voice was stern. 'Puddings? What's going on?'

'They turned up on the doorstep this morning. His mother says he's having memories of a past life. A past life *here*. He... he knows things he couldn't possibly know. Things about Maisie.'

Sunny's eyes filled with concern. He had been my rock, over the last eight years. We'd met through a dating website that Maisie had secretly signed me up for, just a few months before her disappearance. She'd cackled, her face full of mischief, when she'd told me she'd done it, and that I'd got a match. His profile picture hadn't done him justice, the silver hair at his temples making him look older than he did in person. But I had seen straight away that his eyes were kind. And he had a good, strong face.

We'd had a few dinner dates. A trip to the cinema. But once she'd gone, it had been impossible to continue.

He'd driven up to Aberdeenshire that day, the day I found the burnt-down house where Maisie was supposed to be staying. The day I realised she'd gone. He brought a flask of tea and an M&S sandwich, handing them to me as soon as he met me at the police station, and I snapped at him. Later, I tried to explain that my body and my mind were in freefall – I literally felt like I was falling. Shock, panic, nausea. Hollow, bowel-churning terror. Total disorientation. Would you want to drink tea if you were falling out of a plane? Would you be interested in sandwiches at that point?

Things were no better once we got back to Northumberland. During those first months, images of what might have happened to Maisie ran through my head like a gruesome movie, a constant backdrop to whatever I was doing. A dark alleyway. A cellar somewhere. Meaty male hands. Cable ties and plastic sheeting. Her body dumped in woodland, insects crawling around blue-grey lips.

I could just about handle the intrusive thoughts when I was cleaning the glamping pods or dealing with customer complaints for the insurance company in the evenings. But it made no sense to try and enjoy anything. I couldn't even think about a physical relationship, and I'd told Sunny so.

So we'd settled on friendship. Sometimes, I thought about what that might have cost him, over the last eight years. The chance of meeting somebody normal, having kids of his own, maybe. But most of the time I crushed those thoughts down, because I knew I needed him too much.

'I'm so sorry.' His voice was gentle, his brow deeply grooved. 'I think you already know what I'm going to say. They're scammers of some kind.'

'I know. Of course they must be. But I was looking up about it earlier – about past lives. There have been some cases that even the sceptics haven't been able to explain away. Some of the most convincing ones come from India. Have you heard about anything like this before? With your... you know... heritage?'

Sunny quirked an eyebrow at me, in a silent '*Really*?'

But then he went on, with just the smallest of shrugs. 'Hindus believe in a cycle of birth, death and rebirth. It's called *samsara*. Mum could have told you all about it. She'd have been all over this.' He smiled sadly. 'But I guess you could try speaking to my sister. She did a postgraduate course on integrating spirituality into psychotherapy, or something like that. She's worked with Hindu clients before.'

'So *you* don't believe in it, then?'

'Look at me, Teresa. Look at me?' His eyes were fierce and sorrowful at the same time. 'Someone is trying to take advantage of your loss. I'm so sorry this has happened to you. It's unbelievably cruel. Have they asked for money yet?'

'What? No!'

'Have you told them anything? Have you told them about Maisie?'

'No. Nothing at all.'

'Have you heard of "cold reading"?' he went on. 'It's a technique used by mediums and psychics. And scammers, too. It's a way of gathering information about somebody without them realising. They make generalised statements and then narrow them down by paying attention to your facial cues and your body language.'

I shook my head. 'It wasn't like that.'

'What about photos – photos of Maisie around the house? Or is there anything with her name on it?'

'Caroline mentioned the name "Maisie" on the doorstep, before she even came in. And you know I don't have any photos of her on display.'

I'd taken them down off the walls and the mantelpiece a few weeks after her disappearance. It had just been too hard, seeing them all the time. Now I kept them all in a box in my room, where I could take them out and look at them on my own terms.

'They also use "hot reading". They literally look things up about you online.'

The doorbell rang, startling me for the second time that day.

'She's back.' I looked at him sternly. 'Don't say anything!'

6

TERESA

Northumberland
Now

'I got your note,' said Caroline, as she wafted into the hall. 'About George's cut lip. I'm so sorry for the inconvenience.'

'I just happened to be taking the welcome basket over,' I explained. 'And I saw that George had cut his lip quite badly, so I brought him over here to fix him up. But then he had some sort of... episode. I think –'

'Arghhh!' Caroline slumped to one side and groaned. 'Breath-holding, was it? Yes, he used to do that a lot when he was younger, and it still happens sometimes if he gets upset. It's totally harmless. But I'm so sorry, Teresa. I thought he'd be fine for an hour or so.'

She'd been gone for at least three. But I smiled. 'Come on in.'

I led her into the living room where Sunny stood in front

of the fireplace, his feet apart and his arms crossed. His eyes were fierce and dark, his jaw tight.

'This is my friend, Sunny – he's a physio. I asked him to pop over.'

Caroline gave him a brief nod, then crouched down next to George.

'Oh George. You've had these poor people *running around*.'

He stirred under the blanket and settled again.

'Your lip seems fine,' she pronounced, peering in at it. Then she turned to me. 'He can be clumsy, sometimes. He tears around the place without thinking. I really am sorry. He seemed settled so I thought he'd be fine for a bit. But I was longer than I thought. The farm shop owners wanted to try all the samples I'd brought.'

'The samples?'

'I'm a private chef by profession, but it's been difficult to keep that up because of the pandemic, and then childcare, and blah, blah, blah.' She waved a weary hand in the air. 'So I've been branching out into retail. Organic fruit crumbles, sticky toffee puddings, that sort of thing. Restaurant quality, frozen and ready to heat in the convenience of your own kitchen.' She said the words in a practised, sing-song voice. She sank onto the sofa with a sigh, nudging George's feet out of the way.

'Oh, right,' I said. 'And you do that from your house near... Retford, did you say?'

It all felt slightly weird. I had expected to be properly grilled about the breath-holding incident, George's cut lip. But we seemed to have moved on to small talk.

'That's right. Mark inherited the place from his parents. It's a lovely old red-brick manor house. Although it's practically held up by ivy now! I'm worried it may crumble and fall down at any minute.' She laughed, mole eyes twinkling. 'But I love the place. There's a big old kitchen where I can do my stuff.'

I imagined an Aga, and a scrubbed wooden table. Copper pans hanging from the ceiling. Sun streaming through the windows while Caroline worked on recipes.

'Have you lived there since George was born?'

Caroline smiled sadly. 'George came to live with us full time after his mum died, when he was about three.'

Suddenly, everything seemed to shift. 'So you're his... stepmum?'

She nodded. 'That's right.'

I looked over at Sunny, who shook his head at me – a silent warning. But was it possible... was it even remotely possible that George was Maisie's *son*? Was that why those big brown eyes tugged at my heart? Was I looking at my own flesh and blood, my grandson?

'So, what about George's birth mother...?'

'Jan? Well, Mark and Jan were old friends of mine.'

So George did have a mother. *Jan.* A lightning flash of hatred went through me. I told myself to calm down, to stay rational.

'We met at a supper club, back in the day,' continued Caroline. 'Mark and Jan. Me and my slug of an ex-husband, Peter. Then, after three years of marriage, Peter buggered off to Chicago with a twenty-year-old intern from his work.' She rolled her eyes, shook her head. 'Left me high and dry, couldn't afford the rent. Mark and Jan were living up north. But their house in Retford was sitting empty. So they said I could use it as my base until I was back on my feet.'

I nodded, trying not to look impatient. I wanted to hear about George.

'I was a top private chef back then, very in demand.' She said it pointedly, looking at us both in turn. 'I was always shooting off everywhere. A few weeks in a chalet in St Moritz, then a month on a yacht in the Caribbean. That kind of thing. I worked in a castle in Bavaria for a whole summer, for a dear count and his family. But I needed somewhere to come back to. A port in a storm. And Mark and Jan gave that to me.' She nodded, paused for a moment.

'And then Jan got pregnant,' she went on. 'And she had the most awful time. Hyperemesis gravidarum. Excessive morning sickness, you know, like Princess Kate? I drove up and down to the wilds of Scotland, taking homemade meals up for her.'

'Scotland?' A spidery feeling crept down my neck.

'I know, right? A long way to go. But that was the kind of friendship we had. She would only eat fussy little meals – soft, white food. Dover sole in white sauce. Cauliflower cheese with Isle of Mull cheddar. Rice pudding with Madagascan vanilla.'

She looked at me from under her eyelashes, Nigella-style. I half expected her to start reeling off recipes.

'We got her through the pregnancy. But after George was born, she wasn't so great. Very bad postnatal depression that just wouldn't lift. She was in and out of Lendrick View for the next couple of years.'

'Lendrick View?'

Caroline wrinkled her nose and glanced over at George, still sleeping on the sofa. 'An inpatient facility. *Mental health*,' she added in a whisper. 'Mark was crazy busy with work, so eventually I took little George in to stay with me at the

Retford house. I made it my mission to fatten him up, put a bit of colour in his cheeks. Which was no mean feat, when he would only eat sandwiches and sweets.'

She laughed, and for a moment I thought of the witch in *Hansel and Gretel.*

'What's Mark's work?' asked Sunny.

'He's in the wellness space,' said Caroline, tilting her head to one side. 'He's spun up a number of different ventures over the years. Now he mainly oversees them.'

'And Jan...?'

'Ah.' She paused. 'During one of her stretches in Lendrick View, she got hold of a pair of nail scissors. It was all very sad.'

I gasped, before I could stop myself. 'Do you mean...?'

She nodded. 'She ended her life. Yes.'

'I'm sorry.'

'I'm going to be honest with you, Teresa. Mark and I had become close. We leaned on one another, emotionally. With Jan's illness... well, it hadn't been a marriage, in any real sense, for years. So Mark and George both moved into the Retford house permanently.'

'So when did George start talking about his... his old life?'

She narrowed her eyes and looked into the middle distance. 'He's always done it,' she said, shaking her head. 'I remember one time driving past a campsite where there were wooden glamping pods, similar to these you've got here. He pointed at one of them and said "hobbity house". It was strange, as he was only three. He hadn't read any Tolkein. I asked if he'd been to a hobbity house before, and he nodded and said, "Mama".'

My heart contracted painfully.

'Which was strange, because Jan had never taken him

camping, or glamping, or anything like that. She was always too unwell. And he used to babble all the time, while he was playing with his trains, or drawing. He used to talk about "the old time" or "my other life". I thought maybe he meant his life with Jan.'

'It must have been a big change for him, moving to Nottinghamshire with you.'

'I agree,' said Caroline. 'And he was always a sensitive little thing. But then, he started talking about "before I died".'

'That must have been...creepy.'

'And there's the nightmares.' She sighed and shook her head. 'Oh my goodness, nightmares like you wouldn't believe.'

'Nightmares about what?'

'He dreams that someone is trying to lift him out of his bed. Or that he's drowning. "I got drown-ded again," he used to say, when he was younger. Sometimes he gets himself into a right state. He'll go into full breath-holding mode. And he's always soaked in sweat – absolutely soaked. Almost like... well.'

'What?'

'Well, as if he's reliving something. As if his body and mind are trying to recreate it. I do wonder sometimes if he's remembering a traumatic –'

She stopped in mid-flow, and a slightly sheepish expression came over her face. 'Some kind of trauma.'

A traumatic death. That was what she'd been about to say. This seemed to be a common theme, judging from my internet research earlier. Children who claimed to remember past lives often spoke vividly of their deaths, and they were usually horrible – drownings, car crashes, shootings, fires.

And then they tried to flood my mind again – images of

the possible ways in which Maisie might have died. I pushed them away, and my mind presented another picture, one I hadn't seen before.

A yellow dress –

It disappeared as soon as it arrived.

'It's all such a mystery,' trilled Caroline. 'And I suppose we shall never know what these "memories" of his are. Or who "Maisie" was, if she even existed.'

I opened my mouth, unsticking my tongue from the roof of my mouth. 'She –'

Sunny stepped forward, cutting me off. 'If you don't mind me asking,' he said in an icily formal tone. 'How old is George?'

'He was eight in July,' said Caroline in her silky, musical voice.

A little voice piped up from the sofa. 'July the twenty-second.'

The room seemed to swim in front of me.

'What?' said Caroline.

'Have you got any forms of identification for George?' asked Sunny. 'Something you could show us, please?'

I winced. He was going too far, acting like some kind of official, or the police. He was going to drive them away.

Caroline paused, narrowing her eyes for a moment. Then: 'Yes! Yes, I do. I have a scan of his passport on my phone. I needed it for some school trip last summer.'

She fiddled with the phone for a few moments. 'Yes, here it is!'

She presented the phone to Sunny, letting him hold it himself so he could enlarge the image. I saw his Adam's apple bob up and down as he swallowed. He gave a curt nod and handed it back to her.

I shook my head, gave a dry little laugh. So I was supposed to believe that George had been born on the day Maisie went missing? On the day I'd dropped her at school for the final time?

Over on the sofa, George was sitting up straight now. His eyes were fixed upon me, pleading with me.

Don't be angry.

Don't be angry.

7

TERESA

Northumberland
Eight years ago

It was almost the end of term – a lovely warm evening in July – and I'd pinned the French doors wide open to let the summer air flood in. I was making soup while Maisie, just out of the shower after tennis club, sat at the kitchen table doing a jigsaw. Her hair, still damp, was in pigtails because she wanted it to be wavy for the next day.

'What kind of soup is that?' she asked.

'Leek and potato. A bit strange for a hot summer day, I know, but...'

Her mouth dropped open. 'How did you *know*? I've been thinking about leek and potato soup all day!'

'Aha!' I said, with a wink. 'Mummy-Maisie telepathy.'

Since Maisie had been little, we'd often been able to guess what the other was thinking. One of us would hum a tune that had been going around in the other one's head, or

I'd suggest a trip to the beach when she was already scrambling in the cupboard for her bucket and spade.

I felt lucky (and more than a little smug) that she still wanted to hang out with me, at age seventeen. And lucky that I still had her at home with me for another year, until she went off to university or whatever it was she wanted to do. Something arty, probably. School hadn't always been easy with her dyscalculia, and teachers were still saying that she lacked confidence. But she had been predicted to get an A in A-level art.

'Mu-um?' she said in a quiet, wheedling voice, inclining her head to the side.

'Yes, my darling?'

'You know my friend Ally? Well, her family owns this amazing castle place, up in Scotland? She showed me pictures and it's a bit like the Queen's house – you know, Balmoral?'

'Yes, I have heard of Balmoral?' I echoed her rising intonation, just to tease her.

'Mum!' she scolded. 'Ally's invited me to go up there at the beginning of the holidays. For two weeks.' She left a pause. 'Maybe three. Can I go?'

I blew on a spoonful of soup and carefully took a sip. Not enough seasoning. 'Is this Ally who you used to sit next to in French?' I vaguely remembered a quiet girl with thick glasses.

'Yes.' She nodded rapidly, widening her eyes. 'There's going to be a Highland Ball thing that we're going to go to, at this other castle of people they know. Everyone dresses up in tartan sashes and everything, and then they all climb a mountain to watch the sunrise.'

I suppressed a smile. It was nice to hear that she'd made a new friend. I always worried that Maisie, with her shy, quirky nature, was too much of an only child, probably from spending too much time with me. She'd always been charming with adults, talking to them as if she was a mini adult herself, but she tended to withdraw into herself around other kids.

She'd had a best friend a few years ago – the rather stolid, studious Annabelle Punch. But that had ended in heartbreak when Annabelle had managed to reinvent herself, using fake tan and a heavy eyebrow pencil, and had ditched Maisie for the in-crowd. Since then, Maisie had drifted between groups, but nothing had stuck.

My poor love. She looked younger than seventeen, sitting there in her pigtails doing her jigsaw, a smattering of teenage spots marking the tender skin of her jawline. Shouldn't she be glued to her phone, following the drama on Snapchat or Instagram? Maybe this trip would be good for her. It wouldn't hurt her to become a bit more streetwise before heading off to university next year. I had a sudden image of her in a student flat somewhere, during freshers' week, being offered a joint or some dubious white powder. Eyes wide, eager to please.

A castle in Scotland, with parents present, seemed like a good place to start.

It wasn't as if it was going to be a very thrilling summer here in Bamburgh. The glamping pods were booked solid, which meant back-to-back days of cleaning and laundry and dealing with guests. And I was doing an extra job in the evenings, from home – customer service for an insurance company.

'Okay,' I said finally. 'But I want to meet this Ally's mum, to make sure of the arrangements.'

'Muuuum,' sighed Maisie with a hint of an eyeroll as she flipped a jigsaw piece into place. 'I'm not *three*.'

Finally satisfied with the seasoning of the soup, I went upstairs to fetch Maisie's tennis kit from where she'd dumped it on the floor of her room, on top of a heap of other laundry.

I scooped it all up into my arms, and attempted to leave the room backwards, manoeuvring through the detritus of discarded clothes, dog-eared school assignments and half-empty bottles of flavoured water. I stood on a Tampax box and listed to the side, bumping one of her school folders off her desk.

A drawing slid out onto the floor.

It wasn't one of her lovely seascapes or detailed flower drawings. It was a female figure, drawn from behind, standing in front of a window looking out at a night sky. She wore a white dress patterned with silver stars; her wavy fair hair fanned out across her shoulders. But Maisie had shaded in a dark area on her back, the same colour as the sky. It made it look like there was a black hole through her, just empty space, where her heart and her vital organs should be.

A breeze from the half-open window lifted the hairs on my arms. I shuddered, hugging the laundry to my chest. I told myself it was probably just normal teenage stuff. She was just getting angsty feelings out and onto paper.

She'd always had an amazing imagination. When she was five or six, she used to have a little pink plastic table and chair which she would set up at the end of the driveway so she could 'draw everything all around'. But she never drew the outsides of the houses, the pretty window boxes or the neat front gardens. She would draw the things she imagined were going on behind the front doors and net curtains. The dragon that Mrs Finch apparently kept as a secret pet. A pair of ghostly twin girls in the opposite neighbour's attic. She'd once told me that Mr Appleby, the retired civil servant who lived in the bungalow on the corner, cried in his bed every night.

I made my way downstairs, drawing in hand.

Was Maisie going be angry about me looking at her stuff? Heart skipping a little, I placed the drawing on top of her jigsaw and watched for her reaction.

'My drawing of Annabelle Punch?' she said evenly, lifting it off her jigsaw and placing it to the side. 'Why did you bring that down?'

'Ah...' I understood, suddenly. 'The girl with no heart.'

'Yes?' Her voice indicated that this should have been obvious. She scrabbled in the jigsaw box for another piece.

'I thought it was *you*!' I blurted out. 'I thought it was...'

She made a snorting noise. 'Oh, Mum.'

So much for Mummy-Maisie telepathy.

The end of term exhibition took place the following evening. Maisie had been 'forced' to do tours of the English department, showing parents the wall displays about *Othello* and *The Great Gatsby*. So I toured the art block by myself.

I was staring intently at one of Maisie's paintings when I heard a voice behind me.

'She has a real talent. Just in case you didn't already know.' It was Mrs Pierce, the art teacher. 'Her portfolio explores the theme of identity, through the lens of fairy tales and folk tales.'

'*The Little Mermaid*,' I replied. The painting was of a girl at the bottom of the sea. She was upside down, her school skirt billowing around her legs, her hair stuck in an old fishing net.

'Such a fun interpretation,' said a low, gravelly voice. 'Maisie has quite the imagination.' I turned around. The teacher had stepped away to talk to another parent, and another woman had appeared behind me. A short woman with wavy blonde hair, wearing a bright, kaftan-like dress. She looked vaguely familiar – I'd probably seen her at sports days and music concerts over the years, or parked near the school gates.

'You must be Teresa,' she said. 'I'm Ally's mum. We're soooo delighted that Maisie is going to join us at our little Scottish place this summer.'

Little Scottish place? Maisie had said it was like Balmoral.

'It was very kind of you to invite her.'

'Ally's told her to bring wellies and wet weather things, because, you know... Scotland in July.' She laughed. 'Oh, and her swimming costume, in case it's hot. There's a waterfall, a couple of miles up into the forest, with a big pool where the kids go swimming. We call it the fairy pool. And she should bring tennis things, obviously.'

Obviously.

'It all sounds wonderful.' I thought of what Maisie's summer would be like if she stayed at home. Helping me to change beds and prepare welcome baskets. Watching TV on her laptop upstairs in the evenings while I took calls for the insurance company at the kitchen table.

'Is Maisie interested in wildlife? Sometimes we see golden eagles, messing about on the ridges. And we get red squirrels in the garden. She should bring her painting things for sure.'

She took my elbow and steered me to the opposite wall, where she pointed to a woodcut piece. It depicted a red cabbage, sliced through the middle, with tight folds of matter like a brain. The label next to it said 'Alison Jenkins'.

'This is fantastic, too,' I said, trying to push down my feelings of maternal smugness. Maisie's work was in a different league. 'Very... visceral.'

'They've all done so well. Now, shall I give you my number?'

I got out my phone and keyed in the digits as she read them out.

'Lovely. Thank you...' I'd forgotten her name but felt awkward about asking her to repeat it. So I typed 'Mrs Jenkins (Ally's mum)' as the contact name and pressed 'save'.

'And it's Braelochie House, near Ballater,' she said. 'That's Aberdeenshire. I'll message you all the deets.'

'Thank you. I'm so pleased that Maisie has... Well, that she's made a good friend. It sounds like she's going to have a wonderful time.'

'She will.' She touched my arm again. 'This will be *so* great.'

It took me half an hour to track down Maisie, who was in the French department, nibbling at the croissants in the 'French café' that was being manned by her fellow students.

'Ally's mum seems nice,' I said.

Maisie looked up, confused. 'Ally's mum was here?'

'Yes,' I said. 'She was in the art department. She was very complimentary about one of your pieces.' Had she actually been? I was no longer sure.

'Oh,' said Maisie, uncertainty crossing her face like a shadow.

'She was telling me about the fairy pool and everything. It does all sound wonderful.'

Maisie grabbed my arm. 'Let's go back to the car. I'm tired.'

8

TERESA

Northumberland
Now

After Caroline had taken George back to the hobbity house, and after Sunny had left, I climbed into bed and lay there, staring up into the darkness.

I knew sleep wasn't going to come. Maybe I should have asked Sunny to stay the night, like he used to in the early days after Maisie had gone missing. Unable to bring Maisie back, he'd given himself another mission – to make me sleep.

He'd made a deal with me, about three days in. I could sit and watch my phone all day, waiting for contact from her, or news from the police. But then I had to let him take over. He took my phone at bedtime and sat up with it all night in the living room, watching box sets and drinking coffee to stay awake. I made him promise to keep it at full volume, and never more than arm's length away. And I lay upstairs in bed, dozing fitfully, my legs writhing with restless energy.

It reminded me of when Maisie had been a newborn, and

my mother had sat up with her in the night, in those first few fretful days after I'd brought her home from the hospital. We'd taken turns. One of us would rest while the other was 'on shift', walking with her, stroking her back, watching her sleep. Watching her breathe, because that was the deal with parenting. You had to watch them to keep them alive.

And that's where I'd gone wrong. I hadn't been paying attention, letting her go off with a family I didn't know, to an address I hadn't checked. I hadn't been watching.

So now, I watched my phone.

Eventually, Sunny had to go back home, back to his work and his clients. I learned to sleep, very lightly, with my phone on the bedside table. I'd wake at the slightest sound. A curtain rustling in the wind, or the patter of rain. A blackbird warbling in the grey dawn.

I dreaded mornings most. Before, I'd never noticed the tiny moments of joy I'd taken for granted every day. A cup of tea made just right. A hot shower, the texture of a favourite jumper. The yellow glow of lamplight when evening drew in. Now, there was no joy. No comfort. Nothing but that hollow ache until it was bedtime and I could try to doze again for a few hours.

Sunny still came most evenings, though, and we'd watch a bit of television together. I chose teenage dramas about vampires, dating reality shows and baking competitions. Shows I thought she might like, that she might even be watching if she was out there, somewhere. It was a tiny point of potential connection with her. And Sunny would sit with me, bringing me tea and ice cream that my taste buds barely registered, laying heavy blankets over my legs to try and ease their restlessness.

And here I was again, alone in the middle of the night, my

mind filled with George and Caroline, and what it all meant. When the bedside clock showed five past one, I pulled a fleece top over my pyjamas and made my way out of the house, over the dunes, to the beach.

Sometimes, teenagers would gather here on warm nights, lighting fires and drinking. But this evening it was deserted.

The moon hung low in the sky, wreathed in wisps of silver-grey cloud. The three stars of Orion's belt were visible. And high in the sky, the W-shaped constellation of Cassiopeia. I remembered telling Maisie how it had been named after the vain queen of Greek legend, the mother of Andromeda. She'd been amazed.

'So there are, like, stories in the sky?' she'd asked, her seven-year-old face alight.

'Yes, sort of. But they never change, that's the thing. In the olden days, sailors used to navigate by the constellations, when they were out of sight of land.'

I lay back on the sand, knowing I'd be getting it in my pyjamas, and not really caring.

It brought a strange kind of comfort that Maisie was under this sky, somewhere, under this moon and these never-changing stars. Whether she was warm and alive and breathing, or lying quietly under the earth, her atoms transforming into soil and tree and flower.

That was the only reincarnation I was prepared to believe in.

I stared up at the stars, trying to imagine the vast distances between them, the endless expanses of time and space. Then I closed my eyes, listening to the waves rushing onto the sand, letting the sound fill up my mind.

A yellow dress with a daisy print.

The sound of water, gushing onto a hard surface.

A man's hands, the tendons standing out like wires.

Fear. Heart-stopping fear.

I jerked upright, hands scrabbling on the sand. Gasping for breath.

As the adrenaline shock subsided, I tried to understand what I had just experienced. Had it been some sort of dream? But I hadn't been asleep, I was sure of that. I'd been drifting, my mind unmoored from the here and now.

And then I became aware of something else. A creeping sense – a certainty – that I had witnessed something *real.* Something utterly malevolent.

Was this how she'd died?

My fingers and toes were tingling. I tried to breathe slowly.

Was I turning 'sensitive', like George? Was the cold, indifferent universe trying to send me answers, after all these years of longing for them?

I stood up, listing on the sand like a drunk person. I filled my lungs with the night air and expelled it with all my might.

'MAISIE!!'

I shocked myself with the noise I made. The primal howl of a mother separated from her young. But it eased the hollowness inside me, just for a second.

I opened my mouth to shout again. But then, I heard something.

Can you hear me?

It was so faint I barely heard it. Just a wisp of sound, carried on the breeze. Heart leaping, I swung round to the south, where I thought it had come from.

I stood there, bracing my whole body to try and hear. The waves rushed at the shore. My breath came in short, ragged gasps.

'MAISIE!!' I shouted again.

This time I thought I heard something from behind me, on the dunes. But less distinct, this time. It could have been the shriek of a gull.

Should I run down the beach, to where I thought I'd first heard the voice? Should I clamber up the dunes? Should I run home and get a torch? I imagined myself pointing it across the sand, this way and that, the light making crazy arcs across the darkness.

I shouted again. And again.

Nothing. Again, nothing.

Eight years of nothing.

I could walk across this beach, looking for her. I could walk along every beach in the country, every forest track or mountain path. I could criss-cross every town centre, every suburban street. And I would still never find her.

And yet.

Here, now, today, there had been a flicker. An echo of her. There had been *something*.

I brushed the sand off my pyjama bottoms and began to walk towards the path that crossed the dunes, towards the house.

It would be easy to imagine eyes, watching me from the dark sweep of the beach behind me. Feet, moving silently over the sand. The hairs on my neck lifted.

But I didn't look back. There was only one place I needed to be right now.

9

TERESA

Northumberland
Eight years ago

The night before the end of term, Maisie came down to the kitchen in her swimsuit – a black one with a high, rounded neckline that she'd once used for school swimming lessons.

'I can't wear this for waterfall swimming,' she said, her face long and her shoulders slumped down. 'I look like a whale.'

I suppressed a flash of irritation. Maisie was a slip of a girl, with a flat midriff and toned arms from all the tennis she'd been doing.

'Can't I get a new one?'

'It's eight o'clock at night, darling. And you leave tomorrow.' We'd already spent two hours after school getting her nails done – acrylic overlays with a pink flower design on each ring finger. I'd queried whether the nails would survive the waterfall swimming, tennis matches and mountain climbing, and I'd been given a withering look.

'We could go to the big supermarket,' she said in a wheedling voice. 'They'll have swimming costumes. Or even a bikini...'

It would be a half-hour drive each way, but I agreed, thinking I should spend time with her while I could. I knew I'd miss her horribly while she was away.

Once there, she buzzed from shelf to shelf like a bee, gathering items she suddenly, crucially, needed – whitening toothpaste, two extra tubes of sun cream, a box of posh biscuits for the family. She returned to me and tipped an armful of products into the basket I was carrying.

'Can I get this cider apple shampoo? And these face masks? Ally said we should do face masks before the Highland Ball. And can I get these evening primrose oil capsules?' She lowered her voice. 'They might help my horrible skin. And my PMS.'

'You don't have "horrible skin".' I glanced down at the price label on the shelf and tried not to wince. 'They're very expensive, darling.'

'Please, Mum. I really need them. Don't you *want* me to be less moody?'

'Well. I suppose you could try them, see if they help.'

'And I think I should get this bikini, don't you?'

I smiled and nodded, deciding not to stress about the extra expense. She might never get another chance to stay in a Scottish castle, or go to a Highland Ball.

In the queue for the checkout, she prodded my arm. 'Look! It's Kaylee.'

She was one of Maisie's old friends from school. She'd dropped out a while ago after falling pregnant.

'How are you?' asked Maisie, all smiles, when we reached the front of the queue. 'How's Dylan?'

'He's good,' said Kaylee. 'He had his first birthday last week.' Her eyes, heavily ringed with black eyeliner, were flat and expressionless.

'Are you still thinking of going to music college?' I asked. 'I remember hearing you sing at one of the school concerts. *One Day I'll Fly Away*, wasn't it? Just you and the piano. It sent tingles up my spine.'

Kaylee shook her head, not looking up. The scanner wouldn't read the barcode on a pack of make-up remover wipes. She flattened it down and passed it over the laser again.

'That's a shame,' I said. 'You were always so talented.'

'There's an open mic night at the Queen's Arms every Thursday,' she said, as if this took care of her musical aspirations.

I'd heard that Jake, her bartender boyfriend, was into drugs. That he'd got a suspended sentence for breaking someone's jaw in a closing-time brawl.

A smug feeling moved through my body at the thought of Maisie's trip to Scotland. It would do her good to spend time with people who had higher aspirations in life.

In the car, Maisie shot me a dark look. 'Mum, you were really judgey.'

'How come?'

'Going on about music college. She's really proud of her job in Tesco. She was stacking shelves before and now she's been moved to checkout.'

'It's just sad to see her ruining her life. She was so –' A car forced its way out onto the roundabout in front of me. I pressed and held the horn.

'Mum! Stop! GOD!! You're so aggressive.'

I opened my mouth again, about to say something about Jake, and drugs, and falling in with the wrong crowd. But Maisie was shoving ear buds into her ears. Conversation over.

She was still in a bad mood the next morning, when I drove her to school.

'Are you sure you've got everything?' I eyed her holdall and rucksack nervously.

'Yes.' She managed to make the word into a sigh.

She and Ally were heading up to Scotland straight from school. It was a half day for the end of term, and a car was being sent for them at one o'clock. She had looked at me blankly when I'd asked who was going to be driving it, and told me that they had 'staff for that kind of thing.'

'If you think of anything else you need, I can always come and drop it off at the end of school.' I paused. 'I could come anyway, to see you off?' I had been planning to go to the big cash and carry near Carlisle, but I'd change my plans in a heartbeat, if she wanted me to.

No response. She sighed again, very quietly.

Instead of letting her jump out near the school gates, I found a parking space as near as I could get. I got out of the car and held out my arms for a hug. Maisie submitted stiffly, turning her head to look towards the school so that my kiss landed near her ear.

'Have a WONDERFUL holiday.'

''Kay. Gotta go.' She turned and walked away towards the school entrance.

'Maisie!' I called, panic rising suddenly. I'd always been

superstitious like that. Never wanting to sleep on an argument. Never saying goodbye without a hug. When she was little, I used to worry about choking and climbing frame accidents. Then it was meningitis, car crashes, or some depressed teenager going crazy with a gun. I didn't know I was worrying about the wrong things.

She turned for a moment, lifted her hand in a half-wave, and then kept on walking.

I watched her go, aware of the aching pull in my chest. It was a sensation I recognised from a hundred different partings with Maisie over the years. I'd felt it on her first day of school, watching her walk shyly into the school building behind her teacher. I'd felt it when dropping her off for her first sleepover, aged seven, with a rucksack full of snacks for a midnight feast. When she'd left for her first school camp, where they weren't allowed to take phones. The mother-child bond, being pulled like a string. My mother had said something to me once – 'That's how you know you're a mother. It's your job to feel it. You have to feel it and let them go anyway.'

Maisie messaged me later that day. Her mood seemed to have softened a little, because she sent me a selfie of herself in the car. And then a photo of the Queensferry Bridge, the structure rising up ahead like angels' wings. She certainly knew how to take a photo.

I replied straight away:

Amazing! I love you!

I love you 2 Mama

I love you 4

Love you 8

Love you 16

32 x

Going as far as 32 probably meant I was forgiven.

I had tried to sneak number games into everything when Maisie had started primary school and had struggled with maths. I'd make her calculate how many brownies we'd need for three welcome baskets, or the number of eggs the hens had laid in a week. Or I'd get her to sing times tables to her favourite *Swan Lake* theme. Years later, having scraped a C in her GCSE maths, she'd proclaimed that she was 'deleting all maths from her mind'. But the 'I love you' game had stuck.

Another message arrived around five o'clock, with a photo of a picnic table by a river and a polystyrene carton of fish and chips.

Stopping in Dunkeld for tea.

Yum yum. Love you 64 my beautiful girl.

10

CAROLINE

Northumberland
Now

Caroline was too buzzed to sleep. Knowing she needed to wind down, she attempted to make some hot chocolate in the cramped, ill-equipped kitchen area of the hobbity house.

What a day it had been. She remembered the delicious rush of excitement she'd felt that morning when she'd decided to do something *different*, for once. She was supposed to be taking George swimming. Mark had decreed that he must have lessons to overcome his fear of the water. But she hated the whole dreary routine – putting blue plastic covers over her shoes and supervising him in the verruca-ridden changing area, ears ringing from the unchecked shrieks of the other participants. Forcing the squeaky rubber armbands over his elbows as tears of protest ran down his cheeks.

Instead, she'd knelt down in front of him and said, 'Shall

we go on an adventure, George-Pie? Shall we just jolly well do it? Shall we go and find your hobbity house and the road-that-isn't-a-road?'

And his eyes had lit up like headlamps. She'd allowed him to sit in the front passenger seat, giving him a map of the area to pore over as they drove up the A1. She didn't tell him she'd already searched online for 'hobbit houses near Lindisfarne', and had made a note of one particular address.

No, she let him think he'd found the place. It had been quite sweet, really. The way he'd pressed his forehead to the window when the sea had come into view.

Should I go left now, Georgie?

Shall we go that way? That street looks interesting.

'I love this,' he'd said. And then, his little body quivering with intensity: 'I love you, Cawoline.'

And she'd felt a lovely little rush of fondness, and had ruffled his hair.

She was pleased, also, that she'd been able to leave him here in the hobbity house while she met with the farm shop owners. Taking an ADHD-riddled child (Caroline had diagnosed the condition herself) to a work meeting hadn't been an ideal plan. If only he would just sit and play Roblox on his iPad for hours, like normal little boys of his age. But no. Everywhere they went, he had to drag out all his wretched drawing materials and make a mess.

And she never got a clear day, what with Mark insisting she do all the school and holiday club pick-ups herself. As a co-parent, he was a challenging proposition – over-protective, micromanaging, never there.

Caroline looked up from stirring her depressing, unfrothy hot chocolate. Someone was knocking on the door. She opened it to find Teresa standing there, with a pleading look on her face. And *en déshabillé,* as the French would say. She'd thrown a fleece on over floral pyjamas and her hair looked like she'd battled through a thick hedge to get here.

She decided it probably wasn't the right moment to mention that there was no hot chocolate whisk in the kitchen drawer.

'Maisie is... Maisie was –' Teresa swallowed hard. 'Maisie is... the name of my daughter. She went missing eight years ago. On July 22nd.'

Ahhh. Now we're finally getting somewhere.

Caroline tried not to let the thought show on her face. Surprise would be appropriate. Concern, yes. But she had to make sure she didn't look... triumphant.

She blinked rapidly. 'Wow. Just... wow.'

She wasn't surprised, of course, not really. She'd seen the look on Teresa's face when she'd first mentioned Maisie's name – the lightning bolt of hope and pain.

Oh yes, she'd clocked that. She'd known Teresa was lying, or as good as.

'I'm sorry I wasn't straight with you before.'

Caroline widened her eyes again, imagining how she might appear to Teresa – shocked, a little vulnerable. She felt pleased she hadn't taken off her mascara yet.

'Come in. We can chat.'

'Is George asleep? It might be better if we talk out here.' Teresa lowered herself onto the carved wooden loveseat just outside the hobbity house's front door. She seemed to be trembling. Caroline sat down beside her, pulling her cardigan sleeves down over her hands as if she, too, felt nervous.

'Okay,' said Teresa. 'This is all a bit of a leap of faith. But this is the only lead I've had in all this time. I can't just let you walk away.'

'I understand,' said Caroline simply. She left a pause, silently counting three beats as a school drama teacher had once taught her. Then she sat forward, her chin in her hands, her eyes intense (or so she imagined). 'So tell me. Tell me about Maisie.'

'Maisie went to stay with a friend for the summer, when she was seventeen years old. And she never came back.'

'Seventeen?' said Caroline. 'That's so young.'

A defensive look flashed across Teresa's face.

'Oh, no...' Caroline realised she'd have to be more careful. It hadn't occurred to her that Maisie, if she existed at all, had been as young as seventeen. But Teresa had interpreted the remark as some kind of judgement. 'I didn't mean... Well, it's just so young, isn't it? To go missing.'

'I didn't realise she *was* missing. Not at first. I thought she was having the time of her life, at her friend's Scottish castle. But after a few weeks, her messages changed. I began to suspect that something was wrong. Then I drove up to the address I'd been given. And there was nothing there. Just a burned-down ruin.'

Caroline gasped. 'Oh my *God*. How absolutely hideous!' She left another pause. 'So they'd given a false address?'

Teresa looked down at her hands. 'Yes. And there were no more text messages after that. It was as if someone had her phone, and they knew I was on to them. '

'What did the police do?'

'The police?' Teresa's voice wavered. 'They were useless. They thought she'd run away. She was seventeen, old enough to leave home if she wanted to. And she'd been gone for a few weeks by the time I reported it.'

'But they must have done something?'

'Oh, they did, at first. They came to the house and

searched every nook and cranny. Searched the glamping huts and all that, too. They spoke to her friends and teachers. The problem was, what she'd told me didn't add up. She'd said she was going up to Scotland, to stay with her friend Ally's family, in their country house there. But it turned out there was no Ally at the school at all. Only an Alison Jenkins, but she had nothing to do with it.'

'Ohhhh...' Caroline's mind was working. A Scottish country house...

'Maisie had lied, there was no getting around it. She'd apparently texted her friend, Kaylee, saying that she "had to get away". That she wasn't getting on with me.' Teresa's voice wobbled again. 'And she'd taken her passport and withdrawn all the funds from her bank account. Two hundred and thirty pounds. The police thought this meant she'd planned to run away. As if she'd last any time at all on two hundred and thirty pounds.' The unfortunate woman leaned forward and clenched her hands, as if she might vomit.

Interesting, thought Caroline, inching a little further away on the loveseat. So there had been quite a bit of police involvement.

'But you'd met the mother? This Ally's mother?'

'I'd met her at the end of term art exhibition, or so I thought. She gave me the address of the Scottish house, and her phone number. But it turned out the phone number was a pay-as-you-go, with no contract behind it. And the address – well, it led me to that burnt-down house.'

'Well, that was significant, wasn't it?' Caroline forced some indignation into her voice. 'For the police? The fact that she wasn't who she said she was?'

'But nobody else remembered seeing her at the exhibition. The police questioned the staff, the parents, the kids – and nothing. It was like she'd never existed.'

'God.' Caroline watched, horribly mesmerised by a droplet that hung on the end of Teresa's nose. To her relief, she wiped it away with the sleeve of her fleece.

'But then it all changed, because they said they'd made contact with Maisie. They'd texted her number, asking her to get in touch. And apparently, she texted them back. She said she couldn't come in to the police station, as they'd asked, because she was way up north somewhere – and that was consistent with her phone data, the police said. But she said she was fine; she was just taking some time out to figure out what she wanted to do. And she messaged a video of herself, saying she was sorry she hadn't called, and that she was fine. The police showed it to me.'

'But that's good, isn't it?'

Teresa shook her head. 'I've always worried that somebody *made* her send that message. That she was being controlled.'

'Do you think she got in with a bad crowd? Drugs... or a *cult*, or something?' Caroline opened her mouth slightly, placed her fingertips over it.

'I thought it might be an older man. Someone she'd met online, perhaps. But the police downgraded her risk level to medium. They started talking about her being "absent" rather than "missing". They said the case would be reviewed again in twenty-eight days. They'd try to get her to come into a police station in person. But in reality, it was game over. It's a question of resources, you see. Do you know that one person goes missing every ninety seconds in the UK?'

'Crikey. So what did you do next?'

'A missing persons charity tried to help. They made

various suggestions for how to reach out on social media and so on. I went back up to Scotland and did the whole poster thing.' Teresa's upper body drooped forward again. She rested her head on her two hands. 'Edinburgh, Glasgow, Dundee, Inverness. Bus stations, train stations. Homeless shelters and hostels. Libraries and second-hand bookshops. Art gallery cafés and art supply shops. I tried to imagine where she might go.'

'How exhausting.' Caroline wished that Teresa would look up at her, so that she would see the empathy shining from her face. She genuinely did feel exhausted at the thought of trailing round all those dreary places.

'And I was always, always looking. At everyone. On the bus or the train or walking along the street. If I was waiting at traffic lights, I'd be scanning the faces of the people in the next car. The people waiting at the crossing.'

Caroline tutted sympathetically. The reality, of course, was that Maisie probably *had* run away. She had probably been desperate to get some breathing space from her mother, who was clearly the worrying, neurotic type. The police had probably drawn this conclusion too – the simplest explanation was usually the right one.

'And then I took to hanging around the school,' went on droopy Teresa. 'Trying to speak to her friends. Trying to catch sight of Ally's mum again. But the staff told me I had to stop loitering, or they'd have to involve the police. I think someone had complained.'

'What did she look like, this woman? Ally's mum? Could you put out... I don't know... an appeal on social media or something?'

Teresa shrugged. 'She was blonde. She was quite short, with a sturdy sort of build. Afterwards, I went a bit strange and kept seeing her everywhere. I thought I saw her once in Fenwicks in Newcastle, but it wasn't her. And I thought I saw her on telly, in an episode of *Silent Witness*. You can imagine what the police made of that.'

Caroline considered. She thought that she, in that situation, would have pushed the police harder. Maybe she would have hired her own lawyer to make sure the police were doing their job properly. Was that a thing? Did people do that? She supposed that she and Mark were in a certain stratum of society – people who had the connections, the resources, the *nous*, to deal with the situations life threw at you. People who just got things done.

'What about... did you ever consider using a private detective firm?'

'I did go down that route. As far as funds would allow.' Teresa looked down, embarrassed. 'I used a local chap. He kept saying he'd "need more budget".'

Again, Caroline reflected on how she and Mark would have handled this. Mark would have put the job out to tender, most likely. He would have negotiated hard, agreeing payment terms up front. *No find, no fee.* Something like that.

'And then I started staying at home nearly all the time. I figured it was the place I was most likely to see Maisie. The place she'd come back to. She'd know to come home, wouldn't she?'

Caroline opened her mouth to say that her friend's tabby cat had returned home one day after being missing for seven years, had simply come in the cat flap as if nothing had happened. Crawling with fleas, but otherwise fine.

But Teresa got in first: 'Do you know what my worst fear is? That I'll die without knowing. Without ever, ever knowing what happened to Maisie. That thought... it makes me want to just implode. To disappear into a black hole. To just stop. But I have to keep going, don't I? In case she comes back. She might need her mum.'

The night was very quiet. Suddenly, Caroline became aware that her eyes were wet. A strange, ticklish sensation went through her, as if a rare butterfly had landed on her palm. She blinked, causing a single, effortless tear to fall. It cooled on her cheek as she waited for Teresa to look up. As soon as she'd seen it, Caroline brushed it away with a quick movement of her hand.

'It's awful. Just awful.' She left an appropriate pause, dropped her voice to a warm murmur: 'I don't know about you. But I could murder a glass of Pinot.'

And then a noise – a bloodcurdling scream – ripped through the night.

11

TERESA

Northumberland
Now

'Jesus!' I sprang to my feet. 'Is that George?'

It came again – a scream of pain. Utter terror. It made me think of a film I'd once seen about a soldier being tortured in a Middle Eastern jail. He'd cried for his mother by the end, his trousers soaked in waste.

'Here we go again,' said Caroline under her breath. Then she turned to me. 'This is what I was talking about.'

I followed her into the cabin. George was thrashing around on the bed, tangled in the bed covers. 'No! No! He's coming!'

'He's actually still asleep,' said Caroline, perching on the edge of his bed. 'He's having a night terror.'

'Shouldn't you wake him?'

'That can distress them even more.'

George sat bolt upright and pointed to the corner of the room. 'Look! Look!'

The corner of the cabin was deep with shadow. The knots in the wood looked darker, their patterns accentuated. There was one gnarled area that looked almost like the shape of a face, down low near the floor. Was that what had frightened him?

Then his eyes changed. Instead of staring into nothing, he seemed to see Caroline. He crumpled against her body and she held him close, pressing her cheek against the top of his head.

'Come on now, Sausage. It was just a dream.'

'Oh dear,' I murmured. George's hair and his pyjamas were soaked in sweat and the sheet had a large damp patch. To Caroline, I said softly, 'Do you have a spare pair of pyjamas for him? Would you like to borrow something?'

I could hardly believe what I was saying. I was thinking of Maisie's old elephant pyjamas, which I'd kept folded in the bottom drawer of my wardrobe, long after she'd grown out of them. Along with some of her baby clothes, blankets and old teddies. One or two keepsakes from each year of her life.

'Oh, that would be wonderful, thank you.'

I came back a few minutes later with my arms full of fresh bedding, and the pyjamas, with their soft grey elephants printed onto the brushed cotton. Caroline helped George while I quickly changing the bedding.

At the bottom of the bed, between the sheets, I felt something hard. It was a porcelain figurine, about six inches high. An angel, in white and gold robes, with a halo. And there was something else in there. I pulled out a shepherd, who was carrying a lamb. They looked like figures from a church nativity scene.

I placed them on the little bedside shelf.

George was drowsy now, his body floppy and relaxed in

the elephant pyjamas. I opened my mouth to ask Caroline if she could make sure to leave the pyjamas behind when they left, as they had sentimental value. But then I closed it again. If the pyjamas had helped George to feel comfortable and safe, why shouldn't he keep them? It wasn't as if they were any good to Maisie now.

Caroline lifted him onto the bed. He wrapped his arms tight around her neck, clinging to her as she tried to lay him down. A fierce longing rose up in my chest.

'Thank you so much, Teresa,' said Caroline, tucking him under the fresh covers, patting them down lightly over his arms and his chest.

'Poor George. I hope he's alright.'

'Honestly, he'll be fine.'

'Have you considered anything like... I don't know... hypnotherapy, or something? To try and get to the bottom of all this?'

'Hypnotherapy?' She laughed. 'For George? He'd never sit still for long enough!' Suddenly, she looked exhausted.

'It's late. I should let you both get to bed.' I left a small pause, which she didn't fill. 'Shall I bring round some pastries in the morning? I can leave them outside the door for when you get up. A nice treat for George after his disturbed night.'

Caroline tilted her head to the side. 'That's very kind. But George only eats sandwiches and soup.'

'How about a sandwich made with brioche bread,' I suggested. 'With some Nutella and banana as the filling?'

'That sounds lovely. But really...'

I'd gone too far. I'd embarrassed her. 'It's no trouble. Poor George. A nice breakfast is the least I can do.'

My hand on the door, I looked back at George. He was

lying still with his eyes shut tight. But he'd taken the angel from the shelf and was clutching it against his chest, one hand wrapped tight around it.

His lips were moving. Was he... praying?

'Is he okay?'

'Oh yes,' said Caroline. 'He's self-soothing.'

I caught a few of his whispered words.

'Two times three is six... two times four is eight...'

12

TERESA

Northumberland
Now

The waiting room at the Brighter Days practice was warm and welcoming, but I felt anything but comfortable.

I'd barely left the house, over the last eight years, other than essential visits to the cash and carry, or quick walks along the beach. And my trips to Scotland, every few months, to put up posters.

I was always worrying about what might happen if Maisie came back home one day. What if she rang the doorbell, and I wasn't there? I always kept a house key under the flowerpot by the front door, a habit which Sunny fretted about, saying I was asking to be burgled.

A woman stepped out of one of the consulting rooms. She wore a designer navy trouser suit and a crimson silk blouse. Her cheekbones were contoured, her glossy dark hair swept up in a sequinned clasp.

'Aanya,' she said, holding out her hand. 'I only have a few moments, I'm afraid, before my next client. Sunny said there was something you wanted to discuss urgently?'

When Sunny had told me that his older sister was a psychotherapist, I had made certain assumptions. In my mind, she'd been a middle-aged woman with a soft, careworn face. A bit frumpy and maternal. But Aanya was nothing short of glamorous. No motherly vibes in evidence.

She and Sunny both worked here at Brighter Days, a holistic practice in Berwick upon Tweed. It offered various services including psychotherapy and therapeutic massage, holistic physiotherapy and acupuncture. She was the only therapist who was qualified to work with children. In fact, she worked one afternoon a week at Maisie's old school. I'd heard Maisie mention her once or twice.

Annabelle's been sent to Mrs Kaur...

Mrs Kaur gave us a talk about the dangers of social media...

She ushered me into her consulting room and closed the door behind me. Her heeled boots made a soft thunking noise on the carpeted floor as she walked over to her chair.

'What can I do for you?'

'I just wanted some general advice,' I said. 'A steer in the right direction, I suppose. About a little boy.'

A little crease appeared above her nose.

'His name is George. He's from down south, near Nottingham. He's only eight. His stepmother brought him to see me because he's been having... memories, I suppose you would call them. He seems to be remembering a past life. A life *here*. In Northumberland. In my house. Before he was born.'

Her expression didn't change. She'd probably trained herself not to react when patients came out with whacky statements.

'His memories are very specific. He knew his way around my house, even though he'd never been there before. He knows things that he couldn't possibly know. Things about... Maisie.'

The crease disappeared. She sat back on her seat, as if she had it all sussed out now. I was a bereaved mother, driven mad by grief, obsessing over somebody else's child.

The room was very quiet. But I thought I could hear, very faintly, the sound of someone crying in the next room.

'So how did you think I might be able to help?'

'This little boy, George. He's been having nightmares. And night terrors. Dreaming about being lifted out of his bed. About drowning. Yesterday, when we were in the bathroom, he held his breath until he fainted.'

She clasped her hands in front of her, bracelets chinking gently. 'Breath-holding episodes are common in early childhood. And nightmares and night terrors are *very* common. Usually they are a normal part of development and children simply grow out of them. If they're becoming too disruptive, or interfering with his daily life or his progress in school, then his GP could refer him to a sleep clinic.'

'Caroline, his step-mum, seems to think he could be remembering a traumatic death.'

Aanya stared at me for a long time, not filling the silence.

'She was wondering... I was wondering whether hypnotherapy might help. It might shed some light on it all. It might help him to figure out where these memories are coming from.'

'I suppose my question would be this.' She crossed one trousered leg neatly over the other. 'What benefit would all this bring to George?'

'But surely if he could process the memories, it might

help his night terrors and... and everything?' I finished lamely.

'Let me ask you this, Teresa – if George was having nightmares about monsters under the bed, or failing a test at school, would you be suggesting hypnotherapy?'

'I might, if he was very upset by it.'

'Maybe you want to explore his nightmares because the details are interesting to *you*?'

'But –'

She waited for me to finish, regarding me with cool eyes. She was probably unimpressed with how I'd treated Sunny, stringing him along as a 'friend' all these years.

'But some kind of therapy might help him, mightn't it?'

'I suspect what you're thinking of is something along the lines of past life regression hypnotherapy. These methods have been discredited time and time again, and that's why you rarely hear of them outside of Hollywood movies. It wouldn't be appropriate to do such work with a child of this age. I don't know of any reputable therapist who would even consider such a thing.'

'Well, couldn't you just talk to him?' I asked. 'If he's suffered trauma of some kind, whether in this life or not, wouldn't it be appropriate to help him process it?'

She tilted her head to the side, seeming to examine my face more closely. 'Despite what pop psychology and social media articles would have us believe, not all behaviours stem from trauma. And this type of behaviour is not as uncommon as you'd think. Children who talk about past lives don't necessarily have any mental health issues. Think about children who have imaginary friends. We don't rush them off to the psychiatrist, or put them on antipsychotic drugs to stop their hallucinations. We don't pathologise that behaviour, or at least we shouldn't. In the vast majority of cases, they're just being children. It's part of their development.'

I felt like a stupid schoolgirl in front of the headmistress. A mindless consumer of pop psychology articles.

'He takes an angel to bed with him. He sleeps holding a cold, hard porcelain angel. Is that just part of his development, too?'

'Lots of children use transitional objects, or comfort objects.'

'Sunny said you'd know about past lives, and the cycle of rebirth, and everything. He said you'd worked with a lot of Hindu clients, and studied all that.' I felt my cheeks reddening.

'But the child isn't from a Hindu family?'

I shook my head.

Aanya gave a small shrug. 'In cases where past life memories are reported, they usually fade by the time the child reaches about seven or eight. So I would suggest this is likely to be the case for George also. Now, if he has sleep-related anxiety, that's another thing, and a therapist may certainly be able to help with that. But it would make more sense for him to see someone in Nottingham. I have a few names I could recommend.' She paused, her face relaxing into a kinder expression. 'You might also find it beneficial to talk things over with someone. I can certainly put you in touch with a colleague.'

13

TERESA

Northumberland
Now

I got caught up in roadworks on the way home. Rain pelted the roof of the car as I waited at temporary traffic lights, and I had to turn the windscreen wipers to the fastest setting. Caroline and George wouldn't want to stay any longer in this weather – no beach walks today. I resolved to go and see them as soon as I got back. With a twist of anxiety, it occurred to me that they might have left already. There'd been no sign of them when I'd dropped off the breakfast basket outside their cabin door at eight o'clock.

The rain had eased off by the time I got home. I parked the car quickly and jogged up to the cabin. Oh God, they *were* about to leave. Caroline answered the door with her bag already slung over her shoulder.

George jumped up in the air, just a few inches, just once, when he saw me. 'Teresa,' he said. Then he raced past me and began circling the hens' enclosure, making aeroplane noises.

'I'm glad I caught you.' My voice was ragged as I tried to catch my breath. 'I've been to see someone this morning. She's an expert in child psychology. She said that hypnotherapy...' I dropped my voice to a murmur. '*Past life hypnotherapy*... is a no-go. He's too young.'

'Ah well,' said Caroline.

'But you should come back!' I tried to make my voice light and fun. 'George has some sort of connection with the place, doesn't he? Even if it's all a mystery. One of the glamping pods is free next weekend, if you'd like to come back?'

Caroline handed me the key to the cabin and picked up her bag, and a paper bag with string handles, printed with a farm shop logo. 'That's terribly kind of you. Unfortunately, we have plans next weekend. But I'm sure we'll be in the area again at some point. One of the farm shops sounded very interested in the sticky toffee puddings.'

'Can I have your number?' I sounded like some mad stalker.

She hesitated for just a second, glancing across at George. He was spinning in circles now, swinging his rucksack around. I realised he was being a helicopter, not an aeroplane. Clarabelle, the older of the two hens, was eyeing him doubtfully.

'Sure.' Caroline put the bags down and took out her phone. 'I'll send you a text and then you'll have it.'

I read out my own number to her and a moment later her message came through with a little ding. She smiled graciously, lifting her bags again.

My heart sped up. Could I really say what I was about to say? I remembered the tears of empathy that had filled Caroline's eyes when I'd told her about Maisie last night. I decided to take the chance.

'I can't get over how... how similar George is to Maisie.'

She looked interested. 'Really? In what ways?'

'The way he talks. His mannerisms.' I paused. 'This is going to sound insane. I mean... terribly rude, I expect. But I'm just going to come out with it. I can't get it out of my head that George could be related to us. Related to Maisie. That he could be...' I cleared my throat. 'Her son.'

Caroline raised her eyebrows. But her expression was strangely unreadable, as if she was trying to decide how to react, whether or not to be offended.

'By some sort of... I don't know. A surrogacy arrangement? Or a private adoption. I know... *I know*... that it doesn't make any sense. But I can't get it out of my head.'

'Hmm.' Caroline gazed at me. 'I think, Teresa, that this is your grief talking. I was a great friend of Jan's, and I trust Mark *implicitly*.' She closed her eyes on the last word, but there was something in her voice, a slight off-note, which suggested that maybe – just maybe – she didn't. And then she hesitated, just a micro-second too long. 'No, it's just not possible that –'

'I don't suppose... well, does he have a birth certificate?'

'A birth certificate?' Caroline frowned, her nose wrinkling. 'Yes, I'm sure he has a birth certificate. I mean, I *think* he has. Actually... I was looking for it the other day, for something. I couldn't lay my hands on it.' A flicker of doubt moved over her face, as delicate as a moth. Then it was gone, and she smiled. 'I'd have to check with Mark.'

'What would be amazing,' I went on, 'is if I could see it? Just to put my mind at rest.'

She shrugged. 'I mean... I could probably order one online? I *guess*? But no, it's probably at home. I'll check.'

'Brilliant. You're so kind. Look, let me help you carry your stuff.' I leaned down to pick up the paper bag. It gaped open as I took the handles and I saw that it contained unopened food from the welcome pack, neatly stacked inside.

'Come along, Georgie,' called Caroline in a high, fluting voice as I followed her along the path. 'I love what you've done here.' She gestured to the honeysuckle arch that we passed under to reach the sloped rockery and the steps down to the parking area.

'Thank you. I've managed to grow some alpine plants in this sheltered area just here...'

She swept onwards. 'Marvellous. I do like –'

George, whirling up behind us, caught Caroline on the back of her knee with his rucksack. Her heeled boot went from under her. She shrieked and fell backwards, cracking her head off the rustic stone slab that formed the top of the rockery steps.

'My GOD! Caroline? Are you okay?'

She lay completely still, her eyes shut.

I patted her arm. Then her cheek. 'Caroline? Caroline?'

No response. I leaned in towards her, trying to hear if she was breathing. There was something on the step behind her head, a dark liquid pooling very slowly onto the stone. She must have split the back of her head open.

And the edge of the step was green with moss. Slippery.

A hundred thoughts went through my head at once. Hospitals, scans, comas and bleeping machines. A funeral car and a weeping family. Legal action. The public liability insurance documents in my filing cabinet.

'I didn't mean to.'

I became aware of George, kneeling on the path behind Caroline, his face pulled into a long frown.

'I know, I know. It was an accident.' I forced a smile, but my voice came out shaky. I leaned over Caroline and patted her hand awkwardly, and then her shoulder. 'You're okay, love. You've just had a little bump. But I'm going to call an ambulance, just to be on the safe side.'

George rummaged in his rucksack as I dialled the number and waited to be connected. He pulled out the stone angel first and then the shepherd, checking them for damage.

14

TERESA

Northumberland
Now

George was doing a great job with the broad beans. I'd shown him how to pop the long bumpy pods and pull out the beans, then peel the pale, fibrous skins off each one. He'd nearly filled a cereal bowl with the contents.

'See? They're like little green jewels. Like emeralds. Some people eat the whole bean but I like the inner beans. And they're fresher than fresh, straight from the garden.'

'I don't eat inner beans,' he warned. The chair rattled as he swung his legs.

'No?'

'I only eat sandwiches. Or soup. Crushed up soup.'

'Ooh... they'd be lovely in a soup. I've got some nice pea and ham soup in the freezer. We could add the beans to that and blitz it up. I can show you how to work the blender if you like?'

It was strange, talking to a child like this. Somehow

knowing what to say to engage him, to keep him focused on the task, just as I'd used to do with Maisie at that age. It was like getting on a rusty old bike and finding that its wheels turned smoothly and perfectly.

'They're all furry,' he said, running his finger along the inside of the pod. 'Can I keep one?' He looked up at me, eyes pleading, as if he was asking for a puppy.

'It won't stay furry for long,' I said. 'It would go brown and slimy. We can put them on the compost heap, though. Then they can be used for making more beans.'

'In my old life, I nearly had a dog.'

Once again, it seemed like he'd been able to tell what I was thinking.

'Oh yes?'

'His name was Beanie. He used to jump about all over the place. He wasn't real, though.'

I drew in a slow, careful breath. My mother had been to Switzerland when Maisie had been about five. She'd brought back an enormous, stuffed St Bernard's dog as a present. Maisie had called it Bernie. It had 'slept' on her bed for years. Sometimes she'd wake me up in the mornings by bouncing Bernie on top of me, making wild barking noises.

'It's not me,' she'd say, naughty eyes twinkling. 'Bernie woke me up too early.'

'In your old life?' I said to George now. 'Was that...'

'Before I died,' he said.

My heart hammered as I asked my next question. 'What was your name, before you died?'

'Munchkin, I think. Or that might be the other one.'

Or vat might be ve uvver one.

'The other one?'

'The other one of me.'

'Do you mean –' I stopped myself from saying the name 'Maisie.' I had to avoid leading questions. 'What was the other one called?'

He propelled himself off his chair and it scraped back on the kitchen floor. 'I'm hungry.'

'*I'm hungry?*' I queried. 'That's a funny name.'

'No!' he stamped his foot in pretend outrage, a mischievous smile pulling at the corners of his mouth. 'When will Caroline be back?'

'Hopefully tomorrow. Remember, the doctors said she had to stay in so they could do a scan?'

'Like an X-ray,' he said, nodding.

'Yes. Because she lost consciousness for a few minutes after she banged her head. And she's feeling a bit poorly, throwing up and feeling dizzy.'

I'd driven to the hospital behind the ambulance, with George strapped into the back seat. Caroline had been taken straight away, but after forty minutes a doctor had come out into the waiting room and said she'd need a CT scan and that the wait time would be about six hours.

I'd been allowed in to speak to her, had been taken to a bay where she was lying on a trolley with her eyes closed, clutching a grey cardboard sick bowl in both hands.

'The doctor said your scan will be a few hours yet,' I'd said very softly. 'Would you like me to take George home? He's getting a bit restless.' He had been helicoptering around, drawing irritated glances from the people in the waiting room. He'd sat down when asked, but it looked like it was causing him physical pain.

'Yes please, Teresa,' she'd croaked, her eyes still closed. 'I tried to call Mark, but his phone's switched off. He's flying back from Chicago today. He'll be in the air.'

'Don't worry about George. He'll be absolutely fine. I'll take good care of him, and I'll call later to see how you are.'

'She'll be absolutely fine,' I said to George now, echoing my assurances to Caroline. 'And you're going to have a sleep-over with me. Won't that be fun?'

'Can I sleep in my old room?' he asked.

'You can sleep in the room upstairs,' I said carefully. 'The one with the bookcase.'

Later, George helped me to make flapjacks while the pea and ham soup defrosted in the microwave. He stood up on a stool beside me and stirred soft brown sugar into the melted butter with a wooden spoon.

My mouth watered at the warm, buttery scent rising from the pan. I realised that I felt hungry. Properly ravenous, for the first time in years.

'Do you remember you had a bad dream last night?' I asked. 'What was that all about?'

'Probably about getting drowned again,' he said wearily. 'Or maybe about school.' The muscles in his face tightened. 'I can't remember.'

'Three big dollops of golden syrup now,' I said, flipping the metal lid off the tin and handing it to him. Slowly, he lifted a gloopy spoonful and let it drop it into the saucepan.

'Two more big ones,' I said. 'Try twisting the spoon. That's it – well done.'

'It's going all nice,' he observed, pushing the syrup into the sludge of half-dissolved brown sugar.

'Do you think you'll try one when they're ready?' I asked. 'After we've had our soup and sandwiches?'

'Maybe.'

'So... don't you like school?'

He puffed out a breath, making the curls at his hairline lift. 'I'm not good at school.'

'How come?'

'I have to go in a separate room.' He looked down at the floor, the corners of his mouth pulled down in an exaggerated pout.

'Why's that?'

'I do separate lessons with Miss Honey, the TA.' He ran a syrupy hand through his hair and then wiped it on his trousers. I'd have to make sure to clean him up before I returned him to Caroline.

'With the teaching assistant? Why is that?'

'Because I'm like a sponge. That's what Miss Honey says.'

'A sponge?'

'Yes. For people's feelings. If I sponge up too much of them then I just... explode! Boooff!' He flung his arms out.

'Do you want to stir in the oats? Carefully now, because the mixture's hot.'

He stirred, the oats losing their floury look and becoming golden and sticky. 'In the separate room I'm allowed to get off my chair and do star jumps. But I'm still behind. A lot behind, in maths.'

His shoulders drooped, and he gave a great sigh, as if the weight of the world was upon him.

'What?'

'Milo and the boys in my class laugh at me all the time. They say I'm a freak.'

'Maybe Caroline should speak to the school about Milo if he's being mean.'

He shrugged.

'So... what kind of feelings are you picking up? From other people, I mean?'

'Raya gets worried about tests. Milo's parents are fighting all the time. And Miss Mowbray's husband's badly, badly ill. He goes to the hospital every week to get hooked up to some poison. It drips into him – drip, drip, drip.' He looked up at me, his brow furrowed. 'It goes into *him* but it makes *her* cry.'

A shiver rose up my back. 'How do you...'

'And Milo's a red, the worst kind.'

'What do you mean?'

'His sad spurts up like a volcano. Other people, like Miss Mowbray, have blue or green. Just kind of cold and watery like a pond.'

I wondered if this was some kind of exercise he'd been given to help with his emotions.

Can you describe what your pain looks like? What shape and colour is it? Does it have a texture?

'I can feel *yours*, of course,' he said, as if he was stating the obvious. 'But I don't mind.' He tipped his head and laid his flushed pink cheek against my arm.

What did he mean? He didn't even know about me losing Maisie. Unless Caroline had told him. Unless...

Together, we pressed the flapjack mixture into a baking tin. While it was baking, I whizzed up the soup with a stick blender and made a simple cheese and tomato sandwich for both of us.

'Help me carry these to the kitchen table?' I asked George.

He kneeled on his chair, rather than sat. Bobbing up and down, he lifted the top slice of bread off his sandwich to have a look inside.

'It's just cheese and tomato.'

He took a bite, chewed, and then took a tiny, wincing sip of the soup.

'Do you like the soup, George?'

'No,' he said. He slid his lower legs out from under him and settled onto his bottom.

'Oh.'

So was he an empath, or something? Was he psychic? Maybe, when he'd drawn the wallpaper from Maisie's room, he was simply drawing what he could see in my mind.

I remembered my visit to Cheryl Smithers, a celebrated local psychic and medium. I'd consulted her soon after Maisie had disappeared, and the police and private investigator had drawn a blank.

I'd been expecting some sort of dimly lit, tent-like room, draped in gauzy curtains. But she'd just shown me into her very ordinary living room, gesturing towards a squashy leather sofa that was too big for the space. She turned off *Escape to the Country* and tossed the remote control onto the coffee table.

'I'm not getting anything,' she said, after just a few minutes. I'd given her one of Maisie's hoodies to hold, and an old hair scrunchie. She'd drawn several deep breaths, making me think, somehow, of a sniffer dog, trying to catch a scent.

'What does that mean?' Did that make it more or less likely that Maisie was still alive?

Cheryl shrugged apologetically. 'It's just like a radio that's switched off, or out of batteries. There's just no information coming through. That happens sometimes.' And she'd pushed away the cash I tried to hand over when I left.

I used to sometimes wonder if Maisie was a ghost, now. If she was haunting my house. Once, a few years after she'd gone missing, I'd found her favourite mug at the front of my kitchen cupboard. (It had been hidden at the back, where it wouldn't make me cry every time I made a cup of tea.)

I'd never told anyone that, not even Sunny.

Did George have some sort of 'gift' too, like Cheryl? Would it be better to consult her, rather than trying to convince a hypnotherapist or child psychologist to help him?

I watched George now, nibbling at his sandwich.

'What colour's mine?' I asked.

I waited for him to ask what I meant. To clarify that I was talking about my sadness.

'Bright white,' he said. 'A hot, hot fire.' He pronounced the 't's lightly and distinctly, his eyes wide.

I had always thought of my sadness, my pain since losing Maisie, as black. A black hole that sucked all light into it. With a gravitational pull so huge that there was no hope of getting myself out of it. And here was this child, saying the opposite. Saying that it was white, bright, burning like a sun. And if you thought about it, he was right. My never-ending sadness was fuelled by my never-ending love, my love that just wouldn't give up. It was made up, entirely, of love.

15

TERESA

Northumberland
Now

The next morning, I made the mistake of running a bath for George.

'No-no-no,' he said. He flew into the bathroom to put toothpaste on his toothbrush and then ran out again.

'I can't send you back to Caroline when you're all grubby and sticky,' I protested, as he buzzed around the hall with the toothbrush in his mouth.

'Nop gwubby,' he insisted.

'Just an in-and-out bath? A very quick one?'

He gave a high, piercing shriek and ran out, toothpaste foam bubbling down his chin.

I messaged Caroline at nine, while I was making breakfast – early enough to show concern as to her wellbeing, but not too pushy, not suggesting that I wanted George out of my hair.

How are things going? I hope you had a comfortable night.

George was sitting at the kitchen table, pink-cheeked and triumphant, after successfully avoiding his bath. He was wearing one of Maisie's old dressing gowns, a white fluffy one with bear ears on the hood.

'I wonder if Caroline will be allowed out of hospital this morning.' I watched George's face carefully.

'I expect she might need an operation,' he replied. I thought I saw a gleeful flicker on his face, but then it disappeared.

It wouldn't be a disaster, I reflected, if George had to stay another night. Or even a week or two.

Or maybe she would die, and I could keep him here with me forever.

Horrified, I pushed the thought away. But when she did finally message, just before ten, I felt an unmistakeable jolt of disappointment.

CT scan was ok so I'm getting out later today. They're hoping no long-term damage but will need to keep an eye on things. Can't drive for a while.

That sounds encouraging. George can stay here as long as needed so don't worry about him.

Thanks so much. I'm sending a car to pick him up first, and then it'll come on to collect me. It should be with you by mid morning. The driver's name is Raoul. If you could stick our bags in the car too that would be great. Will arrange to collect my car when I can drive again.

I paused for a moment, contemplating possible responses.

Perhaps I could offer to keep him here until she was out of hospital. Or I could drive him back to Retford myself... except that it would mean leaving the glamping huts for a whole day, perhaps overnight.

In the end I simply replied:

No problem. Let me know if there's anything else I can do.

There is one thing. Mark wants me to ask for the name of your public liability insurer. Just to cover formalities, blah blah. Sorry.

My heart sank.

Of course. I'll look out the paperwork.

So I had him for an hour or two longer. I decided to prepare some sandwiches for his breakfast. One with crispy bacon and a fried egg. One with mashed banana with a drizzle of honey.

'Banana sandwiches!' exclaimed George, when I put it in front of him. 'Maisie's favourite!' No sooner were the words out than he clapped his hand over his mouth.

'Who's Maisie?'

He shook his head. He took his hand away from his mouth and busied himself with the sandwich. He whispered something to himself under his breath, so faintly I could barely hear it. 'Shut *up*.'

'Do you remember Maisie from your old life?'

He began to hum to himself.

'I had a Maisie,' I said quietly. 'She went missing. I searched and searched for her.'

He pushed back his chair and scampered away, leaving the sandwich on the table, just one small bite taken out of it.

I gave him ten minutes and then I went to find him. He was standing in front of Maisie's desk, lifting up various bits and pieces and putting them down again – an old lipstick, a pencil sharpener, a bottle of perfume.

'I'm sorry about before,' I said.

'It's okay.' He sniffed the perfume bottle, closing his eyes and drawing a long, deep breath. Then he picked up a plastic bottle full of yellow-gold capsules. He held it up so that they caught the light, seeming, for a moment, to glow. 'Wow. Can I have these? What are they?'

'No, darling. That's evening primrose oil. It's a kind of medicine. It's not a toy.'

His head dropped. 'Okay.'

'We'd better pack up your things.'

He handed his pyjamas to me, and I folded them and tucked them into the bottom of his rucksack. I felt something cold and hard at the bottom and pulled it out.

'Here's your special watch, George. Do you want something to put it in, so it doesn't get broken?'

'It's already broken.'

I shook out the duvet and noticed the porcelain angel and

the shepherd figurine, wedged between the side of the bed and the wall.

'Don't forget these,' I said, handing them over.

Then, when he merely nodded, I asked, 'Do they have names?'

'That's the Archangel Gabriel,' he said. 'And this one's Stanley the shepherd.'

'How come you take them to bed with you?'

He frowned, his face suddenly defensive. I wondered if he'd been teased about them before, or if Caroline had encouraged him to part with them, at least for bedtime. 'I need them to keep safe.'

'What do they keep you safe from?' I asked gently.

'The things in my dreams.'

'What do you dream about?'

'When I died.'

Suddenly, his features seemed to rearrange themselves into Maisie's. The eyes, dark like treacle, staring into mine. The pointy chin.

'Oh, sweetheart.' I wanted to pull him against me, to hold him until he felt safe. 'Are your dreams very scary?'

'Yes,' he said quickly, snatching in a breath. 'I'm running up the stairs – fast, fast, but I can't go fast enough. Someone is coming.'

I nodded. 'What else do you remember?'

'I remember trying to hide. And then I'm dead and drowned. My arms and legs won't move. They're slow like the gold syrup.'

The doorbell rang.

'No!' George jumped up, shot through the hall into my room and tried to hide in the wardrobe.

It took me ten minutes to coax him out while Raoul, the driver, waited patiently by the car. I handed George's rucksack to him, heavy with the stone figurines.

I pressed two flapjacks into George's hand for the journey. He hadn't eaten his breakfast. And I hadn't even brushed his hair – a blonde-brown tuft was sticking up at the front.

'Bye, then, George. It was lovely to have you to stay.'

Suddenly, he threw his arms around my middle. He buried his face against me. I could feel the hot circle of his breath against the jersey fabric of my dress. Stunned, shaking, I held him.

I pushed the thought away, but it came anyway.

My child, for the first time in eight years.

My child.

And I had no choice but to let him go.

He climbed into the car. The engine started up, and I saw the movement of Raoul's arm as he put the car into gear.

And then the window began to open, the glass sliding down half way. George was pushing something out of the window towards me. It was the china shepherd.

I took it from him and the window slid up again.

'George! Don't you need this?' I tapped on the darkened glass. 'George!'

He lifted his hand in a half-wave as the car drove off.

16

CAROLINE

Retford
Now

It was good to be home. A relief, after the ill-equipped hobbit house and the unspeakable smells and sounds of the hospital.

Caroline was kneeling by the filing cabinet in Mark's study. She pulled out a cardboard file that was labelled 'George' and began to arrange the contents on the red and navy Persian rug that lay over the oak floorboards. The room had a reassuring smell – expensive wood polish and old books.

Ever since she'd been a child, growing up in a damp, pebble-dashed council house in Hull, she'd dreamed of living in a house like this. She loved the high ceilings and ornate cornices, the large, square rooms. And the elegant Victorian windows, with the upper and lower sashes each divided into six smaller panes. Everything was generously proportioned, pleasing to the eye.

She glanced outside – the wind was getting up, whistling in the chimneys. (The house had four chimney stacks, standing tall and proud on the four corners of the roof.) The branches of the copper beech, the one at the far end of the garden, danced in witchy silhouettes against the twilight sky. It made it feel all the more cosy inside. The walls of the study – painted in 'Rectory Red' from the paint company's 'Heritage' range – seemed to hold her in womb-like comfort. She took a deep, satisfied breath.

'Can I see?'

She jumped. George was standing behind her.

'This is your birth certificate,' said Caroline, holding it up for him to see. 'See? George Gabriel Jackson. You were born in Aberdeen. It shows your mum and dad – Jan and Mark. And that's your birthday – the twenty-second of July.'

'Do you need that certificate before you can get born?'

'Not exactly.'

'Who decides when you get born, then?'

'It doesn't really work like that,' Caroline murmured.

George curled himself up and did a forward roll across the rug.

'Did you see?' he demanded.

'Yes, I did,' she said. 'Very good, Georgie-Pie. Do another one for me. I'll watch properly this time.'

She drew another file out of the cabinet, and a piece of paper floated free – it was the form completed by the hospital staff in Aberdeen just after George's birth. Caroline didn't understand some of the abbreviations used, but she could see that Jan had lost 900 ml of blood, and that George's birth weight had been just five pounds two ounces. Poor little mite. She remembered how small he'd looked, when he'd arrived to live here at Malham Manor, shortly after his third birthday.

She remembered carrying him up the wide mahogany staircase on that first day, his head turning slowly as she moved, his gaze fixed on the stained-glass window at the middle landing.

She'd thought she'd been prepared. She'd researched 'gentle parenting' techniques and read most of a book on childhood trauma. She'd sourced a beautiful vintage bed for him – one with a railed iron bed frame, salvaged from an old boarding school that had closed down, and had ordered pastel-striped bedlinen to complete the aesthetic. But he'd looked so tiny in it that she'd changed it for a white wooden toddler bed, paired with a dinosaur duvet set. But the new covers hadn't even raised a smile. He hadn't talked much – in fact she'd wondered if he'd had some sort of language delay.

Which reminded her, she was supposed to schedule another meeting with his class teacher. He'd scored just five out of thirty in his recent maths test.

She put a hand to the back of her head, which had begun to throb, as it frequently did since her fall and concussion. She should probably be relaxing in a lavender bath, rather than trawling through paperwork.

She'd had to lie to Mark and say she'd fallen at the farm shop where she'd been touting her puddings. She'd told him that the farm shop lady had kindly looked after George while she'd been seen at the hospital. Unfortunately, he was insistent that she should claim for damages, should demand that the farm shop sent over their insurance details.

Caroline had tried to change the subject. She didn't want to sue Teresa. That unfortunate woman had enough to deal with.

Her chest ballooned with satisfaction as she thought of how she'd managed to get the truth out of her.

There had been a real-life Maisie.

That shadowy presence – like a ghost, living in the house alongside them – was finally starting to come into the light.

The name had popped up every so often over the last few years – she'd heard George whisper it when he was playing with his Lego, or talking to himself before going to sleep. At first, she'd thought he was referring to someone from school. Or perhaps a character from a book or a television programme.

Maisie doesn't like carrots.

Maisie's not scared of the dark.

And then he'd started talking about his 'old life', and 'the time before'. Going on about the 'road that was only sometimes a road', and all that peculiar stuff.

When she'd mentioned it to Mark, he'd just shrugged. He'd never shown much interest in George's imaginative life. When she'd suggested that it was almost as if George was having memories of a past life, he'd stroked her hair, all gooey-eyed.

'It's very special.'

'What is?' she'd asked.

'The strength of your connection with George. He's even got you believing in his imaginary friends.' Then he'd taken her face between his two hands and placed a tiny, gentle kiss on her lips. 'It's adorable. I *love* you. I don't mean to speak ill of the dead, but you're a million times the mother Jan ever was.'

Caroline had waited for the delicious, almost sexual thrill that she used to experience, early in their relationship, when Mark would say this sort of thing. It hadn't quite materialised.

And then there'd been that time, a few weeks ago, when

George had been having his breakfast at the kitchen table, and Mark had been standing by the toaster, ramming down a bagel before leaving for work. Mark hadn't realised that Caroline was in the pantry, writing out labels for jam – raspberry and blackcurrant.

'Caroline's making jam today,' George announced to his father in his high, fluting voice. 'She said I can help put it in the jars.'

That wasn't *quite* true. The jam was destined for the local farm shop, and Caroline couldn't let George's grubby little hands near the carefully sterilised jars. She'd been planning to give him his own jar to play with, if he insisted.

'It's funny,' continued George, his voice puzzled. 'Maisie never used to like jam. But George *does* like it.'

There was a noise. Sudden footsteps across the kitchen tiles.

Caroline peeped out through the pantry door. Mark was looming over George, invading the child's space. George had shrunk into himself, his spine curling like a startled hedgehog's.

'I told you never to mention that name.' Mark's voice was slow and deliberate. 'Not in this house. Not at school. Not *anywhere*. Now, which part of that do you not understand?'

George seemed to have frozen, his eyes wide and his hands clamped over his ears.

'Which part,' Mark said again, 'don't you understand?'

George nodded. Then nodded again, his head bobbing up and down like a puppet's. He scrambled off his stool, the wooden legs scraping against the floor. And he'd run off.

Now, as Caroline photographed George's birth certificate with her phone, she remembered how she had felt something fizzle through her body that day. Had it been excitement? Or something more maternal – a protective urge? She chose to interpret it as the latter.

She was fond of George. Really, she was. All of this was for him.

17

TERESA

Northumberland
Now

When I walked back into the house without George, the emptiness hit me like a wall.

It reminded me of how it had felt, coming home from Scotland without Maisie. I'd returned to a nightmarish, mirror-image world where nothing would ever be the same. Each room in the house had felt different – a disconcerting twin of what it had been before. Her absence, a kind of deadness, filled the air. But at the same time, my body thrummed with a restless energy. The silence pressed itself into the inner parts of my ears, distorting itself into tinnitus shrieks and buzzing. My body's own security alarm, ringing constantly. Too late, of course. Far too late.

The house had never felt like home again. Feelings of safety, of peace, simply weren't available to me any more. I'd felt like Dorothy in her Kansas house, whirling through the air in the cyclone. Never knowing when or how I might land.

But George, in the few hours he'd spent here, had made the house seem bright again – imbued with warmth and purpose. He'd eased the pain of her absence. And I hadn't even realised it. Not until the moment I walked back inside without him.

What did that *mean*? What did that tell me about George?

I imagined Sunny, gravely shaking his head, warning me that George and Caroline were almost certainly trying to take advantage of me in some way.

I tried to focus on my only other form of pain relief – work. I mentally listed all the tasks I had to do – cleaning the glamping huts, making up welcome baskets. Replying to messages on the booking system. Looking for my public liability insurance paperwork. Normally, I would launch into these jobs, making them fill up the day so there would be no time to think about anything else.

But there was a dragging, heavy feeling in my limbs, a fogginess in my head. My body was telling me I was exhausted. So I lay down on the sofa and pulled a blanket around me.

I didn't allow myself to think of it often – that day when I realised she'd gone. I'd been sitting eating toast for breakfast and that text had arrived:

'I love you too.'

In that moment, my instincts had kicked in. I went to my car, without even packing a toothbrush. Things like toothbrushes wouldn't matter, if I was right about this. And they wouldn't matter if I was wrong, either. I pictured myself pulling Maisie into a long hug, that chemical hit of having my baby in my arms again. And then, perhaps, convincing her the holiday had gone on long enough, to get her things and pack them into the car to come home. We could stop at

McDonald's on the way home, get one of her favourite strawberry milkshakes.

And then, the worst moment – when I reached the address she'd given me. The blackened ruins of that house. The police had confirmed that it belonged to property developers who wanted to turn it into a hotel. Nothing to do with Alison Jenkins' family, or any family at all, for that matter.

If I had known, back then, that eight years would pass with still no trace of her, I wouldn't have been able to go on. My heart would have simply stopped beating. My ribs would have given up their pointless task of rising and falling.

But then, I wouldn't have lived long enough to meet George.

I closed my eyes and let my mind drift over everything that had happened. I thought about George's stone angel and the shepherd. About how he had been able to sense my pain, and see its colour. Was he like a little radio, tuning into what had happened?

A yellow dress with a white daisy print.

The image came out of nowhere, just as it had on the beach a few nights ago. It started to subside, to fade, like a dream on waking. I kept my eyes closed, focusing hard, trying to retain it.

The clammy shock of hands under armpits.

My heart sped up. I could feel blood pulsing in my fingertips, my skin tingling. I kept completely still, hoping not to break the spell.

A silver watch with a navy-blue face.

Water. The sound of it gushing onto a hard surface.

And then it was gone. I couldn't get it back again. I opened my eyes and took in my surroundings – my own living room. The dead, empty house.

It must have been some kind of strange dream, my brain firing out images at the threshold of sleep and waking. Trying to process the strangeness of the last few days.

But what if it had been something else? What if I was becoming *sensitive*? Like George? What if I was seeing something that had actually happened?

I messaged Sunny.

'Fancy coming over tonight?'

He arrived just before seven, while I was checking in the filing cabinets for the third time, trying to find my public liability insurance paperwork. All I'd been able to find was the renewal reminder from last year. With a horrible lurch in the pit of my stomach, I wondered if I'd forgotten to phone up and pay the premium.

'Phone them tomorrow,' suggested Sunny, as he poured us both a cup of tea.

'I will.' But my thoughts were racing down a rabbit hole. What if Caroline made a claim against me, and I wasn't covered? What if it bankrupted me, and I had to sell my home, and the glamping huts, and move away? What if Maisie came back to the house and I wasn't there?

'Come and sit down,' said Sunny. 'You look stressed.'

'I don't know what to do,' I said later, when we were installed on the sofa with Sunny's homemade veggie lasagne and *Call the Midwife.*

'How come?'

'What if he *is* Maisie? What if it's true? I've just let him go.'

Sunny sat frowning, deep in thought, for a minute or two.

'I know he seemed to be familiar with the house, and Maisie's room. But did he actually *say* he was Maisie, at any point?'

Typical Sunny, he'd put his finger on something that had been niggling me. I tried to think back. 'He did talk about Maisie. He said banana sandwiches were her favourite breakfast. But then he clapped his hand over his mouth, as if he shouldn't have said it.'

'That's interesting.'

'It was almost as if... as if he thought he'd get in trouble if he mentioned her. But that doesn't make any sense. Caroline had already brought up the subject of Maisie. She did that straight away, at the door when she rang the bell. She asked if the name "Maisie" meant anything to me.'

'So he's allowed to talk about Maisie. But at the same time... he's not?'

'I know none of it makes any sense. But this... this *feeling* I get, when I look at him. It's like I'm looking at *her*. It's like she's in there, behind his eyes.'

'But, T, you're sort of primed to believe that, aren't you?'

'Primed?'

'Yes. Because of your grief, because you miss Maisie so much.'

'It's not just that. It's not.'

Sunny stared up at the wall, thinking carefully.

'I asked Caroline if I could see his birth certificate,' I said. 'If he really was born on the day she left for Scotland, then it would be impossible for him to be...'

'Maisie's child?' Sunny finished gently.

'Yes. There was no way she was about to give birth. Her stomach was completely flat – she'd been parading around in her swimsuit the night before. But seeing his birth certificate would put it beyond doubt, I guess.'

'Yes. But what if we're looking at this the wrong way? What if George *is* related to Maisie, but through her father's side? That could explain the similarity between them. He could be a cousin, or a nephew. Could Jan or Mark have a family connection to Maisie's father? To the Australian side of her family?'

'Joel? But he's dead.' I tried not to sound impatient.

'You looked into it all a while back, didn't you?'

'Yes. Maisie went through a phase of asking about her biological father. I was worried she was going to try and get in touch with him, and I knew it would only end in disappointment.'

'Why were you so sure it would?'

I shook my head. 'Joel only cared about himself. He didn't slow the slightest bit of interest when I said I was pregnant. He tried to deny that the baby was his.'

'A drunken party, I think you said.' Sunny's voice was solemn. He'd lived at home while doing his physiotherapy degree, caring for his elderly widowed mother and stacking shelves in the evenings.

'Yes. We weren't together at the time. He used to call me his "ex with benefits". It's not something I'm proud of.' I remembered shouting at Joel down the phone to Australia: *'You lying, spineless, selfish prick!'* The second-long delay on the line had made it less satisfying, especially when he'd simply laughed. I'd ended up slamming the phone down.

'So when Maisie kept asking about him, I messaged an old university friend on Facebook. I asked her if she knew what had happened to Joel. And it turned out he'd died of sepsis, after contracting meningitis. Only a year after arriving in Australia, actually.'

'So he'd never married, or had kids of his own?'

'Nope. And after Maisie went missing, the first thing the police asked about was her father. They confirmed it with the Australian authorities – that he'd died. There were no other "persons of relevance" in Australia, they said.'

Sunny frowned. 'So Maisie and George can't be related, that's what you're saying?'

I shrugged. 'I can't rule it out, I suppose. But they can't be closely related enough to explain it. The similarities between them, I mean. All the things he knows.'

Sunny sat and thought for a few minutes. When he spoke again it was slowly and haltingly. 'Might it be possible that... that Maisie *worked* for George's family, in some capacity, before his mother died? As a nanny, or an au pair? Maybe he's remembering someone who looked after him, in his 'old life' as he calls it. It could explain why he's picked up some of her turns of phrase, like the silent trousers and so on.'

'But then why would he remember this house? Her room?'

And the eyes. Why would the eyes look the same?

'It is strange,' Sunny conceded. 'But I suppose that side of it could be explained, if it is some kind of scam. Perhaps they could have seen inside the house, somehow.'

I sighed. 'I mean, they could have seen the elephant doorstop if they'd come around the back of the house and looked in the utility room window. But they wouldn't have been able to see Maisie's room.'

'Not unless they'd used ladders,' said Sunny his face still serious.

I imagined Caroline, teetering on a ladder in her high-heeled boots, her Liberty print skirt ballooning in the wind. I caught Sunny's eye and his mouth quirked into a smile.

'Okay, okay,' he said. 'But is it possible Maisie posted pictures of her bedroom on Instagram, or something like that?'

'I doubt it,' I said. 'She wasn't really into social media. She'd deleted Instagram and Snapchat and everything from her phone. Said it was too distracting.'

'Hmm,' said Sunny. 'What about Mark, then? What if he's been here, posing as a workman? A plumber, or a... a window cleaner, or something like that?' He looked alarmed, suddenly, at the thought of rogue window cleaners.

'I did try to look him up online. But there are so many Mark Jacksons. Caroline said he was in the 'wellness space'. I found a Mark Jackson who's a CBT practitioner in Nottingham. Another one who owns a string of aesthetics clinics in the South East – Botox and that kind of thing. There were a few references to a psychiatrist called Mark Jackson, who wrote some papers on new drug trials back in the noughties, but nothing recent. And one who's named as a director of various companies on Companies House, but I don't know if they have anything to do with wellness.'

'Yeah,' said Sunny. 'I looked him up, too. If you search for "Mark Jackson" on the Companies House register, it comes up with two hundred and thirty-one thousand results.'

'And I couldn't find anything on Jan. Or Caroline either, which is a bit strange, given she's supposed to have her own private catering business. Although she might not even go by the name Jackson. Now I come to think about it, I don't even know if she and Mark are married.' I sighed. 'It's so difficult. I can hardly interrogate her, can I? And I can hardly demand to talk to Mark. They'd both think I was completely nuts.'

Sunny placed his lasagne tray on the floor. Then he sat

forward, looking at me intently, his hands clasped. 'Do you think we should take all this to the police?'

The 'we' made my heart melt a little. He had always tried to make me feel that I wasn't alone in all this. He couldn't cross the threshold of my private hell. That was a prison especially reserved for me. But he had spent the last eight years standing on the other side of the bars, steadfast and immoveable, while my other friends had drifted away.

I imagined myself going to the police again, asking for yet another review, wittering on about pencil cases and flowery wallpaper. 'Do you think they would do anything?'

He shrugged. 'They might follow it up with George's family.'

'But Caroline would never speak to me again, if the police turned up at their door asking questions. I'd have blown it completely.'

'Blown what, though, T?'

I could read in his face all the things he wouldn't say. That this whole business was a dead end at best, a con at worst. That George was nothing to me, and it was unlikely I'd ever see him again.

'You think I should drop it, don't you?' I said, a wobble creeping into my voice. 'You think I need to stop obsessing about her. You think I need to... move on.'

He turned his whole body so he was facing me. His face was filled with hurt. 'When did I say that? When have I *ever* said that?'

I curled my body forwards, burying my face in my hands. Then I felt him pulling me close, rubbing my back in long strokes and cradling my head against his chest.

STOP, shouted a voice in my head. I felt a seizing up in my body, like the grinding of gears.

'You're okay,' said Sunny. 'Let it all out.'

'I'm killing you,' I sobbed. 'I'm killing you, aren't I?'

'You're not killing me.' I could feel his voice, the buzz of it through his grey jumper. 'Don't be silly. I'm not having that.'

'*You* could be moving on. You could be with somebody else; somebody you can have a proper relationship with.'

He sighed softly and laid his cheek on the top of my head. 'I'm fine, T. Let *me* worry about me.'

Held tight in his arms, I wept. I wept at the thought that Maisie might have been a nanny or an au pair, living her life without bothering to let me know she was okay. I wept at the thought she was more likely dead, her body decomposed in a ditch somewhere. And I wept for George, with his sweet brown eyes and his hair the colour of Maisie's.

Finally, I drew a deep, shuddering breath. 'I'm thinking of going to see Cheryl Smithers again. The medium. See what she makes of all this.'

I couldn't see Sunny's face. But I could imagine him casting his eyes heavenwards. 'A medium?'

'Yup. Remember, I spoke to her before? After Maisie went missing.'

Sunny's chest rose and fell slowly. Once. Twice. I could almost feel his anxiety, his deep need to protect me, radiating through his body.

'Fair enough,' he said, giving me a squeeze. 'It's worth a try, isn't it.'

'Could you come over tomorrow after work? Just... keep an eye on the place while I'm out?'

He knew I was always anxious about leaving the house.

'Of course. No problem at all.'

Sunny. My Sunny.

A sensation began to spread through my body, warm and

slow and sweet, like butter melting into soft brown sugar. And then – the grinding of gears again.

STOP.

18

CAROLINE

Retford
Now

Caroline was in the kitchen – her domain, as she thought of it, the place where she created her magic. She wasn't creating magic now, though. She was making yet another sandwich for George, who'd been whining for over an hour. Her head was throbbing, despite the extra-strong painkillers she'd taken.

She pulled out the wooden chopping block and placed it on the kitchen island. Yet again, she retrieved cheddar, tomatoes and butter from the fridge. She twisted the stalks off two of the tomatoes – nice red juicy ones she'd bought from the greengrocer, as the ones at the supermarket were always tough and tinged with green.

She always tried to source as many ingredients as possible from small local suppliers – not just the greengrocer but the butcher, the French *boulangerie*, the mediterranean deli on the high street which claimed to have been in business for a hundred years. She particularly loved going in there as it made her think of her father – he'd run his parents' Spanish restaurant in Hull before dying of a heart attack aged forty-three.

So the receipt she'd found in Mark's briefcase last week had struck her as rather... odd. The receipt, dated last month, showed that he'd purchased thirty Tesco ready meals and the same number of pre-packaged desserts – cartons of Ambrosia custard and rice pudding, plastic pots of mandarins and peaches. A bottle of orange squash, some single-portion blocks of cheese and some Ryvita crackers.

Under the warm glow of the pendant light that hung low over the kitchen island, she sliced the tomatoes evenly and precisely. The knife made a satisfying chopping noise on the thick board and Caroline envisaged, just for a moment, how she might look on camera if she were starring in her own television cookery show. With the back of her wrist, she nudged a swathe of expensively highlighted hair away from her face.

George zoomed into the room and circled the kitchen island.

'What's that you've got?' asked Caroline.

He was holding something in his right hand, a thin circle of plastic. She grabbed his wrist, mid-zoom, and he skidded to a halt, emitting a little yelp. The thing in his hand was a hospital ID bracelet. It must have been in the file she'd been looking at last night. Had she dropped it on the floor? Her throat tightened when she thought of what Mark would have said if he'd found it. If he'd realised she'd been snooping around in there.

'Give that to me, Georgie-Pie.'

The tiny bracelet bore the words 'Baby of Jan Jackson' in

black biro, with a tiny smudge at the foot of the 'n'. Below that was his date of birth, and a long ID number.

'It's not a toy.' She tucked it into the pocket of her trousers. 'Don't do that again. Don't take things without asking.'

Caroline arranged the slices of cheese on the bread, laid circles of tomato on them, and placed the second slice of bread on top to complete the sandwich. But then she removed it again, and tucked one of the dark, spidery tomato stalks inside before replacing it. Finally she cut off the crusts and sliced the sandwich into triangles.

'Silly sausage,' she said, handing him the plate, feeling that familiar stab of exhilaration mixed with guilt.

It wasn't as though he'd actually *swallow* the stalk. He always checked inside his sandwiches before eating. In a way, it was a little game between the two of them.

She summoned thoughts of self-love and self-compassion. She *was* a good parent to George. It was for George's sake, really, that she was pursuing all this business about Maisie. And at great risk to herself, too. She held a hand to the back of her head again. There was no telling how Mark might react when she finally worked out the truth, when she confronted him.

She heard his key in the door, the thump of his laptop bag landing on the hall floor, and her heart ticked up a little. She took a deep, cleansing breath. He sauntered in, pulling his tie loose.

'Good day, PQ?' That was his nickname for her – it stood for 'Pudding Queen.'

'Not bad.' Caroline carefully removed a Le Creuset casserole dish from the Aga and ladled out a portion of homemade beef bourguignon onto a warmed plate. She placed a quenelle of celeriac mash on the side and added a few stems of steamed broccoli.

She'd decided she was going to ask him about the receipt. She was going to give him one chance to tell the truth, before she proceeded with... well, everything.

It was embarrassing, really, as if she was challenging him about having an affair or entertaining a mistress – something she'd always been far too classy to do. She placed the receipt by the side of his plate, tapping it lightly.

'Why have you been shopping in Tesco?' It came out wrong, as if she was outraged that he hadn't gone to Waitrose or Marks & Spencer.

But he was too smart not to realise the significance of her question.

He took a few long moments to finish off his mouthful of beef, dabbing his linen napkin to the corners of his lips before speaking again.

'We had a patient going home after a long-term stay. One of our funded patients. She was moving into council accommodation. We wanted to make sure she had some bits to get her started.'

'Oh. Is that a new thing?'

'What?'

'Getting "bits" for patients?'

Mark smiled. 'If you don't like living here, PQ, we can always send you back to *your* council house. You could try touting your wares to the residents of Hull.'

He loved to remind her that she was only here, in this beautiful manor house, fannying around with artisan ingredients all day, because he was bankrolling it all.

'Haha,' she said, mirthlessly.

He smiled again, but he was eating faster now, almost

gobbling down the beef. She sat there watching him, and tried to envisage the different ways her plan might play out.

She imagined a worst case scenario – herself, tragically killed by a furious Mark, and George left motherless. The story would be in the press, perhaps even in a true crime documentary one day. Or another version – Mark dead, Caroline in prison, wearing some smelly orange uniform, and George bundled away by social services.

Then she tried to visualise a happy outcome – herself and George, hopping on a plane to sunnier climes. Or even better, some version where Mark was excised from their lives, like a cancerous tumour, but Caroline got to keep the house, with its fabulous kitchen and its Rectory Red walls.

19

TERESA

Northumberland
Now

It was raining, a cold breeze blowing, when I arrived at Cheryl's bungalow.

'Rubbish weather we're having.' She showed me into the living room, shuffling in slipper boots that were shaped like fluffy dogs. 'Absolutely shocking.' She had a Scottish accent, her voice low and husky. She motioned to the squashy leather sofa, where two cats – a skinny black one and a white Persian - lay curled up side by side. The room had a faint smell of damp, overlaid with a cloying, chemical odour. Cheryl was a mobile nail technician as well as a medium, and there was a table in the corner with a UV nail lamp and a rainbow display of nail polishes.

I sat down. The two cats didn't move, although the white one's ears twitched, as if it was listening.

'I don't really know why I'm here.' But as the words came out of my mouth, I realised that I did know. I wanted to speak to someone who wouldn't think that all this talk of past lives was a load of rubbish, or a con. Somebody who wouldn't pity me, or worry about me.

At the same time, unease was building inside me. I was terrified of what I might hear, even though I wasn't sure I believed in any of this. I remembered how my blood had rushed in my ears, that first time I'd consulted Cheryl, as if I was at the hospital to receive scan results, or the findings from a biopsy. If Maisie was dead, I wanted to know. But I also knew it would be the end of me.

'I was really sorry to hear about your mum,' Cheryl began. 'Christmas Eve, wasn't it, that she died? So awful for you.'

I'd first met Cheryl when she'd been doing mum's nails at the care home. She'd visited every week, setting up her manicure table in the in-house hair salon. I'd seen her with my mother, talking in conspiratorial tones while she rubbed scented balm into her wrinkled hands and gently massaged the joints. She never seemed to be in a hurry. On Cheryl's final visit, Mum had taken twenty minutes just to choose what colour of polish she wanted, before finally opting for electric blue nails with silver sparkles.

And she'd met Maisie too. She'd done her nails the day before she left for Scotland, fitting her in after the ladies at the care home.

'Thank you. Poor Mum – she went quickly, in the end. Pneumonia.' She'd been asking for Maisie, through her delirium. She'd never had a chance to say goodbye. I could hardly bear to think of it.

'It's been a tough year for you, I expect.'

I nodded, and then blurted out: 'I met a little boy.'

She shivered. 'I just got a huge influx of goosebumps.' She frowned and rubbed her arms. 'Go on.'

'He thinks he remembers a past life.'

Cheryl nodded and blinked, mascara-clogged lashes tilting up and down.

'He says he used to live in my house, in Maisie's room. And he knows things he shouldn't know. Things that only Maisie would know.'

'And you're looking for an explanation.'

'I catch myself wanting it to be true,' I whispered. 'And then I hate myself, for wanting it. What kind of mother would want...' My words disappeared.

Cheryl rubbed her arms again. She knelt down and put on the gas fire, clicking a red plastic firelighter until it whooshed into life. The noise seemed to transport me back to simpler times. Visiting Gran, being offered chocolate biscuits and juice in a spotty tumbler.

'You're a good mum. Don't you worry about that.'

For a moment, I wondered if Cheryl and I could become friends. My old 'mum friends' had drifted away after Maisie had gone missing. And making new friends was hard – I didn't like to tell people about Maisie, to see their faces change as they recalibrated their opinions of me.

The mother whose daughter ran away.

The mother who let her daughter get killed.

There was probably all sorts going on at home...

There was usually a flash of judgement, mixed in with the pity. Because I must have done something wrong, surely? Something that *they* would never do.

I had to be different from them. I had to be moved to a separate category. Otherwise, nobody was safe.

The worst thing was, I agreed with them, most of the

time. I constantly scoured the past for occasions when I might have done the wrong thing, said the wrong thing. Times when I might have upset Maisie without knowing it, or made her feel she couldn't share her worries. I ransacked all my precious memories of her – for gaps, for spaces, for omissions. I tried to spot the questions I should have asked, the cues I should have picked up on. I tried to identify the one glaring moment – because, surely, there must have been one – when I could have stopped this from happening.

But Cheryl's gaze held no judgement at all. A warmth emanated from her, an air of total acceptance, just as she'd had with the dementia patients at the care home.

I reached into my bag and pulled out the china shepherd. 'He sleeps with an angel in his bed every night. And with this shepherd. He's scared of something. He has nightmares and night terrors. He dreams about drowning. His step-mum thinks he might be remembering a traumatic death.'

Cheryl took the shepherd and turned it over in her hands. She had long, pale-blue fingernails and I could see darkened areas on her skin where fake tan had settled into the creases. 'The veil is thinner for children,' she said. 'When we're young, we see far more of what's really around us. But we get told we're imagining things, that the shadow people in the corner, or the creatures under the bed, aren't real. So we train ourselves not to see them. And we suppress so much of ourselves, to be able to do that.' She shook her head and sighed. 'Your clever little boy has found a strategy to help him deal with what he sees. Did he give you this shepherd?'

'Yes. He seemed to think I needed it more than him.'

She gave a low whistle. 'His capacity for empathy must be... extraordinary.'

'It is! It's causing problems for him. He's having a difficult time at school.'

'The purer the soul, the more the world will bruise.' She shifted in her chair and silently suppressed a burp.

'So are you able to tell me anything? Do you think that George is... used to be... Maisie?'

She shivered suddenly. Then she frowned. 'What's his name?'

'George. George Jackson.'

Cheryl's face changed – an involuntary spasm, as if she'd been splashed with cold water. And when her features settled again, she looked older, somehow. Infinitely sad.

'George?' she said in a thin, cold voice. 'Why are you asking about him?' She looked away from me and into the gas fire, the blue jets hissing in their wire cage. 'George is dead.'

20

CAROLINE

Retford
Now

Mark was upstairs soaking in the bath – a Victorian roll-top antique, freestanding and double-ended, not that they ever shared it, these days. Caroline had run the water for him, pouring in some of her own precious Jo Malone bath essence, even though it was almost finished. He'd had a stressful day at Chesters, his flagship wellness centre and 'therapeutic community'. He'd been dealing with threatened legal action, from some C-list celeb who'd spent the last month drying out there.

The celeb had clicked that Mark was 'that' Mark Jackson. The one who'd left his NHS post suddenly, some years ago, after allegations had been made by a young mental health nurse. It had been before Caroline's time, and all she knew was that the nurse had withdrawn the allegations, but Mark had resigned anyway. He'd brushed it off, when she'd asked about it, simply saying that he'd fallen foul of 'the woke brigade', but it had all worked out for the best, as it had been the impetus he'd needed to abandon the 'sinking ship of the NHS'.

Mark mainly handled the business side of the wellness centres these days, as he no longer enjoyed 'getting his hands dirty' with the patients. Thankfully, the photogenic Dr Bea, with her ninety-eight thousand Instagram followers, was more than happy to be the public face of the business. And Mark's bumbling old colleague, Dr Gordon, was always around to lend gravitas, if needed.

It was all a bit of a bore. But at least Mark's bad mood had given her some uninterrupted time with her laptop.

But now she needed to get on with dinner. Closing the laptop, she went to the fridge to find some ingredients for soup, and then poured a generous slosh of Merlot into a tall-stemmed goblet.

Humming along to one of her classical music playlists, she fried off some *sofrito* – enjoying the vibrant colours of the celery and carrot amongst the pearly, translucent nibs of onion – and added a pint and a half of fresh chicken stock. Then she chopped some florets of organic broccoli and plopped them in.

Puccini was playing now – the famous soprano aria from Gianni Schicchi. *O Mio Babbino Caro*. Caroline took a long sip of wine and tilted her head back, eyes closed. Mark had taken her to see it at the Royal Opera House in Covent Garden, back in their magical early days. She remembered the thrill that had travelled down her spine when the soprano's voice had soared up into that final crescendo, the audience seeming to hold its breath. She could feel it again now, the hairs on her arms lifting under the sleeves of her cardigan.

With a satisfied sigh, she picked up the remaining part of

the broccoli crown to put it back into the fridge, but then dropped it quickly back onto the worktop.

'Ugh!' The base of the crown was crawling with little grey caterpillars. With a shudder, she chucked it in the pedal bin, letting the lid slam down.

George appeared in the doorway. 'What's wrong, Cawoline?'

'Nothing, Georgie-Pie.'

'Can I have my sandwich soon?'

'Sandwich and soup,' corrected Caroline. For the second time that day, she took cheese, tomatoes and butter out of the fridge. She sawed a couple of slices off the farmhouse loaf which was a couple of days old now and going a bit hard.

'What's a poo box?'

Caroline swung round. George had opened the lid of her laptop.

Caroline was at the table in a flash. George was peering at the screen, at the web page that explained how to set up a private PO box. She slammed the laptop lid shut.

'Look at me. *Look* at me! Don't *ever* do that again. My laptop is private. You don't look at my private things, you little freak. Is that understood?'

The corners of George's mouth moved down, his chin dimpling with the effort not to cry. He fixed his eyes on the floor.

Clenching her fists at her sides, Caroline returned to the soup pan. She knew she shouldn't be angry with him. He was only a small child.

Really, it was Jan she should be angry with. Mental illness or no mental illness, she'd abandoned her own small son. Left him for her, Caroline, to look after, as if she didn't have her own life to live. As if her own plans were of no importance.

Once, bored in a dentist's waiting room, she'd read an article written by a woman who couldn't have children. She explained how, every day, she grieved for the life she'd always thought she'd have. She described a sort of ghost life, running alongside her own. One with nappies and climbing frames and messy paints and Lego. Parents' evenings and teenage tantrums and college admissions.

Sometimes, Caroline wondered if she had a ghost life. The life she would have had if she hadn't had to drop everything and care for George. Did anyone ever bother to think about that?

Looking closely at the soup, she saw that two caterpillars were floating on the surface, in a small circle of yellow-green scum. Sighing, she glanced at her watch, and then pulled the stick blender out of the drawer. She thrust the bladed head deep into the saucepan and turned it on, whizzing the soup into a nice thick consistency.

A bit of extra protein never hurt anyone. And George never ate more than a spoonful or two of soup anyway. It was hardly worth the bother of making it in the first place, let alone making it again, *sans* caterpillars.

When she'd settled George at the kitchen table with his meal – she and Mark would eat later – she poured a second glass of wine and made her way up to the study. She opened her laptop and resumed her search. It was amazing, really, how easy it was to set up a PO box address. It was the work of mere moments.

And it was amazing how easy it was to access DNA testing these days. Some companies even offered next day results. She looked at all their websites, checking the procedure for each one – how long the testing kits would take to arrive, how to post back the completed tests, when and how the results would arrive.

Then came the part she had been stressing about. She drew out the pack of blank, prepaid A4 envelopes that had arrived that afternoon, and fed one of them carefully into the printer.

She created a Word document, set the margins the way she wanted them, and typed in an address. Next, aware of a fizz of adrenaline deep in her stomach, she pressed 'Print'.

The envelope that emerged from the printer was perfect. Nobody would think to give it a second look. She squealed and gave herself a little clap. This was going to work.

21

MAISIE

Killendreich
Eight years ago

Maisie had been expecting a castle, with grey towers and turrets like Balmoral. Perhaps with a flag waving at the top, and a little pack of corgis racing out to meet the Land Rover.

The big white house, standing in a dim clearing between the trees, did not have that vibe at all. Each of the windows on the top floor had its own little peaked roof, which gave it a witchy look, a bit like the gingerbread house in *Hansel and Gretel.*

Its walls were tinged with green – moss, or mildew, maybe? And the gravelled area around the house was spotted with weeds. Maisie had a sudden impression of the surrounding forest creeping in, trying to claim the house for its own. She imagined how she might capture this in a drawing, the colours she would use. It might even work well as a lino cut; the triangular shapes of the gables flooded with dark ink.

They shouldn't have built the house in this damp, sunken spot.

But actually, she kind of liked it. It tugged on something at the back of her mind, as if she'd seen it before in a dream, or in a children's book.

She wished she could send a photo to Mum. But she'd lost phone signal forty-five minutes ago, at the point when the rolling hills suddenly gave way to mountains with sharp peaks and ridges, and the road had to climb and twist its way up the glen. She'd had to concentrate on not throwing up.

The driver, Jock, who seemed to be some sort of groundsman or gamekeeper-type person, had barely said a word on the journey. But his driving had been wild. He'd nearly ploughed head-on into a tractor on the single-track road, almost as if he hadn't seen it coming.

Now, she stepped out of the Land Rover and fresh air rushed into her lungs. It smelled of damp moss and pine needles. Of woodsmoke and wet rocks and long summer grass. Jock carried her bags from the car and let her into the house. She'd been hoping for a housekeeper in a smart, tweedy suit, but there didn't seem to be anyone else around.

She found herself in a large, square hallway with a blue-grey tartan carpet and wood-panelled walls. There was a wide staircase with polished banisters, and a big window at the turn of the stairs. The movement of looking upwards suddenly made her feel sick again. She had to take a moment to steady herself.

To her right there was a fireplace, stacked with logs and kindling. Above it loomed a painting depicting the crucifixion in dark oils. It looked old – seventeenth century, perhaps. One of the Spanish religious painters, she guessed. She tried to remember her art history classes.

On the opposite wall hung a stag's head. Very traditional. But for a horrible moment, it was as if she could see the stag dying on a rocky mountain slope, blood spilling from his throat. His eyes rolling back in his head. His final, ragged breaths rising like mist.

Ugh.

She took a step towards the staircase, assuming she'd be sleeping in one of the rooms upstairs, but Jock cocked his head towards a small door on the left, built into the panelling. It led into a narrow, twisting corridor. Framed black and white photographs lined the walls – groups of people, standing in front of the house. Shooting parties, maybe? Turning a corner, Maisie looked up and did a double-take – there was a full-sized door in the wall, ten feet above her head. If someone had come out of the door they'd have fallen into thin air. The house must have been chopped and changed around, at some point in its history.

They passed double doors to what looked like a big, industrial kitchen, and then reached a second staircase, which was narrow and steep, the steps grey and rubbery.

'The rooms on the staff side are, uh, quieter,' Jock said, leading the way up.

Quieturr... Maisie loved Jock's accent.

Her room, when they reached it, was... well, it was fine. Maisie did a quick mental adjustment. She'd been expecting something more luxurious, in the style of a country house hotel. But this was nice in its own way, with a faded red rug laid over the floorboards. There was a metal bed frame, with a pile of fresh bedding for her to put on. A plain wooden cross hung above the bed. She felt like Jane Eyre, arriving at

Thornfield Hall. Or the nameless governess in *The Turn of the Screw*, arriving at Bly.

There was a window on her left, tucked under the eaves. She could see the forest, rising steeply behind the house. And the crags above the tree line, far above, grey with tumbled rocks.

'When will Ally get here?' Maisie asked Jock for the third or fourth time.

'I don't know anything about that.' He shrugged, not meeting her eye.

She'd been dismayed to learn, earlier that day, that Ally wouldn't be travelling up with her. He had been asked, at very short notice, to accompany a team to a tennis tournament in Paris. One of the other coaches had fallen ill, apparently. He'd promised to join her as soon as he could.

She had told a couple of teeny lies to her mother.

The gist of it was true – she and Ally *were* friends.

But she hadn't exactly met him at school. And he wasn't exactly a girl...

He wasn't a girl in any way, shape or form. Maisie's insides fluttered as she remembered their first time together, in the changing rooms at the tennis club, once everyone else had left for the evening. He'd laid her down gently on the wooden bench and...

Okay, he was her tennis coach. Technically. But he was nineteen, just two years older than her. It wasn't as if he was a paedo or anything.

Of course, she'd implied to Mum that he was ancient and boring – his full name, helpfully, was Alan.

They'd grown close because he'd needed somebody to talk to. He was supposed to be going to some exclusive tennis academy in the US, but he'd had a knee injury. A potentially career-ending knee injury. The tennis academy probably wouldn't take him, now that his future fitness was in doubt.

And then, one evening, he'd actually cried. Who would he even be, he'd sobbed – *what* would he be, without tennis? She'd allowed him to rest his curly blond head against her chest, had dropped a shy kiss on top of his hair. And he'd sat up and looked at her, like she was an oasis in a desert.

She'd hardly been able to *breathe*, on the bus home, for thinking of it.

He was so much more mature than the boys at school. Mature enough to take charge in a difficult situation.

If he ever got here. Maisie turned to face Jock again. 'Have you –'

But Jock had gone.

~

Maisie unpacked, hiding the 'modern' things she'd brought with her – hair straighteners, iPad, various chargers – in one of the drawers, so as not to spoil the Victorian governess aesthetic of the room. But she placed her ballerina musical box, the one containing her drawing pencils, out on the dresser.

Next, she made the bed and tucked her pyjama top and shorts under the pillow, pleased she'd brought the white ones with the delicate floral pattern. She placed the book she was reading – Agatha Christie's *Hickory Dickory Dock* – on the bedside table. When she'd finished, she emerged from the room into the small attic corridor.

'Hello?' she called.

She opened the door of the adjoining room and found a bathroom with a big porcelain bath – an old-fashioned one like on *Downton Abbey* or something. She used the toilet, which had a square wooden seat and a water tank high on the wall, with a metal chain to pull the flush. The water from the taps ran brown, accompanied by a clunking noise, which seemed to come from the pipes. She hoped there wasn't a problem with the drains or something. She washed just the tips of her fingers and smelled them before drying them on her jeans.

Slowly, she made her way to the end of the corridor, where she noticed a heavy door, propped open with a door stop. It had a green 'Fire Exit' sign on it, with a graphic of a stick man running away, which rather ruined the Victorian vibe. She made her way downstairs, back along the narrow, twisting corridor.

'Hello?' she called.

She listened out. For a moment she thought she heard a gasp of high, excited laughter, coming from somewhere within the maze of the house.

But perhaps she had imagined it. There really didn't seem to be anyone around.

'Hello?' she called again.

She reached the main hall where she'd originally entered the house, and spun around slowly, taking everything in. She noticed a mahogany table in the shadowy panelled corner under the turn of the stairs – with a landline phone on it! She rushed to it and picked up the receiver, but there was no dialling tone.

Just behind the table was a door – to an under-stairs cupboard, perhaps? But when she opened it, she saw a set of steps leading down into darkness. A whiff of dank air rose up, and she closed the door.

Turning, she noticed a hall table by the front door. There

was some kind of note on it, a thick fold of cream paper. It was propped up against a framed wooden triptych, showing a pale-faced, haloed Mary with baby Jesus, and two angels with golden trumpets on either side.

Hey Ally and Maisie!

We've had to go out – an emergency with Jan. Please make yourselves at home. There are loads of meals in the freezer – defrost whatever you both fancy.

See you soon.

Love, Dad (Mark)

'What the actual...?' she said out loud. 'You have *got* to be joking.'

She was supposed to stay here, all by herself, in this house? In the middle of nowhere?

Her first instinct was to complain to Mum.

She closed her eyes and growled in frustration.

22

CAROLINE

Retford
Now

It had been a wonderful massage. Caroline had drifted off once or twice, as if floating on a warm sea, to be gently brought back by the warm press of Magdalena's fingers, working expertly around her shoulder blades.

She let thoughts of George, and Maisie, and Mark, float around in her head. Trying to get the pieces to fit. Every time one part of the puzzle seemed to click, another would slide out of place, like one of those annoying Rubik's cubes she'd hated as a child.

The DNA test company envelopes were hidden at the bottom of her underwear drawer. Like weapons, ready to be put to use. Surely Teresa would take the bait and ask for a test? Caroline thought of the seeds of doubt she'd carefully planted – the lie about George's birth certificate being missing; her worried frown as she'd assured Teresa that she trusted Mark implicitly. She could drop in some more, if need be, when she collected her car on Saturday.

She exhaled, visualising a dirty, dark cloud of negativity leaving her lungs.

She inhaled, visualising golden light filling her body.

She managed an hour and ten minutes in the thermal spa area afterwards. A pity, really, that she had to curtail her visit so that she could collect George from holiday club.

As she was validating her parking ticket at the front desk, she felt a tap on her arm. 'You're Mark's wife, aren't you? I've seen you in here together.'

Caroline's heart sank as she turned round to face the woman. It wouldn't be the first time that one of Mark's 'mistresses' had decided to make herself known to Caroline. Typical that it would be when her hair wasn't straightened, and she hadn't applied full makeup.

But the lady in front of her was too old for Mark, surely, given his preference for younger women. She was lumpy and overweight and wore a cleaning tunic.

'That's right?'

'I'm Marion. I volunteer at the Oxfam shop on the high street. Saturday afternoons. Could you let him know that there's been a load of new DVDs handed in?'

'I see,' said Caroline, frowning.

'I know he likes to snap them up as soon as they come in,' said Marion, her moon face beaming. 'There's a box set of the *Father Brown Mysteries*, and a few series of David Attenborough.' She gave a satisfied nod, as if pleased she'd gone above and beyond in her work.

'I shall pass that on,' said Caroline, her tone imperious.

She let herself into the car and slammed the door. She

drew a scarlet Chanel lipstick from her handbag and applied it carefully, using the mirror under the sun visor.

She thought again about the receipt for all those ready meals.

And the fact that she and Mark didn't own a DVD player.

23

MAISIE

Killendreich
Eight years ago

The man standing by the door looked grey in the face, exhausted.

'Maisie?'

'Yes! Hi!'

'I'm...' He shrugged. 'Well, I'm Mark.' His voice sounded very deep, very BBC English, echoing around the high-ceilinged space of the hall.

Suddenly, she was seized by shyness. 'It's so nice to finally meet you.'

GOD! She hated how she sounded, her meek, formal little voice. What must he think of her? Thank goodness she'd pulled a hoodie over the strappy pyjama top she was wearing. But the pyjama shorts only came down to her mid-thighs. Goosebumps had risen on her skin in the cool air.

'It's a shame Ally couldn't make it up today.'

'Has he messaged with any update?' Maisie asked. 'I can't get a signal here.'

Mark had set up a WhatsApp group, for the three of them, to make arrangements for the trip. He'd named it 'Team Maisie'.

'Sorry about that. The phone line's down again, because of the storms last night. It means the Wi-Fi won't work either, but I've requested an engineer call-out. Don't worry – I'm sure Ally will be putting in an appearance soon. In the meantime, did Jock explain that he lives in the cottage out back? If you ever need anything while I'm not here.'

With slightly hooded eyes, and the weathered skin of someone who spent a lot of time outdoors, he had a bit of a lizardy look about him. But he had the wiry physique of a cyclist or a rock-climber, not like an old person at all, and his silvered hair was carefully textured and tousled – she pictured him standing in front of a mirror trying to achieve the right effect.

Usually, Maisie could tell right away if she liked someone. She could get the measure of a person, in a way that her mother had always found uncanny. But in this moment, all she could think about was herself, and how awful she must look, with her face puffy from crying. She pressed the backs of her fingers against her cheeks, trying to cool the skin.

'We've had a bit of a day – well, a night and day. Jan went into labour just after midnight. A few weeks earlier than expected.'

Maisie drew in a sharp breath. Jan had been *giving birth*? Nobody had told her that the baby was due so soon. Why had she been invited up here, in that case? Why hadn't somebody told her not to come? This was so embarrassing.

'She's okay, they're monitoring her closely. But the baby is...' He dragged his hand down over his stubble, stretching his face so that the bloodshot whites of his eyes showed under the irises. Then, slowly, he shook his head.

'Oh no! I'm so sorry. I didn't realise –'

'So I'm going to pick up some overnight things and head back up to the hospital. Jan's sleeping, but I want to be there when she wakes up.'

'Of course, of course.'

Suddenly, she noticed a streak of blood near the collar of his shirt. And a red smudge on the cuff of his sleeve – he'd pushed them roughly up to his elbows. She imagined him taking an active role during the birth. Comforting his wife, encouraging her to push, perhaps even watching from the 'business end', or cutting the umbilical cord.

She felt her cheeks reddening.

'Are they going to be... okay?'

'Jan will be fine. Physically, at least. The wee one... well, it's a miracle he's made it this far.'

He snatched in a shuddery breath through his nose, his nostrils flaring.

Maisie acted instinctively. She stepped forward and put her arms around him. The tartan carpet felt soft under her bare tiptoes.

He smelled of fresh sweat, like he'd just stepped off the tennis court after a long match. With the tang of something sour underneath – fear, stress.

'I'm sure they'll be alright,' she said, uselessly.

'My son,' he cried, in a deep guttural voice. And then a whisper: 'My little son.'

A picture of Ally popped into her head, the way he'd

cried over his anterior cruciate ligament. The way he'd pushed his curly mop of hair against her breasts.

'What's the baby's name?' she asked softly.

'George.' Mark's voice was steady now, in control again. 'We've named him George.'

'There's a ton of food in here.' Mark lifted the lid of the chest freezer. Inside were small plastic boxes, like Chinese take-away containers, all stacked up and neatly labelled. 'You can stick them in the microwave. And there are some bits in the larder. Cereal and porridge and so on.'

He handed her a box with 'Haddock mornay' written on it in stylised, loopy handwriting. Beneath that, the label said:

> *A good source of protein and calcium, plus vitamins B6 and B12, magnesium, niacin, phosphorus, and selenium. Haddock also contains Omega 3 which is a crucial building block of baby's nervous system! Enjoy!*

Without warning, tears stung Maisie's eyes. She thought of the poor baby in the hospital. All the care and love that had gone into getting him this far, all that niacin and protein and everything, only for...

She wiped her cheek with the back of her hand. 'I really need to call Mum. I promised I would, as soon as I got here. She'll be freaking out.'

'If you give me her number, then I'll text her from the

road as soon as I've got a signal. There's a service station with a Starbucks where I usually stop for a coffee.'

Maisie nearly asked if she could come too, if he could drive her back to the real world, where there would be phone service and a Starbucks and... well, *anything*, apart from this gloomy house and the endless trees. Then she realised how inappropriate that would be. She could hardly turn up at the hospital with him. She had to let the man tend to his wife and his ill baby.

'I'll just go and grab my phone.'

'You kids.' He tutted and shook his head. 'In my day, we actually had to *memorise* phone numbers. Can you believe that?' He arched a charming eyebrow at her. He reminded her, just a little bit, of Hugh Grant.

She was out of breath when she got back downstairs again, sweat prickling on her forehead. She went into her contacts and found Mum's number.

Mark held out his phone while she tapped the number in and saved it under his contacts.

'I don't know how you can type at all, with those nails,' he laughed.

Suddenly, she felt embarrassed about her pink acrylic overlays – they seemed over-the-top, out of place here in the Scottish wilderness. As if she was some airhead who might try to climb a mountain in high heels. Perhaps Mum had been right...

'No landline number?' asked Mark.

'Nope.'

He nodded. 'I'd ditch our bloody landline altogether, if I could. It's always going down in bad weather. Listen, if you want to message your mum tomorrow, you can try walking up the track at the back of the house. There's a zig-zag path through the trees and then about a mile up the track it opens out and there's a viewpoint. You can sometimes get a weak signal there. It should be enough to send a text message, although you'd struggle to put through a call.'

'Will I be able to find the track?'

'Sure. It's just at the back of the house. There's a signpost saying 'Footpath to Braemar'.

He lifted his phone and typed the beginning of a message to Mum:

MAISIE HERE ON MARK'S (ALLY'S DAD'S) PHONE.

Maisie raised her eyebrows at him in a wry look.

'What? Is that a bit naff, is it? Well, what about recording a video message?' He opened the camera app on his phone and handed it to Maisie. 'I'll send it from the road.'

'Hi Mum!' Maisie began, waving into the camera. 'I'm really sorry I haven't phoned. The phone line is down and there's no Wi-Fi. But everything is absolutely FINE. I promise. I'm okay.' She paused. *Was* she okay? 'I'll be in touch properly soon, I promise. They said that if you go up some forest track for a mile you can get a weak signal. So I will try to message you. And I will call you when we go into town for supplies etc. I love you. And I love you 2, 4, 8, 32, 64...' She paused, looking up the ceiling. 'And 128! Bye!' Mark lowered the phone, but Maisie signalled him to start recording again. 'And you can contact Ally's Dad on this phone if you like, because he's travelling to Aberdeen tonight! Love you 2, 4, 8, 32, 64.' She waved again and blew a little gale of kisses towards the screen.

Mark gave her a long, level look.

'What?'

'Very cute,' he said. 'Butter wouldn't melt, eh?'

Maisie shrugged. It was none of Mark's business how she talked to Mum. They had their own little language, their Mummy-Maisie code.

'You will have to tell her at some point, you know.'

Maisie felt her insides shrink. 'I know.'

24

MAISIE

Killendreich
Eight years ago

Maisie rose at eleven the next morning and forced down half a Weetabix with some UHT milk she found in the larder. She needed some strength to attempt the walk to the viewpoint.

At first, she couldn't find the start of the track Mark had mentioned. She followed his instructions too literally, walking in a straight line up the rise from the back of the house, because she could see a patch up there where the trees looked thinner. One foot slid into a ditch, at the place where the trees began, and she ended up on her bum in the dirt. Then she found herself in a small clearing, littered with fallen sticks and branches, coated in grey lichen. Poking through, she could see a number of stone markers.

Our Beloved Daisy, age 7

Our dear boy Bailey, age 12

She shrank in horror. Who were these dead children?

Bouncer, age 11

Ah... so it was some kind of pet graveyard.

She turned in a circle, looking around herself carefully. Through the trees to the west (she presumed, since that was where the sun had dipped over the mountain ridge last night) she could see a small cottage. And there was some kind of storage hut a hundred yards or so beyond that.

And there it was. She didn't know how she'd missed it – a signpost. As she made her way towards it, she could see that it said 'Footpath to Braemar'. A spindly tree trunk had fallen across the track, but she climbed over it easily.

She'd thought the walk couldn't get any worse than stumbling across a literal graveyard, but it did. It began to rain – a mist of fine droplets that soaked into her hair. The trees were deep and dark on either side of the path, obscuring any view. The track was thick with mud, and at one point she tried to walk along the grasses at the edge, only for her foot to disappear into a hole full of boggy, stinky water. The wrenching pain was so sharp that she sank to the ground.

Scenarios floated through her mind... She'd probably broken her ankle and would die of exposure. Or she'd be eaten by animals or something. Mountain goats. Nobody would even find her body, out in this wilderness. She gave a shriek of frustration.

But she found she was able to stand on her ankle. She pressed on up the path – Mark had said it was only a mile (although she felt she must have walked at least twice that already). Finally she came to a sign for the viewpoint, and turned off the main path, arriving at a wooden bench a little way along. Whatever view there might once have been was long gone, obscured by conifers that had grown up and up, several feet over her head.

But... yes, there was one bar of a signal!

She keyed a text to Ally.

> When are you coming? I need you to help me talk to them.

A reply appeared a few moments later.

> I might be able to come up on Monday. They've said they need me here until at least then.

But *she* needed him. Monday was three days away. What was she supposed to do until then? Just for a moment, she wondered if he was coming up at all, if he really cared about her the way he said he did.

She'd made a decision, early on, to always think the best of him. She didn't believe those rumours about the other girls he'd coached, particularly about Josie in the year below at school. Not a word of that was true. Or if it was, Josie must have lied to him about her age. But Ally was sensitive about it all, had said they should keep their relationship under wraps, just in case. Just for now.

Mark had agreed that was best, too. He was trying to help Ally, to find ways he could get ahead in his tennis career. They would discuss that too – Mark had said this Scottish trip would be a kind of 'life summit'. They were going to work everything out.

So why wasn't Ally here?

With a little burst of fury, she dialled his number, not caring if he was in the middle of coaching. But the call wouldn't connect. When she looked at the screen, the one bar of signal had gone.

She stood on the bench and waved the phone above her

head, with no idea whether that would help or not. But the one bar did reappear.

Quickly, she texted her mum.

Hello Mum! Having an amazing time.

She paused and tried to imagine what she and Ally might have been doing, in the fictional version of the trip she'd sold to her mother.

Had a lovely family dinner last night.

She paused, trying to think what might impress Mum. Venison, maybe?

Venison wellington!

Was that even a thing? She decided it was.

Went swimming in the waterfall pool with Ally this morning. Was beautiful, clear water. But FREEZING! OMG mum I'm not joking I nearly died.

A message arrived back!

Oh darling Maisie! So lovely to hear from you. Be careful in the water won't you! Did you like the venison?

Maisie thought of the haddock mornay from the freezer last night, how she'd thrown it away because she hadn't microwaved it enough and it was still cold in the middle. Nausea surged inside her.

Yes, it was delicious!

Glad you liked it! What else are you up to today?

What else was she up to? Maisie envisaged the day stretching on ahead of her. Sitting alone in her bare, cold room, pretending to be a governess. Wondering if Ally would come. Wondering if Mark would come. Thoughts of dead babies going round in her head.

She couldn't even. She just couldn't.

Got to go mum. Stepped in hole thing and foot all wet. Had to climb up massive hill to message you bc house in dead zone. And still no Wi-Fi.

Ok. Take care on the way back. Love you so much.

It was amazing, really, the way her mother's love managed to reach her here, half way up a mountain in the middle of nowhere, and even through all of her lies. She allowed it to warm her, just a little. She sent a reply in the usual Mummy-Maisie code.

Love you 2!

Love you 4 xxxx

A sudden wave of sadness came. She folded herself over, pressing the phone against her heart, pressing her eye sockets against the bony hardness of her knees. And she cried until her leggings were as wet as her poor, soggy foot.

25

TERESA

Northumberland
Now

Caroline came to collect her car the following Saturday. My heart soared when I saw that she had George in tow. He zoomed past her into the house.

'I'm so glad you're fully recovered,' I said, setting her cup of tea down on the kitchen table. 'And again, I'm so sorry about what happened.'

She waved her hand airily. 'These things happen. And, just to put your mind at rest, I'm not going to follow it up with your insurers or anything like that. I'm fine, at the end of the day. No lasting damage, that's the main thing. I may be a bit loopy, but that's nothing new!' She rolled her eyes back in her head and let her tongue hang out.

'Oh, well that's good to know. I appreciate that.' I tried to downplay it, to hide my relief.

Through in the living area, George had shaken his drawing things out of his rucksack – an explosion of colouring pencils, sharpenings, pens and scraps of coloured paper – and settled down at the coffee table. Seeing that he was absorbed, I seized the moment.

'I'm going to be totally honest with you,' I began. 'Remember how we talked before? About my worries that Maisie could be... related to George?'

Caroline shifted uneasily. 'I did have a look for his birth certificate, but I couldn't lay my hands on it. I don't want to annoy Mark with it, when he's so rammed at work. Sorry, Teresa. It hasn't been top of my list, what with my concussion and everything.' She put a hand to the back of her head.

'That's okay. I understand. But I have a HUGE favour to ask.' I gave her a pleading look. 'I ordered a DNA testing kit. On the off chance that you would say yes. If George and I both do swabs then it should just get that question out of the way, if you see what I mean?'

Caroline frowned. 'I'm sure I can order another copy of the birth certificate. Wouldn't that be easier? I think you can do it online.'

'But paperwork isn't always... failsafe. Is it? I mean, you weren't there personally, were you, when George was born? When his birth was registered?'

'Oh my goodness. What a peculiar conversation.' Caroline blew out a long breath and raised her face to the ceiling, as if she was trying to think. 'Of course, for my part, I trust Mark *implicitly*.' There was that slight off-note in her voice again. 'But you've been through something unimaginable. And I suppose, really, you're trying to process your grief. And I'm in a position where I can help you with that, in a small way.'

'So... will you?'

She gave a heavy sigh, then looked back at me and

nodded. 'So yes, I *guess*...?' She shrugged. 'I'm happy to do it. I would just ask, though, that we make sure George's DNA doesn't end up on some database somewhere. I'm afraid I wouldn't be able to consent to that.' She bared her teeth in something that was half way between a grimace and a smile.

Something stirred inside me. A hint of wariness, mixed in with my relief. I hadn't expected this to be so easy.

'Of course – no databases.' I emptied the envelope from the DNA testing company onto the table and passed the information booklet and the forms to Caroline.

'Gosh. You mean *now*? You don't hang around, do you?'

'I chose Surity DNA. It seems like a very reputable company. The way it works, it tests for a specific relationship, so I ordered a grandparent test. Please feel free to look through the terms and conditions. I'm sure we can tick a box to say no to databases.'

'Georgie-Pie,' called Caroline. 'We have a little job to do here, if you don't mind.'

The process was quite easy to complete. I removed the test kit from the plastic wrapping and handed the long cotton swab to Caroline.

'Open up,' she said to George, in a sweet, sing-song voice. Looking worried, he opened his mouth an inch and looked at me.

Briskly, Caroline swished the swab around the inside of George's cheek and then handed it carefully back to me.

'George's sample complete.' The way she said it made me think of a surgeon, confirming steps in a procedure. Or a pilot, reporting back to the air control tower.

I took it and sealed it inside a labelled plastic bag, then copied her intonation: 'George's sample bagged, sealed and labelled.'

We exchanged brief nods.

Then I repeated the process with my own swab.

'Teresa's sample bagged, sealed and labelled,' said Caroline. She winced and put a hand to her temple.

'Are you okay?'

'I don't suppose I could trouble you for some paracetamol? I get these crushing headaches that come on suddenly, since the accident. I forgot to put painkillers in my bag this morning.'

'Of course!' I jumped up and went to the kitchen cupboard, thinking, guiltily, of the rustic, moss-covered rockery steps. 'Paracetamol? Ibuprofen?'

'I'll go crazy and go for both,' said Caroline. 'If it's not too much trouble.'

I filled a glass with water from the kitchen tap and handed it to her with the tablets. She swallowed them and exhaled in relief.

'Right. Where were we?' She turned her attention to the papers on the table and picked up the A4 return envelope. 'So you just pop the sample bags in here. And the completed form.'

I did as she instructed, then pulled the sticky strip off the seal of the envelope and pressed it down firmly.

She smiled. 'Now, you must promise that you won't be upset, Teresa. When the test results show what we all know.'

'Oh, totally. It's just to exclude it, as I say. I'll take this along to the post box for the one o'clock collection. It's a nice day for a bit of a walk.'

'George,' said Caroline. 'Would you like to stay here with Teresa while I go and do my thing at the farm shop?' She turned to me. 'If that's okay with you?'

'Of course! Would you like that, George? You can walk to the post box with me?'

We saw Caroline off and then set off along the street in the direction of the main road and the post box, the envelope tucked safely under my arm. Although George ran, rather than walked – scooting off ahead and then circling back to me like a puppy. When we arrived at the post box, I lifted him at the waist so that he could feed the envelope in. He stared into the slot, cupping his hands around his eyes.

'Letter gone in post box,' he confirmed, in the same serious tone that Caroline and I had used while completing the test kit. Then he wriggled down and hared off along the pavement in the direction of home.

But instead of going straight home, I directed him down the sandy little track towards the dunes. It would be good for him to run off some of his energy on the beach.

George looked up at me, his face twisted with anxiety, when I suggested that he could take off his shoes and socks and paddle. The tide was coming in, little white-tipped waves racing in to the shore and foaming back over the wet sand. Gathering his courage, he teetered on tiptoe towards an incoming wave and let the water rush over his toes. He screeched in terrified delight, the wind carrying the sound away.

'Have you never played on the beach before?' I asked as we wound our way back towards the house.

He shook his head, the wind whipping his hair so that it flew out behind him. He walked with his hands cupped in front of him, cradling a small pile of seashells he had collected from the beach, watching them closely.

'Not in this life. I'm not keen on water.'

'It must be quite confusing, having two lives,' I said.

He nodded gravely. 'I'm a freak. That's what everybody says.'

'Well that's not nice,' I said. 'Caroline should speak to your teachers about that.'

He shook his head, his brow furrowed. 'They're already dealing with so many issues.' I guessed that he was parroting Caroline's words.

'It's important to report bullies, though,' I said.

'They're just silly, silly sheep. Copying what the other sheep do. That's what Miss Honey says.' He pressed his lips into a disapproving line and shook his head in a way that reminded me of Maisie, telling me about what the bad boys had done at the swing park, or about Annabelle Punch's failed fake tan attempts.

Arriving home, I opened the door and let him go in ahead of me. Still holding the shells, he tried to prise one trainer off with the toe of the other one.

'The last time you were here,' I said carefully, 'you were telling me about when you died. You mentioned something about...'

'Oh yes – when I got drowned.' He managed to get his other trainer off and nudged them both to the side of the hallway.

'That must have been very scary.'

'He lifted me. Out of my bed. Then there was lots and lots of water. Inside my eyes and ears and down my throat.' As before, he enunciated each of the 't's distinctly, as if he was trying to make himself very clear.

'Where did that happen? Where was the water?'

'In the bathroom,' he said. 'Where can I put my shells?'

'I've got a bowl of seashells right here,' I said, lifting a coloured glass bowl from the hall windowsill and holding it out to him. 'Nice ones I've found over the years.'

It had been Maisie, in fact, who'd collected the shells. There was a plastic box in her bedroom that must have contained hundreds of them.

'So you can put them in here if you like?'

Carefully, he tipped his treasure into the bowl.

'And when you said you were running up the stairs?' I continued carefully. 'You said you were running away from a man?'

'Yes?'

'Where was *that*?'

'That was here,' he said, with a touch of impatience. He held out his hands for the bowl and I transferred it to him.

'Here? What do you mean?'

'Here.' He nodded in the direction of the stairs.

I swallowed hard. 'The stairs you were running up were... these stairs here?' I pointed towards them, the carpeted treads spiralling up towards the shadowy landing. 'In this house?'

'Yes,' he said, nodding emphatically. 'And then I died. Upstairs.'

I moaned softly. Was it possible? I'd always thought Maisie had been taken, somewhere far away. Had she never in fact left?

Had she been killed? Here in her own house?

'It's okay.' He jiggled from one foot to the other and the shells clattered gently in the bowl. 'It's okay, don't cry. That was my old life. It's not now.'

My mind whipped back. The police had searched the house, even though I'd told them that was pointless, that she was up in Scotland somewhere. And they hadn't found any signs of... anything. No blood stains. No signs of a struggle. But of course, that had been weeks after she'd left. It wasn't likely that there would be anything, by that time.

Was it possible? My mind raced frantically, trying to refute what George had suggested.

I'd been out that day, the day she left. I'd been away doing a big shop at the cash and carry. If she *had* come back to the house... well, I'd have been none the wiser.

Was it possible she'd never travelled to Scotland at all?

But that couldn't be right. She'd sent a photo of the Queensferry Bridge, that first day. And one from Dunkeld, of her fish and chip supper. And then, she'd texted me about eating venison wellington. About swimming in a waterfall pool. About falling into a hole and getting her feet wet.

Unless someone else had sent those messages.

I looked down at George, who was kneeling low over the bowl of shells, his bottom raised in the air. His focus was intense as he turned the shells over, examining their gritty edges and smooth, pearlescent interiors, tracing his fingers over the coils and whorls.

'This one is like outer space,' he said.

'Oh yes, do you mean it's like a galaxy, with its spiral shape, and the pinky colour running through it? Yes, I see what you mean.'

He held another one up to his ear. 'I can hear it! I can hear the sea!' He held it out to me, his expression urgent.

The shell was only a few centimetres wide, but I held it up to my ear anyway and closed my eyes, willing myself to hear it. To imagine, like George could, that the shell was a tiny portal to the vast, crashing ocean.

My phone rang, and I jumped, almost dropping the shell. It was Caroline.

'Some urgent work stuff has come up.' It sounded like she was breathless, almost panting. 'I don't suppose you could do me a *hee-yoooge* favour?'

'Of course,' I said, wondering how anything relating to puddings could be urgent. 'How can I help?'

'Could you hang onto George for me? Just for a couple of nights while I sort all this out.'

'H-hang on to him? You mean you want him to stay here...with me?'

'Only if that would be okay,' said Caroline. 'I know it's a big ask.'

When I put down the phone, the strangest sensation came over me. My interactions with George had been like the sun peeping through the clouds on a grey, cold day. A grey, cold life. But this... being able to keep him here with me... for a few *days*. It was like a summer sunrise. Golden warmth spreading over everything.

This was joy. For the first time in years.

I was holding two completely opposing realities in my head.

My child was lost. Long dead. Killed in her own house.

And my child was here in front of me, warm and safe. Exploring the universe in a bowl of seashells.

26

MAISIE

Killendreich
Eight years ago

The Victorian governess vibe was wearing a bit thin now. Maisie hadn't seen a soul for two days and the Wi-Fi still wasn't working. She was in the kitchen, reading her book while she waited for a carton of ricotta-filled ravioli to heat through in the microwave – why was all the food white around here? – when she heard the crunch of tyres on gravel.

She abandoned the ravioli and hurried through the higgledy corridor to the main hallway. The Virgin Mary's face stared up at her mournfully from the triptych on the hall table as she waited for the front door to swing open.

Mark came in first, carrying two holdalls, his face grave. He shook his head at Maisie, as if trying to communicate something. Did that mean she was supposed to get out of the way, to give them privacy?

Before there was time to decide, Jan appeared. She didn't

seem to notice Maisie, and walked towards the stairs, looking straight ahead. Her black hair was cut in a helmet style, the blunt fringe emphasising the structure of her face, the bone and cartilage beneath the skin. She wore a long black jersey dress which stuck out in a bump at the front. Maisie had a sudden image of an insect, its abdomen distended with eggs.

How horrible she was, for thinking such things. Maisie knew your figure didn't just snap back into place after having a baby.

'H-hello,' she said, lifting her hand in a little spasm of a wave.

Jan turned on the stairs, glancing back at Maisie for a moment. Her thin lips curved into a sickle shape.

Maisie nearly jumped back in fright.

'I'll get out of your way,' she said to Mark's back, as he followed Jan up.

'I'll be down in two ticks,' he called. 'Wait for me in the drawing room.'

She went into the large room off the hall – the one she assumed was the drawing room – and sat herself down with *The Turn of the Screw.*

After a paragraph or two, she put the book down and surveyed the room. In front of the window stood a grand piano, its lid covered in some kind of tasselled cloth. To her right, Jesus and his disciples loomed down from a dark painting above the fireplace. To her left was a large bookcase with rows of leather-bound volumes on the top shelves, and some more modern books lower down. They mostly seemed to be about psychiatry and psychology.

Madness and Civilisation

The Divided Self

She found herself thinking about her phone, and wishing

it would work here. Even though she'd deleted Snapchat and Instagram months ago, she still felt the phone's addictive pull, coupled with the familiar spike of anxiety at the thought of checking it. She'd been trying to cure what she privately thought of as her 'phone PTSD' by doing safe, soothing things on it, like looking at cat videos, or playing Scrabble online. Also, she wanted to message Mum. And Ally – to find out where the hell he was. It wasn't fair of him to abandon her here like this.

The room was cold. She looked over at the empty fireplace, its grate swept clean. The room would look so different with a roaring fire. Maybe she could find some wood from somewhere and light it. She wondered how difficult it would be to cut down one of those trees in the forest. With so many, nobody would ever miss it.

She heard Mark's footsteps on the stairs after about ten minutes, and lifted the book so that the cover would be easily visible when he walked in. She wanted him to know that she wasn't just an airhead, an irresponsible teenager. She was a teenager who read Henry James.

He went straight over to the drinks cabinet and poured himself a whisky.

'Want a juice or something?' he asked her.

Maisie shook her head. 'What's... what's happening?'

Mark sat down and closed his eyes, flung his head back against the back of the sofa. 'The baby has a chromosomal abnormality. It was born with part of its brain missing. We knew from the scans that there were... issues. But... yeah. They say his condition is "incompatible with life". He's being moved to hospice care tomorrow morning.' He squeezed his eyes even tighter shut.

Maisie felt a strange sensation in her body. Something

seemed to swell in her chest, to fill it up so she could hardly breathe. A little tsunami of grief for this poor child who she'd never meet, who was to have no life at all.

'I'm so sorry,' she whispered. 'So, so sorry.'

'We'll go back up to the hospital first thing,' he went on. 'I wanted Jan to have a night in her own bed. The doctors have given her something to help her sleep. She'll need all her strength to get through the next few days.'

And then, with a slow, creeping horror, Maisie realised what it meant for *her*. For the things she needed to discuss with Mark, and Jan, and Ally. How could she talk about her right to choose, when Jan and Mark – and poor baby George, lying in some hospital incubator with half his brain missing – had no choice at all?

She felt as if a big black iron cage had clunked down over her head.

Oubliette. Wasn't that the name of those dungeons they'd had in medieval times? The ones with no way out? So that prisoners were just left there to die. She'd seen one on a school trip to Alnwick Castle, and they'd been told that the name came from the French for 'to forget'. She'd felt faint and had been allowed to go and eat some of her packed lunch on the grass.

She needed to go home. It had been stupid to try and cut Mum out of this.

As soon as it was light, tomorrow morning, she would walk up the track and text her. She would ask her to come and fetch her, while Mark and Jan were away at the hospice, watching their baby son die. Panic rose in her throat at the thought of it. How could they bear it?

She'd leave a note and slip away with Mum. She'd get out of this rotting house and back to Northumberland, where she could breathe in the sea air and see for miles in every direction.

But when she reached her room, her phone was nowhere to be found. With shaking hands, she emptied out all her pockets, turned the hoodie she'd been wearing earlier inside out. Had she dropped it on the track up to the viewpoint? It was too dark to go out and look for it now – outside the window was nothing but black, so thick that the glass might have almost been painted over.

Oubliette.

'I can't find my phone,' she said to Mark, who was still lying back on the sofa, arms and legs spreadeagled. 'And I need to message Mum tomorrow, or she'll be worried. I know you've got more important things on your mind but...' She tried to keep her voice steady, but she was on the edge of tears.

Mark opened his eyes. 'No, no,' he said. 'My goodness. A teenager can't be separated from her phone.'

He rose to his feet and raked a hand through his hair, looking around the room as if disorientated. 'We've got a spare phone somewhere. My mother used it when she was in the care home. It's just a cheap pay-as-you-go, but it'll tide you over. I'm sure yours will turn up. It must be somewhere in the house.'

He went away to fetch the phone, and plugged the charger into the wall. After a few moments, the screen lit up. 'There we go. Hang on, let me see if I can airdrop this.'

He fiddled around with his own phone, and then the contact pinged up on the new phone, showing Mum's photo with her phone number underneath.

She held the phone up to her lips, relief flooding through her.

There was another ping and Ally's number appeared too.

'Thank you,' she said. And then: 'Mum's going to go mental about all this, you know.'

Mark frowned. 'That's a rather childish thing to say.'

Maisie felt her cheeks flush. She stared down at the new, rubbish phone. She wasn't going to cry. She wasn't.

'You need to have a grown-up conversation,' went on Mark. 'Adult to adult. Try and see things from her perspective. Think about what she will be bringing to that conversation, in terms of her past experiences, and the events in her own life.'

'I know that. I *know*.'

'Think about what it must have been like for her, bringing you up as a single mother, not much older than you are now. Think about what she might have had to give up.' He glanced up at her, and said more gently, 'You're shaking, Maisie. Breathe slowly now – nice slow belly breaths. I'm here to help now and everything will be okay.'

27

MAISIE

Killendreich
Eight years ago

Maisie woke at eleven the next morning, butterflies in her stomach. Coming down to the kitchen for her Weetabix, she saw that the car in the driveway had gone. Mark and Jan must have left for the hospital already.

She threw on some clothes and walked up the forest track, looking for the viewpoint and the bench where she'd managed to get a signal last time. It was even further away than she remembered, and at one point she thought she must have gone past it. She had a horrible thought that maybe the trees had marched forward during the night, swallowing up the bench, what was left of the little clearing. She thought of Birnam Wood, the trees moving to fulfil the witches' prophecy. She'd studied *Macbeth* for GCSE English.

The butterflies felt more like eels now, slithering around in her guts.

She rehearsed the conversation she needed to have with Mum. Mark was right – she needed to tell her what was happening – to talk to her like an adult. But Mum was in for a hell of a shock.

When Maisie was younger, she and Mum had always been able to guess what the other was thinking. It had been a sort of connection between them that hadn't needed words. 'Mummy-Maisie telepathy,' they used to call it. But recently, that had changed.

Maisie had learned to think of herself as having doors in her mind. Doors she could open and close as she wanted. As long as she kept certain doors closed, around Mum, she could still be Little Maisie, Maisie-Munchkin; the sweet, happy version that made Mum's face light up with love.

If she hid bad stuff behind the doors, it was because she didn't want Mum to worry. And because she wanted Mum's love to be uncomplicated. Unpolluted. Un-disappointed, if that was a word.

But now, all doors would have to be opened. She would need to tell Mum that it had happened – the thing she'd been dreading all her life.

In her mind, she replayed the conversation she'd had with Mum – ages ago now, around the time she'd started high school. Mum had told her that she'd been conceived at a student party when she'd 'got together', briefly, with her ex-boyfriend. By the time she'd realised she was pregnant, the ex had moved to Australia. She'd whispered his name like it was a sexually transmitted disease – 'Joel'.

'But did you tell him about me?' Maisie had asked.

She still remembered the careful look on Mum's face. 'He chose not to be involved. His loss, darling.'

Mum had explained she had left uni to move back home and have the baby that turned out to be Maisie.

'I never regretted it for one minute,' she'd said. 'It wasn't what I planned, but sometimes life throws you a curve ball and you make the best of it.'

Make the best of it. Maisie remembered how she'd felt when Mum had said that. Like she wanted to shrivel up and disappear.

Despite what Mark had said last night, Maisie was well aware of all the things Mum had lost out on. The different careers she could have had, if she'd finished her degree. The neat, traditional family she might have had, if she hadn't already been saddled with a baby.

And Mum's worst nightmare was that she, Maisie, might go the same way. She'd seen that in her face, in her judgey, frowny expression when she'd heard about Kaylee getting pregnant. Or if Maisie ever talked about people at school going to parties, or drinking on the beach. Maisie had never asked Mum if she could go, mainly because she wouldn't be seen dead with any of that crowd anyway, but also because she didn't want Mum to get all stressy.

Maisie wondered if Mum still blamed Joel for ruining her life. Even though he was irrelevant, now. Not to mention dead – according to Mum's Facebook friends.

She paused for breath on the pine-needly path. She drew herself up straight, feeling determined. Truth and honesty – that's what their relationship needed, like fresh air rushing into a stuffy room. Mum would be shocked, at first, when that door was flung open. She would see messed-up Maisie. Scared Maisie. Maisie who had questions.

But first, she had to find the viewpoint. Her legs felt weak. Her bowels spasmed, as if the eels were trying to escape.

Her mother's voice seemed to come into her head, saying the thing she always said when Maisie felt like giving up.

'Take a breath, my love. Then just take one step at a time.'

So she did. She trudged further along the path to another hairpin bend. And there it was – the clearing and the viewpoint.

She took out her phone and typed a message.

Mum? Are you there? I lost my phone so I'm borrowing a spare one for now.

She sat waiting, wishing she'd brought a coat as well as her hoodie. It wasn't raining, but the sky was lead grey and there was a cold breeze.

A reply arrived.

Hello Maisie Munchkin. I have mobile phone insurance with my bank account and I'm sure it covers both our phones. Didn't we register yours on Boxing Day after you got your new iPhone?

Ah yes, that was right. Mum could order a new phone under the insurance and post it up here. Not that it would do her much good, in this awful dead zone.

Cool. Give me one more day to see if I can find it. It's either in the house or lost in the forest.

She pressed 'send' and then paused for a few moments, listening to the wind moving through the trees, starting like a whisper and then building to a soft roar.

From somewhere down the hill, in amongst the trees, she

thought she heard a noise. After a minute or two, it came again. It sounded like her name, carried on the wind.

May....seeeeee...

It sounded like... no. Mum was on the other end of this phone, down in Northumberland, not tramping around these lonely woods. It was some sort of bird, probably. If she had any sodding data, she could google whether there was some kind of weird forest bird that sounded like that.

She typed another message.

How's Gran? Did you speak to them about her radio going missing?

Another few minutes elapsed. It was annoying. Mum usually replied right away. It must be the dodgy signal up here, making it take longer than usual. Maisie stood on the bench and waved the phone around above her head before dialling Mum's number. It wouldn't connect, cutting off immediately with three beeps. She sat down again and waited impatiently.

Yes, I spoke to Sandy. They think another resident picked it up. Mrs Garrick, maybe, when she was on her travels.

Mrs Garrick, a lady with advanced dementia, was the bane of Granny's life. She was always wandering into Granny's room to 'have a blether'.

Mum?

Yes darling. What's up?

There's something I need to talk to u about.

Maisie used the ensuing pause to psych herself up. She did six deep belly breaths and straightened her back.

What is it, Maisie Munchkin?

I haven't been totally straight with you. I'm sorry.

Just tell me.

We tried to be careful.

It wasn't exactly true. That time in the locker room, thoughts about taking precautions had drifted through her head, but her focus had been on other things.

What are you talking about? I'm worried now. Please tell me.

The messages were coming more quickly now – the weird time-lapse thing must have corrected itself. Either that or she had Mum's full attention.

Ally's not a girl. He's my boyfriend. He's 19 and coaches at the tennis club. I've been seeing him for a while.

You lied to me?

Yes. And now there's something else. Mum, don't be mad. It's the worst thing you can think of.

Spit it out.

Maisie frowned. This wasn't going how she'd planned.

Mum was supposed to say that Maisie could tell her anything, anything at all. That she'd never think any less of her.

I'm pregnant. I wanted to come here with Ally so that we could really think about things and make good decisions.

You have got to be joking.

You are joking, aren't you?

No

There was no reply. Maisie wrote a second message, tears filling her eyes.

You're disappointed in me.

I need some time to think about this Maisie.

Mum please. I need you.

I said I need some time.

Maisie dialled the number again. As if to punish her, the one bar of signal disappeared completely, and the phone declared 'no service'.

She waited until the bar came back and texted again.

Mum? Will you come and get me? Please Mum. I'm scared.

She waited ten minutes, but no reply came. She tried again.

Mama? I love you 2 4 8 16 32

No answer. The wind surged up again, so loudly that it sounded like the trees were angry with her too.

She had never, ever felt so alone.

28

TERESA

Northumberland
Now

George was finally asleep, tucked up in Maisie's bed, after six stories and three circuits around the house, but no bath. Exhausted, I took myself off to bed with a mug of apple and chamomile tea.

I needed to check back through Maisie's final messages. At the time, I'd thought some of them were odd, so much so that I'd hared up to Scotland when she'd messaged 'I love you too'. But later, when the police had shown me that video of Maisie – saying she was sorry she hadn't called, but that everything was fine – I'd had to accept that the messages *were* from her.

But now, I needed to check them again. What if that video had been faked, somehow, and she had never gone to Scotland at all? What if she'd died in the house, as George seemed to be suggesting?

I scrolled back to 22nd July – the day she'd left – and the photos of the Queensferry Bridge, and the fish and chip supper in Dunkeld.

It was possible, I supposed, that she hadn't actually been in those places. Somebody could have given her those photos to send on. She could even have even lifted them from the internet herself.

There had been nothing strange, though, about her messages at that point. They still sounded like her, even if they were a little breathless and over-excited.

Then I reached the messages of 25th July, a couple of days after Maisie had gone.

Mum? Quick question. Do you have mobile phone insurance for my phone?

Hello Maisie Munchkin. I have mobile phone insurance with my bank account and I'm sure it covers both our phones. Didn't we register yours on Boxing Day after you got the new iPhone? Why do you ask?

I nearly lost it yesterday when we went waterfall swimming!

Wow! Do be careful, won't you? Careful on slippery rocks and things.

I will. How's Gran? Did you speak to them about her radio going missing?

That message, surely, had been from Maisie herself. My mum's radio *had* gone missing, the day before Maisie left.

But the message about the phone insurance... it was just very slightly odd. I'd once had to answer a bunch of questions like that on the HMRC website, to prove my identity to them.

When did you last take out a mobile phone contract?

What is the name of your mortgage provider?

Was it possible that Maisie had been trying to prove *my* identity, to make sure it was really me? That didn't make any sense. But then I remembered the strangely long pauses that had elapsed between each message and the next. That had been unusual for Maisie, whose thumbs had always moved over the phone keypad like lightning. Thinking back now, it was almost as if the messages were being... analysed? Processed, somehow?

At the time, I'd put the pauses down to the poor phone signal. I'd just felt touched that Maisie was thinking of her gran.

Yes, I spoke to Sandy. They think another resident picked it up. Mrs Garrick, maybe, when she was on her travels.

Mum?

Yes darling. What's up?

There's something I need to talk to u about.

What is it, Maisie Munchkin?

They've asked if I want to stay a teeny bit longer than the two weeks. Maybe three or four? If it's ok with you, I would like that. It's so amazing here. The mountains are so beautiful and I love swimming in the waterfall pool. Because there's no telly or Wi-Fi we have to do other things in the evenings like playing Scrabble and Monopoly.

And there it was – another slight oddity. Maisie had always detested Monopoly, because of having to add up the money. I'd bought a set once, when she'd been about seven, as part of my plan to try and make maths fun. Within five minutes, she'd thrown the set across the room, refusing to pay rent for landing on Old Kent Road.

When I'd first received the message, I hadn't thought about that. I'd been trying to hold back my disappointment, at the thought of her wanting to stay away for longer.

Oh gosh darling. Are you sure?

I will miss you but I would like to if its ok

I guess you could stay a little bit longer if you really want to. As long as you keep in touch, yes? When will the Wi-Fi be fixed?

I remembered the long pause that had followed. I'd imagined her turning to Ally, excitedly telling her that she could stay longer.

Not sure but I like coming up here to message you. The view is amazing! GTG now, just off to play tennis with Ally and her parents. I love you 2 4 8 16 32

I'd replied straight away.

Love you 64 my darling

Now, I closed my eyes and held the phone against my chest. I doubled the numbers in my head, imagining my heart expanding with each sum. There was no limit to the love it could hold.

128, 256, 512, 1024, 2048, 4096...

I was woken by a noise. I sat upright, scrabbled with the bedcovers, trying to swing my legs out of the bed.

There was someone there. A shape, standing by my bed.

Adrenaline flooded my body, shooting down my arms to the tips of my fingers. But then, as I came to properly, I realised that it was George. In the light that filtered in from the hallway I could see that his eyes were wide open. He was pointing to the corner of the room. 'There! He's there!'

I turned my head to where he was pointing – the dark corner between the wardrobe and the far wall. An unusable space under the eaves.

A wave of prickles went down my body. I slid my shaking legs out of the bedcovers. Every instinct was telling me NOT to approach the wardrobe, or the crooked little space under the eaves. But that's what parents were supposed to do, wasn't it? Show your child that there *were* no monsters in the shadows? That it was safe to go back to sleep?

George gulped in a breath.

'He's THERE!' he screamed. And then he clapped his hands over his ears. 'No, no, no!'

I wanted to scream too. I wanted to snatch him up and run out of that room. But instead, I walked over to the wardrobe and shone my phone torch into the shadows.

'There's nothing there,' I said, unsure whether he could hear me or not. 'Nothing at all.'

I thought of what he'd been telling me earlier. That he had died, upstairs in this house. I had no idea why he thought this to be the case. But – I told myself firmly – this wasn't a ghost, or an intruder, that we were dealing with. It was trauma.

He threw his head back. 'Help me!!'

I flew over to him, resisting the urge to wrap him in my arms. Instead, I placed my hands on his shoulders and guided him back through to Maisie's room.

Once in bed, he seemed to settle down, his breathing becoming more regular. I noticed that his porcelain angel had fallen onto the floor, and I tucked it under the covers beside him.

I settled in the pink velvet chair by Maisie's bed and waited for dawn to come.

I didn't sleep, of course. I sat with my phone, searching the internet for help. I scanned through the websites of psychologists, psychiatrists, psychotherapists, play therapists and hypnotherapists. And art therapists, music therapists and drama therapists. Therapists who worked through horses... One who worked through alpacas, and another who worked through sheep.

It was clear I wasn't going to be able to arrange anything quickly. Most of the websites required you to fill in a contact form so they could get back to you. Many referred to waiting lists, or not taking on new clients until further notice. And they all seemed to require an initial discussion session with the parents before needs could be assessed and an appointment with the child could be set up. I didn't have time for that. I needed someone who could see him within the next day or two, before Caroline returned.

I searched for: 'therapists in my area urgent'.

And to my surprise, on the fourth page of results, Cheryl's website popped up. She described herself as an 'intuitive medium healer'. In her 'About me' section, she said that she had recently completed a qualification as a life coach, after several years of working as a spiritual medium and experiencing the positive effect this could bring to people's lives. She considered her highly tuned intuition to be her 'superpower', something she brought to every client session, available to be brought into the process in any way that might be helpful.

It all sounded pretty reasonable.

> *I have an ability to help people connect with what lies beyond. For some people, this might mean the spirit world, but for others, it might mean the parts of themselves that are lost, forgotten, abandoned, or simply beyond their understanding. I can use this ability to provide support and healing for any person who needs it*
>
> *You have probably found yourself here, looking at my website, because other types of therapy haven't worked for you. People often approach spiritual healers as a last resort, and because there seems to be nowhere else to turn.*

If that's you, you have come to the right place. I can help.

George thought that he had died. And he seemed to think that whatever he had encountered there, in that place beyond, was coming back for him. He slept with a china angel in his bed. If anyone's problems were spiritual, his were.

I pinged Cheryl a WhatsApp.

29

MAISIE

Killendreich
Eight years ago

Another day, another trudge up the viewpoint to try and get a signal.

Mum? Have you had enough time to think?

Maisie tipped her head back and looked straight up into the dull grey sky. It was the only direction she could look and not see trees. After a minute or two, a rising tone from her phone signalled a reply.

So many lies, Maisie. You've broken my trust.

Maisie longed to be able to go back and close that awful door she'd opened. To make things go back to how they were before.

I'm really sorry Mum. Please say its okay. I know I've messed up but I need your help.

I think I've protected you too much in the past and that's why you haven't learnt to be responsible. I always jump in and save you from your own messes.

What was she even talking about? What messes? Maisie thought of herself, dutifully sitting at the kitchen table every evening, doing her homework and keeping Mum company while she cooked. Helping change the bedding in the glamping huts. Never attending drunken house parties like the other kids at school. Okay, there was the business with the shared nudes... but Mum didn't even *know* about that.

Please, Mum.

If Ally's parents are willing to help then maybe you should let them. I don't want to be part of this decision. I can't stand to think of you having an abortion. I can't stand to think of you keeping it and ruining your life.

Like I ruined your life when you had me?

There was a pause of several minutes.

I'm too involved to help you with this.

Too involved? You're my MOTHER.

I feel like I don't even know you any more.

Maisie stared at the phone, hardly able to believe what she was reading.

Mum hated the Maisie behind the door.

She felt pain. Real, physical pain, like someone had pushed a hand inside her ribcage and was twisting, squeezing. A hot tear slid down her cheek. And then another.

She placed a hand over her stomach, feeling a sudden rush of pity for the little being inside her, who had never asked to be brought into existence.

From down in the trees, she thought she heard a faint noise, like a voice carried on the wind.

She listened again, but there was nothing. Just her imagination. She was going mad, from isolation. She'd heard of that happening to people.

Later that evening, when she was scraping a half-eaten bowl of spaghetti carbonara into the bin, Mark appeared behind her. Maisie hadn't even realised he was in the house.

'Come and sit with me in the drawing room. Jan's gone up to bed.'

'How is Jan?' asked Maisie, as she followed him through the twisting passages to the main house.

'She's exhausted with all the bleeding, the poor thing. And her milk's started to come through which is just... quite devastating, in the circumstances.' He shook his head gravely. 'There've been a lot of tears today.'

When they reached the drawing room, he went straight for the drinks cabinet and picked up the whisky decanter.

Maisie perched herself down on the edge of a lumpy tweed armchair. She couldn't think of a single thing to say. She stared up at Jesus and his disciples, in their painting above the fireplace, pretending to be absorbed in it.

Mark sat down opposite. He took a sip from his whisky and released a long sigh.

'And… how's George?' she asked eventually.

'We brought him home this morning. He's upstairs with Jan. They're sleeping.'

'Oh!' said Maisie brightly. 'That's good, isn't it?'

Mark raised an eyebrow, and tipped the rest of the amber liquid into his mouth. 'He's under the hospice team, now. Nurses will be visiting to make sure he's comfortable. He's a fighter, God love him. The neonatal team didn't expect him to hang on this long.'

'Oh. I see.'

'It won't be long now,' he added, in a low voice. 'It won't be long.'

She shifted uncomfortably on her chair. There was a little tapestry kneeler by her feet, with some kind of psalm or something on it. She pushed it gently to the side with her toe.

When was Mark going to bring it up? The great big elephant in the room. She imagined it trumpeting and swinging its trunk, knocking Jesus and his disciples off the wall.

'I…I…' What could she say? 'I'm very sorry.'

'Let's talk about you,' he said. His face was pale this evening, and she could see the dark mottling of sun damage on his skin, across his nose and cheeks.

'I think I should probably go back home,' she said. 'I'm just getting in the way here. And it doesn't look like Ally's coming up any time soon.'

'Your pregnancy,' he said. 'Have you thought any more about what you want to do?'

She squirmed again. This was so embarrassing. Although he was a doctor, wasn't he? Psychiatrists were doctors. She'd try to imagine he was her doctor, and not a strange, almost-family member.

'You're under no pressure, of course. But most women find it...' He cleared his throat. 'Easier, shall we say, if the procedure takes place earlier on in the pregnancy.'

He took some leaflets out of his inside jacket pocket and spread them on the coffee table. 'I picked these up from the hospital today.'

She lifted one of them and scanned through it, horrific phrases leaping out at her.

Dilation of the cervix...

Insert special instruments...

Suction and curettage...

And on the back of the leaflet was an image that she knew she'd never be able to unsee.

Her head swooped. Nausea surged. Didn't people just take pills for it, these days? She wanted her mother.

'It doesn't feel like the right time to be talking about this,' she said. She felt like she couldn't breathe, let alone think. There wasn't any space to think about what she wanted. Not in this house, sunk deep in the forest. Not with baby George upstairs, and Jan leaking blood and milk and tears like some nightmarish Sleeping Beauty.

Not with Jesus staring down at her dolefully from above the fireplace.

'One option,' went on Mark, 'is that you continue with the pregnancy here, supported by us. And once the baby's born, Jan and I could step in. That happens more often than you'd think – grandparents bringing up a child. You and Ally could have as much or as little involvement as you like. You could be like another set of parents, alongside us. Or you could treat the baby more like a sibling. So you'd still be family, but not have any responsibility – you'd be able to live your own lives. You could go to university, art school, whatever. And Ally could keep on with his tennis.'

Maisie considered. Was this a third way, a way out of the awful decision? 'Wouldn't you and Jan want to… to try again? To have your own baby?'

Mark shook his head. 'This was our last shot, I'm afraid. We've been trying for a baby for twelve years. We'd gone through multiple fertility treatments, three rounds of IVF, two miscarriages, and then, finally… George.'

'I'm sorry,' said Maisie. It just didn't seem fair that she'd fallen pregnant by accident, through sheer carelessness, when they'd gone through all this.

From somewhere, up above the ceiling, she thought she heard a sob. Rising high and hysterical, almost like laughter. She looked nervously at Mark, but he didn't seem to have heard it.

'We've been told that any child we may conceive in the future has a chance of having the same genetic disorder. The chromosomal translocation that's led to George's birth defects. It's on Jan's side, so there's no possibility of using a sperm donor.'

Maisie felt her cheeks were on fire. She didn't want to be discussing sperm with Mark. She looked down at her hands.

'It's different for me, having a biological child from before the marriage. Jan wanted a biological child. She really, really wanted that.'

For a moment, Maisie wanted to speak up for poor little George. He was a child, wasn't he? Even if he only had a few days to be alive.

'So, have you spoken to your mum yet about the pregnancy?'

'Yes, but she's being weird. She says I need to make my decision, and she doesn't want to be involved.'

'She'll come round. It's just been a bit of a shock, I expect. Why don't you message her again tomorrow? You could invite her up? We could all sit down and discuss things.'

She looked at him doubtfully. 'Discuss... like... everything? Properly?'

'We're all adults, Maisie. And we have a problem to solve – all of us together. We need all cards on the table.'

Maisie frowned, confused. He was the one who'd said, a few weeks ago, that it was necessary to 'carefully manage the flow of information' to Mum, because of how angry she was going to be when she found out. He was the one who'd suggested she should invent a female school friend and a summer holiday invitation, to 'create a bit of breathing space'. And he'd even arranged Mum's meeting with 'Ally's mum' at the school exhibition, to 'close off the problem' of Mum wanting to meet her.

Which was odd, if you thought about it. Maisie had assumed he'd sent Jan to the exhibition, but that made no sense. Maisie couldn't imagine Jan even existing anywhere outside this horrible rotten house, let alone wandering around the art exhibition at Westcoates Academy. And why hadn't Mum said something about her being heavily pregnant and looking like a character from a Halloween movie?

For a moment, she had a sense that Mark was carefully managing the flow of information to *her*. That they were playing some kind of game where she couldn't see the pieces. But Mum would know what to do, when she got here.

'Okay. I'll ask her. I was going to message her tomorrow anyway.'

'Good stuff. Listen, I'd better go up and check on Jan.'

When he was half way out the door, he turned. 'You know, I was thinking, if you are going to stay here for a bit, how about revamping your room and making it your own? It's rather bare at the moment, but it could be really cosy. Your own private space.'

Maisie nodded. She'd been wondering why she couldn't have one of the rooms in the main part of the house. One of the proper, bigger bedrooms where she wouldn't feel so cut off. But actually, a private space sounded good.

'And by the way,' Mark went on. 'I'm sorry you have to stay in that wing of the house, the staff side. It's because Jan really needs to rest. She's very fragile. I'm not sure she could cope with seeing a pregnant woman walking around the place.'

Sometimes, it was as if Mark could read her mind. A bit like Mum used to.

'I understand,' said Maisie, carefully. 'Some stuff for my room would be nice.'

30

CAROLINE

Scotland
Now

Caroline, free from George, sang in the car all the way up to Scotland. She belted out a playlist of old classics – Aretha Franklin, Gloria Gaynor, Tina Turner. During the final chorus of 'Respect', she realised that the speed dial had edged past ninety – in the intoxicating rush, she'd forgotten to ease her foot off the accelerator.

Somewhere near Perth, she stopped for a green tea at Costa, pausing in the queue to take a few deep, cleansing breaths. And then she selected a playlist of moody Scottish folk music which she turned up loud as the rolling hills of the Central Belt gave way to mountains, their jagged ridges and hanging valleys wreathed in low cloud.

It was a pity, she felt, that there was nobody here to see how appealing she must look. Singing in her low, resonant voice to the sad harp music, like a character from *Outlander*, some winsome Scottish lass with a tragic backstory.

She stopped singing, however, when she turned onto the track up to the house some time later. Since the last time she'd been here, the road had deteriorated. In fact, it was less of a road than a forest track, pitted with unacceptably deep holes. Every few yards, a little stream trickled over the track, coming off the wooded bank to the right of the road. There had been heavy rain over the last few days.

It was early evening now. Gloaming, as the Scots would call it. She became uncomfortably aware that it was getting darker, almost black, in the spaces between the pines. Anything could be lurking behind the fronds of brackeny undergrowth, or beneath the spear-like trunks of the fallen trees. Forests freaked her out.

She couldn't be here long – she didn't want to get benighted in the middle of nowhere. She'd lost phone signal a while ago.

The car struggled around a final bend, tyres spitting gravel everywhere. And Inverkillen House came into view. It was a former shooting lodge in the traditional Scottish style – white walls with a grey roof. On the upper storey, each of the six large dormer windows had its own gabled roof, with an ornamental wooden trim. But moss had grown around the timbers, and had begun to encroach onto the roughcasting under the eaves, giving the façade an unfortunate greenish appearance. A number of severe black drainpipes added to the rather bleak impression.

Caroline sighed heavily. A bit of delving around in Mark's files had revealed that he'd lied to her about getting rid of this property after Jan died. It still belonged to the family – well, some sort of trust, anyway. But he'd let the house go to rack and ruin from the looks of it. And the forest, all choked up and overgrown, clearly hadn't been properly managed for years.

She donned the hi-vis jacket and lanyard she'd ordered from Amazon, and grabbed the clipboard and tape measure she'd brought with her. Then she marched up to the front door and rang the bell. When there was no answer, she decided a little bit of breaking and entering was in order, given the time it had taken to get all the way up here, to the back of bloody beyond. And given that it was family property, after all.

There was a stalker's cottage somewhere round the back, she remembered. Some old denizen – Jock, was it? – used to take parties up onto the hills for deer stalking, back in the day. Mark had said it had been quite the country house retreat. Summer picnics, shooting weekends. Swimming in peaty mountain lochs.

She glimpsed the cottage through the trees as she made her way around the back of the house, picking through the tall weeds that poked through the gravel. And beyond that was an old hut with slatted windows for drying out deer carcasses – Mark had told her that was what it was for, anyway. It didn't look as if there was anyone around. Turning to survey the main house, she realised she was facing the back wall of the kitchen, judging from the extractor fan unit that protruded from the wall, its vents furred with gunk. Peering inside a grimy window, she saw stainless steel units, industrial-looking kitchen fittings.

Ah yes. She remembered this from when she had brought up frozen meals for the pregnant Jan, before Mark had arranged a courier company to do that. She'd carefully stacked the milky rice puddings, potato gratins and cauliflower cheeses in the big chest freezer.

There was a utility room adjoining the kitchen, with its own back door. It was the work of a few moments to break the pane of glass and turn the lock from the inside. She was in.

Swiftly, quietly, she moved through the utility room into the kitchen, aware of her heart thumping harder than usual, the buzz of being somewhere she wasn't supposed to be.

She vaguely recalled the way into the main house – along a cramped little corridor with doors off to one side – a cleaning cupboard, a cupboard with a fuse board and a bathroom with a rust-stained toilet.

Finally, she emerged through a wood-panelled door, and the space opened out. She was in the main entrance hall with its big, dark staircase winding up to the first floor. The tartan carpet was threadbare in places, furred with dust along the skirting boards.

A tacky stag's head leered down from high on the wall, a small cobweb trailing from one of the antlers. She hadn't noticed these cringey details before, when she'd driven all the way up here with Jan's meals, desperate just to lay her eyes on Mark. She remembered that chemical intoxication – the delicious, appalling shock – of finding she was in love with her friend's husband.

The furniture in the drawing room was draped in dust sheets. She could make out the shape of a couch and three armchairs, a grand piano. Really, it was like a haunted house, something out of *Scooby Doo*. A hunchbacked caretaker would surely appear at any moment. The room to the rear was empty, apart from six high-backed dining chairs, stacked on top of each other.

At the top of the main stairs, the landing split into two corridors. Caroline worked her way along the one to her left, opening each of the doors – bedrooms, which clearly weren't being used. In the first one, she found a four poster bed with a bare, stained mattress. In the second, a carved mahogany bed frame heaped up with mouldering pillows and piles of blankets, making her think of *The Princess and the Pea*. Everywhere, a stale, sweetish smell, as if air freshener had been used to mask blocked drains.

At the far end of the corridor she found a bathroom with an old-fashioned toilet and a coffin-shaped Victorian bath with a mahogany surround. The peeling window frame was littered with small dead flies.

What was that?

A noise downstairs?

The close of a door.

Footsteps.

Her heart thumped painfully. What should she do? Hide, up here, locked in the bathroom? Or should she brazen it out?

She strode purposely to the top of the stairs, scribbling notes on her clipboard.

A man was already on the stairs, his head twisting up to look at her, his mouth fallen open slightly.

Ah, she thought to herself as she noticed the shape of his eyes. The poor chap was special needs. And he was only young. A teenager. She could manage this easily.

'Hello there,' she piped cheerily. 'I'm Carrie. I'm from the surveyors. Just here to take some measurements.'

The man placed his hand on his heart and sagged forward slightly. 'You made me jump,' he said thickly. 'I thought you were the ghost.'

Caroline allowed her face to expand into a wide smile. 'Sorry I startled you. I rang the doorbell but there was no answer, so I just let myself in. You must be...' She twirled a finger as if she was trying to remember his name.

'Adrian.' The man nodded. 'I keep-an-eye-on-the-place,' he said mechanically, as if that was his job title.

She wanted to ask him more about the ghost. That was intriguing. She tried to think of a reason why a surveyor might ask about such a thing.

Walking down the stairs, she graced him with her most charming smile. 'You're very brave, Adrian, looking after this place on your own.' She gave a feminine shiver. 'I'd get freaked out.'

Adrian's chest puffed slightly.

'Do you see the ghost often?' she murmured.

He frowned, the corners of his mouth turning downwards. Reaching the bottom of the stairs, he crossed his arms and took a more solid stance, spreading his feet out.

'Can I help you with anything else?' he asked.

Caroline paused, wondering whether to say she still had rooms to measure. But she didn't want to be here for long in case anyone else turned up. Surely Adrian couldn't live here on his own, couldn't be the only caretaker.

Then a thought flickered into her mind. 'I just need to check the kitchen,' she said.

The young man nodded. 'That's in the staff side.' He turned and led the way through the higgledy-piggledy part of the house that Caroline had already seen.

'Do you live in?' she asked airily, trotting along behind him.

'Nah,' he said. 'We live in the cottage out back.'

Who was *we*? For a moment, Caroline imagined a small army of caretakers, coming to apprehend her. She definitely needed to make an exit as soon as possible.

Adrian threw open the door to the kitchen, so hard that the spring on the door stopper boinged.

'Kitchen,' he said, waving a bored hand towards the centre of the room.

Caroline made a show of measuring the width of the two windows. Then, with a confident flourish, she turned to the big chest freezer and lifted the lid.

Piles of Tesco ready meals, a few dozen of them.

She nodded. Her instincts had been correct. She thought of the receipt she'd found in Mark's briefcase.

'Ah!' she said, pointing to one of the packages at the top. 'I like chicken curry, too. Is that your favourite?'

Adrian shrugged, uninterested. 'I hate all that stuff in there. We usually have sausages or burgers.'

She didn't want to press him on the point – but if the meals weren't for him, who were they for? She looked around the rest of the kitchen, which showed no signs of use.

'Do you like working here?' she asked, as he led her back through the house.

'Yes,' he said quietly.

'You must be very brave,' Caroline tried again. 'Here all on your own.'

She left a pause. He didn't challenge her.

'And with it getting dark, too.'

'Dad's poorly. He can't walk up the stairs any more. So I have to do the rounds.'

Ahh. Was he talking about Jock, the old deer stalker guy?

Adrian's eyes widened, and his hand moved to his mouth. 'But don't… Please don't say anything.'

'I won't.' She smiled widely. 'Thank you so much for showing me round, Adrian. You've been fantastic. A true professional.'

'It's the crying,' he said suddenly, as he showed her out of the front door. 'It's the crying that bothers me.'

She swung round on her heel. 'What?'

But now Caroline could hear slow, unsteady footsteps, approaching from somewhere on the other side of the house.

'That's Dad,' said Adrian.

She hurried out to her car and got the hell out of there.

31

MAISIE

Killendreich
Eight years ago

Mark was in the kitchen when Maisie went down to get some breakfast.

'I've got to nip out this morning,' he said, as if the house wasn't hours of driving away from anywhere. 'Can I make you some porridge?'

Maisie nodded. 'Yes please. Thank you.' She still couldn't get rid of that high, eager-to-please voice when she was around him.

An awkward two and a half minutes followed, with just the sound of the microwave buzzing as the bowl of oats rotated inside.

'I couldn't help noticing,' said Mark, when the ping finally came, 'that you seem to have a lot of anxiety around your phone.' He placed the bowl of porridge in front of her, handed her a spoon.

'All of us teenagers do.' She laughed, but it came out as a

nervous giggle. 'It'll be a good chance to have a phone detox, being here with no signal.'

'When you were handling it the other day, your fingers were so full of tension that they were trembling. And when you realised you'd lost it, you were on the verge of a full-blown panic attack. Sweating, pupils dilated…'

Maisie sagged in her chair. Why was he like this? Why did he notice all the things that she wanted to hide? Was it because he was a psychiatrist, albeit some kind of entrepreneurial one who owned a bunch of high-end 'wellness clinics'?

She hadn't told anyone about her phone PTSD. Not even Mum.

But Mark didn't need protecting, like Mum. She didn't have to be Little Maisie with him. She didn't need to be sweet Maisie-Munchkin. The relief, at this thought, made her eyes sting.

'There was a whole thing at school,' she began. 'This girl, Annabelle Punch, she shared nudes of me on Instagram.'

Mark simply nodded. If it had been Mum, she would have hit the roof. She would have been on the phone to school in a nanosecond, or driving over to see Annabelle Punch's parents.

'How did it happen?'

'Once, at school, I logged in to the app using her phone, because mine was out of battery. The phone can save your login, if you do that. So later – it was weeks later – she logged in as me. And she'd used my phone, too, one time when hers got confiscated. She must have found the nudes on my camera roll and sent them to herself. I hadn't shown them to *anyone*. They were just, well, I was just trying to see how I looked.'

She cringed at the memory of the photos, so achingly experimental. She'd been trying to work out who she was, who she was meant to be. In the ones Annabelle had shared, Maisie's lips were glossy and slightly apart, her hands cupping her breasts in what she'd thought was an artistic, thought-provoking pose. She remembered wishing she could use the pictures in her A-level photography portfolio, because of the beautiful way the light played on her skin.

'She shared them to my story so everyone at school could see. They thought I'd posted them myself.'

'Did you tell the school?'

'No. I deleted them as soon as I realised. But people – some of the boys – saved them and re-shared them in private groups where I couldn't see.'

'So what did you do?'

'At first, I tried to control it. I kept asking people what was being shared, and where. I kept telling people to take down the posts. But the more I did that, the more they shared them, because it was all a big joke. One of the girls told me the boys had faked a porn video, with my face on it.' She remembered how the girl had tried to look concerned for Maisie, but had barely been able to suppress her glee: 'If it was me, babe, I'd want to know.'

'In the end, I suppose it made me ill.' It was the first time she'd admitted it.

She had a sudden flashback – standing in the school toilets before registration, awash with nausea. Taking travel sickness pills and antihistamines that she'd found in the bathroom cabinet, in the hope that they would take the edge off the panic.

She saw herself again – her image in the mirror above the

sinks, with her dark-ringed eyes and greasy-looking hair. She was ugly, but worse than that, she was pathetic. A total joke.

And she could feel the sensation again now, even as she sat in front of Mark with her porridge – her insides shrinking, liquifying, like a slug covered in salt. The urge to simply stop. To cease existing.

'Did you speak to your mother?'

Maisie shook her head. She hadn't wanted Mum to see that version of her. Mum was the one person in the world who still loved her, even if it was the old version she loved.

'I just wanted to deal with it myself. I deleted Instagram and Snapchat. I came off all social media. That's when I took up tennis and met Ally.'

And she hadn't needed social media after that. She hadn't needed any of them.

She tried to shut off the horrible memories, to be Little Maisie again. But Mark was looking at her as if he could see straight through her, like all the doors in her mind were made of glass. Some sort of psychiatrist's trick, probably.

'Sometimes, we go through times in our life when it serves us to stay small.' Mark made a box-like shape with his hands. His face was all animated, as if he was giving a TED talk. 'We need to protect ourselves. We can't all be social media influencers, or the most popular person in school.'

Maisie shrugged.

Mark went on, leaning in as if he was sharing a secret. 'What I've seen, in my life, and my work, is that some people can stand up to bullies, and others can't. Sometimes, all you can do is remove yourself from the harmful environment.'

But how *could* you stand up to them, she thought, when things were being said online, and you didn't know who, or where, or why? When it was all happening way faster than you could even keep track of?

'People can be cruel, Maisie. People *are* cruel. Believe me, I know about cruelty. I've studied it, through my work. It's surprisingly easy to dismantle a person. To destroy their sense of themselves. It's just a question of knowing what to do and when. Sometimes that's necessary to build a person back up again.'

What was he talking about? His wealthy, substance-abusing patients?

'And unfortunately, teenage girls have a proficiency for cruelty. It's instinctive for them. The competition must be destroyed. But you won't be competition any more. Not now you're taking this different path. They'll literally forget all about you.'

Oubliette...

'But I still want to go to art college. Having a baby – that's not my *path*, or anything.'

'You can still go to art college, Maisie. There's nothing stopping you. From the examples of your work that I've seen, you're a decent artist, for someone of your age.'

The slug-in-salt feeling returned. She squirmed on her seat.

'A year out will give you a chance to build up your portfolio, perhaps with the benefit of a bit more maturity. We can all get a bit ahead of ourselves. Think of this time out as a bit of a reset. A chance to recalibrate.'

What did that mean? Did he think she was rubbish at art?

She had a sudden vision of Mum, towering and furious. Deftly, she closed that door. With Mum and Mark, it was probably better that she only thought of them one at a time.

'What about taking your camera out today? The light's amazing this morning.'

She found herself wanting to take a picture that would wow him. That would show him she wasn't just a stupid schoolgirl.

'But I must go up and see Jan before I go,' he said, sliding his porridge bowl into the sink.

Maisie got her coat and shoes and made her way up to the viewpoint. Sun was poking through the trees today, filtering onto the littered pine needles, and a resiny scent hung in the air, making her think of summer holidays and picnics. She breathed in a big lungful of air and felt a bit better. She took out her camera and took a shot of the last wisps of morning mist, clinging to the tops of the pines.

She was out of breath by the time she reached the bench. She keyed a message into her phone.

Mum?

Hi Maisie. How are you?

A bit meh.

Are you taking your vitamins? How are you finding the new evening primrose supplement?

Her eyes blurred, and she felt two tears wobble on her lower lashes.

Mum! Vitamins are hardly going to fix this, are they?

I suppose not.

They said to ask if you want to come and stay for a bit? Discuss things properly and all that.

There was a long pause.

Sorry but I'm very busy with the glamping huts at the moment. We're booked back-to-back for the next few weeks. The Stevenson clan are back with their entire extended family.

Maisie remembered those Stevenson people from last summer. They'd been a total pain.

Okay

Must dash. Got another two welcome baskets to make up before check in.

Love you 2 4 6 8

She waited, but no response came.

Nothing. Nothing. Nothing.

32

TERESA

Northumberland
Now

Cheryl replied at quarter past seven. She said she'd see George later that morning, just as soon as we were up and ready.

George was still dead to the world in Maisie's bed. Trying to make myself comfortable in the pink chair – I was stiff after spending most of the night in it – I pored over Maisie's messages again, the ones she'd sent from Scotland.

I scrolled to the ones on 27th July, five days after she'd left. I remembered thinking, at the time, that the tone of the messages had gone a bit flat, and I'd half-hoped that the novelty of the Scottish high life was wearing off. I'd longed so much for her to come back home.

Mum?

Hi Maisie! How are you?

Good thanks. A bit tired.

Are you taking your vitamins? How are you finding the new evening primrose supplement?

Really good thanks.

Great!

I asked Ally's parents if you could maybe come up to visit. But there's a big hunting party coming up next week and they'll be a bit short on space.

Oh don't worry darling. I'm very busy with the glamping huts at the moment. We're booked back-to-back for the next few weeks. The Stevenson clan are back with their entire extended family!

I remembered how my eyes had stung as I'd written that. I would have given anything to come up and see this Scottish estate where Maisie was living it up. Sandra, the lady up the road who helped out with the glamping huts sometimes, would have overseen things for me here if needed, albeit at an eye-watering cost.

Okay

I'll message again later. Must dash for now. Got another two welcome baskets to make up before check in. Are you sure you're ok, darling? You sound a bit down.

Perfectly ok.

Love you 2 4 6 8

Love you 16, 32, 64, 128

I shook my head now. I should have picked up that something was wrong, should have left the sodding welcome baskets for later. If I'd been more patient, if I'd kept her talking, would Maisie have told me the truth? Would she have said what was really bothering her?

But maybe not – not if somebody had been watching over her, making sure she didn't reveal too much. I had a sudden image of a shadowy figure standing behind her, telling her what to type.

The messages tailed off, over the following days. She said she'd been busy. She'd hardly had a chance to walk up to the viewpoint where there was a signal. She'd be coming home soon, although she wasn't sure exactly when.

And then I reached the messages of the nineteenth of August, four weeks after she'd left for Scotland.

I'd texted her on waking that morning.

Good morning my darling. I love you so much.

And then, half an hour later:

I love you too

That's when I'd hurried to my car and driven up there.

And then a little memory popped into my head – of George, rummaging around on Maisie's desk the other day. He'd picked up a bottle of evening primrose oil capsules, and asked if he could keep them.

Which meant Maisie had never taken them with her.

What if I'd been right after all, when I'd driven up to Scotland that day? What if the messages seemed odd because Maisie hadn't written them?

Then something else occurred to me. I got up from the chair and tiptoed over to Maisie's desk, trying not to wake George. I picked up the bottle of capsules and turned them round to look at the information label.

EVENING PRIMROSE OIL 1500 MG WITH VITAMIN A AND E

Why hadn't she taken them with her, when she'd been so desperate to try them?

And then, in small letters at the bottom:

NOT SUITABLE FOR PREGNANT WOMEN.

Cheryl had *A Place in the Sun* on the television when we went in, and George launched himself down onto the rug to watch, his chin propped on his hands, his feet waving.

She was wearing a floaty purple dress today, paired with the fluffy dog slippers again, a combination that seemed to emphasise her stoutness. She leaned over to switch on the gas fire, and I worried for a moment that one of her long bell sleeves might catch light.

'Need to take the chill off the place. I've only just got back from the care home. Those roadworks on the main road are a nightmare.'

She crouched down next to George. 'I'll fetch you some juice, pet. And what about a Twix?'

'Yes please,' said George, eyes fixed on the television. Cheryl's white cat sidled up to him and rubbed her face against his hand. He stroked her very gently, his fingers outstretched like a star.

'So that's George,' I said to Cheryl, when she'd taken me through to the kitchen to make tea. 'The boy you told me was dead.'

'I'm sorry, love,' she said, throwing two teabags into mugs. 'I didn't mean to cause upset. Sometimes things can be a little… murky.'

'It's interesting, though. Because he keeps talking about when he died.'

'I wonder what he means by "death", though? We have a very negative view of death in our culture. In many belief systems, death is simply a state of transition. Between life and rebirth. Between earth and heaven.' She splashed some orange squash into a glass tumbler. 'In tarot, it can signal transformation. Moving from one phase of life to the next. Maybe that's what I was picking up, when I said that.' She shrugged, seeming unconcerned.

'Oh no, he means *death* death. And he says he died…' I had to pause, clear my throat. 'In my house. Upstairs in my house.'

She frowned and looked upwards, moving her hands in circles as if encouraging inspiration to come. One of her gauzy purple sleeves nearly trailed into the orange squash. 'I'm getting the sense of… an interruption. He's been through a transition, a death of sorts, or an ending. He's come through it, but some part of him is still stuck there. That could be the root of the nightmares.'

The kettle boiled, sending plumes of steam up towards the ceiling. I noticed that there was a black mouldy patch on the wall near the window, and condensation gathering in the corners of the glass.

'He thinks he died by drowning.'

'Hmm. Fear of drowning is often associated with repressed emotions. A fear of being overwhelmed by them. I could do a lovely visualisation with him. Something that's just very reassuring and calming.'

She placed everything on a tray – George's juice, the mugs of tea, and a plate of Twixes, fanned out in a semi-circle. She carried it through to the living room, moving like a ship in full sail, and set it down on the coffee table.

'Now, I want you to get comfy, George. Here, sit here against this cushion. Would you like to do a visualisation? That just means thinking lovely thoughts and making ourselves feel very safe and happy.'

He shot a glance at me. I raised my eyebrows in a 'why not?' expression.

'Imagine a set of steps,' said Cheryl, when he was settled. I had thought she might speak in wispy, mystical tones, like the rather unsettling voices on some of the mindfulness apps I'd tried. But her voice was warm and confident, more like she was suggesting nail polish colours to a client. 'You can choose what you want them to look like, pet. This is *your* visualisation. They could be old stone steps, with green moss in the cracks, and dandelions growing at the edges, like in a secret garden. Or there could be a soft carpet under your feet, like stairs in a cosy house.'

I shifted nervously. Perhaps I should have told Cheryl that George's nightmares often featured stairs.

'Or golden steps, in a fairytale palace. Have you imagined your steps, George?

He nodded.

'What are your steps like, sweetheart?'

George wriggled his legs. 'They're, like, rubbery. Grey.'

'That's good, George. So I want you to imagine you're going down those stairs. And with each step you go down, your body feels more and more relaxed.'

George opened his eyes again to see if we were looking. Cheryl had her eyes closed, but I winked and shot him a reassuring smile.

'So, with the first step, I want you to relax your hands and fingers. Imagine they're floating in a lovely warm bath.'

George's hands clenched even tighter, and a frown line appeared between his eyes. Cheryl shot me a 'silly me' look, rolling her eyes before returning her attention to George.

'Or if you like, just imagine you're resting your hands on a lovely soft cat or a doggie,' she went on.

Slowly, his hands unfurled.

'And with the next, I want you to relax your face, to soften it. Allow that softness to move down from your hairline. Relax your forehead. Relax your eyes. Your ears. Your lips and your tongue.'

By the seventh step, George did look quite chilled out. His mouth was slightly open, and his breathing had slowed. Uneasiness moved through me – this seemed a lot like hypnotherapy, from what I understood that to be. Hadn't Sunny's sister, Aanya Kaur, said that would be a bad idea?

'At the bottom of the stairs there's a door. I want you to open it. And imagine you're standing in a hallway. What's the hallway like, George?'

'Dark. Grey, like stone.' I was reassured to hear his voice, sharp and clear as a bell. Maybe he wasn't in a hypnotic state, and was just concentrating on the visualisation.

'Okay, good. Now, there's a door in front of you. Do you

want to know what's behind it, George? You can open it right now.'

His hand moved, as if he was closing his fingers around a door handle.

'Now, I want you to imagine the most lovely place you've ever been. Tell me what that's like, George.'

He thought for a few moments. 'A picnic in the woods.'

'What's the weather like, George? Is the sun shining?'

'Yes. It's a hot, hot sun.'

'Tell me what you can hear.'

'Birds laughing.'

'Brilliant. Nice work, George. And what can you smell?'

'The sun. Warm trees.'

'Lovely.'

I took a deep breath of my own, imagining a pine forest. The sun filtering through the branches, the scent of the pine litter, dry after a long, hot summer. Birdsong. The cracking of twigs. The babble of a stream nearby.

Then I could hear the noise of Cheryl's lips and mouth unsticking. 'And what can you *feel*, George?'

Was this the point where it would all become clear? Some hidden trauma, rising to the surface?

Gently, he closed the tips of his fingers together. 'A sandwich.'

Of course.

'A sandwich,' repeated Cheryl. 'What kind?'

'Cheese.'

'Cheese,' repeated Cheryl softly. 'And what about a lovely cool drink? What's your favourite, drink, George?'

'Fanta.'

'I want you imagine a big, tall glass of Fanta, with ice clinking in it, and tiny bubbles rising to the top, and the glass is so cold that it looks all frosty. Take a deep drink from it and imagine how nice that feels.'

He swallowed carefully. Nodded.

'Now, George – *this* – what you can see, and hear, and smell, and touch– this is what's on the other side of this door. And now I want you to imagine that you're the happiest you've ever been. Your whole body is filling up with happiness like a balloon. Warm, golden happiness, like sunlight. Okay, George, are you doing it?'

His chest rose as he drew in a long, deep breath.

'And now I want you to imagine there are people all around you, holding hands and making a bright, white circle. They're your ancestors, come to watch over you and keep you safe. They're the source of all the love that went into making you. All the love in the universe flows through them and into you. Like a bright, white river. And I want you to imagine that all that love goes into you and now you're *even* happier than before. Twice as happy.'

'What's ancestors, again?'

'Our mums and dads and grans and grandpas. Our uncles and aunts. All their parents and grandparents before them.'

He nodded.

'Breathe, George,' she commanded. 'Breathe nice and easily. Imagine that bright white happiness flowing into you with every breath.'

He let his breath out in a loud burst.

'And you know that nothing bad can *ever* happen. Because whenever you want to, you can come through this door, and all this love will be waiting. And thinking about that makes you feel twice as happy *again*. Can you feel it, George? Twice as happy and peaceful?'

He took another deep breath, holding it high in his chest.

'Lovely. And now we're going to leave the woodland picnic for now, but you can come back here whenever you like. Remember that, George. The door is *never* locked. Now, let's go back into the hallway. Remember, the grey stone hallway that we came through in the beginning.' She paused. 'Now. Just take a moment to look round at the hallway. There's nothing bad about it, nothing scary. It's just an in-between place.' She looked up and shot me a meaningful look. 'And look, there's a door in front of you and it opens easily. You can come back up the steps again. Back into Cheryl's living room.'

His eyes were moving beneath his eyelids, darting back and forth.

'What's the other door?' His voice was suddenly tight.

There was a small clicking noise from Cheryl's throat as she swallowed. 'There's a door right in front of you, George. There are steps, remember the rubbery grey steps? Those steps will take you back up to where we started.'

'No, the *other* door. The big black door.'

'Another door? In the hallway?' Cheryl was frowning now, trying to keep her voice light.

A shudder moved through his body. His eyes shot open and he scrambled to his feet, knocking over his orange squash. The liquid flooded over the ceramic tiles of the fireplace surround.

He flew into the hall and we heard the noise of him pulling the handle of the front door, trying to open it.

'I think we'd better go,' I said to Cheryl.

'This is all very interesting,' she said, narrowing her mascara-ringed eyes.

It had been a mistake. A terrible mistake. I remembered back to what Aanya Kaur had said about no reputable therapist subjecting him to hypnotherapy, and that it would be for my benefit, not his.

I hurried him out. As we went out of the front gate, I looked back at Cheryl, who was at her front door, watching us leave, one purple arm lifted in a wave.

George was trotting so fast it was hard to keep up with him. 'What was wrong, George? Why did you get upset?'

I felt his hand strain against mine as he tried to pull away, to zoom off down the pavement. 'It was that hallway she made me go in. The one in the silation.'

'The one in the visualisation?'

He nodded. 'Yes. It had a smell. It smelled damp and horrible. Like in the killing house.'

'Like the *what* house?'

'In the killing house.'

An image came into my head. Of Cheryl's living room, the walls patterned with arcs of arterial blood. Dark, sodden patches on the carpet. A cloying, clotting smell, like raw meat left out of the fridge.

'Okay,' I managed. 'Let's leave it for now. I'm sorry, George. I'm so sorry.'

33

MAISIE

Killendreich
Eight years ago

Later that afternoon, a parcel arrived for Maisie. A parcel! Watching the delivery van trundle off along the drive, she had a sudden impulse to run after it. Maybe she could hitch a lift to... well, to anywhere. Somewhere there was a decent phone signal.

She told herself to stop being silly. Once the current crisis had passed (she thought, guiltily, of Jan's baby), she would ask Mark to drive her to the nearest town.

Which was called... she looked down to check the address on the parcel... *Killendreich*. And that was odd. Because that hadn't been part of the address she'd originally been told, the one she'd passed on to Mum before leaving. She took a photo of the address label with her phone.

She carried her parcel upstairs and spread the contents out on the floor of her room. It contained art materials – high-end watercolour pencils, sketching pencils, an acrylic paint set and brushes, and a big pad of A3 cartridge paper. A dozen tubes of oil paint.

What would she draw? The mountain crags, looming above the endless trees? The stag whose head was on the wall downstairs – but alive, standing on top of a rocky ridge? Or an imaginary forest, inspired by fairytales, like her art project at school?

What came to her, when she closed her eyes, was her own bedroom at home. She visualised the thick pink carpet, which had make-up stains under the dressing table and a flattened patch where a Disney princess castle had once stood. The wallpaper, with its green leaves and intertwining flowers. She pushed the rug to the side and laid out one of the big sheets of cartridge paper on the floor. With a fine brush, she began to paint the pattern of her wallpaper from memory.

Then, when she'd done that, she drew a gingerbread house surrounded by trees. Some of the trees had faces, formed by the knot holes and lichens on the bark. Some had vine-covered branches that looked like outstretched limbs, reaching for the marzipan roof tiles and the candy cane guttering.

After some period of time – it could have been ten minutes or an hour – she heard a little cough behind her.

'Don't let me disturb you,' Mark whispered. He looked entranced, as if he'd stumbled across a rare animal in its natural habitat.

He hadn't been up to her room before, and she felt a strange electric buzz move over her skin from the sense of him being in her space. She also remembered, uneasily, that she'd taken down the wooden cross that had hung above the bed, and shoved it in one of the drawers. Would that be commented upon?

But he seemed transfixed by the gingerbread house she'd drawn. 'Your work is really coming on,' he said, as if she'd been studying for months at the Royal College of Art, instead of stuck in a mouldering Scottish house for a week. He shook his head and squeezed his eyes shut, before pinging them wide open again. 'Wow!'

'Thank you.' She felt heat rising in her cheeks. A swelling in her chest that was the opposite of the slug-in-salt feeling. 'Was it you who sent the package?'

'I thought you might appreciate it,' said Mark. 'We can't have our special guest twiddling her thumbs.'

'I've been thinking about the room – making it more my own, like you said.' She reached for her wallpaper sketch. 'Could we order a wallpaper that looks like this? And maybe a pink carpet, and a pink velvet chair? I mean, if I'm going to be here a while...'

It was strange, because she'd been fed up with all that pink while she'd lived at home. But now, she found she wanted it again. 'It'll be... pinktastic. I suppose we could always get some blue things as well, if...'

A big grin split Mark's face. It was the first time she'd really seen him smile. One of his canines was slightly turned inwards, giving him a lopsided, wolfish look. Suddenly, he looked much younger. Boyish, excited, like Ally when he'd won a big game. 'You're going to keep the baby?'

'Yes. I've decided that I do want to keep it. And it's very kind of you and Jan to offer to step in. But...' She saw something change in his face, like a dark cloud moving over the sky. She went on, making her voice warmer, brighter. 'I do want you to be involved, definitely. I want you to be hands-on... very hands-on grandparents. We could even stay here for a bit, while the baby's young. Until me and Ally can get a place together.' In her mind's eye, she saw herself and Ally going back to Northumberland, moving into one of Mum's glamping huts. Maybe he'd tear some other important tendon and have to give up tennis permanently. He could get a normal job.

'But if I'm having the baby... well, I want to be its mum.'

'I'm delighted, Maisie. I couldn't be more delighted. Once Ally gets up here, we'll sit down and work it all out. And in the meantime, yes, you must make this place your own. Anything you want.'

'Could I get a bookcase? And some books?' She thought she might like a full set of Agatha Christies to go with *Hickory Dickory Dock*.

'Absolutely. And you know you can always use the home cinema? The streaming won't work at the moment while the internet's down, but there's a DVD player and a big screen. I think Jan even has one or two meditation DVDs that you could borrow if you wanted to have a bit of relaxation time. I'm sure that would be good for you – and good for the baby.'

Good for the baby...

That made it all feel very real. That strange buzz moved over her skin again.

'Yes, I should probably try something like that. Some yoga, or meditation or something.'

'Feel free to go down and have a look. Any time. It's in the basement – the stairs are through the door under the main staircase. Maybe you and Ally can have a cinema night when he arrives. We could get Caroline to send up some frozen pizzas in the next order.'

Maisie tried to picture Ally arriving here. *Actually* arriving. And found she couldn't. He didn't belong here, in this sunken green place. And neither did she. It was exhausting her, sucking all the energy out of her.

She had the sudden, rather alarming impression of the house being a living thing. She imagined how she might draw it, like a Venus flytrap, closing around her.

'I haven't been sleeping,' she blurted out.

Mark frowned. 'We can't have that. Is the room too cold? Or is your bed not comfortable?'

'I just... I have things on my mind. I keep playing them over and over, and I can't fall asleep. The noises round here keep me awake.'

Sometimes she heard sounds that didn't make sense – the fast, light thump of small footsteps, running along the corridors somewhere in the house. Or a burst of children's laughter, coming from behind a wall. The echoing noises from the woods that sounded like someone calling her name.

Mark patted her arm. 'I can give you a mild anti-anxiety medication, if you like?'

For some reason Maisie thought of her mother, who would have offered a milky drink or a drop of lavender on her pillow. Who had once sat up all night with her, in the chair beside her bed, when she'd been so worried about her maths GCSE that she couldn't sleep.

'Wouldn't that be bad for the baby?'

'I'm happy to prescribe something very mild, very safe for both you and the baby. Something that will help to ease you back into your own natural sleep cycle. You could just take it for a few nights, to get back on track. You need your sleep – you're growing a baby! Trust me, you'll feel like a new woman.'

Suddenly, reflected through his eyes, she did feel like a

woman. Not a silly schoolgirl who had got herself into a mess.

'How's Jan?' she asked.

'She's sleeping,' said Mark. 'Best thing for her, right now. Gives her a break from everything, for a bit.'

So Maisie had to sleep, so she could grow her baby. And Jan had to sleep, so she could forget hers.

'And... George?'

'Still hanging on. He's a fighter.' He smiled and shrugged. 'We Jacksons don't give up easily.'

34

CAROLINE

Retford
Now

Caroline raised her eyebrows and nodded when she saw the envelope on the doormat. She was impressed. The PO box service had forwarded it on to Malham Manor with next day delivery – very efficient. She might leave a good review for them later. She enjoyed being generous, brightening somebody's day for no reason other than that she could.

She took the envelope upstairs, carrying out a cheeky little salsa move on the landing. Settling herself at the desk in the womb-red study, she put on her reading glasses. She thought they made her look old. But there was nobody else in the house, so it didn't really matter.

She changed the music on the Sonos system to a Gregorian chant, to aid focus and concentration. She imagined monks of long ago, their voices echoing around some ancient church.

A sense of hallowed awe – holiness, even – filled the room, soaring up to the original cornices. It reminded her of attending church services with her grandmother, back when she was a young girl.

She opened the envelope to reveal Teresa and George's bagged samples – the ones they'd taken at Teresa's house – and the accompanying form.

Teresa, bless her cotton socks, had been so careful. Caroline had watched her reading the form through three times, and then double-checking all the labels and making sure the correct samples were in the correct bags.

But then, Caroline had held out the specially printed A4 envelope she'd brought with her from home, Teresa hadn't given it a second glance. She'd popped the samples and the form inside, and she and George had taken it to the post box.

The first thing Caroline did now was make a small amendment to the form Teresa had filled in. She made a note of Teresa's email address, and then crossed it out on the form, leaving only her own email address as the one to receive the results.

Then she sealed Teresa and George's samples into another envelope bearing the address for 'Surity DNA' – the correct one, this time.

She took a deep breath and placed that envelope at the side of the desk. She closed her eyes and let the cleansing Gregorian chant wash through her. She wondered, fleetingly, if the monks – or her grandmother, for that matter – would approve of what she was doing, but brushed the thought away. She was only fighting back against the wretched patriarchy. A woman had to make her own way in this world.

A key turned in the front door and her heart jumped. Then she remembered it was the cleaner's day.

For a moment she had thought it might be Mark. And it really wouldn't do if Mark were to return early from his work trip – some psychiatry conference in Madrid – and find that Caroline had left George with a virtual stranger in the wilds of Northumberland.

Mark wouldn't even let George go for playdates at his classmates' houses. On the rare occasions when a playdate was arranged, the small person had to come over here, for Caroline to feed and clean up after. And she had to collect George from school herself, every day without fail, an arrangement that had totally stymied her career. Even when Mark wasn't away for work, he was always too busy to do it himself.

Yes, he'd dumped George on her completely. It was strange for a father to be so over-protective, and yet so uninterested in spending time with his son.

And this approach of Mark's – it hadn't just cost Caroline; it had cost George. He'd never settled in, socially. He became anxious when social arrangements were mentioned, and would start bounding around the room like a neurotic puppy, or jiggling on his seat.

When Caroline had registered him at pre-school, she'd had to explain that he had been living in a remote part of Scotland. He'd never been to nursery, or even playgroup, before, and that was why he was behind his peers, socially and developmentally. That, and his ADHD, or whatever variety of spiciness he had – Mark had always refused to get him tested.

And when she'd registered him with the local GP, there'd been a complete faff as they hadn't been able to find the correct records for him. Mark had got on the phone and shouted at the receptionist, pulling rank with his medical status.

All these things. He was insulting her intelligence, really. However much George had been foisted upon her, he was family now. And she had a right to know who her family really was. Mark was *forcing* her to use this sub-optimal route.

'Right,' she said to herself. She had to finish this before the cleaner came up, wanting to do the study.

She opened the second test kit she'd ordered from Surity DNA. She brushed the long cotton swab against the inside of her own cheek, bagged it and popped it into the return envelope, along with the extra sample she'd taken from George, the day before yesterday. She remembered how she'd poked the final swab quite sharply into the inside of his cheek, so that he'd winced and lifted a hand to his face. She'd felt a little electric thrill as she'd scraped it back and forth against the soft pink tissue – as if her anger was discharging, like lightning, into his body. That was wrong, wasn't it? She should probably book another massage, get her stress levels under control.

Then Caroline filled in a second form with Teresa's details, but using the US date format for her date of birth, with the month shown first.

So, once Caroline had sent off both envelopes, there would be two profiles for Teresa on Surity DNA's system. She wrote them out on a spare piece of paper, to make sure she'd done it right.

Teresa Jones DOB 3/11/1980 (UK date of birth format, profile linked to Teresa and George's genuine samples).

Teresa Jones DOB 11/3/1980 (US date of birth format, profile linked to the 'alternative' samples).

If Caroline's suspicions about Mark were correct, she would end up with two different results – the first would show a positive DNA match between Teresa and George, and the second would show no match. Which result would she send to Teresa? Well, that would depend. She'd already created a special email address which she would use to send the report to Teresa, with the name of the DNA company in the first part of the address. It was too easy, really.

Finally, she took out the test kit for the other company she was going to use, 'Advanced Life Tech Labs'.

She'd had to phone this one up and ask how to carry out this test, to make sure the results would tell her what she wanted. It required an ordinary DNA test, and something else called a YDNA test. She also had to pay extra so that she could supply a used tissue of Mark's, rather than a cheek sample.

To think she'd failed GCSE chemistry, and only got a D in biology. And here she was totally *owning* this.

35

TERESA

Northumberland
Now

After we got back from Cheryl's, I made a late lunch of cheese and tomato sandwiches and heated up some tomato soup. George wanted to have it as a 'picnic' in his room, so I wrapped the sandwiches in baking parchment and put the soup into a Thermos. I packed them into one of the wicker baskets I used for the welcome packs, along with two apples, a packet of Penguin biscuits and two cartons of juice.

We sat on the floor, him leaning against Maisie's bed and me against the pink chair. After inspecting the sandwich carefully, he ate most of it and took one bite of a Penguin. Then he asked to draw, and took out his paper and pencils.

'I'm sorry that Cheryl's visualisation upset you,' I said.

'It was fine,' he said graciously. 'It was very, very easy for me. Before I died, there was nothing to do except imagination.'

He began to draw a picture of a children's play park. He sketched in a long slide, a climbing frame, and then a seesaw with a small figure sitting on either end. The figure on the higher end was suspended slightly above the seat, his hair pointing upwards, as if he'd been bumped up with the force of the other end hitting the ground.

'Your drawing is so great,' I said. 'Your imagination must help with that too.'

But George merely shrugged.

'So... you know how you said you used to live in this room? With this wallpaper and everything?'

He nodded. 'Like in my drawings.'

'Yes. I wondered what else you remembered about it?'

I'd decided to go very carefully, to stop talking about it immediately if there was any sign he was about to get upset again.

I thought he wasn't going to answer. But after a minute or two, he piped up again. 'It was *like* this room, but I think there were different things outside the window.'

'What was outside the window?'

'Trees. Lots of tall, tall trees going up and up.' He looked up at me, his mouth quirked, as if he knew it didn't make any sense.

Maisie's bedroom window faced the street. I stood up and looked out. There were some bushes in the small front garden, and to the left, I could see the shrubbery around the glamping pods, and the honeysuckle arch over the path down to the parking area. One of the neighbours down the road had a beech hedge and another had a gnarled old apple tree. But there were no tall trees.

'What do you mean, going up?'

'Going up to the top of the mountain.'

A prickly feeling came over me. Had Maisie gone to Scotland after all, then? Had she been held somewhere? In a room that looked exactly like her old bedroom at home? Was that what George was remembering?

I tried to keep my voice neutral. 'Did Maisie like the trees and the mountains?'

No answer came. When I turned around, George was staring down at his drawing, his hand pressed over his mouth.

I took a deep breath. I hated myself for this. I wished I could just leave him alone to get on with his drawing. 'Did Maisie used to be *your* name? Or did you know someone *else* called Maisie?'

'I had a name called Munchkin,' he whispered, lifting the edge of his hand away from his mouth.

'You weren't called George?'

'Yes. We were both called George.'

'Both?'

'Yes. Me and the other one of me.'

We were clearly not going to get anywhere on the names. George seemed to be very confused.

'So there was another room, just like this one? But in another house?'

'Yes,' he said calmly. 'That's right. Can we have a cuddle nap?'

My eyes smarted. That had been what Maisie used to ask for, when she was little and wanted a nap after nursery.

I nodded and moved up onto the pink chair. He climbed into my lap and nudged his head under my chin, in just the way that Maisie used to do.

I closed my eyes and allowed myself to pretend that I was holding her. Allowed myself to drift into a half-sleep as the afternoon sun dropped in the western sky, a column of light moving over the pink carpet.

The daydream – or whatever it was – had more detail in it this time.

I was looking down at a slim, girlish figure, inert inside a yellow dress with a white daisy print.

Then... the sweaty grip of hands under armpits. The shush of fabric against carpet as she was dragged.

And then, steps. Flares of pain as the edges caught the nubs of her spine.

The shock of cold tiles on skin. The sound of taps, turned on full. The side panel of a bath. Its glaring whiteness.

Two hands, the tendons standing out like wires, flipping open a belt buckle. White shirt sleeves pushed up to the elbows. A wristwatch with silver links and a navy-blue face.

The yellow dress pushed up, tight around her hips. Her bare legs pale, the skin prickled with goosebumps.

She couldn't speak. She couldn't move.

So she moved up, up, into her mind. Away from her body, helpless in its yellow dress.

She hid inside a place of no words. No feelings at all...

I forced my eyes open. George was asleep in my arms, the curve of his back moving up and down as he breathed. I laid my cheek on top of his warm hair.

Had he somehow...*transmitted* this memory to me, as he

lay in my arms? Was this his way of trying to convey what he couldn't say in words?

In a day or two, he'd be gone.

I held him closer and let love, and fear, wash over me in a terrifying tide.

36

MAISIE

Killendreich
Eight years ago

When Maisie woke around lunchtime, she did not feel like a new woman as Mark had promised. Her limbs were heavy, her brain full of mush.

She glanced up at the window and saw rain, slashing against the panes. However much she mentally rehearsed the action of swinging her legs out of the bed and standing up, she somehow couldn't get the signal through to her muscles. She imagined herself struggling up to the viewpoint in the rain, her feet sinking into boggy holes, her hair getting wet and straggly like rats' tails.

It was cosy in bed, and she was pregnant, wasn't she? She shouldn't be going out, falling into holes. She decided that Mum could wait another day for a message. She could stew for a bit, after being so mean to her.

Just thinking of the word 'stew' made her stomach roll with nausea. She closed her eyes and did some slow breathing, placing both her hands on her belly. It felt firm, and ever so slightly rounded under the waistband of her pyjama bottoms.

That was the moment when she realised she didn't feel lonely any more. She and the baby – they had each other for company. They didn't need anything except rest. And if she got hungry, she had two cereal bars and a bruised apple in her bag (Mum had insisted she pack them) and the bottle of Fanta that Jock had bought for her at the petrol station in Killendreich on the drive up. It seemed like years ago now.

Maisie rolled over, pulled the covers up to her chin, and went back to sleep.

After a day or two, or maybe it was three, Maisie decided it was time to get up. She managed to go down to the kitchen to make a bowl of porridge for breakfast. Her head spun as she watched the bowl turning inside the microwave, and she only managed to swallow half of the grey, lumpy paste. But she decided to brave the walk up to the viewpoint. She spent ten minutes looking for the cardboard package the art materials had come in, so she could pass on the updated address to Mum. But it had gone. Mark must have taken it away.

Only then did she remember that she'd photographed it with her phone camera. Was this what they called 'pregnancy brain'? Ugh. She hated it.

And then she couldn't find her shoes. She could have sworn she'd tossed them somewhere in the direction of the door, but they weren't there. She went to the boot room where she'd left her muddy trainers, only to find that they were nowhere to be seen either. There was one old pair of wellies in there, two sizes too small. So she squeezed her feet into those.

Her legs felt weak and jelly-ish, climbing up to the viewpoint, and she was properly gasping for breath by the time she reached the bench. She waved her phone above her head, bringing on a wave of dizziness. She leaned forward and threw up, right in front of the bench. Lovely. She hoped no other walkers would come across the pile of vomit. But who was she kidding? Walkers never came up here, through this choked, unmanaged forest.

She repeated the process until she got one bar of signal. Quickly, she dialled Mum's number.

No answer – AGAIN. Maisie screeched in frustration.

She keyed in a text.

> Mum. I'm sick. Please come and get me. The address I gave you before is not right. It's Inverkillen House, near Killendreich. OK?

No answer.

> OK??

Nausea surged again. She needed to go back to the house and back to bed.

> Just come whenever you can. I need to go home.

A big fat tear rolled down her cheek and plopped onto the phone screen.

She waited ten minutes. Half an hour. When two slow, cold hours had passed, she got to her feet – she could feel blisters that had already formed from the too-small wellies – and stumbled down the hill.

Softly, sadly, and only because she knew she had to do it, Maisie closed a door in her mind.

Back at the house, Maisie dragged herself into bed and under the covers and slept. She had strange, feverish dreams about her mother, banging on the door of Inverkillen House. About her phone sprouting feathers and wings and flying down to Northumberland.

She awoke with a start.

Oh Goddd! It was Jan. Sitting on her bed, staring at her. Her eyes were hollow in the bone-white face, their expression unreadable.

'Jan!' Maisie lurched herself up onto one elbow. Maybe Mum had got her message. Maybe she was downstairs, waiting for her. It was nearly dark outside – she must have been asleep for hours.

Her head began to swirl. She let it fall back. Her greasy damp hair met the greasy damp pillow – gross. She was glad Ally wasn't here to see her like this.

'Maisie.' Jan's lips stretched into something that was maybe meant to be a smile, revealing teeth that were darkened, as if she'd been drinking red wine.

'Oh! Hello.'

'Mark tells me you're going to do up your room.'

'Y-yes. If that's okay with you.'

She gave a big sigh. 'You should have seen this place when I was young. The parties we used to have. Shooting weekends, getting down from the hills all covered in mud, just as it was getting dark. The dogs, so excited, racing round us in circles. Charades in the drawing room. Eightsome Reels around the hall. I remember coming home at the end of term, turning the corner of the drive, seeing the house lit up like a Christmas tree.'

Maisie pictured the house in winter, with the drawing room fire lit and the trees outside silvered with frost. Then she realised with a start that she would be spending Christmas here – she'd be heavily pregnant by then. She thought of Mum, visiting Gran to sing carols at the care home, then going home to have lunch alone.

'The house rang with the laughter of children.' Jan closed her eyes as if she were hearing it now. 'Uproarious games of hide and seek. Can you imagine it, with all the passageways, the nooks and crannies? A house built for children.'

'It sounds... really nice.'

'I have five sisters. They all live in Wisconsin now,' Jan went on. 'And the cousins are even further away – seven in Australia and one in Singapore.'

'A lovely big family.'

Jan nodded. 'Anyway. I thought you'd want to know – George passed away this afternoon.'

For a moment she felt like she was falling, as if the bed, the floorboards it stood on, the house itself, had given way into thin air. Her heart missed a beat and then came back to life with an alarming thump that made her cough and put a hand to her chest.

What was she supposed to do? What was she meant to say?

'I'm so sorry,' she whispered. 'I'm so sorry.'

She had slept the day away, lazy and unthinking, while

this momentous event had happened. While a family had been changed forever.

Jan lifted a hand, so that it hovered over the duvet, near her stomach. For a moment Maisie thought she was going to touch her. Awkwardly, she wriggled up the bed.

'Poor little George,' she said, uselessly.

Jan looked up at Maisie, her eyes empty. 'He's with God now,' she said calmly. 'And God shall make everything anew.'

'But –'

She stood up abruptly and made for the door. 'Mark will be up later with your medication.'

Alone in the room again, Maisie had a sudden sense that there was something behind her. A presence of some kind, watching her from high up on the wall. She turned and saw that the wooden cross was back, fixed to its nail above the bed. Had Jan rifled through her drawers to find it? Or did she have a stash of them somewhere? Maisie shivered and pulled the covers up around her face.

37

TERESA

Northumberland
Now

Sunny had brought some of his famous chana dal over for dinner. George refused to even taste it, despite Sunny explaining it was his auntie's special recipe.

'It's a bit like a very tasty lentil soup,' he said. 'Very good for you. It's like eating sunshine.'

But George had shaken his head and scampered off.

Now, he was asleep on the sofa between us. I'd tucked a soft grey blanket around him.

I'd just been telling Sunny about the visit to Cheryl – the visualisation she'd done with George.

'So it was completely useless, then,' said Sunny calmly.

'Not completely useless,' I protested. 'It was interesting to see how George reacted. He was so genuinely frightened. There's no way he's lying about any of this. I just don't believe it.'

'No.' He tilted his head to the side. 'But we have to consider the possibility that Caroline may have primed George – she may have planted ideas into his head, about his supposed past life. Little details about the house, about Maisie. Little seeds that would grow in his mind over time, and form a story that, to him, feels indistinguishable from a real memory. He wouldn't even be aware of it. Children's minds are so malleable. That's why past life regression hypnotherapy is considered to be dangerous. I've been reading about it, T.'

'But why would Caroline do that? I just can't think of a single reason. And if there is some kind of foul play involved, why would she have agreed to the DNA test?'

Sunny frowned. 'Do you think it would be worth getting a private investigator involved again? We could ask them to do a bit of digging on Caroline and Mark.'

'Maybe. But that private investigator I used before was useless. He spent weeks trying to track down the woman at the school exhibition. The one who claimed to be Ally's mum, but wasn't. He said that was the best lead – and the only evidence to suggest that Maisie hadn't just run away, that there was a third party involved. But he couldn't find any evidence that she existed at all. He charged me nearly five grand, to come up with a big fat nothing.'

'Hmm... the police weren't convinced about her either, were they? Because she wasn't on the school's CCTV?'

'No. But they only had CCTV in the main reception and at the entrance to the sports hall. And I saw her in the art block.'

'And you thought you saw the same woman, afterwards – on television?'

'That was a year or two later. I thought I saw her playing a dead body in a crime drama. But it might not have been her. I thought I saw her another time as well – at one of the make-up counters in Fenwicks, in Newcastle. Just fleetingly, through a crowd of Christmas shoppers. When they moved out of the way again, she'd gone. It was a bit like how I kept seeing Maisie everywhere.'

It was one of the reasons I rarely went out any more. Once, I'd run after an Edinburgh bus, convinced I'd caught a glimpse of her, sitting on the top deck. I'd actually caused an accident – a bicycle had come off the road, swerving to avoid me.

'So what made you think it was her – Ally's mum, I mean? When you saw her on the telly?'

'She was sort of short and wide, and she had this very distinctive face.'

'The human brain *is* very skilled at recognising faces,' said Sunny. 'But remember, you were primed to –'

'Sunny,' I said. 'God! Will you please stop going on about priming all the time?'

He pressed his mouth into a thin line, as if he was trying to stop his words coming out. Then he changed tack. 'Did you make a note of the actor's name? The one in the crime drama?'

'Yes, I did. Andrea Hobson-Jones.'

Sunny began searching on his phone. Then he started fiddling with the television, and BBC iPlayer, fast-forwarding through an episode of a drama series about a hospital. There'd been some kind of road accident, and a teenage girl had suffered chemical burns. She was in a hospital bed, her face covered in dressings.

The camera panned to show the family at the girl's

bedside. The mother was sitting there, wringing her hands and looking distraught.

'It's her!' I shot to the edge of the sofa. 'That's Ally's mum! Pause it!'

Sunny peered closer at the screen. 'I thought you said Ally's mum had blonde hair?'

'She did. But it's the same woman. She's just dyed her hair. But her face – it's sort of toad-like.'

Sunny's face creased into a sceptical frown. 'Toad-like?'

'Yes. I would recognise it anywhere. Let it play. See if she stands up. She's quite short – about five foot two.'

We fast-forwarded through the rest of the episode, but the actor didn't reappear.

'Let's find something where she stands up. And where she speaks,' I insisted.

Sunny went through her acting credits on IMDB, and discovered she'd been in an episode of an old comedy from 2013. We paid for the episode on Prime and sat watching it, glued to the screen. She played a health club receptionist.

'Only one towel per session,' she said, giving her customer a haughty look.

'It's her! See her height? And her voice – it's all... toady.'

'Toady?' Sunny sounded bewildered. 'How do toads speak?'

'Sort of low and gravelly.'

'But you told the police this, at the time, yes? That you'd seen her playing the dead body?'

'They came back pretty quickly, saying they'd ruled her out as having been involved.'

'What about looking her up on Twitter, or Twix, or whatever it is they call it now?'

Within moments I'd found her profile. 'I'm going to send

her a DM.' I could feel rage, flowing through my veins, just looking at her profile picture. 'It's her, it's definitely her. Fuck it, Sunny. I've been too accepting of what the police have told me. All along. All through this. Why should I listen to them, when they've completely failed to find Maisie? I need to trust my own gut.'

'Hang on,' said Sunny, holding up his hands. But I was already typing.

Hi Andrea, I am Maisie Jones's mum. We met once before at the end of term exhibition for Westcoates Academy, Northumberland.

I looked back at the calendar on my phone to find the exact date.

You introduced yourself as Ally's mum and we looked at the artwork together. Please could you DM me back urgently?

Sunny shook his head, giving me a warning look. Ignoring it, I began to search the internet for any other information about her. 'It says she lives in London with her wife and their two dogs.'

'She's written a piece about addiction.' Sunny was one step ahead of me. 'Says she had to go to a rehab place in 2017, that she managed to turn her life around with their help. She's run the London marathon twice, raising money for addiction charities.'

'What rehab place?'

He shook his head. 'Doesn't say.'

I went back onto her profile, only to see a message that I had been blocked. Adrenaline surged in my chest.

'Oh my God! Sunny, that proves it.'

He shook his head. ‘Not really. She might just think you’re a… an unwell lady.’

‘She can think what she likes. I’m going to tell the police.’

Sunny shook his head. ‘Tell them what, though? They’ve already ruled her out as having any involvement. If anything, you could get charged with harassment.’

‘I’ll tell them about George.’ I whispered his name – he was still asleep between us.

‘But – the DNA test. You should wait until that’s back. If that shows a match then absolutely, the police might be interested.’

My racing thoughts came to a sudden, dull stop. I sighed heavily. ‘I don’t think Caroline would have allowed the test if there was any chance of it being a match.’

‘Probably not,’ he said evenly. ‘But still, I think your best bet is to get close to the family. Try and make yourself into a sort of bonus granny.’

‘A bonus granny?’ I frowned.

‘Yes. Find some reason to be near Nottingham and get yourself invited to stay. Look around the house. Find out more about them. Find out if there’s any connection between them and this Andrea Hobson-Jones. *That* would be something to tell the police.’

I made a face at him. ‘How am I going to get myself invited to Nottingham? I can’t just turn up there. I’d look like a total nutter.’

‘Maybe looking like a nutter is your best bet. You could pretend you’ve been driven over the edge by Maisie’s disappearance.’ He gave a slight wince, as if he was thinking I wouldn’t have to pretend too hard. ‘Play the sympathy card, and get yourself into the house. Get a good look at this Mark fellow. He seems like a slippery character.’

'I don't want to be a crazy bonus granny. *You* can do it.' I punched him lightly on the arm. 'You can be crazy. We can say you need to see Mark to ask him about improving your wellness.'

'I *will* need to see about my wellness, at this rate,' said Sunny under his breath, returning to his phone research.

38

MAISIE

Killendreich
Seven and a half years ago

Maisie stared in the bathroom mirror as she washed her hands over and over again, trying to get her head around the sheer horror of what had happened. She hadn't thought that things could get much worse than they were – pregnant at seventeen, holed up in this rotting house with no phone and no company. But now...

She'd been going back and forth to the toilet all night with a funny tummy, and her bones ached as if she had the flu. She suspected it was something to do with the fact she'd stopped taking her medication, the little white pills Mark had prescribed for her. They gave her a fuzzy head, and she didn't like how they made her sleep for long stretches of the day. She hadn't left the house in weeks, even to walk around the weed-pocked gravel that surrounded the building.

But now... This awful, *awful* thing had happened. Two fleshy lumps, protruding from her bum hole.

She clung onto the edge of the sink and tried to breathe slowly.

Okay... okay. Could it be... piles? Maisie shuddered. People got those when they were pregnant, didn't they? Something to do with the extra weight? She had a huge baby bump now.

Well, it was either that or some sort of bum cancer. Her lips felt tingly at the thought of it. Little black dots began to appear in her vision.

Okay, she *definitely* needed to speak to Mum. This had gone on long enough. She needed proper medical care. She needed to see a midwife.

Mum had used to watch *Call the Midwife* on Sunday nights, and Maisie had secretly liked it too. For a moment, she imagined Sister Julienne and Nurse Trixie turning up at Inverkillen House with their beaming smiles, bearing a home delivery pack wrapped in brown paper.

Back in her room, Maisie had to sit on the edge of the bed to pull her trousers on, like some kind of old person. And it was bloody freezing, now that it was December. This was literally the worst day of her life.

But she had a plan. Mark was always out during the day, and she'd been told not to bother Jan. But nobody had said anything about Jock, the groundsman. She waddled downstairs and left the house through the kitchen door, making her way along the rough path to Jock's cottage. She rapped on the door until he appeared from a shed around the back of the house.

'Yes?'

His beard was all straggly and his eyes kept wandering off to the side. She wondered if he'd been drinking, even though it was only nine in the morning.

'Please would you drive me to the nearest town? It's very, very important.'

'Sorry. Not today,' said Jock, turning away.

She put a hand on his arm. 'Please. I need to...' Something stopped her from saying she needed to call her mother. 'I need to visit the pharmacy. It's urgent.'

Jock jerked his arm away. He disappeared off into his shed, muttering something that included the F-word.

Maisie almost screamed in frustration. What was she supposed to do now?

Then the front door of the cottage opened, just a crack. A pair of wide eyes peeked out.

'Hello?' said Maisie.

The door opened a crack more. It was a teenage boy. She could see from his facial features that he had Down's Syndrome – he made her think of Danny, the charming young catering assistant at Gran's care home. And then she felt a guilty lurch as she thought of Gran, unvisited by Maisie for all these months.

'I'm Adrian.'

'Hello, Adrian. I really need to get to the nearest town.'

'Killendreich.' He spoke with great authority.

'Yes. That's the one. How can I get there?'

Adrian puffed out a breath, looking very doubtful. 'You'll have to ask Mark. Dad can only drive on a good day.'

Maisie remembered the drive from Northumberland to Inverkillen, back in July, and how Jock had nearly ploughed the Land Rover into an oncoming tractor. Perhaps it wasn't a great idea to ask him to drive her to Killendreich. Then she had a sudden thought.

'How do you get to school? Is there a school bus or something? Where does it pick you up from – the main road?'

School buses were always laid on for students in rural areas, weren't they?

'I don't go to school any more,' said Adrian.

'How come?'

'Bullies. Dad's home schooling me.'

Maisie raised her eyebrows, imagining Jock drunkenly trying to teach Adrian his times tables, or explain how an oxbow lake was formed. Then she had another idea.

'What about... do you have a mum?'

'Not any more.'

Maisie felt a sudden wave of longing for her own mother. As if in response, the baby moved inside her, a little wriggle of limbs. She put out her hand and leant against the door frame.

'How can I get to town?'

'You'll have to go now. I'm not allowed to talk to strangers.' Adrian narrowed his eyes. 'Dad's very protective.'

'Okay, okay,' said Maisie. 'I'll go.'

Later on, waking from a nice long nap (she'd given in and taken one of her pills), Maisie reflected on Adrian and Jock's situation. Jock might be a dishevelled old drunk, but at least he'd tried to protect his son from the bullying. Sometimes, these days, she wished she'd told Mum about the shared nudes incident, that she'd let her take it up with the school. Maybe she'd have let her move schools, or even leave school altogether, like Adrian.

After it had happened – her social death, as she thought of it – she'd started fantasising about her biological father, about the man she only knew of as 'Joel'. With barely any information to go on, it had been easy to imagine his laid-back Australian drawl, his white smile and his huge house, facing the ocean. A life of barbecues on the beach and fiery sunsets. A place as far away from the casual cruelties of Westcoates Academy as it was possible to get.

She'd cried, secretly in her room, when Mum had told her that Joel was dead, that there was no point in trying to track him down. She'd said it so bluntly, without a thought for Maisie's feelings. She'd lost her dad, even if he was only an imaginary one.

So many things to be angry with Mum about.

But Mum had things to be angry with Maisie about, too. She would have gone *insane*, for example, if she'd known about Maisie uploading her DNA onto the ancestry website.

And she would *not* be happy about the fact that Maisie now seemed to be hooked on prescription medication…

Yes, it would be best to get herself off the medication before she tried to speak to Mum again. She'd be off them soon. This afternoon's pill was just a blip. And they couldn't be that strong – Mark had said they were safe for the baby.

There was a knock on the door of her room.

'Can I come in?' It was Mark. He wasn't usually home this early.

'Hi,' said Maisie, trying to pull herself and her bump further up the bed.

'How are you doing?' He sat on the pink velvet chair and clasped his hands, resting his elbows on his knees.

'Not great.'

'A little bird told me that you're in need of some medical advice?'

Maisie frowned. For a moment she wondered how far his seemingly psychic abilities went. Or perhaps he had set up hidden cameras in the bathroom and had seen her staring at her bum with a hand mirror that morning. But then she remembered – Jock.

'Come on, then. Let's have it.' He smiled encouragingly.

She felt blood rising in her cheeks. But he was a doctor, wasn't he? 'I think I might have...' She sighed heavily. 'Piles, maybe? I had a bad tummy last night and these little, like, lumps, have come out? It's really sore when I sit down.'

'Ah, the bane of pregnancy. Poor Maisie. So uncomfortable. But they're very common and nothing to worry about.'

Her face felt like a flaming beacon now. 'Can I get some... I dunno. Some cream, or something?'

'Let me check the medical store.'

Store? Most people had a medicine cabinet.

'I'm sure we'll have some. Jan was plagued with piles during her pregnancy.' He leaned forward with a conspiratorial smile. 'But that information is more than my life's worth! Don't breathe a word!'

Maisie smiled, in spite of herself. 'I won't.'

'We'll have you sorted in two ticks.' He stood up.

'Mark?' said Maisie. 'I want to try and stop taking the medication. It's making me sleepy all the time. I can't be bothered to get up and do anything.'

He sat back down on her bed, his face creased with kindness and concern, a bit like Dr Turner in *Call The Midwife*.

'Oh, Maisie. I know things have been tough for you. But it's your depression that's making you feel that way. The meds are there as a safety net – to prevent you spiralling even further down. But of course, you have choices. If you want, we'll wean you off the meds as soon as it's safe – after the baby's here.'

He'd talked before about her having depression. She'd been a little surprised but supposed it must be obvious to him, a psychiatrist.

'Don't I need... midwife appointments?'

She hoped he wouldn't offer to check her over himself. Her cheeks reddened again.

'Absolutely,' he said. 'You'll be meeting your midwife soon. She'll be coming to do some checks, and talk you through everything.'

'Really?'

'Yes, a lovely young woman called Zuleika. She'll be staying on for a few weeks as a maternity nurse, too, to make sure you get lots of rest.'

It all sounded a bit too good to be true.

'I really need to message Mum. Do you know when the Wi-Fi will be working again?' Her words came out childlike and timid. She hadn't asked him about the Wi-Fi in a while – she didn't like hearing the note of irritation in his usually patient voice.

'I'm sorry, I know it's not ideal. They're saying the old system needs replaced with some sort of satellite set-up. But we need to get planning permission. It's just a bureaucratic headache.'

That all sounded a bit odd. But she was too tired to argue.

'Could you send a message to Mum for me? When you next go out?'

'Absolutely.' He drew his phone out of his pocket and brought up Mum's contact page. He handed the phone to her.

After all this time, Maisie couldn't think of any words. She sat straight up in bed and took a selfie, showing off her bump. She checked the image and quite liked it – the winsome smile was just right, hinting that she might be nearly ready to forgive Mum.

'Send her that. Say the baby will be here soon.'

~

The next evening, Mark came to Maisie's room again. He handed her his phone. Maisie's heart leapt – had Mum replied? Maybe she was on her way up right now. Her eyes began to fill with tears of relief.

There *was* a message.

Thanks for the update. 👍

A *thumbs up emoji*? Maisie had sent Mum a picture of her own grandchild (inside its bump, anyway), and that was the best she could do?

With a sad smile, Mark held out the dosette box that contained Maisie's medication.

'Get a good night's sleep,' he said gently. 'Things will seem better in the morning.'

Maisie checked the time after he'd gone. It was only seven o'clock, but it had already been dark for hours, so she might as well go to sleep. On these short winter days, the sun slipped down behind the mountain ridge soon after noon, its rays barely touching the tops of the trees outside her window. Wearily, Maisie headed for the bathroom, planning to have a pee before the pills carried her off to sleep. The baby was wriggling around, bouncing its head off her bladder.

She stopped short as she noticed the door at the far end of the corridor, the one with the ugly green Fire Exit sign. It led to the narrow stairs down to the kitchen and the rest of the house, and usually, it was propped open. But not today. Today the door was closed.

And when she reached out a hand to open it, she realised that it wasn't just closed. It was locked. Bolted shut from the other side.

39

CAROLINE

Retford
Now

Caroline was in the kitchen, stirring up a huge cauldron of sticky toffee pudding mix, when the email pinged into her inbox.

She put on her glasses and read it through twice, and then nodded slowly. She'd been correct. The test – the one with the genuine swab from Teresa – showed there was a high probability that Teresa was George's grandmother. The email warned that the result couldn't be totally accurate without the mother's DNA. But it would be enough for Caroline's purposes.

Well, well, well, Mark. What have you been up to, you dirty dog?

She had expected to feel a huge, exhilarating rush, at the enormity of what was coming next. But she felt a little dull. Regretful, even, that her current life with Mark would be coming to an end.

That was the point though, wasn't it? Her life had never really been *with* Mark. It was always just her, good old Caroline playing house, while he was away extracting money from wealthy drug addicts. That first, intoxicating rush of forbidden love hadn't been able to survive Jan's death. Or the arrival of George at Retford, poor little sod.

Spain looked like it would be the best option for now – she still remembered a few words of the language from her grandparents. She opened her laptop and searched for the rental house she'd been drooling over the night before. It was perched on a hillside overlooking a bay, the stone a blinding white against the deep Mediterranean blues of sea and sky. The interior photos showed cool, tiled rooms and a slate-grey Poggenpohl kitchen. And that final photo – a sun lounger by a glimmering pool, the wall behind ablaze with bougainvillea. A frosted margarita glass on a table to the side, next to a Marian Keyes novel.

Was it too much to want these things?

This apartment, sadly, was a one bedroom, and didn't take kids.

Her ghost-life flickered tantalisingly into view. The one where she'd stayed a single woman, without ties. Where she cruised around islands in the Caribbean, or got spirited off to St Moritz for the season.

She opened another tab, to look again at her favourite of the two-bedroom options. This one did allow kids – she'd already checked the terms. It was nice, too. There was a small plunge pool in the shady back yard.

She wondered what would actually happen if she took George. Would Mark get the authorities onto her, claiming child abduction, kidnap, blah blah blah? It seemed unlikely, given the nasty can of worms that Caroline was prepared to open. Mark would not want police crawling all over his life. Over every inch of Inverkillen House.

Then she thought about how she'd feel if she never saw Georgie again. If she never had to make him another sandwich, or blend another soup. Never had to go to another meeting with his teachers about his poor grasp of maths. If she never again had to change his soaking pyjamas, or smell the salty, animal tang of fear on his skin after a nightmare. If she never felt his arms around her neck again, his hot breath on her cheek.

She tried to anticipate a feeling of loss. But if she was honest, it wouldn't quite come. She'd always occupied an uneasy space in his life, somewhere between a nanny – a kindly, capable Mary Poppins type – and a wicked stepmother. The 'mother' spot had already been taken. It had never been hers to fill. The occupant of that space seemed to exist alongside her in this old house, in shadows and corners and in things never said.

She gazed at the sun lounger again, the cool margarita. A warm, bright, un-haunted place, where the sun could sink into her skin and warm her blood.

This was her new life, the one she deserved. She just had to step forward and claim it.

40

MAISIE

Killendreich
Seven and a half years ago

The baby was asleep, having finally settled at about half past five. Maisie knew she would hear Zuleika's footsteps on the stairs soon, coming to take him away for the day. But for now, it was just the two of them. Maisie thought of this quiet, cuddly time as their 'golden hour'. Even though it was a cold February morning, still dark outside, the window misted with condensation.

She lay very still, holding him close against her chest, but not too tightly. And with her cheek pressed against the top of his head, with its silky whorls of fine dark hair. She couldn't believe that she had made him. She lifted her left hand and gently pressed the nub of his little nose with her finger. His lips began to work, making sucking movements. He must be dreaming about milk.

After the birth, Mark had asked, teary-eyed, if he and Jan could have the 'privilege' of naming him. Maisie, lying flat on her back with her legs apart while Zuleika had tried to stem the bleeding, had hardly been in a position to argue. She'd been told they hadn't quite decided on a name yet, even though he was two weeks old now.

'Munchkin,' she whispered now into the top of his head.

She thought about the empty day stretching ahead – how she would spend it alone in her room, sleeping, or trying to sleep.

Mark had promised she'd start to feel better after having the baby, but she might feel worse at first. He'd said she had developed severe perinatal depression. A breakdown, to use the common term, probably caused by the breakdown in her relationship with her mother, just at the time she was about to become a mother herself. And being abandoned by Ally, who had returned to the US to have some ground-breaking operation on his knee and continue his tennis career. He'd sent a video of himself explaining why he had to grab the opportunity, or he'd always regret it.

She could hardly believe that neither of them had turned up, not even when the baby was born. She'd sent Mum a photo of the baby, via Mark's phone, saying 'I want you to be in our lives.' Two days later, she'd received an Interflora bouquet, with the words 'Congratulations!' written on the card in the florist's handwriting.

'We're looking after you now,' Mark had said firmly. 'We're your family now.'

Sometimes, when she lifted her head off the pillow, she thought she was back in Northumberland. With the new wallpaper and carpet, and the pink velvet chair and heart-shaped cushion, she could have been back in her little attic room at home.

In fact, she sometimes played a game of pretending she

was back at home. She'd close her eyes and imagine it so hard that some childish part of her almost believed that she – and the baby – might be transported back there. She seemed to remember children doing that in the Narnia books. It had worked for them.

It didn't work now, of course. She began to feel too hot. She still felt achy from the infection she'd picked up from the birth. And her back was hurting from staying in the same position for so long, with the baby on her chest.

It was seven o'clock now and she was starting to wonder where Zuleika was. She'd stayed on to help with the baby, taking him for walks every morning, strapped to her chest. Feeding him with the ready-prepared bottles of formula that had appeared when Maisie hadn't managed to breastfeed properly.

She remembered the birth only in flashes, not as a story where one thing followed on from another. And that was okay with her.

She didn't even want to think about the pain. The labour pains, like the worst cramps you could ever imagine. She'd imagined her innards being wrenched and stretched using medieval torture devices.

Oubliette.

She'd screamed for her mother. Forgetting, in the grip of the pains, how her mother had abandoned her. How she had never come for her.

She remembered the horror of seeing Zuleika – kindly Zuleika, who she'd trusted – reach for small sharp scissors, which disappeared between her legs. She remembered the snipping noise, and the great bellow that had emerged from her throat. The searing pain of stitches, afterwards, through ragged flesh.

She couldn't remember the baby being put on her chest for skin-to-skin contact. That had been part of the 'birth plan' she'd agreed with Zuleika, although they had both struggled with the language barrier. She only remembered hearing him cry, from somewhere that sounded far away. And the hollow ache for him, deep in her chest. As if her heart was being pulled out by a string.

She did remember the panic when she stood up for the first time afterwards. How all her insides had slid out of her, in a great wet rush. How she'd cupped her hands underneath to try and catch it all. There was a big brown stain on the pink carpet to remind her. Zuleika had helped her to the toilet and that was when the tears had come.

That was why they took the baby away, Mark had told her. Because she had become 'dysregulated'. They had needed to make sure the baby was safe, while Maisie calmed down.

Now, a pattern had been established. The baby was always taken away for the day, to spend time with Jan. But he was returned at night, when Zuleika was off duty.

The baby, she had come to suspect, was in withdrawal. It made her shrink in shame, every time she thought of it.

Maisie wasn't stupid. It was clear to her, even through her fuzzy head, that she'd become dependent on the drugs she'd been given during her pregnancy. Tranquillisers, or something, she didn't know what. Mark had said she'd needed larger doses, as she'd become more and more unwell, to avoid a 'total psychotic break'. He'd said she should trust him, and not to believe the hyped-up nonsense she'd probably read on social media about people becoming addicted to their prescription drugs. He'd said they could easily wean her off them when the time was right.

So the baby was jittery, restless, seemed always to be in pain. All of the day and night, apart from that golden hour in the morning when he surrendered to deep sleep, his body splayed out, rising and falling on her chest.

She knew he cried all day, because she could hear him. There was a room on the other side of her bedroom wall – one of the big bedrooms in the main house. She'd worked that out on one of her walks. She hadn't made it up to the viewpoint for months, not on her tottery, weak legs. But she occasionally did circuits of the 'garden' – the weedy, gravelly area around the house – to breathe in the fresh, damp, piney air.

The fact that the door at the end of the corridor was kept bolted did not mean she wasn't allowed to go out. Mark had taken great pains to explain that. He'd said the security arrangements were for her own safety, because of the 'inherent unpredictability' of her condition, and because her medication might cause sleepwalking, or even sudden blackouts if she overdid things. Maisie had felt too exhausted to argue. And a shameful part of her knew that she cared more about having an uninterrupted supply of the little white pills than she did about a locked door. Where would she have gone, anyway? Her room, now she'd decorated it as she liked, was surely the nicest, cosiest one in the house. Sometimes, she visited the home cinema in the basement to watch *Mamma Mia!* or old people's films, like *The Sound of Music*. But it reminded her too much of an *oubliette* down there, with its damp, dank smell.

It was just past seven when the footsteps eventually came. But it wasn't Zuleika who appeared, it was Jan. Maisie hadn't seen her since the birth, when she'd watched, white-faced, from a chair across the room.

Maisie suspected that Mark had told Jan she needed to be more 'hands on', to prepare for when Zuleika wouldn't be here any more. She looked distracted, and kept glancing away – towards the door, and to the window behind her.

'How has he been?'

'He's had a bit of sleep this morning,' Maisie said. She always tried to put a positive spin on things. She didn't want to make it sound like she was incapable of looking after him.

'Oh, was he restless again?'

Restless...?

That was one way to describe it. She thought of the relentless screaming, his body rigid as she tried to hold him close. The enraged expression on his face, balled-up with crying.

'He's got good, strong lungs,' said Jan in a deep, exaggerated voice, like one you might use to talk to a dog. 'He's a good, strong boy.'

'He's quite strong,' agreed Maisie.

Jan reached out for the baby and Maisie slowly detached him from her chest, feeling him stiffen. Jan lifted him by the armpits until their eyes were level.

The baby's face crumpled. Suddenly, Maisie felt worried for him. Properly, desperately worried. She longed to snatch him back from Jan.

Wah-wah-waaaaaah!

'Hello, George,' said Jan.

'George?' said Maisie, over the noise. 'Is that what you've decided to call him?'

'Didn't Zuleika tell you?' asked Jan.

'But... but your other baby was called George.'

Jan smiled, her face suddenly alight. As if she was

burning on the inside. 'Don't you see?' she said. 'This is God's will. His love, made flesh.'

'What?'

'There is only one George. A single, perfect gift from God. Whole and unbroken.'

'But –'

'He heals the broken-hearted and binds up their wounds,' said Jan. She closed her eyes and held her breath, as if she was in the grip of an exquisite pain.

'Are you okay? Shall I take... the baby?' She didn't want to use the name Jan had given him. It sounded wrong.

'Death will be no more. Neither will there be any mourning or crying or pain,' Jan explained happily. 'For the old order of things has passed away. He who sits on the throne said, "Behold! I am making all things new!"'

Terror gripped Maisie's heart. For a moment, she wondered if she was in some kind of nightmare. She felt a sudden, fierce longing for her mother.

Her mother who didn't love her any more.

She glanced at her watch, calculating how long it would be until Mark brought her dosette box and the next little white pill.

41

CAROLINE

Retford
Now

'Ah!' said Mark when she walked into the living room, the larger one at the front of the house where the windows overlooked the lawn. 'Here she is. My Sticky Toffee Diva.'

She gave him a stiff smile. This was his other nickname for her – marginally better than 'PQ', she supposed. She pulled in her stomach instinctively, then remembered how much she hated the patriarchy, and let it hang out.

He leaned forward in his armchair, his glass of Glenlivet in one hand, and stared at her feet, his expression full of mock confusion.

'I don't think I can believe what I'm seeing,' he said.

'What?'

'She's wearing orange shoes with a purple skirt,' he said, as if talking to himself. 'What's come over her? Do I need to call the doctor?'

Caroline sighed. He was right – it was a poor combination. 'I couldn't give a fuck, Mark.'

'Well someone's a scratchy cat this evening,' he said.

She sat herself down on the sofa. Now that it was time, she felt nervous. And furious with herself for feeling nervous.

'Where's George?' Mark settled back into his chair and picked up the remote control.

Caroline brushed an imaginary piece of fluff from her Liberty print skirt. 'Oh, we've been having great adventures,' she said in a careful, cooing voice. 'We managed to find the place he says he used to live. In his old life. Before he died.'

He smirked and downed the last of his whisky. 'Ah... before he died. Yes, right.' He raised his eyebrows and nodded mockingly, playing along. 'Are we talking about the fabled hobbity houses? The "road-that-isn't-a-road"? You found those, did you?'

He gave a half smile, so that just the tip of his crooked canine was visible, giving the illusion that it was the only tooth in his mouth. Caroline felt a surge of disgust. She tamped it down.

'We *did*!' she said, twinkling. 'It took a bit of tracking down, but we got there in the end.'

Mark frowned. He tapped the whisky glass with a fingernail – twice, three times. 'So where's George?'

'George has gone to spend some time with his old family.' She ran her hands over her skirt again, smoothing the silky fabric over her knees.

'Eh?' There was a pause. She could feel his eyes on her. 'What do you mean?'

'Up in Northumberland. Georgie was desperate to find the place. But silly me – you know where it is, don't you?' She looked up and met his gaze. 'You know *exactly* where Maisie lived.'

The name sparked in the air like static. But Mark adopted a charming, baffled expression. 'What in the name of Mike are you burbling on about?'

'What was it? A surrogacy arrangement that went wrong? What happened, hmm?' She watched his face closely. 'Did she refuse to hand over the baby when it came to it?'

Mark laughed. 'Come on, Caro. Where's George? At a friend's house, is he? You know how I feel about –'

'Do you have Maisie locked up somewhere? Or did you kill her and make sure all the loose ends were tied up?'

'Do I have George's imaginary friend locked up somewhere?' He gave a great, spluttering laugh. 'Good Lord, Caroline. Listen to yourself!'

'You won't have thought about it, will you? What you put her mother through? That woman is ruined. A husk of a person. She's been looking for her daughter all these years. Alone, because nobody believed her until now. Until I came along.'

She felt a flicker of self-righteousness for a moment, before she remembered what she was about to do.

'How did you manage to befuddle the police enquiry? I suppose it doesn't matter now. They'll be able to untangle it all now, with this new information.'

'What "new information"?' He still looked baffled.

'The DNA test results,' said Pudding Queen.

Ha! He didn't have an answer to that. His tongue shot out, lizard-like, running over his dry lips. He looked older, suddenly.

'Yes,' said Caroline, trying to hide the annoying shake in her voice. 'Maisie's mother wanted to do a DNA test, and now

I have the results. Teresa is George's grandmother. So Maisie is – or *was* – George's mother.'

Mark got up, walked over to the window and gazed out at the lawn, with its perfect stripes, sloping down to the belt of trees at the bottom of the garden.

'Ah dear.' His voice was soft now, gentle. 'Do we need to get you to see Dr Gordon, my love?' That concern in his voice – one might almost mistake it for love.

'I don't think so. Even if you manage to convince people I'm nuts, it won't matter. Because once I send on that DNA result to Teresa, you'll have to explain yourself to the police. They'll be all over Inverkillen House with their forensic teams.' She paused. 'And their police dogs. Sniffing around.' Wide-eyed, she gave a great, pig-like snort, and then laughed.

He turned to face her. 'What is it that you want, Caroline?' He sounded weary now, resigned. As if she'd orchestrated all this because she wanted another kitchen extension, or a new shoe wardrobe.

'There... *is* another option.'

'What's that, then?'

'I did another DNA test. One comparing my DNA to George's, to generate a negative result, but with Teresa's details on it. Long story short, I could arrange for Teresa to receive the negative result. Then Teresa will believe that George and Maisie aren't related. And all of his mysterious talk about past lives and so on will remain just that – a mystery. We can all go back to normal.' She left a pause. 'Almost.'

'What do you mean? Come on, woman. Spit it out.'

'I want five hundred thousand pounds. Just enough to go away and start somewhere new. Think of it as a divorce settlement. What I would have been entitled to if we'd actually married. If you agree, and you pay half up front, then I'll forward Teresa the negative DNA result. And I'll go and get George back for you. Once he's back, you can pay me the other half. And I'll be out of your hair.'

He gave a low whistle. 'Wow. That's quite the scheme you've dreamed up, PQ.'

'Yes. And just to be clear – if you don't pay, Teresa gets the correct DNA result. And it'll be police... dogs... questions. And social workers, I would imagine.' She pulled a babyish, pouting face. 'No more Georgie-Pie.'

42

MAISIE

Killendreich
Seven years ago

Maisie was lying in bed with George on her chest, rubbing his back in circles. He had been brought to her early today – before dinner, instead of at bedtime. This was happening more and more, now that Zuleika had gone. Jan couldn't cope with a six-month-old on her own. Not for more than a few hours.

There was an air vent above the skirting board, about half way down her bed, where the sound seemed to travel. If she scootched down the bed and held her ear near to it, she could make out what was going on behind the wall – in Jan's bedroom, she guessed it was. Her hearing seemed to have got sharper since having George, as if her body had attuned itself to respond to his cues. She could often hear him crying, and Jan's voice rising in frustration, becoming shriller as the day went on.

Once she'd yelled at him to 'just shut up, you little fucker'. The outburst had been followed by a stream of prayers, and a psalm sung in a wavering voice.

God, she detested Jan. She longed to be able to just push her hands through the wall and take George back. But she always had to wait until Mark was back from work, and brought him up to her, along with two bottles of ready-mixed formula to last until the next morning. Once, she'd spilled a bottle all over the floor and George had cried the rest of the night, his little tummy rumbling with hunger.

This evening, Jan and Mark were arguing.

'You should have kept Zuleika on.' Jan's voice was sharp and accusing. 'Maisie's clearly a fruit loop.'

Maisie gasped in outrage, her mouth staying in an 'O' shape as Mark cut in, his voice stern.

'Please don't use offensive language, Jan.'

'She's not capable of looking after a baby. George is so unsettled in the mornings when you bring him to me. It seems like he's barely slept and he just grizzles all day.'

'I don't think that's entirely fair,' said Mark. 'Maisie can still be dysregulated at times. She'll always be prone to psychosis, I suspect, but she's made leaps and bounds in the last few months.'

Maisie thought of her listlessness, her fuzzy head, and the days when she hadn't been able to get out of bed. The red, raw days after George's birth, when tears had rolled silently down her face from dawn to dusk. The endless nights, when her own distress and George's had merged into one, and her shushing and stroking and rocking had had to comfort them both. Had that been psychosis? Had it really? Or was it just...

'She's devoid of moral character,' said Jan. 'Addicted to all those drugs.'

'She's on a careful regime of medication,' countered

Mark. 'I'm confident that she'll recover with the right balance of meds. I'm weaning her off the more addictive ones so that soon it'll just be the mood stabilisers.'

'Why are you even bothering? Just let her go and she can sort herself out. Or just get rid of her, like you did Zuleika.'

'I'll ignore that last comment,' said Mark with a frosty dignity. 'Maisie is family now. And if that all breaks down, if she leaves us, she may well end up in an NHS setting, seeking help for her dependence on medication, and her mental health issues. That could be a big problem for us. Social work would almost certainly become involved. If she points them in our direction, George could be taken away from us. You're hardly a stranger to mental disorder yourself. And I can't be here to supervise all the time. There may even be police involvement, given the way in which Maisie… ah, came to us.'

Maisie wondered what he meant. She'd come of her own free will, hadn't she? Or… had she?

'Can't you just send her off to one of your rehab clinics? Chesters, maybe?'

'Even at Chesters, the protocols would be different. My colleagues there would have an obligation to notify social work, if there was a child involved. We really don't want anyone official poking around here at Inverkillen House, do we?'

There was a note in his voice that almost sounded quite… menacing. But then he spoke again.

'I *believe* in Maisie. I think she's doing a reasonable job with George, and having her here takes the pressure off you. It's good for us and it's good for her. Here, she can continue to have a role in George's life, but in a supported setting. In the outside world, her addictions and disorders would be brought to light, and George would be removed from her. She's not stupid. She knows that.'

'I don't like her being here,' said Jan. 'I feel like my skin's on fire when I think about her being here in this house. Having a free rein with *our boy*.'

'Maybe we should revisit your meds too, then. But Jan, you need to trust me. And trust in God's plan for our family.' A sly note had crept into Mark's voice. 'He works through me, through my training and skills as a psychiatrist.'

They stopped talking after that, but Maisie could hear a series of grunts and thumps as if... ugh. She couldn't bear to think of it.

She had to get off the drugs. That was the key to all this. Once she'd done that, she could get the hell out. She could escape somehow, and take George with her. Surely the NHS, or social workers, or whoever, would help her, if she was off the drugs? They might let her keep George? Or she could just run away for long enough to contact Mum. Whatever had gone wrong between them, it could be fixed. Couldn't it?

Tonight, she'd only pretend to take her pills. She'd flush them down the toilet. If she went cold turkey, she could probably be off them in a week or two. Whatever mental disorders she had, she'd just have to toughen up and get over them.

But when it came to sleep time, and she had to decide whether or not to swallow her nighttime pills, she began to doubt the wisdom of her plan. She'd seen *Trainspotting*. She knew what withdrawal looked like. She couldn't do that while she was trying to look after the baby.

Maybe it would be easier just to go along with Mark and his plan to adjust her meds. He seemed confident that he could get her better. She'd still be getting off the drugs, just in a more controlled way, and under supervision. And in the meantime, at least she could see George, and make sure he was okay after spending time with Jan. She could cuddle up with him every night. Then, once her meds were stabilised and her mental disorders were better, she could get herself away from Inverkillen House.

'We'll sort things out, Munchkin,' she whispered into the top of George's head, as the merciful calm from the pills spread through her body. 'Not too much longer now.'

43

TERESA

Northumberland
Now

Sunny turned up for dinner still wearing his cricket whites. He'd been playing with the Bamburgh team on their famous pitch beneath the castle – one of the last fixtures of the season.

I'd warned him not to indulge too much on the half time refreshments – the homemade cakes and scones. I was making special macaroni cheese for dinner and George had promised to try it.

George helped me to grate cheddar while Sunny sat at the kitchen table, looking through George's drawings – he'd done dozens of them over the last few days. Some were of forests, or boats sailing in the sea. There were seven of Maisie's bedroom.

'Wow,' said Sunny. 'You're very good at drawing.'

'That's what Miss Honey says.' George shot Sunny a pleased little sideways look before returning his attention to the grater.

'That's the nice teaching assistant who works with George sometimes,' I explained.

'She's better than *nice*,' said George, his nose wrinkling.

Sunny was peering closer into one of the drawings of Maisie's room. 'What's this on the wall, in the drawing?'

George looked over and shrugged.

I wiped my hands and went to look myself. George had drawn a cross shape on the wall behind the bed.

'A cross?' I leafed through the other drawings of Maisie's room. 'That's interesting. Why is it only there in some of the drawings?'

George looked at us like we were nuts. 'It was only there sometimes.'

Only vere sometimes.

'So this is the room in the other house? The one where you lived in your old life?'

No response.

I tried a different tack. 'George, you know how you were talking about when you died? When you drowned, in the bathroom?

He nodded.

'Priming,' muttered Sunny.

I pressed on anyway. 'Was it the bathroom in this house, or in the other house?'

'This house.'

'Can you show me what happened?'

He led the way upstairs to the bathroom, and pointed at the tub from the doorway.

'Okay. Did someone... make you go into the bath?'

'Yes.' George pressed both of his palms to his forehead, the fingers outstretched. 'I was sleeping and then he lifted me out of my bed and drowned me.' He took a step forward and peered into the bath tub.

I spoke softly and carefully. 'Who was that man, George?'

'Dad.'

It was like a punch to the chest. I swallowed and moistened my lips. 'Your Dad – Mark?'

He nodded.

I couldn't stop myself. 'Did Mark... did your dad drown Maisie?'

His eyes widened. He curled forward, as if he had a sudden pain in his stomach, and crossed his arms over his body.

'George?'

There was something wrong with him. His face was going pale. Too pale.

'No, no, it's okay, darling. You don't need to hold your breath.'

I called over my shoulder to Sunny, who was hovering outside. 'Help!'

He saw immediately what was happening. 'Lie him on his side. That's it. He'll be fine in a moment.

I draped a fluffy pink towel, warm from the heated towel rail, over George, and knelt there on the bathroom floor, waiting for his chest to move. Sunny linked his hand with mine and squeezed it.

'We're staying calm,' said Sunny. 'We're staying calm. He's quite safe.' He glanced at his watch. 'He's been out for less than a minute. I'm timing it, don't worry.'

He'd clearly looked up what to do during a breath-holding episode.

For a moment, it flashed into my mind – the father Sunny

might have been. The family we might have been in another life. If I'd had another chance.

Perhaps things had gone so horribly wrong, for George, that his clever little mind had invented a do-over.

'There we are,' said Sunny. 'He's back.'

'It doesn't make any sense,' I said later. Sunny and I were standing outside the bathroom while George was brushing his teeth before bed. He'd swallowed three mouthfuls of macaroni cheese before asking for a cheese sandwich.

'If Mark killed Maisie,' I continued, 'why would she have come back again as his son? Wouldn't she want to be born into another family, as far away as possible? Or don't you get a choice? Is it something to do with resolving unfinished business? What does the Hindu religion say about it?'

Sunny sighed. He squeezed his eyes shut, as if he was trying to avoid rolling them. 'Of *course* it doesn't make any sense, T. That's because you're asking the wrong question.'

'What's the right question, then?'

'What the hell has Mark been doing to his son? It sounds like some kind of abuse.'

'Then we have to find out what's happened. We have to get him to tell us.'

Sunny shook his head doubtfully. 'We need to be very careful of asking leading questions. We have to be careful of...'

He managed not to say the word 'priming'. He cleared his throat. 'In fact, I don't think we should be asking him any questions at all.'

Guilt flooded through me. 'I know. I know.'

George emerged from the bathroom, leaving his towel in a heap on the hall carpet.

I tucked him into Maisie's bed. 'I'm sorry about before,' I said. 'I'm not going to keep asking questions, as I can see that's upset you. But I just want you to know.' I leaned in close and stroked his hair, just once. 'I want you to know that you can tell me *anything*.'

'But I can't, Mama.' His eyes were sorrowful pools in the half dark. 'I can't.'

He turned towards the wall and pulled the duvet up so that it covered his face.

44

MAISIE

Killendreich
Four and a half years ago

'Can we go my picnic again today?'

Maisie loved George's babyish way of talking, and she never corrected him. Bloody Mark and Jan could do that if they wanted to.

She looked up at the window, at the ceaseless rain, moving in sheets across the darkening sky. It had been falling all day. Not that it made any difference to them, stuck in here with the door locked at the end of the corridor. Adrian had left sandwiches and fruit for them earlier, with his usual cheery shout of 'Morning!' And Maisie would probably be allowed down to the kitchen at dinner time, to microwave something and bring it up. Some kind of squishy pasta meal, no doubt.

But yesterday had been magical. Maisie had been allowed to take George out, under Jock's supervision – something that had only happened a handful of times. She'd asked if they could look for the legendary waterfall, the one she still hadn't seen. But Jock had said, in his gruff voice, that it was a six-mile walk to the waterfall and back, and 'the bairn' wouldn't manage it. Instead, he led them a half mile or so along a rough, pine-needle-covered track. The noise of water grew louder until the river came into view, a silvery ribbon in the sunlight, carving its rocky way down the valley. In this part of the forest, the trees were taller, further apart, their tall trunks covered with grey lichen.

Jock looked like a character from *The Lord of The Rings*. He had a straggly white beard these days, and he carried a wooden walking staff that was topped with some kind of bone handle – made from a stag's antler, maybe? He directed them to a clearing in the trees, and Maisie set out a picnic blanket. She and George ate cheese sandwiches while Jock stood nearby, watching them. Then she and George played a game, throwing sticks for Bernie, their imaginary dog. Afterwards, they lay down on the picnic blanket and looked up, up through the branches of the trees, finding shapes in the clouds. Elephants, goblins, vast mountains and seas.

On the way back, Maisie spotted a delivery van, disappearing off up the track away from the house. Her heart leapt. For a moment, she wanted to run after it, to beg the driver for a lift to Killendreich. But then all the reasons why not seemed to tumble on top of her. She had to get herself off the drugs first, so she could convince someone – Mum? Social work? Mark, even? – that she was capable of looking after George. That he didn't need to be taken away from her.

In the kitchen, Adrian was unpacking two large crates of frozen meals. He smiled when he saw them, his whole face lighting up.

Maisie gave him a little wave. 'Hi Adrian!'

'Hiy-Ayd-yan!' repeated George.

But Jock had marched Maisie and George through the kitchen and up the stairs. In the corridor outside her room, he'd turned on her, his face contorted. 'Don't you ever talk to my son, do you hear? *Ever.* Or you can forget about coming out of your room again.' Flecks of white spittle had flown out of his mouth as she'd backed away.

'Please my picnic?' George was saying now, tugging at her arm.

'Not today, Munchkin.' She kissed the top of his head. 'It's nearly dark outside, look?'

'Aww.' He pouted, pushing his bottom lip out. Maisie felt a rush of pity for him, stuck in here with her all day. What was the point of living in the countryside if they couldn't explore the outdoors? Maybe Jan took him out, on the days she looked after him. Although somehow, Maisie doubted it. She suspected that Jan plonked him in front of the television most days. She pictured him in the dark, windowless home cinema in the basement, watching children's cartoons on the state-of-the-art screen. Or recorded church services, perhaps – sometimes, she heard hymn-like singing drifting through the passageways of the house.

'*Please* can we go my picnic?'

'Shall we go there in our imaginations?'

She set out two sheets of A4 and positioned her musical box pencil case in front of him. It was just as well that George liked drawing, or instructing her to draw. More and more, he was being brought to her during the day, as well as at nighttime.

George ignored his paper, but grasped the mechanism on the pencil case, winding it up to make the ballerina turn. The melody from *Swan Lake* tinkled in the quiet room.

Maisie drew the clearing in the trees, shading in the blue sky, the dark trees, and lighter patches on the ground to show the sunlight filtering through the branches.

'If you close your eyes, can you hear the river, rushing over the silvery grey rocks?'

George closed his eyes obediently, but his wiggling feet suggested a restlessness, a warning that he might not tolerate the drawing activity for much longer. Maisie tried to make her voice calm and soothing.

'Can you see the blue sky above, like when we lay down on our backs?'

'Silent trousers,' said George solemnly.

'That's right,' Maisie giggled. 'Just enough blue in the sky to make a pair of silent trousers. Or sailor's trousers, it is really.'

George's eyes flew open. Maisie realised her mistake, mentioning sailors.

'And can you smell the lovely piney smell?'

'Yes. Can we play pirate ships?'

Maisie suppressed a sigh. She had learned to go along with his sudden pivots in attention. Sometimes it was frustrating. But she could hardly blame him for being restless when they were stuck here in this room most of the day. She took out another sheet and began to draw a ship, blue-green waves cresting around its bow.

George brought his hand down on the paper with a smack. 'No – *play* it.'

Maisie cleared away the paper and pencils, piling them on the desk. Then she pulled the blanket off her bed and laid it out on the floor of the room, folding it at the front to make a bow, and at the back to make a stern.

'*Ahoy, me hearties!*' she exclaimed, forcing enthusiasm into her voice. One of her molars had been bothering her all day. And all of the night before.

George emitted a loud 'Eeeeee!' and jumped onto the blanket.

The game consisted of Maisie – the pirate captain – looking through a telescope (an empty loo roll tube) and pointing out sea monsters in the 'sea' (the carpet surrounding the blanket). George, the junior pirate, would then have to jump in and 'net them'. She made sure he did a lot of jumping in and out of the 'sea' – it helped him to burn off his energy.

Sometimes she would jump in too, and pretend to be an octopus or some other tentacled monster. Wrapping him up with her arms and legs and tickling him until he screeched and squealed.

She waved her loo-roll telescope around, already wondering how she'd entertain him once he was tired of the pirate game. They could play zoos again, she supposed. This involved drawing all the animals and propping the drawings up against the walls, and they would go round visiting each one. She and George would take turns to impersonate them. The angry silverback, defending his territory. The shy giraffe, with her long-lashed eyes.

Guiltily, she looked forward to bed time, when she could take some stronger painkillers for her tooth. And maybe two of her little white pills. Two pills wouldn't be enough to completely knock her out – she wouldn't risk that while George was asleep in the bed beside her. But it would be just enough to feel nice and cosy and calm. She'd been trying to cut down on them, to reduce them to just one per night. But she hadn't slept much, the night before, with her tooth. And if she had to entertain George all day tomorrow as well, she'd need a decent night's sleep. She'd try cutting down again once her tooth had stopped hurting.

George charged up to her. 'Do octopus arms!'

She wrapped him up tightly, making loud sucking noises, and George shrieked at the top of his voice.

Suddenly, the room was plunged into darkness. The power had gone out.

She heard George gasp.

'It's okay, Munchkin. It's okay. The power has just gone out for some reason.'

'Put on, put on!' he cried.

Maisie tried the light switch. Nothing.

She thought quickly. 'How about a story? I could tell you the story of *The BFG*. Or *Matilda*?' She'd read them to him enough times that she practically knew them by heart. He wouldn't know the difference, anyway. He wasn't even three yet, and just wanted to hear the sound of her voice.

'No! No no no no! No like it!'

She pulled him closer, feeling his heartbeat fluttering against her own chest.

This was bad. Sometimes, when George panicked, he held his breath until he passed out. The first time it had happened, Maisie had thought he'd died.

She had to keep him calm. But all the stories had gone out of her head.

'Two times two is four,' she began. It had come out of nowhere. Suddenly, she saw herself at the kitchen table with Mum, doing her maths homework. A plate of biscuits and a tumbler of juice at her side.

She felt him crane his head up, as if he was curious now, trying to see her face in the darkness.

'Come on, under the covers. Haven't you played night time maths before? I used to play it with Mama.'

'Mama?'

'Yes.' She lifted him into her bed and climbed in beside him. 'We'll go and visit her one day. She lives by the sea, and there are hobbity houses in her garden.'

She felt a sudden surge of longing for home. George pressed his face into her chest, as if he could feel it too.

'Two times three is six,' she said, squeezing all of the fingers of his left hand in turn, and the thumb of his right.

'Six,' he repeated.

'Two times four is eight.'

By the time they reached sixty-four, she felt his fingers relax, and his little body softened into hers.

She reached across to the dosette box on top of her bedside cabinet. Would she take one pill or two? Her tooth was still really sore. But if she managed with just one pill, it would be proof that she was managing to come off them.

Who are you kidding? You've been trying to come off them for three years now.

An intrusive thought. She'd learned to try and ignore these voices in her head. Mark had explained that they weren't helpful, that critical self-talk was something that we learn from our parents without realising it – we absorb their negative emotions like little sponges, and start to attack ourselves.

So what on earth was George absorbing from her?

She dropped a kiss onto the top of his head and squeezed her eyes tight shut. Mark had said she should try to replace her negative thoughts with positive ones.

I'm safe here and I'm recovering.

I'll be able to stop my medication when the time is right.

She decided to take both the pills.

45

TERESA

Northumberland
Now

George and I were setting up paints and paper at the kitchen table when an email pinged onto my phone. It was from the DNA testing company. I opened up the attachment to see columns of figures with a box at the bottom.

Probability of a grandparent/grandchild relationship: 2.4%

And then more wording below:

A 2.4% probability of relationship is considered an exclusion; no relationship can be demonstrated.

It felt like a physical blow.

'What's wrong?' I felt small, slightly sticky fingers, tapping my arm.

I hadn't realised, until that moment, how much I'd been

hoping that George was Maisie's child. That I'd somehow misremembered Maisie's flat stomach, and she'd been pregnant with him when she'd left, after all. That she'd had a life I didn't know about, and had gone on living that life, after leaving here.

But if not, what was this feeling? This feeling that I was inextricably linked with George. If that wasn't down to our DNA, some matching pattern spiralling inside our cells, what was it?

Did it make the other explanation – the past life explanation – more likely? Did it mean it was more likely that Maisie had died?

With great difficulty, I pulled myself together. 'Sorry, George. I'm okay. Shall we finish setting up the paints?'

My phone pinged again while I was helping George to fill jam jars with water for painting. It was Caroline this time, saying she'd come and pick George up at lunchtime if that was convenient.

I watched him over the next couple of hours, trying to commit him to memory. His teddy-bear groove, his pointy chin. His golden-brown hair, which would never stay in place. The energetic buzz of him, hopping on and off the chair, switching from one paint colour to the next. His wide-eyed questions about whether the green paint would taste like soup, if he ate it. Or if he would die again, if he drank the murky water in the jam jars.

I placed his painting on the sunlit windowsill to dry – two small figures riding on the back of a gigantic dog, its white fluffy tail streaming out behind them.

'Is that...'

'Beanie,' George confirmed. I turned to see him executing a perfect forward roll across the kitchen floor.

Caroline arrived at lunchtime, in a peacock-blue dress with a Peter Pan collar.

Her face was strangely expressionless when she said hello. She looked tired, her velvet hairband scraped back to reveal dark, slightly greasy roots.

'Did you get the email?' she asked. 'A negative result, like I said.'

'I know,' I said. 'Thank you so much, though. You've put my mind at rest.'

George came down the stairs, bumping his rucksack down behind him.

'Have you got all your bits and pieces, George?' asked Caroline. And then, to me: 'Thanks for looking after him.'

'Any time,' I said. 'Any time at all.'

'That's kind of you.' She put her hand on the front door handle.

'So it's still a mystery, isn't it?' I said, trying to strike up a conversation. 'Why he seemed to recognise this place.'

'Maybe he *was* here in a past life,' said Caroline. 'No DNA result could tell us that.'

'I suppose.'

'It'll always be a mystery.' There was a blankness in her words. No sparkling curiosity in her eyes any more. It was as if her mask had dropped.

'Would you like to stay for a coffee?'

'Thanks, but we've got to get going.'

No, no, no… this wasn't how it was supposed to end. I was supposed to become a bonus Granny.

I followed them out to Caroline's car. George climbed into the back seat, and she did up his seatbelt, then closed the door a little more forcefully than seemed necessary.

Panic flooded my body, hot and cold at once. I was letting

him go. I was letting her take him away from me. I might never, ever see him again.

'Keep in touch!' I said brightly, desperately. 'Do come and visit if you're up this way again!' What else could I say? 'I'm going to be in Nottingham in a few weeks, for a... I'm going to be visiting friends. Shall I look you up, while I'm there? I could drop you a text?'

'Lovely.' Caroline flashed a tight smile and raised her hand to wave as she got into the driver's seat.

George turned to me, his face heavy with sadness. He placed his hand flat on the window. I mirrored it with mine, the glass cold under my fingers. And then he mouthed two words as the car began to move away. They might have been 'Thank you,' or 'See you.'

But I was sure they were 'Love you.'

46

MAISIE

Killendreich
Four and a half years ago

The room was so dark that Maisie couldn't even see her hand in front of her face. There was no moonlight tonight, and not even a scattering of stars. Heavy cloud had rolled over the glen a few days ago and hadn't lifted.

The power had been switched off in their part of the house again. Maisie had noticed that it usually happened when George had been particularly noisy, jumping off furniture onto the floor, or making aeroplane or helicopter noises. The darkness would descend suddenly and completely, as if someone had dropped a cloth over a bird cage.

Or maybe it was because Jan had seen that she'd taken the wooden cross off the wall, when she'd dropped George back after lunch. She only brought him herself on days when neither Jock nor Mark was around. Usually, Maisie could hear the lighter tread on the stairs and she'd shove the cross back up there, above the bed. Today, she'd had to do it while

Jan screamed from the doorway – something about letting the devil in. George had shrunk down, covering his ears.

She didn't like to think of the cross, hanging there in the dark above their heads.

Usually, once the power was off, it was off for the night. When this happened, even if it was at five o'clock on a dark winter afternoon, she had to pretend it was time to go to sleep, to avoid all-out panic from George, or a breath-holding incident. So she'd learned how to keep him nice and calm, tucking him up close beside her, under the duvet. She would tell him to imagine that Bernie the dog was curled up beside them. And she would tell him stories, whispering them into his ear.

If they ran out of Roald Dahl tales or *Famous Five* stories, she'd tell him the stories her own mother had told her, about a made-up school called St Winifred's. She told him about the horrible Miss Agatha, who made the girls do cross-country running during thunderstorms, and the lovely librarian who used to supply hot buttered crumpets to those in need.

Tonight, she was just at the part where the girls were devouring their end-of-term midnight feast. She was beginning to drift off herself, and was half imagining that her mother was there, reading the stories to both of them.

But then she realised the voice wasn't her mother's. She could hear someone through the wall, and they weren't happy.

Were Mark and Jan arguing again?

With George still held against her chest, she wriggled closer to the air vent on the wall. He didn't wake, but he dug his fingers tighter into her fleece.

She could hear Mark's voice – calm and slightly patronising, like he was talking to a patient. 'You're jumping ahead of yourself. You've only been on that higher dose for a few days. Let's just take a breath and see how that goes.'

'But I'm not getting any better!' wailed Jan. 'I think it's this house. I can't leave, but I can't stay, either. Sometimes I think it's cursed. I can sense something – can't you? I can feel it coming through the walls, creeping in around the curtains at night. Rising up from under the floor.'

'You're spiralling, Jan. You really must resist getting sucked into that sort of thinking.'

There was a pause, and a loud sob from Jan.

'I know your faith is being tested,' said Mark. 'But you must stay strong. Think only of good things. The things we pray for will be given to us – wellness of body and spirit.'

He sounded so unlike himself that, for a moment, Maisie wondered if it was him at all, or there was another person in the room with them. But no... it was definitely Mark's voice. He was channeling weird priest energy, or something.

'I'm praying every day,' said Jan.

'And you need to pray *more*. The answer is to have *more* faith, not to start questioning things. And try to engage with the boy more. There's no harm in giving God a bit of a helping hand.'

'I *do* engage,' said Jan.

'You leave him in front of the television. When you're not sleeping, that is. Do you think that's what God would want?'

So Maisie had been right. She planted a defiant kiss on George's forehead. Although just for a moment she wondered if she *would* stick him in front of the television, sometimes, if that were an option.

'But the meds make me sleepy. And he's *exhausting*,' wept Jan. 'He won't sit still, but it's not just that. Sometimes, when he looks at me, it's like he can see right into me. It's like he *knows*... and he hates me for it.'

'Paranoia,' diagnosed Mark, sounding like himself again. 'The new higher dose of the quetiapine should help with that.' He cleared his throat. 'And try praying. Deeper, more frequent praying.'

'I've *been* praying,' Jan said. 'Trying to understand why I can't love him – our perfect boy. Our whole, unbroken boy. And I've realised that the problem isn't really him. The darkness in him comes from *her*. The problem is *her*.'

Maisie gasped. What a total bitch.

'You do love him, Jan,' said Mark, sounding tired. 'You just haven't bonded with him properly. It's a symptom of postnatal depression.'

Jan's voice rose in anger. 'How am I supposed to bond with him when *she's* here? He only wants *her*. That's what makes me doubt things. That's why –'

'I agree,' Mark cut in. 'I've decided I'm going to phase out Maisie's involvement.'

Maisie pulled George closer to her chest, holding her palm over his little ear. Holding her own breath so that she could hear better.

'I'm seeing some worrying behaviours in the boy,' said Mark. 'Which he displays after spending time with her. And yes, I think it may be interfering with the bond between you and George.' He paused and then continued, switching from his psychiatrist's voice to his holier-than-thou priest's voice. 'We thought we were doing the Christian thing, giving her a home and a purpose, but we have to think of the boy. I probably shouldn't say this, as a psychiatrist, but I think she's basically a person who lacks moral fibre. She can't muster up enough self-control to get well. She's still dosed up to her eyeballs, every day. Enough is enough. I'll make the necessary arrangements.'

Maisie had a sudden image of Mark as a chameleon, his lizardy eyes blinking, watching Jan carefully as she teetered on the edge of whatever madness this was.

'And you think she'll just leave quietly, do you? What if she takes him with her? Have you thought about that?'

'Then we would call the police,' said Mark. 'He's our child, remember. She has no right to take him anywhere.'

'He's our child *on paper*.'

'And in God's eyes, of course,' he added. 'But paper will be enough.'

'But what if she goes to the police?'

'And tells them what? Who are they going to believe – a psychiatrist, whose name is on the child's birth certificate? Or a drug addict with a history of psychosis?'

'We need a fresh start,' wailed Jan. 'Somewhere away from here. We could go to Wisconsin. I'll be better among my own family.'

'Jan,' said Mark. 'You have severe, disabling agoraphobia. You've barely left the house since we brought the baby home. How are you going to go halfway across the world to Wisconsin?'

'You could give me something to relax me. For the journey.'

'We have everything we need here. Try and have a little more faith.'

'Sometimes I think the best way would be for me to go back to God. George and I, together. Whole and unbroken. I could take him with me. It would save him so much suffering.' She paused, and then a sly note came into her voice. 'There are lots of ways.'

'Stop it, Jan. Just stop it.' He sounded angry now – more real. 'All I've *ever* done is try to make you happy. To give you what you wanted. Haven't you any idea what I've done for you? You're throwing it all back in my face.' He paused and began again more gently. 'Your baby died. It's the worst thing that could happen to anyone. But God has given us –'

'God has given us WHAT?' spat out Jan. 'A little whore's baby?'

'Jan...'

'I'm sorry, Mark. I'm so sorry. I didn't mean that. He's our little George, of course he is. Praise be to God for his unbroken body. Blessed be.'

'Blessed be,' repeated Mark. 'That's my girl. Positive thoughts only. And we'll try a higher dose of your meds this evening.'

Then Maisie heard a faint noise, a sort of electronic chirping noise. She'd heard it before, through the wall, from time to time, and had assumed it was some kind of alarm going off.

But then she heard Mark's voice. 'Mark speaking? Are you sure? Can't Bea deal with it?' Then there was a pause before he spoke again. 'Okay then. I'll come down tomorrow.'

Then his voice changed as he spoke to Jan. 'I've got to go down to Chesters. It's all kicking off. I'd better drive down tonight.'

The chirping sound had been a *landline phone*. Mark had taken a phone call. Here, at Inverkillen House.

Maisie gasped as she understood the enormity of what had happened.

There was a working phone line in the house after all.

But worse than that, more shocking... was that Maisie had believed – she had actually *believed* – that Mark had still been trying to get the phone line fixed *after three and a half years*.

'Will you be okay for a couple of nights?' Mark was saying. 'I'll get Jock to sort the meals and things. He'll bring George to you as usual, but maybe just for an hour or two, yes? Give you a bit of a break.'

'Of course,' said Jan, her voice calm now. 'George will be safe with me. In my Father's house are many rooms. I will come again, and will take you to myself. Wherever I am, there you shall be.'

Maisie stayed awake all night, making her plan.

The only reason she stayed here, like a prisoner in this damp, rotting house, was for George. He needed somebody proper to look after him, who was going to play with him and read to him, and not just put him in front of the television while they napped. He needed someone to cuddle him at night when the lights went out, and make sure he didn't stop breathing.

But now Mark was turning on her. He was talking about, what... 'Phasing out her involvement'?

And Jan was clearly a psycho, threatening to go back to God and to take George with her.

She had to get him out of here. Even if that meant social workers, and mental health settings, and all the things that Mark had darkly referred to.

There were a few problems, of course.

First, they were locked in. She'd need to find a way around that.

Next was the fact that they were literally in the middle of

nowhere. From her hazy memories of the journey here, the nearest phone signal was a good half-hour drive away. And it might take hours just to walk up the track to the nearest B road. She couldn't risk going to a farmhouse or cottage, even supposing there were any. Not when they might know Jan and Mark.

But maybe they'd be able to flag somebody down, get a lift to the nearest town. If she could make it back to Northumberland, and speak to Mum in person, perhaps she could make her understand.

Maisie felt that door – the one that she'd kept closed, in her mind, for so long – creak open a little. Her heart hammered with the enormity of it. She might fall through, step straight into nothingness.

She held George closer to her, tucking his warm head beneath her chin. This was for him. She had to be strong. She couldn't buckle.

The next problem was that she didn't have any proper shoes, and neither did George. They'd been locked in the boot room, only brought out if Jock was taking her and George out for a walk.

She had a pair of summer flip-flops that she'd packed three and a half years ago, and never worn. They'd have to do.

As for George, well, she'd just have to carry him. And she'd have to carry her rucksack, too, with enough snacks and water to last until they could get help. She felt weak, suddenly, at the thought of it, of how she'd actually manage.

And she wondered how she'd manage without her medication, and the painkillers she'd got into the habit of taking each night, since her teeth had been bad.

From nowhere, she had a wave of certainty that Mum

would help. She would book an emergency dentist appointment, and take her to the doctor. She'd make leek and potato soup and warm compresses and she would wrap Maisie in her arms and tell her that anything could be achieved if she just took one step at a time.

It was like the working phone line, shut away in the room behind the wall; the thing she most needed had always been there. She just hadn't been able to reach it, because of Mark.

She gulped in a sob. George stirred in her arms.

I love you, Mama. We're coming home.

47

TERESA

Northumberland
Now

I lay in Maisie's bed for two hours after George had left, watching the shadows move across the ceiling. The atmosphere in the house had thickened again. The silence filled my ears, shrill and insistent, like the buzz of a disconnected line.

Unease moved in waves across my skin, churned through my guts. It was the upset of George leaving, I told myself. I'd be better later, when Sunny came over to watch television.

Was there something here – a sense of presence?

I thought of Maisie's favourite mug, moving itself to the front of the cupboard, years ago now. A tiny breadcrumb, the merest hint of her, a trail that ended... nowhere.

And then I thought of all the strange things George seemed to know. I turned them over in my mind. The silent trousers. The theme to *Swan Lake*. The wallpaper and the

Hickory Dickory Dock book. The elephant door stop. Bernie the dog... or had it been Beanie?

Finally, I messaged Cheryl.

> George has left. DNA test says he's not related. But that makes it all even more strange. How did he know the things he knew?'

She replied almost immediately.

> Hi Hun. Huge goosebumps on reading your message. What RU thinking?

> What if Maisie did die here? What if her presence is still here in the house? What if she was trying to tell me something, through him?

An image came to mind of Sunny, raising his eyebrows in a gentle query.

Another message from Cheryl popped up.

> I've got a client at four but I could pop over quickly and take a look?

I felt like I'd contacted a plumber about a blocked toilet or a leaking tap.

When she arrived, a vision in a fluffy white jumper and a pink tulle skirt, she asked me to show her into every room. She lingered in Maisie's bedroom, touching the books in the bookshelf, the items of make-up still cluttering the desk. The bathroom also seemed to interest her. She leaned low over the bathtub and turned one of the taps off and on again. She opened the medicine cabinet and lifted a plastic bottle of paracetamol, giving it a little shake. In my bedroom, she stood in the middle and spun around slowly, looking up as if she was inspecting the ceiling for damp. She kept sighing and wincing, sucking air through her teeth.

'What do you think?' I asked, once we'd come downstairs into the hall.

'I'm not really getting anything except a whole load of sadness.' She shook her head. Then she glanced quickly over her shoulder. 'Although there's something about those stairs.' She gave a slight shudder.

'Oh! George said he remembers running up those stairs before he died. Trying to get away from someone.'

She nodded. 'That figures. It could be your anxiety about the stairs that I'm picking up, then.'

'When George said that, about dying in the house, I looked at Maisie's messages again. The ones she sent from Scotland. I've been trying to work out if they're really from her, or not. Some of them do sound like her, and others seem… odd. But then, there's the video message that the police forwarded on.'

'What was that?'

'When the police got involved – that was about four weeks after she went missing – they said they'd managed to make contact with her. They sent me a video from her. She said she was fine, and she was sorry she hadn't been in touch. How could she have sent that, if she died in this house, on the day she went missing?'

Cheryl frowned. 'Do you still have the video?'

I nodded, and brought it up on my phone.

There she was, my beautiful Maisie, smiling and waving.

'Hi Mum! I'm really sorry I haven't phoned. The phone line is down and there's no Wi-Fi. But everything is absolutely FINE. I promise. I'm okay. I'll be in touch properly soon, I promise.'

There was a glitch in the video, and then she re-appeared with her chin slightly dipped, as if the recording had stopped and started again. 'I love you. And I love you 2, 4, 8, 32, 64... And 128! Bye!' She lifted her fingertips and blew kisses towards the camera.

Cheryl asked me to replay it. She took the phone from me and held it close to her face. At the point where Maisie started blowing kisses, she paused the video and enlarged the image with her fingers.

'You're saying she sent this video on... what date?'

"The twentieth of August. She left for Scotland on the twenty-second of July, four weeks earlier.'

'And I did her nails before that, right? You brought her over to the care home after school.'

I nodded. 'You did them the day before she left.'

Compassion flooded her face. 'I'm so sorry, pet. Look at the nails.' She held out the phone. 'See them? They haven't grown out at all. I'd say this video was recorded no more than a few days after I did the nails.'

I swallowed hard. 'There's no way it could have been taken later?'

She shook her head. 'Not four weeks later. No way. I'm sorry.'

'Could she have got her nails done again?'

Cheryl shrugged doubtfully. 'See the little white flower on the nail of the ring finger? I did that, hun. I know my own work. Anyway, wasn't she supposed to be in the middle of nowhere, with no phone signal? I can't imagine there being many nail bars up there, in the wilds of Scotland.'

'Oh God. She's dead, isn't she?'

'I don't know.' She flicked a glance at her watch. 'Listen, I need to go. But tell me – where in the house do *you* feel Maisie's presence the most?'

'I don't know... her room?'

'Okay. Here's what I recommend. You go and sit there for a while. Carve her name into a candle and then light the candle. Speak to her. Say all of the things you wish you could say to her. Sit with your sadness and your loss. That's where you access your truth.'

She hugged me on the doorstep. 'Good luck, lovely. Let me know how you get on.'

When she'd gone, I went upstairs and took a rose-scented candle from Maisie's wardrobe, one that my mother had given her for Christmas. I remembered helping Mum to choose it from a stall at the care home's Christmas fair, giving her ten pounds from my purse to pay for it. With one of Maisie's kirby grips, I carved her name into the side of it, feeling foolish. But feeling strangely reckless, too. My heart began to race.

I didn't take the candle into Maisie's room, but into the kitchen – the place where we used to have all our chats. I lit it, placed it in the middle of the kitchen table and drew up a chair.

Say all of the things you wish you could say to her.

'I miss you so much,' I said out loud.

Silence, too much silence. It seemed to swallow up my words.

'I'll never, every stop loving you. I don't understand why you went away.'

The silence was broken by a low whoosh from the utility room – the boiler starting up.

'If I did something to make you go, then I'm sorry. I'm so

sorry I wish I could protect you from whatever has happened to you. I cannot bear to think of you alone or scared or in pain. Sometimes I wonder if you cried for me, when it was happening.'

Tears poured down my face, dripping off my nose and chin.

'Please come back to me, my darling. I cannot live without you. I just can't.'

My body began to shake, like it was holding all my grief at once – all of it, from every day of the last eight years. And the grief of all mothers and children, from every place and time, all separated eventually.

I thought of my mum, during her last few days of life. Weak and bald, incontinent and helpless. She'd cried for her own mother, as if she was the only one who could love her like that. And I, in turn, had longed for her – the calm, reassuring mother of my childhood – in those awful weeks and months after Maisie had gone. Generation after generation. Loss after loss, a howling black hole of absence.

Sit with it, Cheryl had said. But it was too much. It was going to break me, split me apart right down the middle.

I sat up straight, slowed my breathing and opened my eyes. It was okay, I told myself. I didn't have to do this. It was probably all nonsense anyway. I shouldn't have listened to Cheryl.

Straight ahead of me I could see the open doorway to the utility room. A pale wash of moonlight illuminated the tiles. There was a darker shape by the door, with a curved back like a crouching creature.

A chill moved down my back and my arms. Had I conjured up some... entity, some *thing*, with Cheryl's ritual? I wanted to get up, turn on the lights, blow out the candles, but my limbs were frozen.

It took a few moments for me to realise what the dark shape was. It was the elephant door stop, distorted by its own shadow. I almost laughed out loud at myself. But then two thoughts entered my head, almost simultaneously.

I thought of the first day George had come to the house with Caroline, how he'd asked to see the elephant door stop that I kept in the utility room. It had been one of the strange things that made me believe he was familiar with the house.

But... I had won the elephant door stop in a Mother's Day raffle at the care home – I had bought a strip of raffle tickets for Mum, and one for myself. It had been just after I'd had the utility room redone, because I remembered hoping that its wrought iron base wouldn't mark the new, gleaming white floor tiles.

Which had been six years ago. Two years after Maisie had gone missing. She had never seen the elephant door stop. She had never even known of its existence.

I folded forward, my heart collapsing.

George wasn't Maisie. Of course he wasn't. He wasn't her son, as the DNA test had proven. And she wasn't communicating through him, either. It was all nonsense.

I'd been played. Someone was using me, taking advantage of my grief. My impossible, unmanageable grief. The grief that made other mothers shrink and turn away when they saw me. What was it Caroline wanted – money? If so, why hadn't she asked for it?

I picked up my phone, hands shaking. I dialled Caroline's number, no longer caring what she thought of me. I would demand answers. Threaten the police, if she didn't give me them. There was nothing to lose now, was there?

But I got a recorded voice saying that the number I'd called wasn't recognised.

Sitting there as the room darkened, I tried to work it out.

Nothing made sense. But there were two things I had to accept.

George – if his name even was George – was nothing to me.

And Maisie, however much I longed for her, was gone. She was never coming back.

48

MAISIE

Killendreich
Four and a half years ago

There was a window in the bathroom, high up between the sink and the toilet, looking out onto the back of the property. And there was a small area of flat roof below and a bit to the left – for one of the storage rooms near the kitchen, she thought. She could probably drop down onto the flat roof and use the drainpipe to scramble down to the ground. But George, even though he was a little monkey, always climbing everything, wouldn't manage that.

Perhaps she should wait until the next time Jock took them on a walk.

But then Jan's sly voice came into her head.

I could take him with me. There are lots of ways.

Maisie had read, in old boarding school stories, about people tying sheets together to climb out of windows.

George was still asleep, lying on his back with a hand curled up by his face. She pulled some spare sheets out from the wardrobe in her room. She used her craft scissors to cut them into wide strips, and tied them together with knots she'd learned long ago, in Girl Guides.

George's rucksack, the one he kept his toys and his drawing things in, would have to do as a harness.

It was five in the morning, the sky just starting to get light, when she woke him and manoeuvred his sleepy limbs into the straps. She fed the sheet-rope through the straps and fastened the clasp at his chest. She tugged at it as hard as she could, glad that it seemed to be made of very sturdy plastic. Then she used the sheet-rope to lift him, experimentally, to check the rucksack would take his weight. Wide awake by this point, he threw back his head and laughed.

'Again! Again! Fly me.'

Kneeling down in front of him, she explained what she was going to do – they were going to fly out of the house because they were going on an adventure.

She had to stand with one foot on the edge of the sink, and one on the closed toilet seat, to lift him onto the window sill. He looked up at her with wide, trusting eyes as she lowered him down.

'That's it, Munchkin.'

And then, a couple of feet from the ground, the clasp of the rucksack gave way. George made a squealing noise as his arms slithered out of the straps. She heard the sickening thunk of his head hitting the scrubby ground. Followed by an outraged wail.

Maisie scrambled out of the window and swung herself down onto the flat roof. Then she shimmied herself down the drainpipe, jumping the last few feet when the pipe began to pull away from the wall. She landed beside George, wrenching her ankle.

'I'm sorry! I'm sorry!'

She could see that it was the stitching attaching the clasp that had given way, not the clasp itself. But duh! She should have thought of that.

There was a cut on George's cheekbone, and there were bits of gravel and mud in it.

But Maisie could deal with that – she had come equipped. She reached into her own rucksack for the baby wipes she'd packed.

'There we go,' she said, cleaning the graze. 'There we go. Please be quiet as a mouse, Munchkin. Remember, our adventure is secret?'

George regarded her reproachfully, using his anorak sleeve to wipe a trail of snot from his nose. Maisie pulled out another baby wipe to clean him up and then hoisted him up onto her hip.

Her plan was to walk through the forest, to stay off the track itself. Mark might have been called away to Chesters, but Jock was still around. He might realise that they'd gone and come after them. But she hadn't reckoned on the sheer number of poky branches, the small stones, the boggy bits, the broken twigs underfoot. Within minutes, her feet were bleeding in the flimsy flip-flops, and there was a shooting pain in her ankle from where she'd wrenched it.

'Take a breath, my love. Then just take one step at a time.'

Maisie could almost hear her mother's voice in her head. Although this was a bit more of a challenge than doing her maths homework.

She hadn't realised how cold it would be. She stopped to pull the hood of George's hoodie up – his cheeks were pink and cold, and his nose was running again.

The muscles in her arms were burning. She tried carrying

him piggy-back style instead, but it was just as exhausting. It didn't help that he kept trying to wriggle off, that he didn't care that he didn't have shoes on.

'Want to *run*,' he kept saying, and she'd have to haul him higher up onto her back.

They reached the B road just after ten o'clock. George had finished off the snacks she'd packed. She had to hold him firmly by the hand to stop him flying off into the road.

She let a tractor go past, in case the farmer was a friend of Mark's. They stepped back into the cover of the trees at the side of the road. George watched the tractor drive past, his little mouth drooping in disappointment.

Ten minutes later, a Post Office van approached. Maisie lifted a hand to flag it down, hardly believing their luck as it slowed to a halt. She gave the driver a story about her car having broken down, a mile or two back, which he seemed to accept.

As they drove towards the town, the driver chatted with George about his van, while Maisie watched her phone.

As soon as one signal bar came up, she phoned her mother. When there was no answer, she keyed in a text.

Coming home. Bringing George. Need help Mum. PLEASE be there.

49

CAROLINE

Retford
Now

Caroline arrived back at Malham Manor with a splitting headache. George had been restless on the drive from Northumberland, twisting and wriggling in his car seat and making strange moaning noises. He'd kept saying he needed the toilet, no matter how many times she'd told him to just hang on. She'd reached around and shoved his iPad into his hands, almost swerving into the wrong lane as she did so.

'Roblox!' she'd snapped. 'Just bloody play it, and shut the freak up!'

Now, he sprinted upstairs as soon as she opened the front door. She heard the bathroom door slam. What a drama queen that boy was sometimes. He'd try the patience of a saint, she told herself. She took a deep, self-compassionate breath and released her shoulders.

Mark was in the living room. He looked rumpled and handsome and a little sad. He was wearing cords and a heavy-knit Barbour jumper that made him look like he'd stepped out of a country clothing catalogue.

She hardened her heart. 'George is back. So can I have the rest of the money now, please?' He'd transferred a hundred thousand that morning, before she'd left, and had promised the rest when she brought George back.

'I'll have to arrange a CHAPS transfer,' he said, holding up his hands as if he was expecting her to kick off. 'There's a daily limit for online banking. I can do it over the phone.'

Caroline nodded, suddenly exhausted. She kicked off her shoes and slumped onto the sofa.

He dialled a number on his phone and strode around the room, giving instructions to a telephone banking representative on the other end.

'My voice is my password,' she heard him say, twice. And then a few moments later: 'Thanks so much for all your help, Janice. Have a good day, now.'

'When will it be in my account, then?' demanded Caroline.

'It'll be Monday now.'

'Okay.' She gave an exaggerated sigh.

'Rough day, PQ?' His voice was almost tender. 'Me too, if I'm honest. How about a gin and tonic?'

She realised that she was *longing* for a gin and tonic. Mark made really good strong ones, with loads of ice and just a dash of tonic. She nodded and followed him through to the kitchen.

'Why are you being nice?'

He shrugged and sighed. 'If you want out, Caroline, you want out. And agreeing a one-off payment and a clean break is a decent way of doing it. Better than involving lawyers and separation agreements and all that stuff. With us not being married, the legal position wouldn't be straightforward, and the lawyers would soon have us at each other's throats. We'd spend thousands on fees alone.'

He chopped a slice off a lemon and slid it into her glass.

'You really didn't need to force my hand, with all this nonsense about George.' He handed her the glass. 'What's the point of making someone stay? If one party feels it's over, then it's over. That's why I've never really believed in marriage. It's a sort of legal prison.'

He gave a sad, reptile-like smile. For a horrible moment, she wondered if he'd poisoned the gin and tonic. If it would be easier for him just to get rid of her. He'd got rid of Maisie, somehow, hadn't he?

She put down her drink, the glass thunking the worktop so hard that she thought it might shatter. 'What did you do, Mark? What did you do with Maisie?'

He was silent for such a long time that she wondered if he was going to answer at all. 'She had an unwanted pregnancy. She agreed to let me and Jan adopt her baby.'

Caroline nodded. 'I thought it was something like that. You were clever, the pair of you, the way you faked Jan's pregnancy. The hyperemesis gravidarum, and all that. It was an excuse so that she could lie low up in Scotland, wasn't it? I can't believe you had me slaving away making all those white meals, though. I put a lot of love into making those, you know.'

It hadn't exactly been *love*. She had always found Jan quite annoying, if she was honest. It had been Caroline's raw attraction to Mark that had fuelled the 'friendship' between the two couples, even when Peter had still been around.

'Jan and I... our own baby died.'

Caroline blinked. She hadn't seen that coming. 'I'm... I'm sorry.'

'And you needn't worry. Maisie's out there somewhere, living her own life. We're not in touch any more. She used the payment we gave her to start a new life, away from her mum. She found her... intense. Suffocating.'

Caroline frowned. 'So why are you giving me the money I want, then? Why not just let me reveal all to Teresa?'

'We had to do the adoption off the books.' He waved a hand, as if it was merely a matter of paperwork. 'Technically not strictly legal. It would be an inconvenience, to have to explain it all to the authorities. And I could get struck off. The GMC don't look too kindly on psychiatrists with criminal convictions. It's just a whole world of pain where I don't particularly want to go. And the money – well, we have been effectively married for the last five years. You've helped me out with George. I suppose I've taken you for granted. It always takes two, doesn't it, for a relationship to fail?'

Caroline stared at Mark. Had she misjudged him? The problem was there had always been two Marks in her mind. This kindly, capable, strong one that stood before her now in his Barbour jumper. And the other one. The one who showed through in flashes and glimpses but disappeared if you tried to look too hard. Like a shape in the mirror, seen from the corner of your eye in a dark room. She had never been able to get the measure of him.

But the good thing was she no longer needed to try.

'I hope you'll be happy.' He held out his own glass to chink hers. 'Are you really sure about this? We'll miss you, you know.'

50

TERESA

Northumberland
Now

'I think it's encouraging,' said Sunny, pausing the television for the fifth time. 'The elephant doorstop development, I mean. And the fact that Caroline has ditched her phone.'

He always found a way to be upbeat. Sometimes it drove me mad. Mostly, though, it made me feel safer with him than with anyone else.

'How can you possibly think that?'

We were sitting on the sofa together, part way through an old episode of *The Great British Bake Off*. Sunny had brought a 'picnic' with him, since I hadn't thought I could eat anything. He'd brought flatbreads and cheese and juicy red grapes. A box of flaky samosas and two chocolate eclairs.

'It's proof that it's been a scam of some kind,' he went on. 'I didn't believe that George was channelling Maisie, or had been Maisie, or whatever it was they were saying. But the elephant door stop proves it – because that wasn't within

Maisie's knowledge. So we are further on than before. We have a piece of definite information.'

'But what was the scam? They never asked for any money, or anything like that. And Caroline agreed to my idea of the DNA test, which suggests she had nothing to hide.'

'When George first arrived, he knew things that he could only have learned from Maisie – that's a simple fact, yes?'

I nodded. At least he wasn't disputing that, implying it was all in my head.

'Then he – or somebody he was close to – must have spent time with her. Like I was saying before – she could have worked for the family, or nannied for them, or something like that.'

We both sat back on the sofa, our heads laid back so we were staring up at the ceiling. I tried to force my brain to come up with scenarios – any scenario at all – where any of what had happened might make sense.

'If Maisie had been his nanny, why would Caroline bother following it all up?' I said eventually. 'George's "memories", I mean. It would be obvious where they'd come from.'

'Maybe Maisie was in George's life before Caroline. From when his mother – Jan? – was alive.'

'But Mark was always around, wasn't he?'

'Could it have been...' Sunny paused and bit his lip. 'Well, hmm. What if Maisie was...'

'Ugh!' I sprang upright on the sofa. 'What if Maisie was some kind of secret lover? Is that what you were going to say? God, Sunny, she was only seventeen.'

I put *Bake Off* back on, trying to drive the images out of my head. But after ten minutes of watching the contestants make gravity-defying sponge constructions, Sunny picked up the remote and paused it again.

'Now that Caroline has cut off contact, the "bonus granny" plan seems to be off the table. So I think we should change tack. I think it's worth putting a call in to the police.' Sunny's face was earnest, his cheeks tinged with pink. 'You can tell them about all this – that we believe George may have spent time with Maisie. That the family has contacted you, with the aim of manipulating you in some way.'

I sighed. 'But if we suggest she was employed by the family, or something like that, they'll just see that as proof of their theory – that she chose to go missing. That she set up another life for herself.'

'You can also tell them what Cheryl said about the video of Maisie – that it was recorded around the time she left for Scotland, and not four weeks later. That points to foul play, doesn't it? And at the very least, the police might question Caroline and Mark. They might slip up. You never know.'

'How can they question them, though? Caroline's phone isn't working any more. And we don't even know where they live.' I'd pored over the DNA results report for contact details, but only Caroline's email address was shown.

'The police will be able to find them. She was seen at the hospital, wasn't she, for her concussion? They'll have an address for her.'

I picked up my phone and stared at it. I still had DI Strachan's number in my contacts list. I'd used it several times over the years, asking for updates, or passing on what I thought were leads.

Such as the time somebody from a public library in Fort William had seen one of my missing posters and phoned my number, saying she thought she'd seen a girl fitting Maisie's description, around the time she went missing.

Or the time a man had called from a woollen mill shop in

Skye, one rainy morning in March, four or five years ago. He said that Maisie had been in the shop, just minutes before. He had been so convincing, describing her in exact detail, that I'd got in my car and driven up there. When I arrived, seven hours later, the shop owner gave me strange looks, saying she knew nothing about it. Some kind of hoax, she suggested. She offered me a free cup of tea and scone in the café, and recommended a B&B where I could stay the night.

The DI's number always went to voicemail. Every time, I'd get a call back from somebody in the team, saying that they would look into it.

'I'll call in the morning,' I said. 'It's late.'

'I should go.' He heaved himself to his feet.

'Sunny...'

STOP, said a voice in my head.

'What is it, my ...' He cleared his throat. 'What's up?'

He'd been about to say, 'My love.' I could see it in his face.

'I just don't want to be alone,' I said. 'What if I get that terrible feeling again?'

'The feeling about all the mothers and daughters?'

I nodded, no longer caring if I seemed nuts. 'Would you stay?'

Sunny never stayed – not since the very early days after Maisie disappeared, when he'd sat awake every night on the sofa, watching my phone so that I could sleep.

So it was strange that it seemed like the most natural thing in the world to climb the stairs together, and head to my bedroom. I used the bathroom, brushed my teeth and got into my pyjamas, but he stayed fully dressed. We got under the duvet, and he encircled me in his arms. My cheek rested against the textured wool of his jumper, my face rising and falling with his breath.

A feeling of peace – impossible as that was – flooded through me.

I relaxed all my muscles. I breathed from my belly, instead of high in my chest. I allowed myself to drift.

And then, like some kind of creature from the bottom of a pond, something slid free and swam straight across the back of my mind.

Lying very still in Sunny's arms, I turned my mind's eye around, so that I was looking straight into myself. Into a memory.

I was lying on someone's bed, in my university halls at Leeds.

Janet. It was Janet's room. A girl I hadn't thought about in years. She'd been studying medicine, not psychology like me, but we both sang in the chapel choir.

I was lounging on her bed, sucking a Strepsil, while she stood in front of her wardrobe in her underwear, pulling the hangers apart, looking for something to wear.

We were getting ready for a party. A group of boys – Joel, my flaky ex-boyfriend, Jan's boyfriend, Michael, and their two other flatmates – were going off travelling for the summer. Jan was going home to Scotland. I would be working in Woolworths on the high street, back at home in Chester-Le-Street.

I allowed my mind's eye to travel around the room.

There was a radiator under the window – one of those big clunking ones, like in a school classroom. She'd hooked a small drying rack to the top of it, pairs of her pants and socks hanging there to dry. Nike socks. She always wore Nike socks.

There was a wooden crucifix on the wall by her bed, with a twisted lead figure of a sad-looking Jesus.

And beside it, a framed picture. It showed a dark old

house in the middle of some trees, the name scrawled on the corner in black charcoal.

'It's a bit grim, your place,' I said, teasingly. 'Like something from a Brothers Grimm fairytale.'

'Thanks a bunch.' Janet could be a bit brittle sometimes. Laughing one minute, sulking the next.

'Have you found anything yet? Something nice and summery.'

It had been a rainy May and June, no lying about on blankets on the university lawns. Revision had been done in the library, rain drumming on the roof. And now I'd come down with tonsillitis for the third time that year – I'd spent the morning at the student health centre trying to get antibiotics.

'You'd better borrow some of my make-up too,' Janet said. 'You look like one of the cadavers up at the medical school.'

And then the memory slithered away again, disappearing into the murk at the far reaches of my mind. I kept very still, eyes closed, and tried to capture it again. But it had gone.

But now... now I couldn't move. Something was over my face, suffocating me. Something was gripping me, tightening around my limbs like the coils of a snake.

It gripped tighter and tighter, closer and closer.

I was going to die. I was...

Dreaming?

With a huge effort, I popped my eyes open. Nobody was suffocating me – it was just Sunny's grey jumper, my face still pressed against it. Just his arms, close around me. I gasped in a lungful of air and sat upright.

'It's okay,' said Sunny. 'You've had a nightmare, that's all.'

He reached out his arms, and I sank into them again. Felt his hand cradle the back of my head.

'Shush now... shushhhh.'

I could hear the sound vibrating through his chest.

Suddenly, I thought of the times Maisie had crept into my bed as a small child, entwining her limbs around me so tight, as if she wanted to climb right inside my body. Wasn't that what we all really wanted? To know another person as well as we knew ourselves?

And to be known, inside and out? My hand wandered to Sunny's waist, as if it wanted to slide under his jumper, to feel the warmth of the skin there.

STOP...

I felt that grinding sensation again. Like a drill hitting metal.

I pulled my hand back. 'Perhaps you should sleep on the sofa.'

51

MAISIE

Killendreich
Four and a half years ago

The driver of the Post Office van dropped them off at the petrol station in Killendreich.

Still no reply from Mum.

Maisie fretted. What if she couldn't reach her at all? What if she was away on holiday, or something? Although Mum never went on holiday, not with the hobbity houses to look after.

She hoped that Mum still kept a spare house key under the flower pot by the front door. Her own keys seemed to have gone missing. She'd turned over her room that morning, looking for them.

Maisie went to the ATM. Her card wouldn't work. She checked the expiry date – two and a half years ago. How could she have been so stupid?

She had twelve pounds and forty-eight pence in her purse.

It was all going to be impossible. She wondered if she'd better just go to the nearest police station. Then she remembered Mark's comments about kidnapping. She thought about how George had no shoes.

'I hungry,' said George in a whiny voice. The excitement of the adventure had waned long ago, minutes after the final cereal bar.

They went into the mini supermarket on the high street. Heart racing, Maisie stuffed a bunch of snacks – sandwiches, muffins, water – into George's rucksack and left without paying. Well, they needed to eat, didn't they? She told herself that she could come back one day, one day in the future when she was safe again, and repay them.

They waited at the bus stop. If they could get to Perth, perhaps they could hitch rides down south. Or would that be too obvious a route? Maisie kept looking around her. She thought of the sheet-rope, still hanging out of the window at Inverkillen House.

The bus – a coach, with soft, upholstered seats – was heavenly, even if the ticket had used up almost all her money. George – who had thankfully been allowed to travel for free – was enchanted, and Maisie wondered if he'd ever actually travelled on a bus before. He'd spent most of his short life holed up at Inverkillen House, as far as she could tell. He was up on his knees like a meerkat, looking out of the window, before he suddenly yawned and curled up, laying his head on her knee.

Soon, she realised that she was feeling unwell. Her right hand was shaky, and she felt queasy with the rocking motion of the bus. As her brain swelled and throbbed inside her skull, her mind wandered to the little white pills she'd left behind at Inverkillen House. She'd known she would have to manage without them, because she'd need to stay awake and alert, but now, she wished she'd brought them. Even just half of one pill might have settled her system a bit.

Then the stomach cramps started, like a hand gripping and twisting her guts. George woke up with renewed energy, and started to wander up and down the aisle between the seats. A couple of old ladies looked round at Maisie, disapproving. She had to grab him and hold him on her lap as he wriggled, kicking the back of the seat in front.

'George, please,' she pleaded. He looked back at her sorrowfully and kept kicking. He seemed incapable of sitting still.

'You're a pest,' she muttered, through gritted teeth. 'A terrible pest.'

When they arrived at the bus station in Perth, she had to rush into the public toilets.

'Maisie not well,' came little George's voice from outside the cubicle. She thought of him, standing on that dirty floor in his socks, and willed her guts to stop churning.

It took nearly two hours, but they managed to hitch a lift with a shaven-headed lorry driver who was heading down to Hull. Maisie didn't like the way he looked at her as she climbed in with George. But what choice did she have?

He eyed her up and down. 'Running away from boyfriend?' His voice sounded Eastern European, his tone mildly amused.

'Visiting my mother,' she said primly. She could feel moisture beading at her hair line. A sweaty, prickly feeling down her back.

'Mama,' confirmed George. He looked tiny in the middle seat, swinging his dirty socked feet.

'Boyfriend hit you?' queried the lorry driver, taking a long drag from his cigarette.

'No,' she said. 'My boyfriend is meeting us there.'

It occurred to her that she could message Ally. Except that he hadn't bothered to message her in literally years. He was probably still in the US. And who knew what he would do, anyway? He might get straight on the phone to Mark.

Perhaps, if she could borrow the driver's phone, she could log on to Instagram or Snapchat. She could find people on there and message them, could ask for help.

Kaylee? Was she still slogging away at Tesco? Singing in the pub on a Thursday night? Her baby would be four now, would be starting school soon.

Annabelle Punch? Absolutely no way. A shudder moved through her body at the mere thought of that sly, smug bitch. And she would be away at university now, with her top grades. Having June balls and black-tie dinners and probably watching boat races and stuff.

Maisie had never felt so alone. So left behind. She kissed the top of George's head and gave him the phone to play with. It might keep him still for five minutes.

At a quarter to five, a text message arrived from her mother. George held up the phone to show her.

> Ok. I'll try and be there. I'm driving up from Milton Keynes so you may get there first.

Her heart leapt. And then began to sink, slowly. It was hardly the joyous response she'd been hoping for.

Near Rosyth, she had to ask the driver to pull over in a lay-by off the dual carriageway. Mortified, she squatted behind the truck, her jeans pulled down to her ankles, to release a violent stream of diarrhoea.

A passing van sounded its horn in five short bursts. Moments later, someone wound down their window to shout something.

'Hurry up!' shouted her own lorry driver from the cab. And then something in another language. Maisie had a sudden fear that he would drive off and leave her. Drive off with George.

'I'm coming, I'm coming.' A wave of dizziness came as she stood upright. 'Just one more minute. Please.'

She was pulling down her jeans again, ready for another explosion, when she heard the rumble of the lorry's engine starting up. It began to lurch forward.

'George!' she screamed, trying to pull her jeans back on, and losing her balance so that her bum landed on the ground, only just missing the pile of mess.

The lorry stopped to let her back on. 'Only joking,' said the driver, tossing her a half-full bottle of Coke.

They had to stop again at a petrol station near Dunbar, where there was a toilet around the back. It didn't look as it had been cleaned in months and she had to hold her breath before she could force herself to go in there. Afterwards, she could barely summon the strength to climb up into the driver's cab.

'Poor, poor,' said George, frowning and pressing his hand onto hers.

'Thank you, Munchkin. I'm okay.' She thought how terrible she must look, her hair drenched in sweat now.

Finally, they parted company with the lorry at a service area near Berwick. After using the bathroom, Maisie texted her mother.

Mum, can you pick us up? We're at the services near Berwick.

The reply took ten minutes to come through.

I'm stuck in traffic. See you at home when I can.

But Maisie had a plan. Mum had emergency cash hidden inside a folding chessboard in the sideboard at home. Maisie went into the shop to ask the lady behind the till for the number of a local taxi company.

George seemed to enjoy the taxi ride enormously. He stared out of the window, watching everything as it went past.

They had to wait for five minutes at the level crossing near Lucker.

'Why we have to waiting?' he piped up.

'Because a train's coming, Munchkin. The cars have to wait so the train can come through. If you listen hard, you might be able to hear the tracks rumbling.'

Maisie lowered the window for him, and he stuck out his head. He gasped as the train approached and rushed past, wisps of gold-brown hair lifting from his forehead.

They continued on, driving past fields, farmhouses, a little development of pristine white new-builds.

'Nearly home,' she whispered to George. 'Nearly home.'

'*When* are we?' demanded George, trying to undo his seatbelt.

'Look out and see if you can see it. There are little wooden houses in the garden, with special round doors. Little hobbity houses.' She felt tears stinging her eyes, and suddenly felt as if she was about three years old. 'That's where my Mama lives.'

'Mama,' repeated George. 'In there?' He pointed to a tumbledown barn.

'Not yet...' Maisie said.

He lifted his hand again when they passed a children's playground with a wooden play fort. 'There?'

'Not yet...' She patted his knee.

'Now, keep your eyes out when we turn into this road...'

'Is it here?'

'Yes it is, baby,' she said, taking it all in. The house looked as familiar to her – as right – as if she had never left it. 'Yes it is.'

52

TERESA

Northumberland
Now

'I'm sure DI Strachan will call you back soon,' said Sunny, putting tea and toast on the kitchen table in front of me. He'd spent the night on the sofa while I'd been upstairs, lying awake and fretting.

'Probably.' I tried to inject some positivity into my voice.

He pulled his laptop towards him and began typing. 'I've been searching for Caroline's business. I've found this one – "Queen of Puddings". Is this her?'

He tilted the laptop towards me. Caroline's smug face, beneath a white chef's hat, beamed out from the 'About Us' page.

'We can show this to DI Strachan, when we speak to him.'

'I guess.'

'We need to collate as much information as we can find, on Caroline and Mark, so we can give them the best chance of finding them. I'm also working on another angle. What if we could find the house George was talking about? The one where the wallpaper is exactly the same as in Maisie's room. Now *that* would be interesting.'

'If that house even exists. Like you said, Caroline was probably priming him.'

Our roles seemed to have reversed. I was the one picking holes in everything now, while his eyes were shining with purpose. He picked up a piece of toast, stared at it like it might contain the answers we needed. 'I think we assume for the moment that it does exist. Some of George's memories must be real. Remember how affected he was, when Cheryl did the visualisation with him?'

'I suppose so.'

'It seems like too much of a coincidence that the wallpaper happened to be exactly the same. It looks old-fashioned. Not the sort of thing you could buy these days.'

'Not unless you could find the odd roll on eBay or something. It's an old Laura Ashley print from way back. Vintage, probably. It's been there since I was a little girl, when my granny owned the house.'

'What if...' Sunny typed something into his laptop. 'The wallpaper in George's house was custom made? So that a room would *look like* Maisie's room?'

A small shiver went through me. It was creepy, somehow, to think of someone going to those lengths. 'How would that help us?'

'We could search up all the companies that sell custom-made wallpaper in the UK.'

'And?'

He smiled excitedly. 'I'll show you.'

Sunny spent a few minutes setting up a free email address under Jan's name: 'jan.jackson1971@freemail.com'.

Something stirred at the back of my mind. My university friend, Janet, looking through her wardrobe while I lay on the bed.

Was it possible...?

Janet's surname had been something posh and double-barrelled. I couldn't remember exactly what. Surely she would have kept that name, even if she'd married, rather than becoming... *Janet Jackson*?

We took a photograph of a section of the wallpaper in Maisie's room and uploaded it.

Then Sunny emailed twenty-four different companies with the same message.

> *A few years ago you made up an order of wallpaper based on the design shown in the attached photo. I am looking to order some more, because the wallpaper has been damaged in a flood. I wondered if you still have the previous order on your system so that I can get an exact match? It will have been under my name or possibly my husband's. Jan or Mark Jackson.*

Half an hour later, I received a call.

'Yes, we have this on our system.' The woman sounded neutral. Bored, even. 'How many rolls would you like?'

'Oh, that's wonderful news!' I said, in the wavering voice of a posh, older lady. 'Five rolls, please!'

I glanced up at Sunny. He had his hand over his mouth, trying not to laugh.

'I'll just get my debit card. Hold on. I've left it upstairs, silly me.' My plan was to leave a long, awkward silence, so she'd be eager to get me off the phone and would give me the information I wanted. I got up and began walking up the stairs, imagining I was going up to the third floor of my vast country house.

Vast country house...

I thought of that picture on Janet's bedroom wall, all but forgotten until it had popped up in my mind the other day – of a dark, gabled house with a name scrawled in the corner. It had begun with the letter 'I', I was pretty sure. A Scottish name, for a Scottish house.

Inver something...

Suddenly, I could hear George's breathy whisper in my head, his complaint about the damp smell of the hallway in Cheryl's visualisation:

In the killing house...

George almost always mispronounced 'th' sounds as 'v' sounds. Had I mentally corrected him, without realising? Had he pronounced the first two syllables, in fact, correctly?

Inver... killing house

I walked down the stairs. And then up again, heart hammering. Finally, I said, 'Oh – and can I just check you still have the correct address on file? You might have our Retford house on file, but I want it posted straight up here to Scotland.' I swallowed, and moistened my lips. 'To Inverkillen House.'

On the other end of the line there was a stifled yawn, followed by the noise of fingers tapping on a keyboard. 'I've got an Inverkillen House, near Killendreich?'

'Wonderful,' I scribbled down the postcode as she read it out. 'That's the one.' I sat down on the top step, trying to catch my breath.

'I'm so sorry, but could I call you back in a few moments? I just need to locate my debit card. I'd lose my head if it wasn't screwed on.'

I turned to Sunny, my body shaking with adrenaline.

He laughed, the excited shout of a little boy. 'I can't believe it! We did it!'

He held out his arms. Breathless, giddy with finally making some progress, I walked down the steps to him, let him pull me to his chest.

Some wonderful chemical cocktail was flowing through my veins. I could feel my skin tingling. A fluttering sensation low down in my body. I held his upper arms, feeling the swell of his muscles under my hands. I closed my eyes.

And then...

STOP

The shock of cold water, filling nose and throat and lungs.

Blue-grey fingers, poking out from a scrubby pile of undergrowth.

I pulled myself away from Sunny. 'What have you got on for the rest of today?'

'I'm driving up to Inverkillen House with you.'

53

MAISIE

Northumberland
Four and a half years ago

The key *was* under the flower pot by the front door. And there was still spare cash in the chessboard – more than enough to pay the taxi driver. He drove off with a casual wave, unaware of the miracle he'd just performed.

He'd brought her home.

And the house smelled of home. Of sun-warmed wood and clean laundry and the buttery scent of baking. Maisie sank with relief onto the living room couch, pulling George close beside her.

Everything was going to be okay. Mum would be here soon. In person, Maisie could make her understand. She'd go back to being normal again.

And yes – *Mum* could speak to Mark and Jan about the arrangements for George. She'd sort it all out, speak to Citizens Advice or a family solicitor. Maybe they could... what was it?... share custody, or something. There'd be no need for social services, or any of that. A sense of comfort flooded her body, almost as if she'd taken one of her pills.

But George was desperate to see around the entire house. Her ankle throbbed as she hauled herself to her feet and showed him around.

In the kitchen, she popped him on the counter to look out of the window.

'You can see the sea! See?'

'See, see.' He peered curiously.

'Over that way, there's a castle on the hill, see? And if you look out there – far away in the distance – there's an island? It's called Lindisfarne Island. And there's something called a causeway, which is like a road out to the island. But some of the time, at high tide, the road is underwater. So you can't drive on it then.'

'Only *sometimes* a road.' George nodded slowly. His brain was like a little sponge, she'd noticed, storing up useless facts.

'That's right.' She rummaged in the cupboard, trying to find her favourite mug, which had the word 'Maisie' surrounded by pink hearts. Surely Mum hadn't thrown it away? But no – there it was, right at the back.

George clambered off the kitchen counter, wincing when his feet reached the floor. His socks were dirty and one of them had a huge hole in it. She'd need to put him in the bath and wash him, see if he needed any plasters.

'Can I see *all* of de Mama house?'

Maisie sighed. Her tea would have to wait until later.

George wanted to see the utility room first. He crouched down next to an elephant door stop and patted it tentatively. It was an awful, ugly thing. Mum must have been given it as a present or something. He made an elephant noise, looking up at Maisie for validation. She nodded solemnly and made an elephant noise too.

Back in the hall, he took the stairs in one go, shooting up like he was rocket-propelled.

In her own room, George nodded approvingly. 'Vis is *our* room.'

With the same wallpaper, carpet and bedding as her room – *their* room? – at Inverkillen House, it almost looked like it had been transplanted here. Even the duvet was rumpled on the bed, pulled back from the pillow, as if she'd just been sleeping in it.

It almost felt as if she'd never been to Inverkillen House, as if the last three and half years had all been a dream.

Except for George. He wasn't a dream.

Where was Mum? What had she been doing in Milton Keynes, anyway? Maisie took out the phone and messaged her again.

Where are you? We're at the house.

They snuggled up together on the couch and watched some television for a bit. Sometimes, at Inverkillen House, Maisie had been allowed to take George down to the basement so that they could watch DVDs. They were mostly old-school ones like *Poirot* or *Inspector Morse*. And lots of religious ones about Joan of Arc and St Francis and people like that.

Now, she found some episodes of *In the Night Garden* on BBC iPlayer. George gave a satisfied sigh that almost sounded like a purr. He curled up with his head on her knee.

She was just starting to nod off when she heard a noise – the rumble of a car drawing up on the street outside.

Finally! She nudged George's head off her lap and ran to

the window. But the car was a black Range Rover. She supposed it was possible that Mum might have changed her car... But then a man got out of the driver's side.

Mark.

Her heart leapt into her throat. She grabbed George, who had come up behind her to see what was going on. She pulled him away from the window, into the short passageway between the living room and the hall.

How had he found them? For a horrible moment she wondered if Mum had told him. She was the only person who knew that she and George were coming here. But Mum wasn't in touch with Mark... was she? That would make no sense at all.

The doorbell rang. It rang and rang again.

'Who's vat?' asked George.

'Shh, shhh,' said Maisie. 'We have to be quiet.'

With a plummeting sensation, she realised she hadn't locked the front door. She'd simply slung her keys into the seashell dish on the hall table.

Now there was a knock... three loud, slow knocks, as if he knew she was in here.

Fear seized her. Terror. She could taste it in the back of her throat, like hot metal.

After months – years – of wondering about Mark, and what they meant to each other, she finally knew. She knew, with utter certainty, that he meant her harm. Not because he hated her, but because she was – despite everything – nothing to him. And now, by running off with George, she'd become a liability, something outside of his plan.

From somewhere – spy films? – a word came into her head. *Neutralised*. She would have to be neutralised.

She seized George by the shoulders. 'Upstairs! Run, George, as fast as you can!'

And George ran, his small feet pounding the treads of the stairs. She hurried up after him.

On the turn of the stairs, her wrenched ankle gave way. She fell onto her front, hitting her chin against one of the treads, her body sliding heavily down two or three steps. She felt a hot rush of blood in her mouth. Her tooth, her tooth...

She could hear the noise as Mark tried the handle of the front door, the click of the mechanism. The sound of the door brushing over the mat.

Somehow, she made it onto her knees and scrambled up the last three steps. George stood on the top landing, his face a mask of terror at the sight of her.

She wiped the blood away from her chin with her sleeve.

'It's alright, George. Maisie's alright.'

Then she pulled herself to her feet, trying to ignore the agonising pain in her ankle. They ran into Mum's bedroom and climbed into the big mahogany wardrobe. She pressed herself into the corner, pulling George against her. The wood creaked softly behind her back as she breathed.

'Keep totally still,' she whispered.

How had he found them?

She could hear footsteps on the stairs now. He must have heard them from the hall. The footsteps entered the room, coming closer.

'Am I getting warmer?' His voice was laced with amusement.

The footsteps stopped.

The wardrobe door burst open.

'What on *earth* are you doing in here?' He gave a burst of a laugh. 'You silly loons.'

Twenty minutes later, they were drinking hot chocolate in the living room and Maisie was feeling stupid.

'What happened to his face?' asked Mark.

'Oh... He fell over. When we were...'

She wasn't going to say she'd dropped him, when she was lowering him out of the window on a sheet.

Mark gave an affectionate, frustrated growl. 'It's a miracle he didn't hurt himself more badly. If you wanted to leave, you should have spoken to me. Not climbed out of an upstairs window like some kind of Nancy Drew character.'

Maisie hadn't heard of Nancy Drew. She stared down at the ground.

'I understand,' he went on. 'No young girl wants to be stuck in a house in the middle of nowhere. No friends, no phone reception, no Instagram. I get it, I really do.'

Maisie looked at him, trying to figure him out. He'd locked her in her room, basically, for three and a half years. Like some kind of Sleeping Beauty. If Sleeping Beauty had been kept dosed up with tranquillisers and painkillers.

For the first time in ages, she remembered her art portfolio – the fairy tales theme she'd chosen. She imagined how she might draw a drug-addicted Sleeping Beauty, her beautiful face crusted with sores as the forest grew up around the castle. Instead of thorns and briars, she could draw giant hogweed plants, with their enormous umbrellas of poisonous white flowers.

'The security measures we took, back then, when you weren't well, they're not necessary now. They haven't been for a while. We just stuck to them out of habit, and habit is a terrible thing sometimes. I'm sorry, Maisie. I really am. We can do better than that.'

She gave him a grudging nod.

'So, have a think about it. What would "better" look like?'

Maisie thought back to the conversation she'd overheard through the wall. About how Mark was going to 'phase out her involvement'. Was that just something he'd said to keep Jan happy? Did he want her around, after all? Perhaps he was trying to fix things between them.

An image of giant hogweed burns came into her mind – a child's hand, grotesquely swollen and seeping with fluid. Her own hands smarted at the thought of it. She shook her head to try and dispel it.

'I don't understand what you're saying.'

'We could put things on more of a professional footing – we could pay you for looking after George? And make sure you have more freedom during your time off.'

But George is *mine*, she thought.

'We could give you your own car, perhaps?'

She wondered, for a moment, how that might work. Where would she drive to – to Killendreich and back? At the end of the day, she needed to be where George was.

'Or maybe it's time to make the break,' he said quietly, as if he was sad. 'Go and have a life of your own. A proper life. Go to university, or art school. You're talented. You could do anything. We can get another nanny for George. She won't be as good as you, of course. But I understand. You have your own life to live.'

'I want to speak to Mum,' she said.

Her arms and back were hurting now, as if there was an electric charge under her skin, triggered by the slightest movement. She wondered if he had brought any of her white pills with him.

'Is she on her way?' asked Mark.

'Yes,' said Maisie, defiantly.

'Okay, okay,' he said, looking around the room. 'Shall we kip here tonight, and wait for her to arrive? We can have a family conference.'

Maisie felt like her head was spinning. Half an hour ago, she'd thought Mark was going to run up those stairs and kill her. Now he was talking about family conferences.

Who was he? *What* was he? An endlessly shifting shape. One thing today, and another tomorrow. It was exhausting.

'My have bath?' asked George.

She groaned inwardly. George loved his baths. Normally, she enjoyed this part of their routine, and took time over bathing him in the long Victorian bathtub at Inverkillen House – it wasn't as if they had anything else to do. He loved to watch the peaty water gushing into the tub, swirling shower gel into it to make bubbles.

'Come on then.' She held out her hand.

'Deeper, deeper,' insisted George, capering around the bathroom in his underpants.

She gave him a bath, using a facecloth to get all the ingrained dirt off his feet, which took ages. He kept springing up, shouting, 'Tickly!'

She let him play in the water for a little while. The pain in her tooth was awful again, and she was starting to feel sick. It suddenly struck her that Mum might have painkillers. She would have *something* she could take. Maybe even an over-the-counter remedy to help her get off to sleep. Night Nurse? But there was nothing inside the bathroom cabinet but a plastic bottle of paracetamol.

She became aware of a little jagged reaction inside herself. A hot, fierce flash of anger with her mother – hatred, even – for having nothing stronger than paracetamol. She took a couple of the tablets, washing them down with water from the tap. Then she closed the bathroom cabinet to look at herself. The mirror was all fogged up and she rubbed out a little patch so that she could see her face.

Her eyes were dull, and there was a red lump where a stye was starting to develop on her upper eyelid. There were a couple of sores around her cracked, dry lips. A smattering of spots on her chin.

God, she looked like a drug addict or something.

She smiled at herself. Her lips stretched open to reveal a row of yellow teeth, and a big black gap where one of her premolars was missing. And some of the other teeth had brown, crumbling areas near the gumline, where decay had started in the gaps between the teeth.

The mirror steamed over again, covering up the horrible face.

Taking George to her bedroom to get him changed for bed, she suddenly felt exhausted. Beyond exhausted. A dragging, dizzy feeling came over her, like she just had to lie down and close her eyes.

And it seemed George was tired too. He looked droopy, his eyelids half closed. He didn't even react when she pulled his old, faded Spiderman pyjamas out of her rucksack.

'Put them on, Munchkin.'

She curled up on her bed. Just for a moment. Her body felt heavy. So heavy. She could feel every ounce of her energy draining into the mattress beneath her.

She was to have a night in her own bed, after three and a half years.

Then she felt her boy climb in beside her – damp hair and clinging limbs and soft cotton. She tucked his head under her chin and pulled him close against her body.

54

MAISIE

Northumberland
Four and a half years ago

Maisie awoke with a jerk. For a moment, she thought she was at Inverkillen House, locked up safe in her room. But where was that noise was coming from?

'My GOD! My GOD!'

Who was shouting like that, in the middle of the night?

She wasn't at Inverkillen House; she was at home. At home in Northumberland. And something was happening in the bathroom.

There was a thunking noise, the scrabble of limbs on a wet floor. Choking, coughing.

George...

Maisie swung her legs out of bed, but they had no power in them, they folded under her. She forced herself up and made it to the bathroom, one hand on the wall to steady her.

George was on his hands and knees on the tiles, water running off his Spiderman pyjamas into the large puddle that had formed beneath him. Mark was leaning low over him, rubbing his back as his body convulsed with coughing. A thin trail of watery vomit hung down from his mouth.

Then George reared up on his knees, making a honking, wheezing noise in his throat as he tried to snatch in air. He was deathly pale. Had he been breath-holding again? Was that it?

'George!' She tried to take one of his hands, but he'd clenched them into tight, trembling fists. She rubbed his back instead.

Cough, cough, cough.

She turned to Mark. 'Shall I call an ambulance?'

'Give it a minute. He's okay, I think. He's just taken in some water. He'll clear it himself. He's getting air in to his lungs now – a bit, anyway.'

'What happened?'

Mark's voice was matter of fact. 'You left the bath full. He was under the water when I found him.'

'No! No... I don't understand. We were tucked up in bed. And I'm sure...'

She'd let the water out of the bath, hadn't she? But she'd been so tired and fuzzy-headed that she couldn't be one hundred percent sure.

'You're sure... about what?'

She shrank away from him. 'Nothing.'

'Thank God I heard something from downstairs. Just a little squeak – it must have been him struggling in the bathtub.'

Mark pulled the child onto his knee and wrapped him in a towel. George, still dripping, looked up at Maisie. There were burst blood vessels in the whites of his eyes. But the skin around his lips was losing its blue tinge.

'And what happened to his feet?' demanded Mark.

Maisie looked down. Now that they were clean, his feet looked red and bruised. There was a nasty gash on his big toe.

'We had to...' She cleared her throat. 'I couldn't bring many of George's things with me,' she said in a dignified voice.

'You made him walk to Killendreich *without shoes*?'

'I carried him,' she said. 'I carried him most of the way.' She could feel the ache in her arms, as if to prove it. The throbbing of the muscles, the sore skin, as if she was coming down with flu. She longed to go back to her bed.

'He can sleep downstairs with me tonight,' said Mark, sweeping George up into his arms.

The next thing she knew, she was waking up. And it was like being pulled up, up, through a million miles of blackness. There was a noise, and it was a noise she knew she shouldn't ignore.

Then she registered that she was in her own bed, at home. And Mark was calling from somewhere in the house – downstairs, she thought. Her phone was showing that it was just after six in the morning. Maybe Mum had got back.

She pulled herself out of bed. Her ankle was sore and stiff, from hurting it the day before, and her head began to spin as soon as she stood up. She had to stop half way down the stairs and hold on to the banister for a few moments.

When she reached the living room, Mark was leaning over George, who was laid out on the sofa.

'He's not right,' Mark said. 'He's drowsy and lethargic. His breathing is laboured. He's got all the hallmarks of secondary drowning.'

Maisie's heart plummeted to her feet.

'Get in the car,' he said. 'We'll take him up to the A&E at Cramlington. It'll be quicker than an ambulance.'

She went upstairs to grab her things, stumbling on the top step and falling onto the landing. It was as if she was drunk, or something. Her feet didn't seem to be working in time with the rest of her body.

Although she had no memory of doing it, her things and George's had already been packed into their rucksacks. The bathroom had been cleared up, and the wet towels from last night were folded neatly on the heated towel rail.

'Hurry!' called Mark from downstairs.

George looked like a ragdoll when Mark carried him out to the car, his arms and legs flopping. He couldn't sit up, so she fastened the seatbelt around his waist and tried to hold him semi-upright, his head against her chest.

Mark explained, in a loud voice as he drove, that secondary drowning meant that water had got into his lungs and irritated the lining of the alveoli, causing fluid to build up. She held George close and pressed her ear to the top of his head. She thought could hear a faint rattle with each in-breath.

'Come on, baby. Come on.'

Her tears had made a patch of his hair all wet, but he didn't even seem to feel it.

Mark was taking the corners at speed, propelling her body forwards, or sideways against the car door. Suddenly, nausea rose in her gullet. Her bowels clenched. *Not again.*

She sat holding George, trying to control the spasms in her body, feeling she had never known such utter misery.

Once, she gripped him too hard, and he opened his eyes and stared up at her. He looked terrified. As if he knew he was drowning in his own lungs.

Or maybe he was terrified of *her*.

When they finally arrived at the car park, she unbuckled George and Mark lifted him out through the other passenger door, pulling him under his armpits.

'You wait here,' he said.

'Why?'

'Are you kidding?' He gave a bark of a laugh. 'They'll take one look at you and there'll be social workers crawling all over us. There'll be questions about why you didn't empty the bath, why you weren't watching him when he drowned. Stay here, sit tight, and let me handle it.'

When he drowned.

He was talking like George was already…

She could hardly bear to think the word.

Like he was already dead.

55

MAISIE

Northumberland
Four and a half years ago

Mark was gone for three hours and twenty minutes. At one point, Maisie went in to use the toilet and nearly went up to the reception desk to ask where George had been taken.

But she thought of Mark's words and imagined social workers swarming into the hospital. Police, even. She would have to follow Mark's instructions. At least George would be safe while he was in here, with the doctors and nurses watching over him.

When Mark finally returned to the car, it was without George. Maisie realised that her whole body was shaking. She pressed her thighs down, hoping it wasn't visible.

'He'll be okay,' he said, climbing into the back seat next to her. 'He's on oxygen and an antibiotic drip.'

A swingeing pain went through her. She recognised it as

relief. All her bodily sensations felt like pain, today. But this was good, she reassured herself. George was going to be okay.

'Can I see him?'

'No,' said Mark. 'It's family only.'

The rejection felt like a slap. 'I'll *tell* them I'm family, then. I'll tell them he's my... my son.'

She'd never said that word out loud before, not in relation to George.

Mark didn't miss a beat. 'Incorrect. George is registered as my son. Mine and Jan's. I have a scan of his birth certificate right here. Have a look, if you like.'

He keyed something into his phone and showed her the screen.

'Take it all in, Maisie,' he said patiently. 'Take it all in.'

She took the phone and read through the document. 'This is the wrong one. It shows Jan as his mother, not me. And it doesn't show his correct birthday. This –'

And then she realised. The dead baby. Mark was using his birth certificate as if it belonged to George – to *her* George. Apart from anything else, this document made it look like George was six months older than he was. Would that impact his treatment, she wondered? Shouldn't Mark tell the hospital?

'Where's his real birth certificate?' she demanded.

'There's no medical record of you ever having given birth. No record of it at all.'

She flashed back to that day, felt an aching throb between her legs at the memory of stitches, bleeding. 'But Zuleika...?'

He shook his head with a smile that was almost sympathetic.

'Zuleika entered the UK in the back of a lorry, four years

ago. According to official records, she doesn't exist. Good luck finding her.'

'DNA. I'll insist on a DNA test.'

'Which I, as George's father and legal parent, would have to consent to,' said Mark, a hint of enjoyment in his voice now. 'And what do you think is the likelihood of that happening?'

'A court order... You can get court orders for that kind of thing,' she said weakly. Her stomach was cramping. She was going to have to run back in to use the toilet again.

He laughed. 'Have you any idea how much a legal action like that would cost?'

She thought of the fifty-three pence she had left in her purse. It hadn't even been enough for a can of juice from the vending machine in reception.

'I'll explain it all to the doctors, then,' she said, her heart hammering. 'I'll say it's a complicated family situation. They'll let me see him.'

'You won't,' said Mark evenly. 'Because if you do, all hell will break loose. They'll take one look at you and ask you all kinds of questions, which you won't be able to answer. You'll have to explain why you left George to drown. You'll have to explain about the cuts on his feet and the bruises on his face, which he sustained whilst in your care. And they'll insist on a drugs test. Which you will fail.'

'But *you* gave me the medication. You said I needed it.'

'Can you think how he must have felt?' said Mark quietly. 'Sinking under the water. Knowing that he was drowning. And that he was completely alone. That was down to *you*.'

'I have a right to see him. He's...'

'Now listen, Maisie, listen. How about we do things my way, hmm? The way we agreed. You agreed that Jan and I would bring George up as our own, that we would be his parents, didn't you? That was always the plan. But I've been happy to take you in, to look after you as well. You've not been well, Maisie. And it's not your fault. It was the pregnancy that triggered your psychosis, and I hold some responsibility for that, having encouraged you to go through with it.'

Maisie shook her head. 'I'm perfectly well. I'm off the medication now. I've been off it for...'

Two days.

'Jock's on his way,' said Mark. 'He will pick you up, take you back to Inverkillen House. Your medication is there. I'll tell Jock to give you as much as you need. You can rest and recover from all this upset.'

Her whole body seemed to melt at the thought of it. Taking her pills and sliding into bed. Maybe she could go back. Just for a bit. Just until she was strong enough to... what? To fight for George? At least until these awful stomach cramps and the muscle aches had stopped.

'And when I come up next, we'll talk about the future, and what that might look like.'

'George. I want to see George!'

'There's going to be a change in the arrangements for George. A change of scenery, once he gets out of hospital. He'll be based at my other house, near Nottingham. I've found a lady to look after him. An experienced housekeeper and nanny. And I've enrolled him in an excellent private nursery.'

'I can look after him.' She sounded like a child; she could hear the plaintive note in her voice. 'You don't need the lady.'

'You're not part of the new arrangements for George,' said Mark. 'He may be able to visit Inverkillen House, from time to time. Perhaps for a week in the summer.'

'But what am I supposed to do at Inverkillen House? If I'm there all alone?'

'There all alone, with food, shelter, heating, medication,' he corrected. 'It's a cold, hard world out there, Maisie. Especially for a drug addict with mental health problems. With no qualifications or experience. Maybe we could arrange a correspondence course for you. You could finish your A-levels. And then do something with the Open University, perhaps. Or an art course, to keep you occupied while you try and wean yourself off the meds. Which will be a long, painful process, let me tell you.'

A Land Rover drew up beside them.

Jock. He was here already? Mark must have called him hours ago.

'I'm not going anywhere!' Maisie's voice was rising hysterically now. 'And I'm definitely not getting in a car with *him*.'

'The only way for you to keep in touch with George,' said Mark, 'is to do things my way. You have to accept it – he's *my* son. He's my flesh and blood and I'll never let him go.'

'What about *me*?' pleaded Maisie. 'Don't you care about *me*?'

She searched his face, looking – stupidly – for love. For recognition. For anything.

Nothing. Nothing. Nothing.

56

TERESA

Killendreich
Now

Sunny drove us up to Inverkillen House – a five-hour drive from Northumberland. I spent most of the journey typing search terms into my phone, trying to find a trace of the Janet I'd known at university, trying to work out if there was any way she could be Mark's dead wife. The search results, of course, were swamped with content about the singer.

'She had a double-barrelled surname,' I said to Sunny for the fifth time. 'I keep thinking "De Winter", but that's from *Rebecca*, the Daphne du Maurier book, isn't it? Or "De Ville", as in Cruella, but I don't think that can be right either.'

'You don't have a year book, or anything, from when you left uni?' he asked.

'But I never finished the course,' I reminded him. 'I dropped out when I got pregnant with Maisie.'

Sunny reached across and placed his hand on the back of

mine. 'You were so brave, deciding to bring Maisie up as a single mum. And without any help from her father, as well.'

This was one of Sunny's favourite topics – he loved to tut at how useless Joel had been, moving to Australia and abandoning me and Maisie.

'Yeah. The child support agency said they couldn't get him to pay if he was out of the country. And then, I suppose, he died anyway. Not that I knew that, at the time.'

Sunny shook his head. 'What a useless prick.'

'Totally.' I twisted my fingers nervously, trying to think. I didn't have time to indulge in a Joel-hating fest with Sunny.

The party I'd been getting ready for with Janet – it could have actually been THE party. The one where I'd got hopelessly drunk and ended up pregnant. All I really remembered, now, was arriving at Joel's flat, seeing his kitchen counter crowded with bottles. There'd been a glass mixing bowl filled with home-made punch, with slices of tinned peaches floating around in it. Joel had admitted that he and his flatmates had simply dumped a tin of fruit into a bowl of vodka and Southern Comfort.

And then nothing – until waking up the next morning in Joel's bed, my head throbbing as if it was about to explode. I'd lain there, slowly noticing the other sensations in my body, realising that we must have had sex. I'd walked downstairs to the kitchen on shaky legs, clinging to the banister with both hands. Joel's housemate, Michael, had made me a bacon sandwich. I'd taken one look at it and run to the bathroom to throw up, not quite managing to make it in time. And then, after a few weeks, I'd started throwing up in the mornings for a different reason. I'd been in denial at first, though, putting it down to a sickness bug. I'd been three months along before I'd picked up a pregnancy test in Boots, telling myself that it was just to rule it out.

Suddenly, something popped into my mind. I remembered telling Janet about my pregnancy, one evening after chapel choir. Her face had hardened, turning almost ugly.

'You mucky little whore,' she said. 'May God forgive you.'

Had she hated me so much that she'd tried to take Maisie from me, all those years later?

'I just don't understand what she would have to do with it. It makes no sense.'

Sunny shook his head, frowning in concentration as he navigated the complicated road layout that led to the Queensferry Crossing.

Three hours later, we lost signal after driving through the small town of Killendreich. Looking up from my phone, I realised why – we were in the mountains now, the road following a wide, rocky river upstream. The lower slopes, strewn with grey rocks, had a desolate feel, more like a prehistoric landscape than bonny, shortbread-tin Scotland. Above us loomed steep-sided gullies, gouged out of the rock by glaciers in millennia gone by.

We passed a neat white bungalow, a farmhouse, and then a few miles on, a tumbledown, half-ruined cottage. The road narrowed to a single track, skirting the side of a spruce plantation, and Sunny slowed the car to a crawl. According to the GPS, we'd already reached our destination, and the postcode for Inverkillen House.

'Sunny – look!' Up ahead, partly obscured by trees, stood an old wooden sign, silvered with age and barely legible. 'It says Inverkillen House. And look, there's a turn-off. On the left – see where there's a break in the trees? And the two white stones on either side of the track?'

So we turned off the road and bumped along the narrow, unmade track for what seemed like miles, winding deeper and deeper into the forest.

'I hope there's somewhere to turn round,' fretted Sunny. 'Otherwise we'll be reversing all the way back.'

But, after rounding a final bend, the house loomed up suddenly, in a gravelled clearing between the trees.

It struck me straight away as an ugly, mean-looking house, with its dark, triangular gables, its white walls tinged with green mildew. It certainly wasn't the turreted, romantic Scottish castle that I'd envisaged when Maisie had started talking about Ally's 'Scottish place'.

'It doesn't look like there's anyone about,' said Sunny, drawing up the car by the side of the house. 'Shall we ring the doorbell?'

'You do that, if you like. I'm going around the back. I'm going to try and find a way in.' Sticking to the law, relying on the police, hadn't got me any closer to finding Maisie over the years.

Could she be in there? Was it even remotely possible?

One of the windows around the back had already been broken. It was covered with a bit of board which Sunny pried away easily.

'What if you're struck off? As a physiotherapist?' I asked. 'What if you get a criminal record?'

He turned to me, his eyes shining. 'At this moment, Teresa, you are my only concern.'

I felt myself flushing, a warm glow rising through me. 'We can say we heard someone shouting for help. Isn't that some sort of defence for breaking into a property?'

'Yes,' said Sunny. 'I think I saw that on *Happy Valley*.'

We found ourselves in a large kitchen area, with industrial-looking units. Double doors at the far end led into a dark corridor, floored with peeling lino. I pushed open doors to side rooms and cleaning cupboards, and a cold, poky bathroom. Down another short corridor, a steep staircase rose up to the left, and I hurried up it, my trainers pounding on the steps while Sunny's steady footsteps followed behind.

At the top was a door to the right, with a fire door sign on it. Oddly, for a fire door, it had thick steel bolts, top and bottom. I slid them open. Beyond was a corridor with two doors off it. The first opened onto a bathroom. Its small, high window was fitted with a metal grille. Someone was obviously paranoid about security.

And then, at the end of the corridor, we entered a bedroom.

I noticed the pink carpet and the velvet chair first. Then I took in the wallpaper – green leaves intertwined with pink flowers.

Against the wall by the door stood a small bookcase, containing a collection of children's books – *The BFG* and *Matilda*. Several *Famous Five* books. A couple of Miss Marple mysteries, furred with dust. *Hickory Dickory Dock*.

It was just like Maisie's room at home, except for the security grille that had been fitted over the window.

And the stain.

It was on the carpet by the bed; over a foot wide, the brownish-red colour of old blood. It had sunk into the pile, the sort of stain that no scrubbing would ever remove. That volume of blood hadn't come from a cut finger or a nosebleed.

'We're too late!' I cried out. 'We're too late.'

I sank to my knees, pressing my forehead against the

stain. Maisie had been imprisoned here. Alone and helpless. Probably terrified. Perhaps crying for me.

And I'd given George up to these people, too. To these psychopaths, whoever they were. I'd let them take him away from me, after his years of trying to find me.

I thought of the china shepherd he'd pushed out of the car window into my hands.

I thought of Maisie, walking away towards the school building, that last day. The half-wave she'd given me, her hair blowing in front of her face.

'Let's check the rest of the house,' said Sunny. 'And then we'll call the police.'

'You go and check.' I wanted to stay here, in this place that held the final traces of Maisie. I wanted to stay right here with my face pressed against the floor.

Some time later, I heard footsteps on the stairs again. I heard them coming along the corridor and into the room behind me. I heard the noise of a deep breath being drawn in, and then exhaled.

'Teresa?' said Sunny, crouching down and placing a hand on my back. 'I think you should come down. I can hear a noise, coming from below. I don't know what it is. I think it's coming from the basement.'

57

MAISIE

Northumberland
Four and a half years ago

'It'll take f-five hours or so,' said Jock. 'To get up to Inverkillen House. Hopefully we'll avoid the w-worst of the rush hour.'

Maisie nodded doubtfully and checked that her seatbelt was fastened tight. She couldn't smell any alcohol on Jock's breath. She'd have to hope today was 'a good day', in the words of Adrian, and that he would be fine to drive. She hadn't forgotten the journey from Westcoates Academy to Inverkillen House three and a half years ago, the white-knuckle drive along the twisting, single-track roads.

For a moment, she ached for the girl she'd been that day. For the girl who'd believed that a bright future was still possible, had believed that the Jacksons, with their Scottish estate and their waterfalls and hunting parties, would be able to sort everything out. She'd wanted somebody to take away all the difficult decisions she had to make. And in a way, they had.

But as she sat there, watching the Northumbrian fields slide past, that ache began to change into the strangest sensation. It was as if a string was tied between her heart and George's. And it was being pulled tighter and tighter with every mile they drove further from the hospital.

A distant memory floated into her mind. She remembered her mother, saying that was how she'd felt when Maisie had gone away on her first school camp.

'That's how you know you're a mother,' she'd said.

Then she saw it all clearly, as if for the first time. She was a mother, whatever Mark said. She was a mother, and it was too late.

Because she had left George. She had allowed herself to be driven away. And, at least partly, she'd done that because she wanted her medication.

She was a drug addict, who had given up her child for drugs.

She pulled down the sun visor and looked at herself in the mirror. The sores around her mouth looked angrier than last night. Another crop of spots had erupted, near her hairline this time. And her face was covered in a greasy sheen of sweat. She kept her mouth closed, didn't want another glimpse of the nasty black gap where her tooth should be.

The housekeeper, nanny-type person in Nottingham would do a better job with George than she would.

It was she, Maisie, who had risked his life, lowering him out of the window. It was sheer luck that he'd only cut his cheek and not broken his fragile three-year-old skull. It was she who was responsible for his sore, cut feet. It was she who had left him alone to drown in the bath. She thought of his wary, frightened eyes, gazing up at her on the way to the hospital.

She imagined the life ahead of her at Inverkillen House. Stuck in her room in that back corridor most of the time, but without George's sleepovers and his visits during the day. A life that would be punctuated by pills, by counting out how many she would need to get through each empty day and each restless night.

She imagined herself trying to do some sort of higher education course with no internet access.

Tears slid down her cheeks. It wasn't going to work. Mark wanted her out of George's life, and so that was what would happen.

But the string... She wondered if she could cut that string, and how it would feel. Every nerve inside her seemed to flinch at the thought of it, as if layers of skin were being peeled off her body.

It was probably the withdrawal, she thought dully. She wrapped her coat around herself and tried to sleep, only to be woken with a start when a lorry blared its horn. Jock seemed to have pulled onto a roundabout without checking.

'Could we stop for a break?' she asked, suddenly feeling nauseous. Jock drove on, and she wasn't even sure if he'd heard her.

It was a couple of hours later – they were somewhere beyond Perth – when Jock pulled off the road and into a service station.

'Need fuel,' he said gruffly. 'W-want anything from the shop?'

She shook her head.

When he'd gone into the shop to pay, she stepped out of the Land Rover. She thought of the comforting pills, waiting for her at Inverkillen House. She thought of the mother-string that she would have to cut, in order to survive. The doors in her mind that she would have to close forever.

And then she looked around herself, raising her eyes to the blue-grey mountains in the distance, and the road ahead as it wound up to the north. She didn't know which way she should go. Or where she might get to, on foot and with no money.

She seemed to hear her mother's voice. Her mother from before, back when she'd still loved her.

'Take a breath, my love. Then just take one step at a time.'

58

TERESA

Killendreich
Now

Through in the main hallway of the house, Sunny pointed to a panelled wooden door under the wide staircase. It looked like a cupboard under the stairs, but it gave onto a small flight of steps, heading down.

The air became chilly as we descended, with a smell that was a mix of damp stone and old drains. I'd smelled it before when touring historic properties – in dungeons and cellars and priest's holes. At the bottom we encountered a door, not wooden and rotting, but constructed of grey-black steel.

And then, muffled by the door, we heard a delighted laugh. A few notes of a song.

With both my fists, I banged on the door, as hard as I could.

'Maisie?' The strangled cry left me before I could stop it. 'Maisie!! Are you in there?'

There was a long silence and then the door opened.

It was a small, thin woman with angular features and greying black hair, dressed in baggy white pyjamas with silver stars.

'Please –' I began.

The door began to close again, but Sunny was too fast. He blocked it with his foot.

'We just want to talk.'

I thought, for a moment, of George and Caroline on my doorstep that day. How I nearly hadn't let them in.

The basement space was set up to give the sense of being inside a church. A huge screen was fixed to the far wall, showing an image of a stained-glass window. It depicted Christ with his arms outstretched, backlit so that light seemed to stream from his flowing, coloured robes and his halo.

Two rows of carved wooden pews were positioned in front of the screen. And behind them, a sofa bed, the covers in a state of disarray.

Wide, boxy shelves lined the walls to both the left and right – hundreds of DVDs on one side, rows of books on the other. A few DVD cases were strewn on the floor – old movies, mostly. *The Song of Bernadette. Meet Me in St Louis. Casablanca.* A box set of *All Creatures Great and Small.*

One of the lower shelves of the bookcase, at chest height, was devoted to china figurines. They were arranged in groups, as if someone had been playing with them. I could see a Mary and a baby Jesus tucked into a wooden manger. A man in white robes with a staff. A flock of three or four sheep. Dull, orangey LED candles flickered around them.

The damp stone smell was overlaid with the scent of incense, and the garlicky traces of an old meal. I noticed there was a door off to the left, opening onto a cupboard-like space, with a tiny section of kitchen counter, a small fridge tucked underneath, a microwave on top. On the wall, above the microwave, hung a plain wooden cross.

The woman stood with her back to the sofa bed, as if she just wanted us to go away so she could go back to sleep.

Could it be the girl I remembered from university? The one who'd been half way through a medical degree, and wanted to be a GP?

I studied her bone structure. Her nostrils, flaring slightly as she inhaled. Those eyes.

You mucky little whore.

At university her face had been more rounded, with a creamy complexion. And now it was angular, almost emaciated, her skin papery thin.

'We know each other.' I kept my voice gentle. 'I'm Teresa. From University.'

She didn't react at all.

'Do you know where George is?'

'George?' Her voice was flat, wooden. 'Why are you asking about him? George is dead.'

I flashed back to Cheryl, the same words emerging from her mouth as she'd gazed into the hissing blue flame of her gas fire.

'But… he's with Caroline,' I said. 'Isn't he? He's not… he's absolutely fine.'

Jan hid her face with her hands. But her dark eyes were just visible, peering between the thin, splayed fingers.

'George isn't dead,' said Sunny in his clear, calm voice. 'Teresa saw him yesterday.'

She shook her head vehemently. I heard a bone in her neck crack. 'You're talking about the other boy. The replacement. He's gone now, too.'

A replacement? George had been born to replace a dead child?

My heart seemed to break from its stitchings. I thought of his nightmares and his restlessness, his anxious gaze. I wanted to sweep him up into my arms and tell him that he was wanted. Love, adored. For exactly who he was.

And then I remembered his ambivalence about his own name. The other child who he kept mentioning.

'That's the other one of me.'

What had happened here?

'Where is she?' My voice was pleading now. 'Where's Maisie?'

'How should I know?' Jan shook her head again. 'I haven't seen her in years.'

'But she *was* here?'

'Oh yes. And that child of hers, always hanging off her. Whingeing all the time. Crashing and banging around. Crying through the walls.'

That child of hers.

So George *was* hers – Maisie's flesh and blood. Not some ghost or echo of her. Had the DNA test been wrong? How could that have happened – weren't these things supposed to be failsafe?

'Where is she now?' I demanded.

She shrugged. 'No idea.'

'And what about... Ally?' I had no idea if the girl even existed, but I decided to take a chance. 'Where's Ally?'

'Who the fuck's Ally?' She turned away in disgust.

'Please, Jan. You need to tell me what you know.'

Silence. I decided to change tack.

'Why are you down here in the basement? Did Mark make you come down here?'

'It's better down here. Down here, underneath. Nice and close.'

She stretched out a hand in the direction of the wall, fingers curling like she was reaching for something.

'Close to *who*? What?!'

I spun round to get Sunny's attention. But he'd clocked something on the floor, a piece of paper. He picked it up and put it in his pocket, then straightened up and came to stand next to me.

'Tell us, Jan,' he said. 'Tell us about your baby.'

'Why should I tell *you*?'

She stared at us, her face stiff and contorted like a theatre mask. But there was no real anger in her eyes. Only a great, gaping loneliness.

'Because we want to know about him?' tried Sunny. 'And however short his life was, he doesn't deserve to be forgotten.' He shot me an uncomfortable glance.

She sank down onto the edge of the sofa bed. I saw that her calves were stick thin, poking out from the pyjama cuffs.

I knelt in front of her. 'How did you lose him?'

'The nurses said I could hold him, if I wanted. After the birth.' She paused, jiggling her feet like a child. 'They said it might help, in the long run. It might help me process things. But Mark said not to look at him, because he wasn't really ours, he wasn't the one who was *meant*.' She looked up at us, her eyes desperate, flicking from my face to Sunny's and back again. 'He said God was sending us the other one, the girl's baby. He said it was best not to look, because of the deformities. Our real George, when he came, would be whole and unbroken.'

Silence in the room.

Then Sunny cleared his throat. 'Your own baby had... birth defects?'

'I only looked at him once. He looked fine, really.' Her voice trembled. 'More or less. They'd put a yellow woollen hat over his poor head.'

She looked up at us, her brow furrowed as if she was trying to make sense of it all. And there it was in her eyes – that pain again, the pain that wrapped itself around all mothers and children. That tangled knot of love and loss.

'Mark took charge, when we got home. He settled the baby down here in the basement, where the walls are thick. And he let nature take its course. But I could still hear the crying. That was the problem. And the crying went on after he'd gone. Day and night. He didn't want to be replaced, even though he was... the way he was. Eventually, I came down here. He's nearer to me, like this.'

'I'm sorry you lost your baby,' I managed.

'I only looked at him once,' she repeated.

Sunny and I exchanged glances. There was nothing either of us could say. Nothing had helped Jan, not her nostalgic movies or her figurines or her mocked-up church. Not even another baby. Nothing could put it right.

'Please tell us what you know about Maisie,' I said softly. 'She was *my* baby. And I've lost her, too.'

Her face morphed into a sneer. 'That piece of teenage trash? Why should I know anything about her?'

A blast of sour breath reached my face. I straightened up, took a step back.

'We're going to call the police.' Sunny's voice was kind but firm. 'So it's all going to come out. You might as well tell us.'

'If you want to call the police, you'll need to drive to

Killendreich. Now please will you go. I'm busy.' She picked up a remote control.

'You've killed her. Haven't you?' My whole body flooded with rage. My hands tingled with it. I wanted to squeeze them around her wiry throat.

I felt Sunny's hand on my back.

'What have you done?' I insisted.

'Please leave.' She shook her head. 'Please. If you would be so kind.' She pressed a button on the remote control, and the stained-glass window image disappeared. A scene from the Alps filled the centre of the screen instead – snow-capped peaks, blue sky, a flower-filled meadow, like something from *The Sound of Music*.

No – it *was* actually *The Sound of Music*. Julie Andrews began to sing about the hills being alive.

Jan collapsed back onto the sofa bed and pulled the covers up under her chin.

Sunny passed a piece of paper to me – the one he'd picked up from the floor. It was a receipt from Amazon. For some vitamin tablets. The billing address was not Inverkillen House. It was Malham Manor, Retford, Nottinghamshire.

'Malham Manor?' I turned to Jan. 'Is that where George is?'

But she was staring at the screen, shaking her head, her hands over her ears.

'I didn't think I could love him. I only looked at him once.'

59

CAROLINE

Retford
Now

Caroline checked her banking app again. It was silly, this need to keep double checking, but she couldn't help it. The CHAPS transfer should be coming through any minute now.

She took a sip of her coffee, and nibbled the croissant she'd heated up for herself. It was a beautiful morning, the sun streaming in through the kitchen windows. She wondered for a moment if she'd miss all this. But it was only weak, English sun, she reminded herself. And it was only a Waitrose croissant, not a freshly made pastry from an artisanal Spanish bakery.

She and Mark had actually had sex last night, for the first time in about a year. A strange intimacy had sprung up between them, now that they knew it was over between them. It had almost made her think about changing her mind. But she reminded herself that Mark was perfectly capable of being charming when it suited him. He wouldn't be so charming if he knew she was leaving today, and not at the weekend as she'd told him. And that she was taking George with her.

She tried to envisage his face when he realised, when he came home to an empty house later that evening. It caused a strange mix of emotions to stir within her... fear, satisfaction, slight regret for what had been lost between them. But most of all, a huge adrenaline thrill. She felt *alive*, for the first time in years.

Caroline had applied her electronic signature to a lease, paying for six months up front to secure the apartment immediately. She'd chosen her favourite one in the end, the one with the pink bougainvillea climbing the white walls, and the sun lounger with the ice-rimmed margarita. By a stroke of luck, it had turned out that there was a small box room that the agents weren't allowed to officially call a bedroom. It only had a very small window, more of a vent really, and there was no air con in that particular room. But it would be fine, she was sure. She'd heard somewhere that children didn't feel the heat in the same way as adults.

The move would be good for George, too. Especially in the long run. He would grow up bilingual. He'd study for an International Baccalaureate (she assumed) rather than boring, outdated A-levels. All those benefits.

The suitcase she'd bought for him was made of hard, bright green plastic and it had frog ears, and little wheels so he could pull it along himself. She'd also bought an ID wrist-band for him, with her name and phone number on it, in case he wandered off at the airport.

Labelling him like a suitcase didn't make him hers, of

course. But he was hers as much as he was anyone else's, she felt.

She remembered the day she'd first met him. Mark had phoned at the crack of dawn, saying that Jan had attacked the boy and had tried to drown him. He was trying to get her admitted to Lendrick View, but he needed Caroline to take George while he made the arrangements. He'd instructed her to drive to a hospital in Northumberland, and to park in a specific zone of the car park. All very mysterious. And he'd come hurrying out of the building – from some back entrance that looked more like a fire escape – carrying a bundle in his arms. George had been asleep, wrapped in a car rug.

'Take him,' Mark had insisted. 'Drive him back home to Malham. He's sedated but it'll start wearing off soon. Give him something to eat when he gets home and he'll be right as rain in the morning. I'll see you tomorrow at some point, I expect.'

He'd turned and walked back to the hospital building without so much as a 'thank you'. Or even a kiss. She remembered thinking that the honeymoon phase, the delicious excitement of their affair, had clearly worn off. But that was okay, she had reasoned, because they were entering a new phase.

And she remembered looking down at the bundled-up boy, already a dead weight in her arms. He'd been handed to her with no equipment, no instructions, nothing but the car rug. Almost as if he'd just been born. If it had been a film, or a book, it would have been the moment when she fell in love with him. The moment when she became a mother.

But there'd been a crust of dried snot around the rim of one of his nostrils. And he'd smelt, just slightly, of wee.

But that was all ancient history. And now, she had to finish packing. On her way upstairs, she put on Madonna's *La Isla Bonita*, streaming it loud through the Sonos system. It was important to get herself in the holiday mood.

She checked her hand luggage, making sure she'd packed the Marian Keyes novel. She'd ordered a copy of the exact one – the one that had been shown in the photo of the villa, the one on the table by the sun lounger. She'd read the first chapter already, and was looking forward to reading more on the plane later, with a gin and tonic loaded with ice. She'd bought some antihistamines for George that would hopefully knock him out for the flight.

Next, she went into the study and placed an envelope on Mark's desk. She'd already handed over the results from the first DNA company, and had deleted all relevant emails from her iCloud server while he'd watched. He'd insisted on that, after phoning the bank to set up the CHAPS transfer. But the final DNA test – that extra one from the second company, which had included the YDNA test – had only arrived in the post that morning. She'd read through the results carefully, three times, trying to make sense of it. But none of it mattered now. Mark was welcome to it.

As long as that money came through, of course. She checked her phone again. She'd give it until noon and then phone him at work.

Finally, she went into George's room and kneeled in front of his chest of drawers. She pulled out a few pairs of pants and socks and folded them inside the frog suitcase. And some shorts and t-shirts. A hoodie in case it was cool in the evenings. He'd probably want to take his weird china figurines, the angels and shepherds, but there wouldn't be room. For an amusing moment she imagined them being smashed open by customs officials, to check they weren't filled with heroin.

No, she would pretend to have packed them, and then buy some more once they were there. Spain would be full of those kinds of things. There would be Virgin Marys and angels and saints all over the place. They'd probably have those morbid little shrines at the sides of the roads.

'What's all this?'

Mark.

Her heart stopped. She'd been singing along to Madonna, hadn't heard him come in.

Slowly, she turned around. Looked him straight in the eye. She'd have to try and brazen it out.

'It'll be good for George to see the world a bit. We can share custody. He can spend some time in Europe with me. Then you can have him back when school starts.'

She thought of Mark, on the day before term started, scrabbling around in drawers trying to find all the items of stationery on the stationery list. Realising that George's trousers were too tight, and that his school shoes didn't fit, because Caroline hadn't ordered the next size up. Trying to put together a packed lunch that met George's tedious requirements. She almost felt sorry for him, before she remembered that this would never happen. Once George was in Spain, there was no way she was sending him back.

Mark took a step forward. 'You're not taking him anywhere. I'll have you arrested for kidnap.'

Caroline smiled happily. 'I'll have *you* arrested. We'll let the police decide if you're telling the truth about Maisie and this so-called adoption. They'll dig all your skeletons out of the cupboard. Or out of Inverkillen House, for that matter. *Sorry*.'

Not sorry.

He sighed. His shoulders drooped and he stared at her pleadingly. His eyes looked shiny and for a moment she thought he was about to tear up. 'Caz. Please. Can we talk about this properly? It doesn't have to be like this.'

She thought, for a fleeting moment, about whether he might be right. Whether there was another way. Maybe they could do all this amicably, like a normal divorce. They could co-parent. Maybe they could even live together happily, like Prince Andrew and Fergie.

He made his eyes gooey. 'I love you, PQ.'

He was being Nice Mark, to try and get her to stay. The thing was, she realised, there weren't only two Marks. There were any number. He could make himself into whatever you wanted him to be. A man who couldn't keep his eyes off her, in the beginning. A man who worshipped her in bed, greedy for her curves and her Clarins-soft skin. Who'd wept with gratitude, the first time she'd cooked a Sunday roast for him and his poor, motherless son (even though George hadn't taken one bite). A visionary psychiatrist and philanthropist – or, if you preferred, a brilliant entrepreneur who had seized a gap in the lucrative wellness market. An alpha male who could make her damp, council house childhood seem like a bad dream. A bringer of love, joy and intergenerational wealth.

He could find out your weak points in a hot minute. He could work out what made you tick, and use it to build you up or bring you crashing down.

He could mimic the full range of human emotions with uncanny accuracy. He could make you feel like he was loving you, even while he systematically took you apart.

He took a step towards her, his eyes empty.

'Oh, Caroline...'

Then she felt a sharp pain in her thigh. Her first thought was that she must have been stung by a bee.

But a cold feeling was spreading through the area. Her leg started to feel numb.

She lost her balance, felt herself toppling to the side. She tried to break her fall by putting her arm out, but that had gone weak and useless, too.

Her mouth wouldn't work either. She couldn't get any words out. All she could do was stare at him.

She saw him lift her phone from the top of George's chest of drawers. He tapped on the icon for her banking app, and held the screen up to her face.

'*Let's check it's you*' suggested the text on the screen. Then there was a pinging noise as the software recognised her face. He brought up her bank balance. Her precious, hard-earned bank balance.

He was going to take it all. And he hadn't requested the bank transfer – for the rest of the half million – at all. Of course he hadn't. She'd been so stupid.

Mark typed things into the phone. Then he held it up to her face again. She closed her eyes, tried to twist her face away, but her neck wasn't working either.

'Good grief! How the devil have you blown fifteen grand in two days?'

Another ping came from the phone.

'Anyway,' said Mark. 'That's the money transferred back to me. Thanks, Cazza.'

'Mghhhh! Muhhh!' she managed.

He stood behind her and grabbed her under the armpits, making a loud 'huhhh' noise, as if he was winded from the effort of lifting her. Cheeky fucker.

As Mark dragged her backwards into George's walk-in toy closet, she realised these were probably her final moments. He dropped her next to a big box of Lego and covered her with a layer of dressing-up costumes, throwing a yellow polyester chicken suit over her face.

Her vision started to go, disappearing into purple and black blobs.

All of her body was numb. She could only feel her lips, tingling. At least there wouldn't be any pain. She was glad of that.

Just this ache of disappointment.

In the darkness, in her mind's eye, she thought of the pink bougainvillea. The pool, rippling with light in the afternoon sun. The margarita that she would never get a chance to sip. The novel she'd never finish, its pages lifting in the gentle breeze that came off the sea.

It wasn't fair. It wasn't bloody fair.

60

TERESA

Retford
Now

'It'll probably be alarmed up to the hilt,' warned Sunny, as we wound our way up the long driveway to Malham Manor. 'They clearly aren't short of a bob or two.'

The house looked like something out of *Homes and Gardens* magazine. Square and graciously proportioned, built from old red brick with ivy clinging to the north and west elevations. Tall chimney stacks on the four corners. Large, Georgian-style windows, their frames immaculate white.

There were three wide steps up to the front door, which was painted a gleaming navy blue and flanked by stone columns. I pressed the bell and heard it ringing from somewhere deep within the house.

What would I even say to Caroline, if she came to the door? I'd been trying to rehearse it during the drive down, but I still had no idea. Or was it possible George would come scampering up to the door himself? I'd have to fight the urge to scoop him up and take him away, back to Northumberland where I could keep him safe. I pressed the bell again, feeling quite sick.

'Nobody's home,' Sunny said. 'Are you sure you want to do this?'

I nodded. 'I'll go in, and you can keep lookout.'

'I'll grab my tools from the car. Hang on.'

'Two break-ins in two days,' I commented, as we walked around the back of the house. 'We should get a couple of those stripy jumpers, like burglars wear in children's books.'

'I can be Scarface Sunny,' he said, his face completely deadpan. 'And you can be...'

'Sneaky T,' I supplied.

There didn't seem to be anybody about. I could make out the felt roof of an outbuilding behind the high privet hedge that bounded the far side of the sweeping lawn – a potting shed, perhaps, or a garage.

Sunny suggested we try one of the kitchen windows. He neatly smashed the corner of one of the panes and slid his hand in to undo the catch. The lower sash slid up quite easily, making a gap big enough to climb through.

'Can you give me a leg up?'

'I think *I* should be the burglar.' Sunny's face was suddenly stubborn, as if we were fighting over roles in a playground game. 'And *you* can be the lookout person.'

'No. I know what I'm looking for,' I said, even though I didn't. 'Take the car back onto the main road and keep an eye on things. If you see any cars turning up the drive, phone me and I'll slip out. I'll run behind that hedge and climb over the far wall. I'll get back to the car and we can get away.'

'A getaway car,' said Sunny.

'Exactly.' I stepped towards him, face lifted, as if I was

about to kiss him. Then I remembered, with a strange little shock, that kissing was something we didn't do. I pulled back, looked down shyly, and pushed my hair behind my ears. 'Right. Let's do this.'

Caroline's kitchen was a large, double-aspect room with a dark-blue Aga set into an arched chimney breast. A white ceramic Belfast sink, with a gleaming swan-neck tap, stood in front of one of the windows, the sill lined with pots of fresh herbs. Copper pans hung from a rack over a wood-topped kitchen island.

I slipped my shoes off and tiptoed into the hall, taking in the grand staircase, with its arched, stained-glass window at the middle landing. There was an open door leading into a cloakroom, lined with Barbour jackets, with wellies paired in a rack beneath. Four old tennis racquets and a couple of cricket bats had been stuffed into the rack too. I imagined Sunny facing down Mark on the cricket pitch, doing one of his killer spin bowls.

Everything was immaculate. In the living room, the cushions were plumped perfectly, arranged on three Chesterfield sofas. Even the wooden logs, stacked to the side of the fireplace, looked like they'd been steam-cleaned.

I wished I had more time to poke around and explore. But I was looking for papers, documentation. Something to prove that George wasn't really theirs. Something to prove the link with Maisie.

Upstairs, I found another drawing room, with tapestry chairs and a full-sized grand piano, several silver photo frames positioned carefully on its polished ebony lid. And next door there was the study, with blood-red walls and a Persian rug on a polished wood floor. A mahogany desk dominated the room, its surface clear apart from a green-shaded lamp. I pulled on the desk drawers, but they were locked, apart from the top one which just held paper clips and a couple of pens. There were two filing cabinets – again, locked.

There was a letter lying on the desk. I picked it up. Surely that would be too easy...

It *was* a letter from a DNA testing company – but not the same one we'd used for my and George's swabs. There was a covering letter saying a report was enclosed, and a booklet with further information and FAQs.

I couldn't believe how lucky I was. Was this the real DNA test? The one that would prove I was George's grandmother?

But no – as I read the report, I saw this had been a test comparing *Mark's* DNA with George's. A "YDNA test", it was called. Why on earth had Caroline wanted this? I read the results, trying to understand. The report stated, with its technical, heavily caveated wording, that the test was consistent with Mark being George's grandfather. A positive result.

My mind began to work. So Maisie had got pregnant with Mark's son? And Mark and Jan had stepped in, and brought George up as their own?

But an additional test, on a second sheet, provided some further information. Mark was excluded as George's paternal grandfather.

What?

So this could only mean that Mark was George's... *maternal* grandfather? I paused for a moment, trying to work out what it meant. Mark was... George's mother's father.

That made no sense – not if George was Maisie's son.

Because Maisie's useless father, Joel, was dead. The police had confirmed that with the Australian authorities.

My head was whirling. Was this another falsified result, contrived by Caroline?

Or had I misunderstood Jan – was George not Maisie's biological child, after all?

I thought suddenly of the photographs upstairs – the ones on the grand piano. I'd hurried past without looking at them.

I climbed the stairs again, dashing off a quick text to Sunny to say I was okay, and just needed a bit longer.

The photos on the piano were a mix. There were some of Caroline in exotic locations. There was one of her wearing ski gear and an oversized pink bobble hat, the Matterhorn looming in the background. In one, she was on the deck of a yacht, looking out over an azure sea. There were one or two of George when he was younger. And there were some arty black and white ones, clearly done by a professional photographer.

In the largest one, a man was lifting a horrified George into the air, while Caroline stood, open-mouthed with delight, her hand on his shoulder. Around his wrist – I lifted the photo to examine it more closely – was the silver and navy watch that George always carted around in his rucksack.

And then I saw that this man – the man holding George – he was Michael. Joel's housemate at university.

A wave of dislike went through me. Michael had been a superior, alpha male type, fresh from an all-boys boarding school. He'd thought the sun shone out of his own backside because he was studying medicine, and played for the university's first fifteen rugby team.

Michael was George's grandfather? And he went by the name of Mark, these days?

So Maisie had somehow got together with... what, Michael's son?

But no. The test had said he was George's *maternal* grandfather.

I shook my head, trying to think. None of this made sense. I thought of Sunny, in the car outside. He'd be getting frantic. I'd have to go back.

But then something stirred at the back of my mind – a vague memory. I'd known Joel's flatmate as Michael, but now I thought about it, I had a feeling it might have been a nick-name. A play on the singer's name.

Because – that's right – everyone had thought it was hilarious when he'd hooked up with... Janet.

I sank down onto my knees by the piano. I closed my eyes and tried to summon up the memory again – the memory of lying on Janet's bed in our halls of residence, while she picked out something for me to wear to the party.

I remembered the scrape of hangers against the rail, like nails down a blackboard, as she pulled a dress out of the wardrobe. 'You can borrow this,' she said. 'It will be perfect for a summer party. It's a bit big for me, but it'll be fine on you.'

She threw it over to me. It landed on me, half covering my face, making me laugh. A yellow cotton dress with a daisy pattern.

There in Caroline's opulent drawing room, I drew my arms around myself. The memories that had been haunting me –

they hadn't been Maisie's, bleeding into my mind through George. They had been buried so deep inside that I had never recognised them as my own.

The ground was shifting under me. The walls I'd constructed in my mind, the locked doors to closed-off rooms, they were all falling down.

Now I could remember putting on the yellow dress, pulling it up over my hips. And I remembered arriving at Joel and Michael's house, announcing I'd only have one glass of the homemade punch, because I was on antibiotics for my sore throat. And later, lying down with Joel in a bedroom upstairs. He'd been throwing up and needed someone to keep an eye on him.

There'd been three or four steps from the bedroom up to the bathroom. I remembered helping Joel to stagger up them, my arms locked around his waist.

And sometime after that, once Joel had passed out, unresponsive on the bed, someone must have come in. Because someone had dragged her...

No. Someone had dragged *me.*

Up those steps.

I could almost feel it now – their hard edges jabbing into my spine.

There'd been gushing water. Probably to mask any noise.

And I'd been lying on the floor, my face pressed up to the side panel of a bath, my muscles turned to useless rubber.

I saw it now with perfect clarity – an expensive Swiss watch with a navy face, the hours studded with tiny diamonds. Thick fingers flipping open a belt buckle.

It had been about Maisie, but not in the way I'd thought.

Not her end. But her beginning.

My poor, poor love.

My first thought was that she'd found out, somehow, and that was why she'd gone away. She must have thought I hadn't truly loved her. That I couldn't love the child of a man who'd...

Who'd raped me.

I folded myself over, hands covering my head.

It took three attempts to pull my phone out of my pocket. I had to call Sunny. To let him know I was coming out, to be ready with the car.

What had I been given, that night of the party? I hadn't got into that state from one glass of punch.

And then... what? Michael, or Mark, had found Maisie? And where did George fit into all this?

Saliva flooded my mouth, and I knew I was going to be sick. I managed to scramble to my feet and ran into the hall, pushing open doors, desperately needing to find a bathroom. I found an airing cupboard, full of linen. Another cupboard which seemed to be a kind of bar, shelves stacked with wine and spirits bottles. And then I found myself in a child's bedroom. George's bedroom, bless him. I flung open a door that looked like it might lead to an en suite, but beyond it was just a walk-in cupboard.

At first, I thought it was a toy of some sort. A rubber leg from a joke shop. For a Halloween prank, perhaps. It was sticking out from underneath a chicken costume, with a woman's sandal wedged onto the foot. The toes had red nail varnish, chipped at the edges.

Don't be silly, I told myself. Gingerly, between thumb and forefinger, I lifted the chicken costume.

It's okay, it's okay, it's okay.

A life-sized doll. That's what it was. Wasn't it?

It's okay.

But it was Caroline, her filmy eyes staring straight up at the ceiling.

And there was a faint thumping noise coming from somewhere behind me. Footsteps, coming up the stairs.

61

MAISIE

Retford
Earlier that day

When Maisie began her afternoon shift at the holiday club, the children had just finished their packed lunches. They'd been playing Capture the Flag in the playing fields for most of the morning and now it was quiet time. Most of them were lounging on beanbags watching *Moana*, which was being projected onto a screen at one end of the gym hall. But George was sitting at the art table, drawing.

'Hello, you!' Maisie came in and sat down next to him on one of the miniature chairs. As always, she longed to reach out and bundle him into her arms, to breathe him in. As always, she pushed the feeling down, tried to behave as if he was just another child in her care.

She'd applied for as many holiday club shifts as possible, but for most of them she'd been assigned to the nursery team. This was only the second time she'd seen him in four weeks. During term time she saw a little more of him, as he came to her for help with numeracy a couple of times a week.

She looked down at what George was drawing. It was a hobbity house with two enormous chickens that, despite George's impressive drawing skills, looked a bit like dinosaurs. A small face stared out of one of the windows, and another figure was scattering food for the chickens.

'How are you? Are you having a good day?'

'No,' he said evenly.

'Oh dear. Why not?'

'Something's going on.' He spoke quietly, eyes fixed on the drawing, like a little spy conveying intel to his handler.

Maisie had impressed upon George, during their maths support sessions, that if he ever needed anyone to talk to – about *anything* – he could talk to her.

She hadn't exactly used the words 'guardian angel', but that was what she had meant.

It was one of the stages in her plan, which involved hiding in plain sight, in George's school, making sure he was okay. It was why she'd dyed her hair dark brown, and straightened it, and why she wore clothes from M&S and sensible shoes that made her look older than she was. It was why she'd changed her name, by deed poll, to Maisie Honeywell.

Miss Honeywell, to everyone in school. (Miss Honey, to George.)

She knew she didn't deserve to be his mother. Not when she'd given him up like that, and just let Mark take him. Not when she'd got in Jock's Land Rover thinking about her little white pills. But she could – and would – devote the rest of her life to watching out for him. Making sure he was okay.

'What's going on?' she asked him now, bending low.

He shook his head.

'Has something happened at home?' She knew that George didn't see much of Mark, that he was away for work most of the time. But sometimes, George had told her tearfully, he shouted. Maisie was keeping a note of these instances. She had the phone number and email address for the social work department – the children's services team – stored on her phone. Her threshold for using it would be low. But she didn't want George to end up in care, either.

She wasn't stupid. She knew there was zero chance that any court in the land would give him to her. The charity who'd looked after her, Bright Starts, had vouched for her when she'd applied for a minimum wage job in a chronically understaffed nursery in Glasgow, and then this classroom assistant role. They hadn't questioned why she'd wanted to move to Nottingham, had even helped her to rent a room in a shared house. But a court would investigate further, would see that she'd needed help getting off prescription drugs.

George was okay where he was. For now. Because Caroline... well, she seemed okay. She swanned around a bit, giving minor royal vibes. But George was always nicely dressed, with polished shoes. His face and hands were always clean and he smelled of soap. He always came in with a decent packed lunch, even if the contents didn't seem to vary at all.

And now he was shifting from one side of his bottom to the other, jiggling his feet.

'Do you need to do a run-around?'

George nodded. He slid off his seat and did a circuit of the gym hall, before returning to his drawing.

'What's up, George?' she repeated.

'Caroline was packing a case.'

'A case? What kind of case?' The skin on Maisie's arms prickled.

'A suitcase. I think she's running away. Like in *Five Run Away Together*.'

Running away? Was Caroline leaving Mark? Maisie supposed that nobody could blame her for wanting to leave that pig. For a brief moment, she flashed back to lowering George out of the bathroom window at Inverkillen House. That awful moment when the rucksack strap had broken free from its stitching.

'And she's ordered a suitcase for *me*.' He looked up at her, his eyes hollow. 'It arrived yesterday. It looks like a frog. A silly frog, for babies.'

'Where do you think you're going?' Maisie asked. 'On a holiday, maybe?'

He shrugged. 'When I went to stay in the hobbity huts last week, I just took my rucksack. Not a *frog suitcase*.' He shook his head in disgust.

Maisie paused. 'You've been to the hobbit houses? Like... recently? Not in your old life?' George mentioned his 'old life' quite often, referring to it quite matter-of-factly.

In my old life I didn't have to do maths.

'Yes. Caroline took me there. I stayed with Teresa, the sad, sad lady.'

Maisie's throat felt blocked, suddenly, like there was a great big ball of bubble gum stuck in there.

'Up in Northumberland?' she croaked.

'Up in North. Yes.'

'Why did Caroline take you there?'

'I don't know. She was selling puddings or something.'

'And this lady, Teresa,' she whispered. 'Why was she so sad?'

George frowned. He slid off his chair again. He did two circuits of the gym hall this time, and when he returned, his cheeks were red and flushed.

'She was sad because her Maisie went missing,' he panted. 'She searched and *searched*.'

Maisie's heart contracted. 'She searched?'

'Yes. And now Caroline is running me away.'

Maisie thought very hard for a few minutes. She thought about everything she'd built up, over the last few years, and how easily it could slip away. Then she made a decision. She took George by the hand and led him to the children's bathroom.

'Wait in there for a bit, would you? I'll be back in a minute.'

Then she went up to the holiday club supervisor, Mrs Jack. 'George is being sick, poor boy. Actually, it's coming out of both ends. Quite explosive.' She widened her eyes. 'I just phoned home, and his step-mum can't come and fetch him because she's got a migraine.'

Mrs Jack gave an exasperated sigh.

Maisie went on. 'She said his dad won't be able to make it either, not until six. Shall I take him over to the sick room at the senior school? We don't want it spreading around.' She grimaced, as if she was visualising what holiday club would be like tomorrow if all thirty children started exploding at both ends.

The supervisor nodded. 'Okay. You take him over. I'll ring round and see if anyone else can come in this afternoon. Looks like we might have our hands full.'

Maisie fetched George from the bathroom and picked up his coat and rucksack from the row of pegs in the corridor. 'We're going out on a little trip, okay, George? We're going to figure out what's going on, with the frog suitcase. We're going to pretend to be spies.'

George nodded, his face grave.

Maisie knew the route to the Jacksons' house. She walked past it most days, although she could never see much, glancing between the stone pillars that marked the entrance to their long, winding drive. Once, she'd sneaked past them, and made her way towards the house, keeping hidden by the trees and bushes that lined the drive. But when she'd come into view of the house she'd simply stood there, taking in its size, its elegant grandeur, feeling stupid. How could she, a barely qualified classroom assistant, ever hope to get the better of someone like Mark?

As they walked, Maisie thought about what George had said.

She searched and searched...

The house was only a fifteen-minute walk from school, and today they did it in ten because George was trotting ahead for most of the way.

But when they turned the corner of the main road and saw the stone pillars, the entrance to the driveway, Maisie stopped dead.

Mum's old car. Just parked there, with nobody in it, on the other side of the main road.

What the actual...

She knew the registration plate, because it had 'DOO' at the end. Mum had nicknamed the car, an ancient beige Skoda, 'The Mystery Machine'. Maisie knelt in front of George, swept a lock of fair hair away from his eyes.

'Now George, listen. We're going to go and speak to Caroline, okay? We need to find out what's going on.' She had no idea what she was going to say when she got to the house. No idea what she'd say to Caroline. Or to... Mum? It barely seemed possible.

All she knew was that it was time to act. She had to do *something*. She couldn't let George get taken away again.

'Okay.' He stared up at her, a reproachful look in his eyes.

'What?' She scanned his face, trying to work out what he was thinking.

'How long do we have to pretend you're Miss Honey?'

Maisie swallowed hard. Had George known who she was all along? She opened her mouth to answer him, but something caught her eye, over at the entrance to the Jacksons' driveway.

A man stood there.

Her heart jumped at the sight of him. She'd been primed for seeing Mark. But this wasn't Mark. It was... was it *Sunny*? She'd found him on a dating website, matched him up with Mum. That had been just a few weeks before she'd left. Had they actually stayed together?

He took a step towards them.

'Maisie?' His face was alight, as if he could barely believe what he was seeing. His arms came out, as if he was about to step forward and hug her. But he lowered them again, his movements slow, as if she was a rare animal and he didn't want to startle her. A baby deer or something.

'You look different,' he said. 'So grown up. And look at your dark hair.'

'You were at the hobbity houses!' George stared up at Sunny, his face full of wonder. 'How did you get *here*?'

Sunny crouched down in front of him. 'George,' he said. 'Good to see you, buddy. How's it going?'

George nodded. 'We've come to see Caroline, to find out why she got me the frog suitcase.'

Sunny stood up again and looked at Maisie. She thought for a moment that his eyes were wet.

'It's just a feeling, more than anything,' said Maisie. 'Caroline's planning on taking George on holiday, but something's not right.'

'Caroline's out.' Sunny turned to Maisie. 'There was nobody in when we rang the doorbell, no cars in the drive. But Maisie, your mum's here. She's gone into the house to look for... well, I'm not sure what she's hoping to find.'

'Me?' suggested George.

'Possibly.' Sunny nodded down at him. 'I'm keeping watch. Because, obviously, em, *strictly*, she's not supposed to be in there.' He allowed his eyebrow to flicker up.

'Oh. Okay.'

'She's going to be so pleased to see you,' he said to Maisie. 'She's been waiting for this.' His voice cracked. He cleared his throat and continued. 'For so long. Where –'

'Are you looking for Dad?' piped up George. 'Because he's working from home today. In the stables.'

'In the stables?' Sunny's voice was suddenly tense.

'Yes. The stables around the back. Behind the hedge, but before you get to the woods. That's where he keeps his office and also the cars. Also, he's been doing gardening.'

'What?'

'Yes, he was digging a big hole yesterday, in the woods. A trench, he called it. For growing cauliflowers.'

He was growing cauliflowers in a trench in the woods? A shiver flashed down Maisie's back.

'I'm going into the house,' she insisted.

'No. Wait. I'm going to phone Teresa now. It's not safe for either of you to be in there.'

He dialled her number. After ten rings, it went to voicemail.

'No answer.' Sunny turned to Maisie. '*I'll* go in.'

'You can't be in two places at once. You need to keep watch. And look after George. That's the most important thing.'

George's eyes were like saucers. He nodded up at Sunny. 'We can go in my den. It's in the holly bushes.'

'I know the house,' lied Maisie. 'And Mark and Caroline know me. I can talk them round, if there are any problems.'

'I don't know. We should probably call the police.'

'And tell them what? That Mark's growing cauliflowers, and Caroline is planning a holiday? That Mum's broken into their house?'

Sunny hesitated.

'I'll give you my number,' said Maisie. 'Just ring me if you see him coming. Or anyone else. We can get out quickly.'

'Okay,' said Sunny finally. 'I'll show you the window where she got in. But if you're not out in five minutes, I'm phoning the police.'

62

TERESA

Retford
Now

I swung round, stepping back out of the cupboard and into George's bedroom.

He stood there – Mark, or Michael – blocking the space between me and the door. In his left hand, he held a loaded syringe.

'Well, well,' he said, his voice amused. 'Teresa Jones. What the devil are you doing in my house?'

My legs felt as if they were filling with some thick, hot substance. I couldn't take a single step.

'Where's Maisie?' I managed.

'Long time no see, eh?' He said it casually, as if we were meeting at a drinks party, or a university reunion.

'What have you done to her?'

'What have I *done* to her? Good God, woman. I haven't seen Maisie in years.'

'But you've got George. You took George from her.'

'We took George *for* her,' he corrected, his voice neat and precise. 'When she asked us to.'

'When she asked you to? What do you mean? How were you even in touch with her? How did you find her?'

He curled his lip, looking at me like I was crazy. '*She* came looking for *me*.'

'I don't understand. She didn't know you were –' I swallowed hard. 'Her biological father. My God, *I* didn't even know.'

He gave an exaggerated shrug. I kept my eye on the syringe, still held lightly between his fingers.

'Chill, Teresa. It's a funny story, actually. When Jan had her second miscarriage, she uploaded our DNA onto some website, unbeknownst to me. She wanted it screened for health issues – she was convinced one of us had some sort of faulty gene, and the doctors said they wouldn't order the tests unless there was a third miscarriage. I know,' he said, shaking his head. 'Cruel, isn't it? So she took matters into her own hands, in her usual half-arsed, ineffective way. She didn't pay attention to what she was signing up for, didn't select the right privacy settings. Which meant that our DNA results were searchable for ancestry purposes, too. People looking for DNA matches. Long lost family and so on. I would never have agreed to it. But it was a happy accident, in the end.'

'*What?*' It was almost impossible to take in.

'That's how Maisie found me. She'd uploaded her own DNA. She was looking for her biological father. It was a big thing for her.'

'Her *DNA*? But I'd told her who her father was. I explained to her about Joel.'

Mark nodded slowly. 'Poor old Joel, eh? The convenient scapegoat, over in Australia where he couldn't defend himself. He always said that you were nuts. He said he hadn't shagged you in months, when you claimed to have become pregnant by him.'

My head swooped. The floor seemed to be pitching, like a ship in a storm.

'Maisie did the DNA test because she didn't trust you,' he went on. 'And she was proved right, wasn't she? When she found me. Her real father.'

I could barely speak. 'You will. Never. Be. Her father. Never.'

'Maisie not only *wanted* a father. She *needed* one. She asked me for advice, when she found out she was pregnant. One of life's truly serendipitous moments. She *happened* to be pregnant. I *happened* to need a baby. If I've learned anything in life, it's to capitalise on opportunities, whenever you can. If you don't, others will.'

'Who?' I managed. 'Who got her pregnant?'

'Her tennis coach. Ha! You didn't see that one coming, did you? Yes, it all came out, on one of our calls. About her secret boyfriend. The fact she'd got pregnant.' He paused, enjoying the moment. 'The fact she couldn't talk to her mum about it. Because she'd never been able to talk to her about anything. She broke down, the poor kid.'

The words were like daggers, plunging into my softest, most vulnerable parts. But then I seemed to hear and see Maisie in my mind. I could see her screwing up her face and saying 'What?!?' Like most teens, she'd been able to load that single word with utter disdain.

He'd flipped this around. He was trying to make me into the bad mother, the person in the wrong. I had to resist him, mentally, even if my own legs were about to give way. There was a chair standing against the wall, George's judo costume slung across it. I pulled it towards me, its thin metal legs scraping against the wooden floor. I sat down, pressing my quivering thighs down with both hands.

'Why would she come to *you*?'

He shrugged. 'I think she sensed that I was the sort of person who could sort things out. Who wouldn't make a big song and dance out of things. I offered her somewhere she could have some space and time while she got her head together. She decided she didn't want a termination, so Jan and I stepped in. Took the baby off her hands. It made sense, when Jan could only produce duds.'

'*Duds?*'

'Yeah. It turned out she did have a genetic fault. She passed it down to that thing she gave birth to.'

I thought of Jan, trying to contain herself and her unimaginable loss within the four walls of that basement prison.

'A... *thing*?'

He shrugged. 'It wasn't a baby, not in any real sense. Not with half its brain missing. And we *needed* a baby, a son to be exact. And he had to survive infancy, that was the fucker.'

'What are you talking about?'

'For, ah, for legal reasons.' He looked sheepish, just for a split second. 'To do with the family trust.'

I must have looked blank.

'The trust set up by Jan's father,' explained Mark. 'It settles benefits on those of his children who meet the conditions of the trust.'

'The conditions?'

Mark shrugged. 'Archaic, isn't it? A sort of incentive to produce males.' He gave me a dark half-smile. 'Males don't do well in that family, you see. Jan has five sisters and seven nieces.'

'You didn't know Maisie was going to have a boy.'

'There was a fifty percent chance. Those were odds worth taking, don't you think? Considering the reward in question.' He grinned widely, as if he was telling me about some genius business deal, a gamble that he'd pulled off. I wondered if he'd actually enjoyed the risks he'd had to take.

'So what... You've got access to this trust fund, while Jan rots in the basement up in Scotland?'

Mark nodded. 'For the purposes of Jan's family trust, it was expedient for her to remain alive. For all other purposes, it was better for her to be... contained, shall we say.' He frowned, forming the shape of a box with his hands.

'Why couldn't you just let Maisie go, then? Once you had your... *male child*?' I shuddered.

'I did, Teresa.' He smiled widely. 'I did, *years* ago. She just chose not to come back to you.'

'Because you'd indoctrinated her, I suppose? You'd turned her against me?'

'Oh, Teresa. The sad truth is, I hardly needed to do anything to make your relationship disintegrate. To unravel that precious "mother-daughter bond".' He rolled his eyes. 'All I did was a bit of editing of text messages. You finished it off yourselves. A little bit of misinterpretation here. A bit of hurt pride there. A sulk or two.'

'I knew it!' For a moment I felt triumphant. 'I knew those texts weren't from her.'

'Did you?' He sounded almost bored. 'Well *she* was completely oblivious. She thought you were disappointed with her for getting pregnant. Ashamed of her. She'd made her own bed and would have to lie in it, that sort of thing.'

I drew in a quick, sharp breath. 'I would have never, ever said those things! I would have supported her without question. I would have moved fucking mountains for her. Maisie would have known that.'

Wouldn't she? My heart hurt to think of her vulnerability, seventeen and pregnant and alone. Her bravery in reaching out to me, only to receive those cruel messages back.

'*Why*? Why would you do that?'

'I couldn't have you interfering with Maisie's decisions.' He glanced towards the toy cupboard, then back at me. For a moment, he looked uneasy.

I nodded. 'You have to hate us, don't you? The people you hurt? It makes it easier.'

He eyed me with a mixture of disgust and mild curiosity, as if I was some sort of unusual insect that had crawled into his house. 'I'm not sure I feel strongly enough about you to call it hate. But perhaps it's something along those lines.'

'Did you hate me that night? The night of the party? Is that why you did it?' Still, it seemed unbelievable that the girl in the yellow dress had been me. But Maisie was proof of that. George was proof. 'Is that why you drugged me? And raped me?'

'Teresa, *please*.' He frowned, wrinkling his nose as if I'd released a bad smell. 'That's a rather unbecoming way of putting it. You were totally out of it. What's the difference whether it was Joel who did the deed, or me?'

'I was "out of it" because you drugged me.'

'I wanted something, and I took it. Chaps did, in those days, before all this whining "me too" nonsense. It happened all the time – at parties, balls, nights out. You know it, I know it.'

'You took what you wanted?'

'I always do. That's the mindset that's got me where I am today.'

'But you must have got a hell of a shock when Maisie contacted you. You must have realised you'd be exposed as a rapist.'

He pointed the syringe upwards, and tapped it with his fingernail, as if to bring any air bubbles to the surface. 'Others in that position might have seen it that way. I simply saw an opportunity to contain that information, by containing Maisie.'

'Is everything an "opportunity" to you?'

'Yes, exactly. That's the difference between success and failure. That's why I am where I am, and you are where you are, scraping a living with your one-star holiday hovels.'

'You're nothing but a vile thug.' I drew myself up tall with a shuddering breath. 'But me? I'm capable of miracles. Because I made love come out of it. And here I am, confronted with the disgusting sight of you, and I'm filled with *nothing* except love for my daughter.'

I thought of George's hot, hot fire – his description of the love and the pain he could see in me.

Mark took a step forward, holding up the syringe.

It was happening, the thing I'd feared the most. I was going to die without ever finding out what had happened to Maisie.

My fury erupted into a white-hot plume. I screamed at the top of my lungs.

'*TELL ME WHERE SHE IS!!*'

63

MAISIE

Retford
Now

As soon as she climbed in through the kitchen window, Maisie could tell that Mark was in the house. The air was bristling with his presence, laced with the faint scent of his aftershave.

And as her ears adjusted, she realised she could hear voices from upstairs.

For a moment, she thought about climbing back out of the window again, telling Sunny to phone the police straight away. But what if... what if it was too late by then?

She drew a long knife from the block that stood on the kitchen island. Just in case. Then she crept up the stairs, willing the boards not to creak.

The voices were coming from one of the bedrooms – George's, from what she could see through the slice of open door.

And – oh my God! – she could see Mum.

Older. Thinner. Sadder, Maisie realised with a pang. But also, exactly the same.

Mark was telling Mum about what she, Maisie, had done – uploading her DNA to the website. And Mum just sounded… bewildered. Confused.

'Maisie did the DNA test because she didn't trust you,' Mark was saying. 'And she was proved right, wasn't she? When she found me. Her real father.'

Maisie wished she could run in and explain. She'd done the DNA thing after the shared nudes disaster – after her social death. She'd sent off the sample after Mum had told her that Joel, her supposed father, was dead. She'd been hoping for other relatives – half-siblings, maybe. She'd been clinging to the possibility of that other life by the ocean, under the warmth of the sun, far away from school. And it had been a huge shock when she'd found out that her father was called Mark, not Joel, and that he had never gone to Australia at all.

But now he was twisting everything, clearly enjoying the way he was hurting Mum: 'Yes, it all came out, on one of our calls. About her secret boyfriend. The fact she'd got pregnant. The fact she couldn't talk to her mum about it. Because she'd never been able to talk to her about anything.'

Woahhhh. That wasn't fair. She'd never said that.

Of course, there were *some* things she hadn't told Mum…

But she *had* told her about the pregnancy. At least she'd thought she had…

Now, she could hear Mark crowing about how he'd altered their text messages.

Maisie shrank with shame. She'd wondered about the messages before, and pushed the thoughts away for being too difficult. Somewhere deep down, part of her already knew that Mum wouldn't have said those things. That Mark must have messed things up between them, somehow.

And then she heard her mother's voice again: 'I would have moved fucking mountains for her.'

She was like a tiger or something. A fierce creature who would have torn Mark to pieces, to save Maisie.

And what had she, Maisie, done in return? She'd sulked in her attic room, not bothering to walk to the viewpoint so she could speak to Mum properly. She'd accepted Mark's ridiculous lies about the Wi-Fi and the phone line. She had given up too easily, choosing to believe his horrible, twisted version of Mum.

Oh Jesus, no. What was Mum talking about now? A student party. *Rape?* Mark had raped her? That was how she, Maisie, had been conceived?

Her body went hot and cold at once.

And then it was like everything shifted in her mind, the pieces of her life suddenly slotting together in a different way. She thought of her mother, always so judgey about teenage drinking, about unplanned pregnancies, casual hook-ups. The way her face had gone so stiff and frozen whenever these subjects came up. It hadn't been prudishness, as Maisie had thought. It had been trauma, pushed deep beneath the surface.

And the gloating look on Mark's face during that first WhatsApp call – that made sense, too. He'd said he hadn't the faintest scooby why Teresa had lied to Maisie, why she'd said her father was some Australian dude called Joel. He'd winced, implying Mum would go ballistic if she found out about Maisie uploading her DNA, uncovering Mum's dirty secret.

'Maybe it was an honest mistake,' Maisie had said. 'Maybe she got confused.'

Mark's laugh had boomed out, distorting over the laptop speakers.

Now, she was filled with loathing, creeping up inside her body like a hot, oily, stinking sludge. Loathing for Mark. And for herself, because this – *he* – was where she'd come from.

This was too much. She couldn't breathe. She had to get away. She'd go back down and find Sunny and George. Let Sunny decide what to do.

Then she heard her mother's voice again, rising pure and clear. Totally fearless.

'I'm capable of miracles. Because I made love come out of it. And here I am, confronted with the disgusting sight of you, filled with nothing except love for my daughter.'

Maisie dropped her face into her hands, her eyes squeezed tight shut. Mum *thought* she loved her. But she didn't even know her any more.

Then she heard Mum scream: '*TELL ME WHERE SHE IS!!*'

And she knew with absolute certainty that Mark was about to hurt her.

It was time for Maisie to act.

64

TERESA

Retford
Now

'T*ELL ME WHERE SHE IS!!*'

Then, as if in answer, a figure appeared. Standing behind Mark, with one finger held to her lips. A knife in her other hand, crossed over her heart.

My Maisie. My darling Maisie, my love.

She had long dark hair, with a blunt fringe. And dark eyeliner that made her eyes look smaller. But I'd know her anywhere. Of course I would.

It must have happened, I thought to myself. I must have already died. This was some sort of near-death experience. He'd injected me with his poison without me even registering it.

But I could still feel my legs, shaking against the seat of the chair. I could still feel my heart, the beats pounding my chest.

And I would have given them up. Every heartbeat. Every minute I had left. Just to see her one more time.

Joy came like a lightning strike. Eviscerating me. Almost unsurvivable.

Mark could see it from my face – he knew there was someone behind him. Just as he began to turn, Maisie lunged at him. In the split second it took for her to pull back her arm, ready to strike with the kitchen knife, he grabbed her wrist. He wrenched it behind her back with a sickening crunch. Her face contorted, in the same way it had done when she was a child, when she'd crashed off her tricycle, or fallen off the climbing frame.

Then he plunged the syringe into her shoulder.

With a howl of rage, I lifted the chair I was sitting on and flew at him, driving one of its thin metal legs into the base of his skull. He pitched to the side, trying to right himself, then lurched forwards onto his hands and knees. I went for him again, hacking at the back of his head, and the sound was like an axe splitting wood. His body fell forwards.

I turned. 'Maisie! Maisie, my love. Are you okay?'

She was on her knees by the end of George's bed, curled in on herself like a wounded animal, her left hand splayed over her right shoulder, the fingertips indenting the skin.

I crouched over her, covering her body with my own, rocking her. I could smell her – the faint, petal-sweet fragrance that had clung to her t-shirts and pyjamas as a little girl. The scent that had lingered on her bedsheets for just a few days after she'd gone.

And I could feel her heart, as light and rapid as a bird's. Both our heartbeats together, like when I'd carried her inside me.

'Breathe, my darling. Breathe.'

She tilted her head to the side, her face a rigid mask of pain and fear. 'Mama.'

It wasn't fair. It wasn't fair. I'd found her and now she was about to die. I was about to lose her all over again.

There was a noise behind me. Mark stood over me, lurching from one foot to the other like a drunken sailor. Holding Maisie's knife.

So I would die too. That part, I didn't mind. I didn't want to live any more if it had to be without her.

But this fight demanded every particle of strength I possessed. I launched myself backwards, driving my elbow up in the direction of his groin. There was a crunch of ligaments, a tearing of soft tissues, a strangled expletive. I felt the knife slice my shoulder, then heard it clatter to the ground. I fell to the floor and scrabbled for it, knowing I only had seconds. Mark, groaning, managed to kick it out of my reach.

Quick footsteps sounded on the stairs, outside the room. Behind me.

Mark, bent low over his bruised groin, raised his head to look up.

Sunny – dear, gentle Sunny – was brandishing a cricket bat. He took a step forward and swung it hard into Mark's left temple. Then he raised it again and thwacked the other side of his face. His head whipped to one side and then the other, like he was a boxer, about to go down.

He crumpled onto the floor.

Sunny turned to me, his eyes wild with fear. 'You're hurt.'

'See to Maisie,' I said. Her face was on the floor now, her arms collapsed out in front of her.

Sunny knelt down by her side, and laid his cheek against her face. His eyes were fixed on the far wall as he concentrated on trying to feel her breath.

He began moving her limbs, arranging her into the recovery position. 'Stay with us, Maisie. Stay with us, now.' He lifted his phone and dialled 999, asked for police and paramedics.

I curled in behind her, pressing my face to the back of her neck, breathing her in. Pretending that she wasn't about to slip away. Pretending that we would have more time.

George flew into the room.

'George!' cried Sunny. 'I said to stay in your den. It's not safe.' He glanced behind him at the shape of Mark on the floor. 'Go out into the garden, George. Go out NOW!'

The boy dropped to his knees beside me, crouching over his mother. 'Stay awake, stay awake. Two times two is four... Four times three is sixteen... Love you sixty-four, love you three hundred and twenty...'

65

TERESA

Northumberland
Three months later

I'd resurrected Maisie's old pink plastic drawing table. It had been at the back of the garage, under a huge box of art materials.

George and I had carried the table to the end of the driveway and now he sat drawing, bundled in his anorak, rapt in concentration. Sometimes, he looked up, scanning the houses and gardens at the other side of the street.

'Tell me about your drawing, my love.' I placed a glass of squash on the table in front of him. I was keeping an eye on him, doing little odd jobs around the front garden, getting it ready for winter.

'So this is a space robot,' he said, pointing to a shape made from three ovals, outlined in shadow. 'He's hard to draw because he's white, like an AirPod case. He lives in this other world place, with a sad, sad dragon.' The ridges on its back were grey and rocky like the mountains behind Inverkillen House.

'And what's this one?' I picked up one he'd dropped on the paving stones – it was about to flip away in the breeze. He'd drawn a creature with a navy-blue watch face for a head, its limbs made of links of silver metal. It was on an island, surrounded by a choppy sea where the waves were purple and red.

George shrugged. 'Dunno.'

I shivered in the weak November sun.

George glanced down at it and returned to his dragon.

I went to find Maisie, who was sitting on the bench outside the front door. 'It's amazing. His drawing – it's like an energy source for him.'

She didn't look up. She just sat there with her arms crossed, sunk deep inside an oversized hoodie. The medics at the hospital in Nottingham had assured us that the drugs that Mark had injected her with – a cocktail of strong sedatives and a paralytic drug normally used during anaesthesia – hadn't caused any long-term physical damage, but her reactions seemed dulled, sometimes. Slower than normal. The GP had said it was probably a trauma response, that she'd recover in time.

'*You* did that,' I said, sitting down next to her.

She pulled her feet onto the bench and hugged her knees as if she was trying to disappear.

'You taught him how to escape into other worlds, in his imagination. It's how he regulates his emotions and soothes himself. And how he processes things. That's why he's such a happy, cheerful little boy. And that's why he's got a good heart, a *loving* heart, despite... everything.'

'Despite the fact that a quarter of his DNA is Mark's, you mean?' She spoke in a spiky, challenging voice.

'Despite what he's been through. And that's because of the way *you* raised him, during his most formative years. Because of the love you gave him. And the sheer hard work you put in, in the most enormously difficult of circumstances.'

She never wanted to talk about Scotland, and how she'd spent her days there. But George had told me about how she'd taught him to draw, how she'd played with him 'all day long' and read stories to him 'all night long'.

'He's a hugely resourceful boy,' I insisted. 'He's a delight to be around. And that's down to you.'

George no longer talked about the days 'before he died'. Once we'd explained that those events were part of his own life, his own early memories, he seemed to accept them. The 'road-that-was-only-sometimes-a-road' was now just Lindisfarne Causeway. Inverkillen House was somewhere up north where he'd lived as a baby. The 'hobbity houses' were a somewhat boring part of his everyday life – he helped me to carry fresh towels and welcome baskets to them every morning.

'That's good,' his play therapist had said, when I'd discussed it with her. 'That's normal. He's processed those memories so he can allow them to fade, like normal childhood memories.'

He wasn't going to have normal childhood memories, though, was he? Not after so much loss, so much change.

We'd been trying to piece everything together, since Mark's death. The lengths he'd gone to had been extraordinary.

I'd been right about Andrea Hobson-Jones, the actor I had seen on the telly. She'd eventually unblocked me and messaged me back. Apparently, she'd become addicted to alcohol and prescription drugs when her acting career had failed to take off. She'd been receiving rehab treatment at Chesters, one of Mark's wellness centres, but needed a longer course of treatment than she could afford. Mark had offered to waive the fees if she did a small acting job for him – standing in for his wife at some school event. It had seemed harmless at the time, if a little odd. She'd cried down the phone when I told her what had happened to Maisie.

We still didn't know for sure how Mark had manipulated young Ally. How he'd convinced him to pretend he was coming to Scotland with Maisie, only to cut off contact as soon as she'd left. But the police confirmed there'd been a large payment from Mark to an elite tennis academy in the US, around the time Maisie had gone missing. A 'donation', the tennis academy had called it. And medical bills had been covered by a third party, too – Ally had undergone three different surgeries to repair his knee. But he'd left the tennis academy a year later. He was travelling around South America now, the police had said – to all intents and purposes unreachable. They still wanted to question him about Maisie, and about three other young girls he'd 'coached' at the club, one of them under sixteen.

The police had explained the business with the phones, and it still made my head spin. It seemed that Mark had stolen Maisie's mobile phone as soon as she'd arrived at Inverkillen House, and given her a basic replacement, setting it up with the wrong number saved under 'Mum'. When Maisie thought she was messaging me, she was actually messaging a third phone that belonged to him. And Mark had used her original phone to exchange messages with me, using some of Maisie's words and some of his. And he'd passed on my own messages to Maisie's replacement phone, editing them as he pleased.

Once Maisie had been dosed up with tranquillisers, and had given up walking to the viewpoint, he'd had to write the messages himself. That was when he'd slipped up, forgetting to write 'I love you 2'. He hadn't reckoned on that causing such an enormous ping on my maternal radar. But he'd handled the police involvement like a pro, convincing the officers, via Maisie's original phone, that all was well.

And then he'd been free to continue with his plan, using drugs to slowly dismantle her. To take her to pieces so he could take her child.

'I'm going back to bed,' said Maisie, getting up.

My heart sank. She'd only just got up an hour ago. She spent most of her days either asleep or watching Netflix on her iPad.

When she'd first come back, I had tried to understand it all by telling myself that there were two Maisies. There was the one I'd held safe in my heart during the years she'd been missing. The one with pigtails who'd sat sweetly at the kitchen table doing jigsaws, almost breaking from the weight of her secrets.

And the other one, with dark hair and a heavy fringe that hid her beautiful eyes. The one who had given up art and drawing, and talked in a slow, flat voice, like she just wanted to go back to sleep. The one who had made the decision, four and a half years ago, not to come back home. Even once she'd wrenched herself away from Mark and Inverkillen House.

I loved them both, with a ferocity that kept me awake at night. Even if I sometimes struggled to understand them.

When we'd come home from Nottingham, once the hospital had released Maisie and the police had finished with their questions, we'd sat down at the kitchen table and I'd asked her to tell me everything.

She'd told me – as briefly as she could, as if she couldn't bear to think of it – about what had happened in Scotland, about her escape attempt four and a half years ago, and how she'd pieced a life back together for herself afterwards, with the help of the charity.

She knew, by that time, that I hadn't sent the text messages she'd received, in that area of patchy signal, high up on that forest path. Yet I could see that some part of her was still hurt by them. That somewhere inside her mind there lurked a version of me who'd rejected her.

I kept apologising. 'I'm so sorry I wasn't here, when you brought George back home that time. Mark – although I didn't know it was him, at the time – sent me on a wild goose chase up to Skye. He was using your phone then, too, darling. I had no idea...'

'I know,' she said dully.

'And when you broke away from Mark...'

'I was in the rehab place for a while, Mum. I wasn't in a good place. My teeth were falling out. I didn't want you to see me like that.'

I sat there at the kitchen table, bemused, trying to find words, wondering what I could possibly say that wouldn't sound like a criticism.

You should have come back.

I would have loved you, whatever state you were in.

You left me alone, all that time, thinking you were dead.

'But after the rehab, darling. If you knew that the text messages weren't real...'

'I didn't *know*, Mum. I didn't want to think about them.'

I tried again. 'But if you suspected...'

'I knew they *might* not be real. But I couldn't face the risk that they *were* real.'

I nodded. 'I think I understand.' She'd been so fragile that any risk of further rejection had been too much to face.

But what about me? What about my mother, who had died without seeing Maisie again?

'It's a pity you didn't see my campaigns on Facebook, from when you were missing. You would have realised.' I realised, as soon as I said it, that she would interpret this remark as 'judgey'. And maybe there was a slight part of it that was... not judgemental, exactly, but a bit needy. Loaded with my desperate need to understand.

She sighed heavily. 'I explained, Mum. About social media. I thought Mark might use private detectives to try and track me down, so I stayed off it completely.'

She started picking at her fingernails, breathing heavily through her nose.

'I know, my love. You did the right thing. You couldn't risk Mark finding you.'

Her eyes, half-hidden by the fringe, became sorrowful, like a child's. 'And I thought you would have got over me, by then.'

My heart plunged again. How had this happened? How had my love failed to reach her? How had she not understood?

'I would have walked to the ends of the earth to...' I had shaken my head, a lump swelling in my throat.

She'd writhed in her seat and brought her hands up by her ears, as if trying to block me out.

'I'm not as good as you, Mum. Okay?'

'That's not what I meant, my darling.' I'd kept my voice soft.

That conversation had been three months ago. Since then, I hadn't pushed. I'd said I was always here to talk, whenever she was ready. I told her, dozens of times a day, that I loved her. Sometimes, it felt like watering a plant that was already dying. Flooding it with sunshine, only to see its leaves darken and wither.

Now, Maisie rose and began to walk back into the house.

'Would you like to make George's sandwich?'

I saw her shoulders droop. 'Maybe later,' she said.

Since she'd got home, Maisie had never referred to George as her son. She wouldn't accept that she was a mother. She'd been given antidepressants by the GP. She'd embarked on a course of counselling. None of it was helping.

'Why don't you spend some time with him?' I suggested. 'You could just watch a film together.'

'He's better with you,' she said.

'But you've always looked after him so beautifully, darling,' I said. 'When you were in Scotland with him. And being Miss Honey, just so you could watch out for him.'

'But he's okay now,' she said. 'He's away from them. And he's got you.'

She made her way upstairs. I longed to follow her, to pull her into my arms and hold her. But since coming back, she flinched and stiffened whenever I touched her.

'Where's Maisie gone?' George asked, skipping up the steps.

I planted a kiss on the top of his head. 'She's gone upstairs to have a rest, darling.'

He nodded and ran into the house.

I found them later. Maisie was asleep on her side, facing the wall, and George was lying quietly behind her, with one of his hands, star-like, on her back.

'What colour is it today?' I whispered, sitting down on the side of the bed and stroking his hair.

'Black,' he said, looking up at me with those enormous eyes.

'Nothing is working,' I said to Sunny later, while we were taking a walk along the beach. The cloud hadn't lifted all day and the sea was grey and dull, but George had needed to get out. He raced ahead of us on the sand.

'She won't even look me in the eye.'

'Keep going. It's just going to take time. It's only been a few weeks, really.'

'It feels like a nightmare. I've finally got her back, after all those years of longing for her. And now – it's like it's too hard for her. She's trying to disappear again. Right before my eyes. And I can't do a single thing about it.'

'You're doing everything you possibly can.'

'I feel like I've run out. I've run out of options. I've run out of energy. Sometimes... sometimes I even wonder if it's best for George, after all, staying here. Maybe he'd be better with a foster family, without this sadness hanging over everything, this heaviness.'

'Stop,' said Sunny, his voice low and firm.

'I feel like my heart is breaking. I feel like *I'm* breaking.'

'You won't break,' he insisted.

'I will,' I wailed.

'Well, if you do, I will hold all the bits of you together and keep you safe. Just like you are doing for Maisie.'

'I want her back,' I whispered.

'Keep hold of her,' said Sunny. 'Just keep holding on.'

His voice quivered with emotion, although he cleared his throat, trying to hide it. He was holding on too, of course. I'd been telling him, for years, that I couldn't have a physical relationship while Maisie was missing. That it could never work because of my intrusive thoughts about what might have happened to her. But now she was back, and I still couldn't let him near me.

There was one enduring question, always in my mind. How could I keep us safe?

Sunny had tried, harder than anyone. He'd inflicted the fatal injuries on Mark, that day at Malham Manor, thrashing the life out of him with the cricket bat. He had protected Maisie and George as if they were his own. He had risked his life and his freedom for us.

And it still wasn't enough.

'I'll never forget what you did for us,' I said. 'I know how much you risked.'

Charges hadn't been brought against Sunny – or me. The police and prosecutors had been satisfied that we'd been acting in self-defence, using reasonable force in defence of ourselves and others. But they'd questioned us separately for hours, while Maisie lay in hospital. I'd got back everything I wanted that day, and almost lost it again, too.

I stared out to sea. A gleam of light moved over the surface of the water for a moment and then disappeared. 'That day... It was almost like you loved Maisie as much as I do.'

He gave a short, gruff laugh. 'I've loved you for years. How could I not love them?'

His love was strong enough, free enough, to spill down the generations. Even though I couldn't give him anything back. This kind, gentle man was the most astonishing person I'd ever met.

He lifted his hand gently, moved a lock of hair away from my eyes. Stroked it into place behind my ear.

I felt that STOP sensation again – the grinding of gears. It was no good.

'I have to let you go,' I said. 'I'm killing you.'

Sunny shook his head. 'Why do you keep saying that, T? I'm good. I'm *more* than good. If this – chatting with you, walking along the beach – is as much as you'll ever let me love you, then I'm perfectly happy to keep doing it forever.'

I could feel my hands clenching at my sides. My muscles tensing, as if readying to fight back.

And then a murky memory floated up, of another place and time: the yellow dress. The cold, tiled floor of the student bathroom. Hands, moving over me, full of malignant purpose.

A seizing up in my body. A silent scream, echoing around in my head all these years.

STOP. STOP. STOP.

George raced up to us, colliding into Sunny and flinging his arms around his waist, showering us both with sand.

'Woah! Steady!' Sunny laughed, placing a protective hand on top of George's head. George smiled up in return, completely unguarded, his expression reflecting the lightness in Sunny's face.

Perhaps, to help Maisie heal, I first had to heal myself.

George scampered off, and Sunny turned to face me again. 'I was thinking. There's one thing you haven't tried yet. What about giving Cheryl a call?'

66

MAISIE

Killendreich
A few days later

As soon as Adrian led them around the back of the house, Cheryl went all wobbly. She had to stop and take a puff from her inhaler.

'What a place,' she muttered, her face pained, as if they'd taken her to a sewage processing plant, or a rubbish dump.

Maisie felt irritated. It was she who'd lost years of her life to this place, not this weird Cheryl. She didn't really understand why Mum had insisted on bringing her at all. She'd been talking all the way up in the car, talking about energy fields and things like that.

Adrian led them to a clearing between the trees, up behind the house. An area of torn-up earth.

'This is where the pet graveyard was. The police had to dig it all up.' Adrian shook his head, sucking air through his teeth. 'Most of the bones they found were animal bones. Dogs and cats.'

Cheryl shook her head, her purple kaftan flapping in the breeze.

'I remember Jan talking about her dogs,' said Mum. 'When we were at uni. They used to have springer spaniels – gun dogs – back in the day. They used to take them up into the hills for shooting expeditions.'

For a moment, Maisie remembered the Inverkillen House she'd imagined at first, the version Mark had sold to her, when he'd suggested that she and Ally come up for the summer. A proper country house home, with summer picnics and swimming parties. Tennis matches and shooting weekends. A man who wanted to try and be her dad.

She surveyed the area in front of them, the dark mounds of churned-up earth where the ground had been disturbed. On a small boulder, at the side, lay the little stone markers that had marked the pet graves. And the remains of a wooden cross, held together with wire.

'This bit here is where they found the first skeleton.' Adrian puffed out his cheeks and blew.

The police had confirmed they'd found the remains of a newborn. A male with significant congenital deformities.

At least her little half-brother had died of natural causes, Maisie kept reminding herself. There was nothing she, or anyone, could have done to save him. A kind doctor from the hospital in Aberdeen had explained that, when she and Mum had gone in to view his medical records. His birth defects had not been compatible with life, and his life expectancy at birth had been a matter of hours or days.

The doctor explained that arrangements had been made with a children's hospice in Dundee – specialist nurses were supposed to visit Inverkillen House to provide end of life care for the baby, and support the family through this time. But, unbeknownst to the Aberdeen team, Mark had cancelled the visits, saying they'd decided to return to their other home near Nottingham, where they'd be amongst friends and wider family. He said he'd arranged support from an equivalent service there. The staff had had no reason to doubt him, a psychiatrist working in the field of mental illness.

But instead, he'd let his son die without the care that would have made him comfortable. His death – his little life – had to fall through the cracks. Public records had to show that he'd been born, but not that he'd died.

And Maisie felt that *she* had let him fall through the cracks. She hadn't wanted to think about him. Nobody wanted to think about a baby who couldn't live. Not even Jan.

After George had gone to Nottingham, Jan had taken to the basement. It seemed she'd developed acute agoraphobia, on top of the depression she'd struggled with since adolescence. Mark had kitted the basement out for her, arranged food and supplies to be brought to her, but she'd stayed there by her own choice. After Mark's death, after it all came out, she was moved to a facility in Edinburgh for assessment, and was now being cared for by nuns in some sort of religious place.

'And the second skeleton was here,' Adrian said gravely, pointing to the far right of the torn-up ground. A sudden breeze shivered through the trees and a few droplets of rain fell.

'Zuleika,' whispered Maisie.

It seemed that Zuleika, the woman who'd helped Maisie to give birth, and had provided her and George with care during those early days, had been murdered. Cause of death was blunt force trauma to her skull. She'd been undocumented, and the police still hadn't been able to track down her family. She'd simply known too much. She'd been thrown away like rubbish.

Maisie often wondered why Mark hadn't just killed her too. Sometimes, she wished he had.

'Want to see inside now?' Adrian asked.

He let them through the main front door, into the hallway with the grand staircase. Maisie remembered the first day she'd arrived. How she'd been so nervous to meet Mark, the man who was her biological father. She remembered fancying herself as a sort of Jane Eyre character, embarking on an adventure. She remembered how awkward it had felt, not knowing what to call him. Not knowing what kind of man he would turn out to be.

Adrian led them through the higgledy corridor on the staff side, and up the steep grey stairs. At the top of the stairs, they turned to face a door on their right. A fire door with a deadbolt top and bottom.

She shrank back.

'How about I wait here,' said Mum, pushing open the door. 'I'll stand here and make sure this door stays open while you look around.'

Adrian led Maisie through, with Cheryl following behind, tutting loudly. They passed the bathroom, with its high window, the one from which she'd lowered George in his rucksack harness. It now had a security grille across it.

Her pulse quickened as she entered the little room where she had lived for three and a half years. It looked smaller than she remembered. She could barely believe that she'd slept with George in that single bed, had played and sung and taught him here, that she'd made a world for him out of these few square feet.

And there was the window, the one she'd gazed through

at night to see the stars. The one she'd opened to breathe the pure night air during stifling summer nights. Where she'd sat watching during the day, seeing the tops of the pine trees waving in the wind, and lifted George up so that he could see too.

It had been fitted with a security grille. Black steel rods.

'Cockwomble,' cursed Cheryl, under her breath.

Maisie realised that Mark must have arranged this, when she'd run away to Northumberland with George. He must have ordered Jock to make these alterations, before summoning him to collect her from the hospital. This was what she'd been heading back to, when she'd climbed out of the Land Rover that day, and decided to take one step at a time.

The hospital in Northumberland had confirmed to the police that they'd never treated George. It seemed that Mark had staged his accident in the bath, and sedated him to mimic the effects of secondary drowning, before handing him over to Caroline in the hospital car park. Although Maisie would never be able to prove it now, she was sure he'd also drugged her that night. She understood, now, that this was how he controlled people – carefully tailored 'treatment plans' of mind games and psychiatric drugs.

Maisie had barely been able to take it all in, over the last few months, as details of what Mark had done began to emerge. It was as if she was watching it on some true crime documentary, as if it had happened to someone else.

But now she curled her fingers around the cold, hard window bars, and she finally understood. Her choices had been taken away. Mark had forced his will upon her, just as he had done to her mother at that student party.

She hadn't given her child up. He had been taken.

She would have to think about it all later, and work out what it meant. Now, she followed Cheryl and Mum out of the house, back up the rise to the patch of turned-over earth. The medium stood for a moment, brushing the sleeves of her kaftan, and its long skirt, with her hands, as if brushing off specks of dirt.

Then she held up her arms and began to say something in another language. Gaelic, perhaps. Then she said some words in English.

May you dance with the light in the morning
May you shine in the sky as the sun goes down
May you rest in the earth where new roots grow
May you be held in the arms of your ancestors

Maisie felt a shiver run along her arms.

'You okay, pet?' asked Cheryl, when she'd finished. She reached into her pocket for her inhaler, took another long puff.

Maisie thought carefully and then she spoke. 'There's something about this place. I used to think I could hear things.'

Adrian nodded gravely. 'I heard things, too. Laughing, and the sound of footsteps. But Dad always said that was Jan, down in the basement. He said that noise can travel, through the pipes and things, especially when it's quiet.'

Mum's mouth moved into a thin, pressed line. She wasn't impressed with Jock. He'd told the police he'd always assumed Maisie was staying at Inverkillen House voluntarily. Which, in a way, she was. He'd claimed not to know anything about any dead baby.

But he'd been remunerated very handsomely by Mark –

or rather, by Jan's trust fund. He'd saved enough to make sure that Adrian would be well provided for, after he'd gone – which would be soon, as he had an inoperable tumour in his brain. It had grown slowly since being discovered nine years ago, but it was increasingly affecting his vision, his co-ordination, and now his 'down-below', according to Adrian. Once Inverkillen House had been sold, Jock was going to move to sheltered housing in Killendreich, and Adrian was moving to an assisted living facility.

As Mum had said darkly, a desperate parent would do almost anything to protect their child.

'And Jan heard things too,' Mum continued now. 'Babies crying, voices through the walls. But that might have been a symptom of her illness. Or, I suppose, just a symptom of her isolation.'

Maisie had read about this. Prolonged isolation could make you imagine things – voices, faces. It was your mind, trying to protect itself.

Suddenly, she felt it again – the intense loneliness of being in this house. The way it had pressed down upon her, day and night. The way it had drained her, like an illness. The way she and George had clung to each other, creating imaginary worlds to survive.

She thought of the short, dark winter days, the curtains drawn across the attic window to keep the warmth in. The long summer twilights, shadows stretching across the floor.

'The mind can do funny things,' said Cheryl, 'Sometimes, ghosts are just an echo of what someone most longs for.'

Maisie thought of those voices in the forest, calling out her name. Calling out for what had been lost.

She hung back with Mum as they walked to the car.

Adrian hurried on ahead, with Cheryl, grilling her about ghosts.

'It was awful here,' she said finally, swallowing down a big lump in her throat.

'I know, darling,' said Mum.

She needed to try and explain.

'I was Little Maisie, when I was with you,' she said. 'Good, sweet Little Maisie, with no complications. That's why it was hard to tell you about... you know.'

She'd been afraid that Mum might not be able to love the later version. The one whose nudes had been shared on the internet, the one who'd had sex in the tennis club changing rooms. The one who'd got addicted to tranquillisers and opiates and lay in bed all day. Who'd given up her baby for an easy life.

But that was *Mark's* version of her, wasn't it? She thought again about the bars on the window, how cold and hard they'd felt under her skin. And she realised that, even though he was dead, she would have to spend the rest of her life fighting him.

'I turned into somebody that I didn't like. I thought you wouldn't like me either.'

She thought Mum would rush in with soothing contradictions. But she just laughed, as if Maisie had said something genuinely funny.

And then, for some reason, she remembered how Mum had spoken to Mark in George's room at Malham Manor. The way her voice had risen, pure and clear. Completely, utterly lit.

'I'm capable of miracles. Because I made love come out of it. And here I am, confronted with the disgusting sight of you, filled with nothing except love for my daughter.'

Suddenly, in a wild leap of understanding, she got it. Mum loved each and every and all versions of her. She loved everything Maisie had ever been, right back to when she'd been a clump of cells she should never have wanted. And she loved everything she would ever become.

It *was* some kind of miracle. Something that didn't make any sense.

She wasn't quite able to look at Mum yet, wasn't ready to see all that love in her eyes. But she stopped, there on the gravel in front of that terrible house, and she held out her arms.

67

CAROLINE

Malaga, Spain
Three months later

There was nothing in particular to get up for, so Caroline lay in bed for a while, itching at a swollen mosquito bite behind her knee, and another in the crease of her groin. Breathing in the smell of drains.

There were a few niggly issues with the apartment. An eggy smell wafted up from the kitchen sink, even though she poured bleach down it every night. And the toilet kept getting backed up. Most mornings, she had to have a good go at it with the plunger.

The landlord company had sent a man out, but she hadn't been able to understand what he'd said.

He had gesticulated wildly, jabbing a finger in the direction of the building site just over the road from the apartment. Maybe they were messing up the drainage system, as well as banging and drilling all day long. Sixteen months, it was due to go on for.

She'd be gone by then, she supposed. She'd paid six months' rent up front. But after that, she had no plans. No means of supporting herself. None of Mark's money was due to come to her. It hadn't even *been* Mark's money, as it turned out. It had come from Jan's family trust, and now the lawyers were crawling all over that, talking about embezzlement and breach of trust. Malham Manor had been mortgaged up to the hilt and his wellness business had gone into administration, a bunch of investors all lining up to try and get their money back.

It turned out that neither the locals nor the expats who lived in the area were interested in sticky toffee puddings or crumbles. Not in this heat.

She was going to have to apply for some private chefing gigs. She'd sent off her CV to a couple of agencies. But with five years out of the game, there hadn't been so much as a sniff of interest.

Mark had planned to bury her alive.

The drugs he'd injected her with, in George's room at Malham Manor, wouldn't have killed her, even if the medics hadn't intervened. Apparently, he'd been planning to dump her in a trench he'd dug in his vegetable garden. Would she have woken up, she wondered? With soil in her nose and in her eyes, filling her mouth when she opened it to scream?

Sometimes, in the night, she woke up convinced that she was being suffocated. She had taken to sleeping with the windows and the patio doors open, trying to ignore the whine of the mosquitoes.

She would have to call somebody else out, she supposed. Another plumber, who spoke English.

Perhaps she could ask Terry and Barbara, her English neighbours down the road, for a recommendation. They'd been quite pleasant in their own way, had even invited her to an ex-pats' curry night at some Indian restaurant in the next town.

Not really her type of people, though. Terry who looked like he was in the late stages of a multiple pregnancy, his polo top stretched tight over his belly. Barbara with her smoker's cough and her over-bleached hair. The inspiring quotes that they'd framed and hung on the walls of their downstairs loo.

Laugh, love, eat, repeat!

Positive vibes only!

Mark had planned to bury her alive.

She really should finish that Marian Keyes book. She'd lain out by the pool quite a bit when she'd first arrived, but had spent most of the time scrolling on her phone, unable to concentrate for more than a few minutes at a time. And there seemed to be some kind of problem with the swimming pool filter. The water was murky and had a definite smell to it.

George had sent her one of his pictures the other day. It had arrived in the post – a picture of a family playing on the beach. A man, two women and two little children.

Caroline had dropped it into a pile with the others. She supposed that she should reply to him.

And she should really get in touch with Teresa. But what was there to say?

Thank you for saving my life.

Sorry for the business with the DNA tests – it was nothing personal.

'Blackmail' was such an unbecoming word.

I was trying to escape from a controlling relationship. I wasn't thinking straight.

That was what she'd told the police, when they'd questioned her over and over again. There had been no charges, in the end. No punishment, except... except *this*. To live out this life that she'd wanted.

Her stomach swooped with dread as she thought of the day ahead. Its blinding heat and its emptiness. She could send queries to more agencies, she supposed. She could – and she'd been meaning to do this for weeks now – walk down to the town and buy a postcard to send to George. She could experiment with making some cold puddings – cheese-cakes or English trifles, perhaps – before tipping them into the bin, because she had no appetite, these days. Perhaps the expats would go for them. Not that Terry or Barbara needed any more puddings, from the look of them.

No. It was all too exhausting. Self-care, that was what she needed. She could lie by the pool, and just ignore the smell. She could make herself a margarita and finish the Marian Keyes book.

Mark had planned to bury her alive.

She turned over in bed, pulling the duvet up as far as the bottom of her ribcage – she couldn't tolerate it anywhere near her face. It was only half past ten. She could sleep for another hour, perhaps. Then there would be less of the day to kill.

68

TERESA

Windermere
Six months later

Jan was staying in Nazareth House, a place run by an order of nuns. It was perched high on a hill overlooking Windermere. It wasn't a mental health facility, they'd been keen to stress on the phone. The nuns had no formal training. They just offered a quiet place to stay, on an ad hoc basis, for people whose troubles were spiritual in nature.

George had started asking about the woman who'd claimed to be his mother, back in 'the old time'. So, after careful discussion with his play therapist, Maisie and I had decided to take him to visit her.

We found her in a sunlit room at the back of the house, with large windows overlooking a lawn scattered with the first fallen leaves. She sat with a plastic laundry basket in front of her and she was sorting the items into piles. George hesitated at the doorway, and then approached her.

'Jam,' he said. He bent over his rucksack and took out his

angel and his shepherd. He waved them in front of her, dancing them around with a fixed smile on his face. It was as if he had retained some sort of muscle memory of how to engage with her. And indeed, he was rewarded with a watery smile.

Maisie, who had flumped down onto one of the ancient, chintzy armchairs, held out her arms. George hopped onto her lap with a sharp intake of breath, like a swimmer coming onto land. I hadn't realised he'd been holding his breath.

He looked up at Maisie, and she dropped a kiss onto his forehead.

'This seems like a nice place.' I settled myself onto the sofa. 'The person who showed us in was lovely.'

'Sister Monica,' said Jan, nodding.

'Do you like it here?'

'They leave me to my own devices. But I've started joining in with compline. We sing by candlelight. There was a long time when I couldn't pray at all. But it's different, here.'

Suddenly, I felt we shouldn't have come. What was there to say? I couldn't just start talking about Jan's dead baby, or the years she'd spent in the basement of Inverkillen House. We could hardly sit chatting about Mark and his Machiavellian schemes, his psychopathic traits. Or about how I'd driven a steel chair leg into the base of his skull, before Sunny had finished him off with the cricket bat. I couldn't tell her about how I could still hear the splitting sound of wood and bone when I woke up in the middle of the night.

But Jan turned to Maisie. 'They explained to me about Mark. About the things he did to you. The way he made you give up the boy.'

George tucked his head under Maisie's chin and cuddled in.

'I suppose you're going to say you had nothing to do with it?' There was a splinter of ice in Maisie's voice.

'He told me that it was all God's plan, and I just needed to have faith. He said you were addicted to drugs, that you never wanted the baby in the first place. He said you were just doing it for the money. I didn't know that he'd taken you...' She swallowed hard. 'That he'd taken you from your mother.' And then she muttered: 'I'm sorry.'

Maisie paused, and I wondered what she was thinking. When she and I spoke privately, she tended to refer to Jan as 'that psycho bitch'. But she gave a small sigh. 'We're still here. That's the main thing.'

'Have you been to the house?'

'We did visit,' she said. 'A while back.'

'It's being sold?'

'I think so. The lawyers are dealing with it all.'

There'd been some talk of varying the terms of the trust, of recognising George as a child of the family, even though he was no biological relation to Jan. It would probably take years to sort out.

'Where will you go?' Jan looked confused, as if it was impossible for Maisie to exist anywhere else outside Inverkillen House.

'I'm living with Mum at the moment. But I'm about to move to Edinburgh, with George. I'm starting a degree in creative and therapeutic arts.'

My heart swelled with pride every time I thought about it.

She'd been doing an access to higher education course, building up her portfolio. George had attended the local primary school, and I'd looked after him in the afternoons while she studied. He'd helped me with the welcome baskets, feeding the chickens and the ducks.

'She's amazing at art,' I said.

'My drawings?' said George, bobbing up. He slid off Maisie's knee and ran to his rucksack, pulling out his folder.

'Yes, would you like to see George's drawings?' I said. 'I think you might find them interesting.'

Jan's brow creased as she looked through them, and two deep dimples appeared in her chin. The pictures focused on various activities – swimming in waterfalls, flying on dragons around mountain peaks and castle battlements, walking enormous dogs. There were two small boys in every single one.

Finally, Jan got it. She looked up at me, her eyes wet with tears, her face flooded with something that looked like peace.

George hadn't been able to replace the first George, Jan's lost, longed-for baby. He hadn't been able to take on his soul, no matter how many prayers she had offered up. But, through some mystery that none of us could fully grasp, he carried that boy with him.

Which was not the same thing, of course. But at the same time, it was everything.

When we said goodbye, George paused at the threshold of the room and looked back. I followed his line of sight to the pile of laundry by Jan's side. Poking out from underneath a bundle of paired socks, I could see the rough base of the china shepherd, and the tip of one of the angel's wings.

I turned to him to check that he was sure, but he had scampered off.

69

TERESA

Edinburgh
One month later

'I think that's everything,' I said, placing the last of the boxes on the floor. I could feel the pull in my lower back and hoped it wouldn't be too niggly on the drive home to Northumberland.

'Do you like it though, Mum?' Maisie looked at me, her eyes anxious.

'It's lovely, darling. I'm glad you managed to get something so... nice.'

It was a small, two-bedroomed flat within a student accommodation block, a special one for single-parent students. The windows didn't fit properly in their frames, and one of them was always open a crack because it wouldn't close. There was a split in the plastic-leather sofa, revealing a crumbling yellow interior. Maisie said she'd already reported the problems to the building managers. The room smelt faintly of spices and old cooking.

'Come see my room!' cried George, dragging on my hand.

Maisie had set this room up first. She had bought a second-hand cabin bed, and had spent the last two days assembling it, working out how to do it without the original instructions. She'd decorated it to make it look like a pirate ship, with portholes along the guard rail, and a ladder encrusted with jewelled barnacles. A skull-and-crossbones flag was suspended on a pole at the foot of the bed. And tent curtains, patterned with blue and green waves, were drawn around the space beneath.

'This is my cabin,' he said, pulling the curtain aside. Maisie had hung fairy lights inside the space and made a porthole 'window' from a picture George had painted of a roiling sea, complete with a smiling sea monster. There was a desk area with a miniature chair tucked beneath it. And George had upturned a plastic toy storage box to make a second seat.

'I'm the captain,' he added.

'Oh wow! It's amazing.'

Part of me – a big part, if I was honest – had wanted them to stay at home with me. I'd privately worried over her decision to move to Edinburgh – to move George to a new school, a new home, after all that he'd gone through.

But Maisie's life had been on hold for so long. She was finally setting sail.

'Mum? How do I read the electricity meter?' Maisie's voice drifted through from the kitchen. After we'd done that, she wanted me to help set the correct time on the oven, and advice on how long it would take to cook sausages on an induction hob. George's food choices had widened to include sausages and peas.

When the questions had stopped, I knew it was time.

'I'd better get down the road.' That made it sound nearer than it was. As if I'd be living round the corner rather than an hour and a half's drive away.

I kissed them both, holding their bright faces between my hands, committing them to memory. The exact way they looked, this day, this hour, this moment, because it would never come again.

A tear wandered down Maisie's cheek. 'How will I do it, Mum?' she whispered.

'You're doing it,' I said. 'All you need to do is keep going. One step at a time.'

George pulled me down, his face excited and earnest at the same time. 'Don't worry,' he whispered. 'I'll be here.' He'd seen Maisie through her highs and her lows. He was going to take every bit of happiness that was going, and hold on to it carefully.

I returned to my car, and negotiated a hideous one-way system to get out of the city centre, which distracted me for a while. And then I was driving down the grey, monotonous A1.

This was it. She'd left home. She'd gone.

I thought back to the day she'd started nursery, looking back to see her arms stretched out towards me, as a key worker tried to distract her. The hollow ache in my heart as I'd returned home to an empty house.

I thought of the day I'd dropped her off at primary school. Staring at the yellow duck on her coat peg, watching it go blurry as I willed myself not to cry.

The day she'd gone to tennis club for the first time, insisting that I wasn't to collect her, she'd get the bus home.

The day I'd looked at her work, at the art exhibition, and realised that this young woman, with her extraordinary ideas, her talent, wasn't really mine any more. She had never been mine to begin with.

And the day I'd dropped her off, that last ever day at school. That half-wave, the longing to run after her.

I'd had to let her go, and let her go, and let her go again.

The string inside me pulled tighter, with every mile I drove. I was gasping in breaths, my throat aching in the effort not to cry.

A call came through and I answered on hands-free.

'How did it go?' It was Sunny.

'Oh. You know.' I didn't have to finish the sentence. He knew.

'My last client cancelled, so I got home a bit early,' he said. 'Tonight I shall be serving chicken makhani with home-made flatbreads, followed by vanilla panna cotta and raspberry coulis.'

Since Sunny had moved in, he and I had been taking turns to make the evening meal. We made it into a competition, with George and Maisie as the judges. Last week, I'd won, producing rack of lamb and dauphinoise potatoes in Friday's 'quarter final'.

'I promised George we'd FaceTime him.' My voice cracked a little. 'He wants to see if the panna cotta is properly wobbly.'

'Oh, my love. We'll see them on the twenty-fifth. That's only eight days.'

'I know.' Maisie was going to come with me to try on wedding dresses. She'd made an appointment for us at a posh place in Edinburgh, even though I'd protested that I would feel silly in a traditional bride's dress.

'But this is it, Mum,' she'd said. 'Sunny's been waiting for you for years. You're his fairytale. You need the right dress.'

It had been Maisie, in the end, who'd inspired me, who'd shown me how to move forward. She knew that she couldn't undo what Mark had done to her. She couldn't go back to how she was before. But she had looked, unflinchingly, into the most damaged, broken parts of herself and decided to carry on anyway.

What was broken could still be loved.

If she was brave enough to believe that, then I could, too.

And I'd been going along to Cheryl's shamanic drumming sessions, with a group of other women who'd survived trauma. We met every second Thursday night on the beach, searching for healing in sound and singing and firelight.

'A very ambitious menu,' I said to Sunny now. 'I just hope you can pull it off.'

'I love you,' he said.

'I love you too.' The words soared up into the air, finally free. 'I'll be back soon.'

The clouds parted slightly, a pocket of clear sky appearing. To the east, the sea came into view, its pearly-grey deepening to indigo at the horizon. I imagined George's pirate ship bed, pitching and rolling in storybook storms, or bobbing on calm seas. He was safe now, though – safe inside himself, whatever weather might come. His little face had told me that, when he'd said goodbye.

I had to let them go, and let them go, and let them go again.

Tears streamed down my face as I thought of how lucky I was.

And so I kept on going. Driving south, towards Northumberland, and Sunny, and the 'road-that-wasn't-a-road'. Towards the hobbity houses and home.

A NOTE FROM LUCY

Thank you for reading *The Child Who Came Back*! If you would like to find out what happens next, I have written a mini-sequel called *The House Nobody Wanted,* which I would like to offer you as a free gift and a thank you!

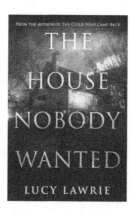

Download it by copying this link into your browser and following the instructions: https://BookHip.com/HHFDZFA

Reviews are so important to us authors, especially those of us who publish independently. I would be really grateful if you could spend a moment to write an honest review on Amazon (it doesn't need to be long or detailed – even a line or two would be great).

Also, if you enjoyed *The Child Who Came Back*, then you'll love my other psychological thrillers, *The Child In My House* and *The Child Upstairs* which are available now on Amazon!

If you would like to get in touch, I would be delighted to hear from you! Please email me at lucy@lucylawrie.com

ACKNOWLEDGMENTS

Firstly, thank you to my husband, Matt. You are a kind of miracle – an endless source of love, encouragement and belief. Thank you for helping me with plot issues when I get stuck, and sorry for when I laugh uncontrollably at our more whacky ideas! The trickiest parts of this book were worked out on a rainy day drive from Glencoe to Fort Augustus. Just as well the weather was too bad to go waterfalling!

Thank you to Lottie for keeping me right on what teenagers would or wouldn't say! And to Ezra, my wonderful son. I'm so proud of you both. You have both brought out the Mummy Tiger in me, and I think that tiger helped to write this book! Thank you to Becca, for being a treasured part of my family, and for making me feel optimistic about young people enjoying reading!

Huge thanks to Lesley McLaren and Jane Farquharson for your creativity, enthusiasm, and your eagle-eyed knack of spotting plot holes and continuity errors! Most of all, thank you for making this process so much fun. There's no way I could do this without you.

Extra special thanks to Jane for editing the manuscript and helping me get it ready to go out into the world. I am so lucky that I can entrust my 'babies' to you!

Thank you to all my readers, and especially those who have joined my email list and who exchange messages with me from time to time. You make this possible. You also make it feel worthwhile, which is more precious to me than you will ever know. I am incredibly grateful for every single one of you.

Finally, to my dad, who died while I was writing this book. You opened up worlds with every novel, poem or play that we read together. You believed, right from the start, that I was a writer. You pointed me towards what is beautiful, in the world around, and in people, and I hope this comes through in everything I write. Thank you for everything and I miss you.

ALSO BY LUCY LAWRIE

THE CHILD IN MY HOUSE

A family riddled with lies. A little girl who won't speak. What if keeping her safe means losing her forever?

Juliet only wanted to see her childhood home one more time – to look at it from the street. She never intended to meet the new owners, let alone talk her way into a position as their new live-in nanny. But it's too late now to tell the truth about who she really is.

Six-year-old Kitty has progressive mutism and cannot speak. Nobody knows why she keeps making silent phone calls to the police. Juliet makes it her mission to find out.

As Juliet settles into the house, nostalgia for her childhood gives way to uneasiness, as troubling memories surface. She begins to realise that her new employers have a connection to her own past, and family secrets she has tried hard to forget. And she is horrified to learn that they have a secret too – one that could blow their world apart.

Juliet faces an impossible choice. Keeping Kitty safe could cost her everything.

The Child In My House is available now on Amazon.

ALSO BY LUCY LAWRIE

THE CHILD UPSTAIRS

She doesn't realise that she ruined my life.

Or that I'm about to ruin hers.

Steffi seems to have everything. She lives in a gorgeous house with her fiancé, Tom, his young daughter and their sweet little baby.

But she hasn't told anyone about the unfortunate accidents that keep happening. That she's terrified to go upstairs in her own house. Or that her old imaginary friend has come back, whispering instructions on how to look after the baby. And she can't tell Tom that she's struggling. Not after what happened to his first wife.

She's starting to realise that people have been keeping secrets from her. That there's something about her childhood that doesn't add up. Something dark, lurking just beyond the reaches of her memory.

Poor Steffi doesn't know who to trust any more.

She certainly shouldn't trust me.

The Child Upstairs is available now on Amazon.

Made in United States
Orlando, FL
27 June 2025

62365660R00267